FEAR NO EVIL

ALSO BY REBECCA HARTT

FEAR NO EVIL

CHRISTIAN ROMANTIC SUSPENSE

THE LOST ARE FOUND
BOOK ONE

REBECCA HARTT

Released December 2024
ISBN: 978-1-64457-732-5

Rise UP Publications
www.riseUPpublications.com

This book is dedicated to the brave missionary largely responsible for the original dissolution of the FARC and the 2016 Havana Peace Accords. God used this missionary to bring hundreds of FARC to Christ. With God in their hearts, killing became distasteful, and striking a peaceful resolution became their goal. Like Maggie, I appreciate God's "subversive" nature—how He works through the humblest of hearts to make His Kingdom come.

∾

For everyone who lives in fear: You are not alone.
For those who protect the rest of us from fear: Thank you. Your reward is coming.

INTRODUCTION

Welcome to the first book of The Lost Are Found Series. This series will feature intriguing Navy SEAL bachelors and independent heroines who find themselves in exotic settings and perilous situations. To survive, they'll need to rely on faith and each other for courage, discovering along the way that they're stronger together than they ever were apart.

PROLOGUE

TWELVE YEARS AGO, PARIS, FRANCE

Maggie Ellis shot another glance at the haggard man sitting alone under the awning of the outdoor café. Dark beard, darting eyes, deep grooves in his weathered face. Of course, he could be a Frenchman with swarthy coloring, but with the beard and the overwrought expression, he resembled a Middle Easterner who'd lost his entire family in a war. The unsettling vibe he gave off kept Maggie from focusing on her boyfriend.

"I have something for you."

Jake's words, uttered in his understated way, claimed her attention. Looking back at him, Maggie's heart skipped a beat at the sight of an emerald solitaire flanked by two diamond chips and sitting in a black velvet box.

"It's a promise ring, so don't panic. I'd like for us to marry in about ten years."

Her rounding eyes rose to Jake's soft-blue gaze as he watched her reaction through his thick lenses. With his glasses and brown hair, Jake resembled a tall Harry Potter. To hide her astonishment, she focused back on the ring.

"Oh, Jake."

The dismay in her voice caused his mouth to firm and his shoulders to slump. "Look, it's only a promise ring. Just please take it."

"No, I love it. Really, it's just…you shouldn't have."

"Why not?" He took the ring out of its box and held out both hands. "Come on. Let's see if it fits."

As he slid the circle up the fourth finger of her left hand, where it lodged securely and comfortably, Maggie considered what it signified: a promise to end up together.

For a moment, she allowed the romanticism of the moment to sweep her away. His gesture was the icing on the cake for a perfect year. It was here at Café du Jour that they'd met at the outset of their junior year abroad—the best eight months of her life so far.

Looking up, she took it all in: the crisp spring air and flower boxes in all the windows. The ubiquitous smell of fresh-baked baguettes. And, in the distance, the gothic bells of Notre-Dame Cathedral tolling 6:00 P.M. The pale-blue sash of sky between the dormered roofs of the buildings on each side of the street had begun to blush toward the hue of France's rosé wines. She would treasure this moment.

Jake still had hold of her hand. "Do you like it?"

She couldn't lie. The emerald popped against her tan skin. "I love it." But nowhere in her future did she expect to be Mrs. Jake Carrigan, let alone Mrs. Anybody. She and Jake would return to their respective colleges—to Georgetown U, in her case, Boston U, in his, ten hours apart from each other. The connection they'd discovered in Paris would pass into oblivion, as all things did.

Caressing her knuckles with his thumb, he hedged, "Listen, Lena."

She loved that he called her that. Only her Venezuelan relatives had ever shortened Magdalena to Lena.

"I know you've got plans to take on the world, and I'm not about to try and stop you."

Yep. She was her father's daughter through and through, a chip off the old block.

"But what we have doesn't come along every day. You have to realize that." Determination glinted in his eyes.

She'd been known to make light of their connection because it scared her. Romance would only complicate her future. Yet everything Jake said felt just right. His sense of humor kept her laughing. From the day they'd met, they'd been inseparable. And when he kissed her, she clamored for more—at which point Jake, with his scruples, always drew the line.

"I realize." Smiling with mixed apology and gratitude, Maggie decided to accept the ring, if only as a memento of this beautiful chapter in her life.

Movement out of the corner of her eye returned her attention to the man under the awning. He'd gotten up from his table and was walking away, leaving his backpack under his chair.

"Oh, sir." She raised her voice so he would hear her. "You left your bag." But he didn't so much as glance back.

Jake craned his neck to see who she was talking to, then to identify the bag. Concern knit his brow, but Maggie was already two steps ahead of him. Growing up in Venezuela, she had seen her share of violent protests.

Her brain downshifted, turning seconds into minutes. The black backpack with its vivid Adidas logo lay not five yards away. The man's weird energy suddenly made perfect sense. He'd left that bag there on purpose; he was planning to wreak havoc on this outdoor café.

The blood drained from Maggie's head.

Jake took in her reaction. "Oh, come on. He probably just forgot it."

She had to warn people, but horror gripped her vocal cords. All Maggie could do was lunge out of her chair, grab Jake by his shirtfront, and haul him toward her, away from the bag. As slim as he was, it wasn't hard to move him.

"Bomb." She managed to get that one hoarse word out. The terrorist was striding down the stone-paved street, intent on distancing himself. Maybe they still had time. "Move!" She wanted to run, to warn people, but Jake resisted.

"We can't just leave. I still have to pay."

Strangers all around them were gaping at her use of the word *bomb*.

Meanwhile, the would-be terrorist had slipped into a small green car. Maggie pointed desperately at the backpack. "That's a bomb!"

"Lena, he probably just forgot it."

But the foreigner was aiming what looked like a remote control in their direction.

"Down!"

There wasn't any more time to convince Jake. All Maggie could do was heave their wrought-iron table onto its side to be used as a shield. Their glasses and empty plates came crashing down.

Even as she hauled Jake down alongside her, a brilliant light burst over them. The heavy table cannoned into them. A high-pitched buzz distorted the roar and the screams that followed.

Stay conscious! Stay alive!

When the roar receded, Maggie found herself curled into a ball, with Jake draped limply over her.

It took ages to get out from under him. Her movements were feeble. She couldn't get her body to do what her brain was telling it to. Bits of shrapnel abraded palms and knees, cutting her skin as she struggled free.

"Jake!" He slumped bonelessly onto the debris. The frame of his glasses hung askew, one lens shattered. Bits of glass shimmered on his skin. His thick brown hair was covered in ash, and the gash on his brow ridge pulsed blood with every beat of his heart. "Jake!" She shook him. "Jake, wake up!"

Little fires blazed on every side. He couldn't die on her, not after giving her the ring.

Jake's lashes fluttered. His soft blue gaze focused on her face. "Lena."

"Yes! I'm here, Jake. And you're okay. *You're okay.*" She ran trembling fingers over his body, seeking injury, not finding any—apart from the head wound. But his eyes rolled back into his skull, and his eyelids melted shut.

Her heart stopped for a second time that night. Had he just died on her?

Checking his jugular for a pulse, she felt nothing but warm skin.

"No!" Bent over him, Maggie cupped his dear face, smearing blood across his temple. "Don't you dare die on me, Jake Carrigan. I promise I'll marry you one day, okay? But you have to live. You hear me?"

CHAPTER 1

CASABLANCA, MOROCCO, PRESENT TIME

Am I dead? Pain seared Maggie's side as she tried to draw a breath. Lying flat on her back in a narrow, bricked alley just a few steps from her apartment in Casablanca, she assessed her injuries, took stock of her situation, and groaned.

The bit of violet sky peeking between overhanging roofs informed her it was nightfall. Raising her arm to check the time, Maggie launched a cloud of flies that had been crawling on her. Her watch glowed 8:37 P.M., which meant she'd been lying here for at least an hour. Summer was the peak tourist season in Casablanca. People must have skirted the comatose and bleeding woman, ignoring her plight. Even now, she could hear somebody edging around her—a woman with a baby. Maggie murmured reassurances, and the young mother scuttled past.

The jig was up. Her cover was blown. As Jake would have said in the Irish Gaelic of his paternal grandfather, *"Nách mór an diabhal thú,"* which loosely translated meant, *Well, aren't you the devil?*

The gut-lurching realization that her true identity was known had hit her on her walk home from work. She was approaching the gate that led to the courtyard of her building when Kamal's bodyguard materialized in front of her—no sign of Kamal anywhere. One look at the dark intent in Farid's dark eyes, and she'd realized both he and Kamal knew exactly who she was. She'd been handily played, all the while thinking herself in control of the game.

But that was hours ago.

By some incredible stroke of luck, she still wore her watch, not yet stolen by one of Casablanca's many thieves and pickpockets. The watch contained a GPS chip, broadcasting her location. So long as she could get to her apartment to place the necessary call, an extraction team would be deployed to recover her. But what if Kamal and his bodyguard suspected as much and followed her? The whole extraction team could be targeted.

Maggie held her breath and listened. Her neighbor's dog wasn't barking, which it did whenever strangers were in the building. So maybe the coast was clear.

Summoning her strength, she rolled from her back to her front. A moan escaped her clenched teeth. *Oh, man.* Kamal's bodyguard had broken at least one of her ribs. Pushing to her hands and knees, she waited for the tsunami of agony to subside.

The CIA had assigned her here only nine months earlier. Her objective was simple: verify the rumors that switchblade drones, earmarked for the Russian Wagner Group, were passing through a waterfront warehouse in Casablanca, a circumstance with frightening implications.

Magdalena Montoya Ellis had been a shoo-in for the CIA. Not only was she fluent in Spanish and French, but her father was a public corruption section chief for the FBI. The Ellises were patriots. Morocco was her third assignment, following Bogotá and Caracas. Here, she portrayed herself as a French fashionista, selling clothing at a boutique not far from the warehouse in question. Befriending the foreman, Kamal, had been laughably easy.

With very little coaxing, Kamal had taken her out to dinner and for leisurely evening strolls along the waterfront. He hadn't pressured her for intimacies, thank God. In fact, he'd spilled everything there was to know about the shipments bound for Russia—their point of origin and how they would get there.

Now, it was plainly apparent Kamal had been testing her. No doubt he had fed her a string of lies, and a mole in the CIA had reported them all back to him, proving Maggie was a spook, as he obviously suspected.

I'm sorry, Kamal. Despite his radical political convictions, she had genuinely liked the man, though he didn't hold a candle to her college sweetheart. And Kamal must have liked her, too, because his bodyguard, Farid, whose fists were the size of hams, could have easily killed her. Instead, he'd roughed her up and walked away. At least, she hoped he had.

I have to get out of here.

With the help of the rough earthen wall next to her, Maggie managed to get vertical. Blood slid from her split lip to her chin before dripping onto her Christian Dior blouse.

Gritting her teeth, she shuffled toward her apartment building, a two-story structure of dried clay, entirely whitewashed. Through her one good eye, she plumbed the shadows, terrified Farid would return to finish the job.

The neighbor's dog began to bark as she reached the building. She stilled, looked, and listened.

Was the dog just barking at her…or was Farid nearby, watching her every move?

The courtyard, with its burbling central fountain and decorative blue tiles, stood quiet. Everyone was having dinner, as evidenced by the aroma of roasting lamb and mint tea.

One ragged step at a time, Maggie dragged herself up the stairs to her second-story flat. The fine hairs at her nape prickled as she spotted her door ajar. Someone had come this way before her, if they weren't still here. Too bad her Ruger was tucked in the drawer by her bed—at least it used to be.

Approaching her door, she listened again. The dog stopped barking, a reassuring sign. What a relief Miles, her half-brother, and his bride, McKenzie, who'd lived with Maggie for several months, had just returned to the States.

Porcelain shards crackled under Maggie's pumps as she waded inside. So much for her collection of ornamental plates, torn off the wall, shattered and scattered like confetti. They were supposed to be souvenirs from her Moroccan tour.

She would be lucky to have herself as a souvenir at this point.

Eyeing her semi-dark living room, Maggie absorbed the scene of cushions and pillows strewn across the Persian rug for which she had haggled fiercely at the outset of her tour. She hoped to see it again one day—only possible if it wasn't stolen by the time the CIA packed up her stuff and sent it stateside.

She headed for her kitchen, where every dish had been pulled from the cupboards and smashed. Glass and ceramic crunched and squealed beneath her soles as she limped toward the sink. God forbid they'd found her Agency phone, hidden in the false bottom of a Lysol spray bottle.

With a groan, she retrieved it from under the sink, removed the false bottom, and breathed a sigh of relief as the phone fell into her hands. *Buíochas le Dia, Thanks be to God*, as Jake used to say.

Following a wary glance behind her, she entered the passcode, then the letters *E-X-I-T* on the alphanumeric keypad. That would bring an extraction team to the escape-and-evasion point within one hour. Maggie swallowed hard and ended the call.

If she could make it there in time, she'd be whisked away. Not exactly a triumphant withdrawal, as had been the case in Venezuela two years earlier, when she'd been rescued with a thumb drive full of price-less intel—not to mention the most astonishing thing of all: Jake Carrigan, her first and only love, had been the SEAL in charge of the extraction team.

What an exhilarating moment that had been! He'd tucked her under his protective wing and delivered her to a U.S. aircraft carrier in the Gulf, only to vanish on her as suddenly as he'd vanished from Paris.

Maggie had made inquiries later, discovering that not only was Jake a Navy SEAL, but he'd been trained by the CIA's Special Operations Group to protect case officers like herself—which was crazy because the time she'd checked on him before that, he'd been working for the Peace Corps. Never in a million years would she have pictured Jake as a Navy SEAL, let alone a SOG.

Limping toward her bedroom, Maggie paused at the sight of her mattress flipped onto its side. The drawer of her bedside table stood open, so the Ruger was gone. Turning away, she skirted the colorful pillows in her wrecked living room to get to her balcony.

How am I going to make it to the exfil site?

With pure Ellis determination, that was how. At her balcony door, she took one last look at the apartment she'd called home. It had never occurred to her that she would be leaving with her tail tucked between her legs.

At least I'm alive.

She stepped outside, pulling the door shut. Her escape-and-evasion plan involved going over the railing, dropping to the flat rooftop of the adjacent building, and crossing that to a fire-escape ladder that would put her on a different alley, one that zigzagged toward the coast. Easy peasy. In a nondescript mosque about a klick away, an asset would be waiting for her. Supposedly, there was a tunnel under the city that led from the mosque to the ocean, where the extraction team would pick her up.

If she made it that far.

Pausing for strength, Maggie inhaled the warm Moroccan air, forever infused with the sweet and savory scents of couscous, *ras el hanout,* and fresh-baked *khubz* bread. Her thoughts flitted to the local baker, an informant who was always glad to share the local chatter, like whose son fancied whose daughter. *I'll miss this place.* Probably because the French-influenced culture here reminded her of Paris and the joyous months with Jake.

A glance at her watch prompted Maggie to get moving. Only how was she supposed to climb when she could barely even stand?

Lifting her gaze to the stars obscured by a desert haze, the words Jake had shared with her more than once came to mind. *"One day, Lena, you're going to figure out that you can't save the world by yourself. If you ever need help, just reach up. God's right there, waiting for you."*

He'd never understood her need to defend democracy. Growing up in Venezuela, she'd seen firsthand what the fall of democracy looked like. Even so, Jake's faith had always inspired her. She gripped the railing on her balcony and swayed. "So...I think I might need help right now."

Getting no response and with no other choice, Maggie lifted a long leg over the railing, sat a moment, then heaved her other leg over. As she slipped off the rail to stand on the outer ledge, she pivoted to face her building. Remarkably, only mild discomfort accompanied her movements.

Next, she moved her hands from the railing to the vertical balusters, then lowered one foot to the bakery's flat roof. Her ribs barely protested. *Huh. Maybe I should pray more often.*

Encouraged, Maggie crossed the roof to the fire escape on the other side. The last time she'd looked at the rickety ladder, some of the rungs were starting to rust through.

While climbing down the ladder backward, she anticipated the pain to return with a vengeance, but it didn't. Her adrenaline must be kicking in. She dropped down into a quiet alley and then made her way downhill toward the mosque.

The unlit street kept Maggie wary. She'd never ventured out at night without a djellaba, the hooded robe most local women wore, and for good reason.

Furtive footfalls had her spinning around just as an old man walked up on her. He gasped in alarm at her disfigured face and gave her a wide berth.

She had to look frightful with one eye swollen shut and her lip oozing blood. Thank goodness the odds of Jake rescuing her a second time were slim to none. She wouldn't want him to see her like this.

The last time Jake had rescued her, she'd been confident and still in one piece, not at all like now.

Maggie checked her watch. Only thirty minutes remaining, and she was just now reaching the mosque.

Arriving at a door thickly layered in gold paint, she used a buzzer to announce herself. Her lower lip throbbed as she waited. At last, the door popped open, and a dark-skinned imam dressed in blinding white robes swept her inside.

"I've been expecting you." His English was perfect. "Can you walk?"

She clutched her side as she swayed on her feet. "Sure."

"Good. The team is nearly here. We have to move quickly."

He pulled her into a dim antechamber, through a side door, and down a hall to an alcove. A push against the back wall sent it rumbling inward, revealing the tunnel into which he ushered her, leaving it open and clicking on a penlight. A curve in the tunnel beckoned them down an angled floor of hard-packed dirt, which took them beneath the ancient city toward the pier where the team would be waiting.

They seemed to walk forever, though Maggie knew it wasn't even one klick to the extraction point. Her pain was returning with a vengeance, shortening her steps.

"Just a little farther."

The man's encouragement kept her going.

Moisture now hung in the air, tinged with the smell of sea salt. When they came upon a door that marked the tunnel's end, she swallowed a sob of relief.

It opened suddenly, and the silhouette ducking under the low lintel was identical to the one that had come bursting into the office in Venezuela. "Jake!"

"Lena!"

When he tacked on a phrase in Gaelic, she knew she wasn't just imagining him. On a moan, she stumbled into him, letting him support her. What were the odds he would be sent to save her twice?

"What hurts?" He held her firmly but gently.

"Everything."

He spoke over his shoulder. "Decker, pass me an auto-injector of morphine."

Maggie dropped her head against his dense chest. She could hear his heart thumping with sure, steady strokes that proved he was really with her.

A jab in her arm sent morphine swirling into her bloodstream, smoothing the razor's edge of agony, turning the world fuzzy. She'd made it to the exfil site. Jake would take it from here.

As he scooped her off her feet, carrying her like a baby, an explosion of semiautomatic gunfire filled the tunnel.

Jake moved so fast that she didn't know what was happening; she only knew that someone had fired at them from farther up the tunnel. *Farid. She'd led him straight to the extraction site!*

"Relax!" Jake bounded with her up a run of steps. "We got this."

By the time they reached the top of the stairs, the burst of gunfire was over. Jake bore her through an open door, out onto a long, dark pier where starlight winked through the haze overhead, and a warm, wet breeze blew over them.

He stepped down into a rigid-inflatable craft that rocked against the pier, then sat with her across his lap. The boat pitched as several more SOGs jumped in. The stealth motor thrummed to life, scarcely audible over the slapping water. Cooler air streamed over her as they pulled away.

Up and over waves they went, kicking up sea spray that swirled around them and dampened every inch of her. The glow of the Casablanca cityscape faded, leaving nothing but a star-studded sky above and waves below that subsided into swells.

Jake asked his men to report in. One of them indicated he'd been nicked by a bullet, but nothing too serious. Another stated that the target was dead.

Jake scowled down at her. "Did you know you were followed?"

She had trouble getting her tongue to cooperate. "Possibly."

"Who did this to you?"

There was no mistaking his fury, but she wasn't authorized to tell him. "My fault. I was played."

He adjusted his hold, cradling her like he never meant to let her go. The thighs she sat across were as dense as tree trunks. The gangly young man she'd loved in Paris had morphed into something more.

She had so many questions to ask him. But she was too drugged to speak.

Their motor cut off abruptly, and a hulking shape emerged from the dark, scarcely visible against the night sky. They coasted silently into an enclosure—the port of a Navy vessel, given the smell of motor oil and steel and the sound of sloshing water. With a low hum, the jaws of the port closed behind them, and the lights blinked on.

Half a dozen sailors stood around what resembled an indoor swimming pool. They helped to moor and stabilize their craft.

Jake managed to clamber off the RIB without handing her off to anyone. Maggie's head lolled on his shoulder. Her wet clothing made her shiver. Even so, the urge to fall asleep was overwhelming. *Stay awake!*

But the morphine he'd given her was most likely dosed for a man twice her size.

His boots rang along a metal corridor before he ducked into a room that smelled of antiseptic. When he laid her gently on a gurney, she clung to the sleeve of his night ops uniform.

"S'ay wi' me."

Her request made him hold her gaze. He didn't wear glasses anymore. The Navy must have corrected his vision.

"You need a doctor, Lena. And I can't stay."

His terse reply betrayed a certain level of frustration. Was he mad at her? Sensing him about to leave, some desperate emotion pushed tears into her eyes. "Don't go."

With a firming of his lips that was all too familiar, he peeled her left hand from his sleeve, regarded her bare fourth finger for a split second, and then brushed his lips across her knuckles.

The sweet gesture made her heart clutch. *Oh, Jake, I miss you!*

"Be well." He released her, then swiveled on his soles, ducked out the door, and disappeared.

Again? Her heart unraveled like a spool of thread. Why did Jake blow in and out of her life like this without any explanation? It was crazy.

CHAPTER 2

S he was crazy. At least Maggie Ellis feared that was the case, though the in-house psychiatrist at the CIA called it PTS, Post-Traumatic Stress—not necessarily a disorder unless it never went away. She shook her head, lamenting her weakness. One bad experience, and suddenly she was falling apart? Ellises were made of sterner stuff than that. But Dr. Richards had prescribed a twelve-month hiatus from casework, and Maggie had been given an analyst's job at Langley.

Just two months in paperwork purgatory was enough to make anyone go nuts; Maggie couldn't fathom doing another ten. Gritting her teeth the entire time, she became a nine-to-five desk jockey while doubling down on convincing Dr. Richards that she was all healed from her nightmare in Morocco.

And apparently, he'd fallen for it, for she'd received instructions this last week to pack a suitcase for an overnight in New York City to meet with her boss's boss. This morning, she'd taken the Amtrak from Union Station in D.C. to Penn Station in Manhattan. She went straight to the hotel to check in and to change. And now she was braving the August heat by walking to the clandestine CIA station instead of taking a taxi.

Her destination was just six blocks from the hotel and only one block from the United Nations Headquarters. A brisk walk past the latter would dispel her jitters.

She wouldn't have been summoned here unless she was about to get briefed on a new assignment. *Buíochas le Dia.* Funny how she never forgot Jake's Gaelic phrases. But what if she wasn't ready?

To bolster her confidence, Maggie wore a black sheath dress under an emerald-green cropped jacket that matched her eyes. It was a little too warm for the jacket, even one with three-quarter sleeves. To compensate, she wore her long raven hair in a ponytail that twitched behind her as she walked.

The staccato of her leggy stride turned the heads of men and women alike, assuring her she looked her best. But even with a newly purchased Ruger strapped to the inside of her left thigh, her gaze darted nervously toward every door and alley as she coursed the sidewalk.

Farid was dead. He couldn't hurt her again. How many times did she have to tell herself that?

Maggie checked her watch—the same one that had saved her in Morocco and even in Venezuela, for that matter. Perfect. She would arrive at the scheduled meeting exactly on time because the United Nations Headquarters was straight ahead of her, with all those colorful flags snapping in the hot breeze. Who wouldn't be inspired by the visible sign of countries working toward a better world? And here was the tall, steel building she was looking for, labeled with a brass placard that read: **U.S. Department of the Treasury**. That, of course, was a front.

As she marched toward the double glass doors, Maggie took her CAC card from her purse while checking the door's glass reflection to confirm she wasn't being followed. She swiped her card under the scanner, and the doors popped open. The cool marble foyer stood empty, apart from a security guard who stared at her entrance.

Standing at five-feet-nine-inches tall, with a face she'd inherited from Miss Venezuela 1990, her mother, Maggie resembled a fashion model more than a case officer, especially now that she'd lost seven pounds from all the running she'd been doing.

"Afternoon, miss. Can I help you?"

"Maggie Ellis. I have a meeting with Deputy Director Hinton."

The portly guard consulted the screen of his laptop, sliding a finger down it until he saw her name. "Oh yes. Well then, you know the drill, ma'am. Surrender any electronics or weapons, look into the retina scan, then come on through the metal detector."

While the guard politely averted his gaze, Maggie reached under her hem to withdraw the Ruger from its holster. Vulnerability assailed her as she placed it in the plastic tub with her purse. She'd left her phone in the hotel so no one could track her movements. Bending over the retina scan, which recognized her emerald-green eyes, she was cleared to step through the metal detector next, then collect her purse. The guard would hang on to her Ruger for the time being.

"Have a good meeting, Miss Ellis. Head to the eighth floor. Turn left off the elevator, and it's the last door on your left."

"Thanks." Could the guard tell her stomach was full of butterflies?

Pull yourself together, Maggie! Her heart trotted as she proceeded toward the elevators. *It's not like you're going to the electric chair.*

Even so, by the time she reached the eighth floor, a cold sweat filmed her upper lip, and she was hoping she still had time to use the restroom. She bolted out of the elevator as it opened, turning left per the guard's instructions and colliding with a very solid individual coming up the hall.

It took everything in her not to startle like a cat with its claws out, fur spiked. "Jake!"

Gentle blue eyes regarded her from a height of well over six feet. Not even a trace of surprise lifted his dark-brown eyebrows, suggesting he was expecting her. "Lena."

The way he said her nickname stirred up dormant feelings. His gaze glossed over her ponytail, swept the length of her body, then rose again, centering on the thin scar that hatched her lower lip, a memento from Morocco. "How are you?" Concern laced his voice.

He couldn't possibly know about her diagnosis. "I'm great." She raised her chin to lend assertion to the statement. Then ruined it by adding, "Do you know where the restrooms are?"

He gestured with his chin up the hall behind her. "I'm headed that way right now."

"Thanks." She wheeled away, aware that he was watching her stride ahead of him. The solidness of his frame was still imprinted upon her senses. In college, he'd been lean and lanky. But now, dressed in a heather-gray suit with a white shirt and no tie, he looked like an advertisement for the Special Operations, all broad shoulders and muscle-corded neck.

Without glancing back, she pushed into the restroom, determined *not* to encounter him again when she came out, but suspecting she was going to.

As she washed her hands a moment later, she noted with dismay the ring on her fourth finger—the promise ring Jake had given her. Had he seen it on her? She always wore it when she was stateside because she loved it, but Jake might get the wrong idea.

Wriggling it off, she dropped it into a zippered pocket on her purse. After drying her hands and patting away the nervous perspiration on her face, she blew out a breath and left the bathroom for her meeting.

Please, let me have a new assignment. Another day stuck in the office, and she'd really lose her mind. *But am I ready?* Squelching the uncertain voice, she left the bathroom.

Jake was not in the hallway. Relieved, Maggie hastened to the office at the end of the corridor. The door on the left stood open, with four men inside, blocking her view out the window, and one of them was Jake. Her heart began to dance a jig.

"Ah, there she is." Her boss from back home, a burly Black man with a megawatt smile, stepped in her direction with his hand outstretched. "How was the train ride, Maggie?"

"Good, Gordon, thank you." Her hands were still cool from just washing them. "No delays."

"Excellent." Gordon turned and guided her toward the other three. "Let me introduce you to the present company."

Jake's gaze folded over her, but he gave no outward sign of knowing her.

"Everyone, this is Magdalena Ellis. Maggie is originally from Venezuela, which is why she's our top choice for this operation."

Top choice? Was she headed back to Venezuela? Her mouth went dry, and her palms turned clammy.

"Maggie, you've met Deputy Director Hinton before, haven't you?"

She sent the silver-haired, rather hefty man a practiced smile, withholding her hand lest he guessed how nervous she was. "Only over conference calls. How do you do, sir?"

"Good to see you again, Maggie."

Gordon gestured next to a slim gentleman with a hooked nose, dark hair and eyes. "This is Charles du Lac, assistant director of the Department of Peace Operations overseen by the United Nations Secretariat. At least that's his cover. Charles is with DGSE, the French Secret Service."

"Enchanté." The Frenchman held out his hand, forcing Maggie to touch her damp palm to his. He clasped her hand firmly. "I hear you went to school in Paris for a time, mademoiselle."

"Yes." She waited for Jake to mention he had been there with her, but he did not. "What part of France are you from, sir?"

"Please, call me Charles. I am from La Ville de Fontainebleau."

Memories of giddy laughter and bone-deep contentment rocked Maggie. It was all she could do not to meet Jake's eyes to see if he remembered that perfect day when they'd toured the castle and hiked in the nearby forest. "I've been to the châteaux there. It's just lovely."

Gordon interrupted. "Maggie, this is Navy SEAL Lieutenant Jake Carrigan. He's a member of our Special Operations Group."

As Charles released her hand, Maggie faced Jake, expecting him to say that, as a SOG, he'd already rescued her—twice. Instead, he just nodded, sketching her the world's smallest smile.

She nodded stiffly back. "Lieutenant Carrigan."

The deputy director inserted, "Charles will be working with you two on a special project."

Oh? Maggie's heart did a backflip as euphoria tangled with trepidation. *I'm working with Jake?*

The director gestured toward the briefing table. "Let's all take a seat, shall we?"

Homing in on the seat near the end of the table, Maggie remained off-kilter when Jake took the chair directly across from her. If she extended her foot, she would touch the toe of his dress shoes—size thirteen, unless his feet had grown. Hinton settled into the high-backed swivel chair at the head of the table with Charles and Gordon on either side of him.

The fact that Hinton would be briefing them told Maggie this assignment was top tier. Normally, Gordon supplied her assignments.

After slipping on a pair of silver-framed reading glasses, Hinton regarded Maggie over the top of them. "Ms. Ellis, do you remember Mike Howitz and Jay Barnes? You worked with both men on your first assignment in Colombia."

Two youngish men who'd worked closely with her on her first assignment at the U.S. Embassy in Bogotá came to mind. "Of course." They'd been like brothers to her, showing her the ropes and making her tour in Bogotá a wonderful experience. Alarm arrowed through her. "Why? What's happened to them?"

Hinton grimaced. "I'm sorry to say they were both abducted by the *Fuerzas Armadas Revolucionarias de Colombia* in March of this year."

Maggie frowned and glanced at Jake, whose poker face suggested he knew this already. "I thought the FARC disbanded years ago. Wasn't there a peace agreement with the government, giving them seats in the House and the Senate?" She clearly remembered that happening while she was in college.

"It did." Hinton tipped his sparse head of hair. "But a handful of dissidents, including the FARC's second-in-command, fled to the mountains in northeast Colombia, allied themselves with the drug lords there, and have sworn to punish anyone associated with the Havana Accord, which they claim is a fraud. They're funding themselves with drug sales and ransom money."

Unbelievable. All that had been accomplished in the peace agreement was for naught. Poor Mike and Jay! What would happen to them?

"Howitz and Barnes were kidnapped right off the streets of Bogotá last spring. Their families have been told to wire five hundred thousand dollars apiece to pay for their release. Of course, the FBI has asked them not to pay a cent and to let intermediaries negotiate for their loved ones' release. That's where you two come in."

Finding her mouth hanging open, Maggie clicked her teeth together.

"The UN's Department of Peace Operations is sponsoring a team to spearhead negotiations for their release." Hinton gestured toward the Frenchman. "Mr. du Lac is a member of said team. Other volunteers include the lead negotiator, who is German, as well as an Italian, a Turk, and a French couple." His gaze went to Maggie, then Jake. "That's going to be your cover."

Maggie's blood pressure spiked. Wait, a *couple*? And Jake, a Frenchman? His French hadn't been all that good twelve years ago.

Gordon seemed to read her mind. "Lieutenant Carrigan has just completed an advanced language course at The Farm. Moreover, we have a liaison agreement with the French Secret Service, who are the only folks who'll know your true identities."

Charles, Maggie's CIA equivalent, sent her an encouraging smile.

"Here's the cruncher." The deputy director laid a pudgy hand over the documents in front of him. "We don't have much time to prepare. You'll need to fly to Bogotá on Monday."

Monday! So no returning to her office in Langley next week. Maggie's relief faltered. She'd better be ready for this. What's more, she'd be working with *Jake*, who would be posing as her *husband*. Was this someone's idea of a practical joke?

Gordon cleared his throat. "This being a humanitarian mission, Maggie, you won't be able to carry any weapons or any overt communication devices of any kind." His chocolate-brown eyes conveyed apology. He, of course, was well aware of her diagnosis.

Hinton tacked on, "The FARC are going to march you deep into their territory in a remote mountainous region. They may strip you of any possessions you carry, so weapons and cell phones are out. However, our intel suggests they'll let you keep your passports and your boots."

Maggie's lips started to tingle—a telltale sign of an impending panic attack. *Keep it cool.* Glancing at Jake, she found him frowning at the tabletop.

Gordon added, "You don't have to take this assignment if you're not ready, Maggie."

Her cheeks flamed as she fixed a chagrined stare at her boss and grappled with her rising panic. She had to be ready.

"Barnes and Howitz were colleagues of yours." Gordon's words echoed the thoughts in Maggie's head. "So I thought I'd give you first crack at this."

A thought occurred to her. "Is Lieutenant Carrigan accompanying me for my *protection*?" If she was going to get her moxie back, she had to do this on her own.

Gordon cocked his head at her indignant tone. "As it happens, Maggie, we're also liaising with the Southern Command on this matter. SEALs from Team Six have already deployed to Bogotá. They've been setting up a Joint Intelligence Center at the American Embassy where they'll track your progress via microchips implanted under your skin. While your job is to discover everything you can about the FARC, including Howitz and Barnes's exact location, the SEALs' job is to extract the hostages, if and when UN negotiations fail."

Jake finally spoke up. "How do I pass on this intel without a phone or radio?"

Hinton gestured dismissively. "We'll cover that later. In addition to finding Barnes and Howitz's location, we want all the intel you can acquire on the FARC's present circumstances. Do they have any allies? How well-armed are they? How many do they number, and what are their vulnerabilities? Go ahead and open your envelopes." He slid two envelopes across the glossy table, one for her and one for Jake.

Quelling the tremor in her fingers, Maggie freed the flap on her envelope and shook out the passport inside. After cracking the cover, she assimilated her new legend with a thrill of excitement and a renewed sense of calm. This was a familiar process, taking on a fresh identity fraught with nuanced details, quickly internalized, and then worn like a second skin.

The name beside her photograph was Madeleine Martin Cotillard. At least she would respond immediately to someone calling her name. She glanced up at Jake. What was *his* name? The pages of her passport, heavily stamped, indicated extensive service to the United Nations Department of Peace Operations. According to the legend sheet that came with the passport, she was an associate human affairs officer working for the UN Secretariat and living in New York City, married to Jacques Matis Cotillard—so that was Jake's new name.

How ironic they were posing as a married couple. She shot a glance at his left hand—no ring, thank goodness. At least she wouldn't be filling another woman's shoes.

The resignation in Jake's otherwise deadpan expression suggested he'd already known what his legend would be.

So be it. She and Jake were professionals with a job to do. Even if he were married, that wouldn't change anything—except he wasn't married, *Buíochas le Dia.*

Hinton sat back in his chair while eyeing them over his reading glasses. "Well, I'm sure you have a million questions, so let's get started."

An hour later, Maggie followed a grimly silent Jake down the hall toward the elevators. He hadn't said much more than a "yes, sir" for the last half hour, yet after reaching the elevator and stabbing the down arrow, he swung around to face her, and the worry carving a line between his eyebrows was apparent.

Maggie drew a tight breath, marshaling her courage. They needed to clear the air if they were going to work together, let alone act like a loving married couple. "Would you like to go out for a drink or something? We have a lot of catching up to do."

His gaze narrowed slightly. "We're going to dinner in two hours." Charles had instructed them to meet him at the restaurant in their hotel, which told her Jake was staying there, too. Over dinner, they would practice their new roles as Monsieur and Madam Jacques Cotillard. She hoped Jake's French was better.

Rebuffed, Maggie tried a different tactic. She notched her hands at her waist. "What's the matter, Jake? Never worked with a woman before?"

His gaze slid over her. "Why are you so thin?"

The unexpected question shocked her into silence. Heat seared her cheeks, no doubt turning her face beet red. "I run." She spoke the words through her clenched teeth. Not even her therapist knew how much she ran—fifty miles a week, sometimes more.

Jake's frown grew less severe. "You can't run in the mountains, Lena—they're too steep. So what are you going to *do*?"

Did he know about her diagnosis? The concern in his gentle gaze made her stand taller. She shrugged dismissively. "Not run, I guess."

To her surprise, Jake raked a hand through his brown hair, betraying frustration. "I want you to turn down this assignment."

The words had her taking a tiny step backward. "Do what?"

"You're not ready, Lena."

She gasped, offended, even though his words echoed what her own mind was telling her. "You don't *know* me. You don't know if I'm ready or not!"

His mouth firmed. Calm as always, he spoke without raising his voice above a murmur. "I know what you went through in Morocco. I can tell just by looking at you that this assignment is going to set you back. *Please*, turn it down."

Was he only worried about her? Maybe he thought she would blow the operation for everyone—not just for Howitz and Barnes, but for the SEALs, too.

What if he was right? Discouragement threatened to undermine her wavering confidence. Unwilling for him to see it, she whirled away from him, eschewing the elevator in favor of the fire exit immediately adjacent.

"Lena!"

Behind her, she could hear Jake muttering something to himself in Gaelic. Tears clogged her throat as she practically flew down the echoing stairwell.

Jake *did* know her. He had just articulated what the fearful voice inside of her was saying. But she *had* to be ready. Mike and Jay were her colleagues. It could have been *she* who'd been kidnapped by the FARC, her life and her future snatched away from her. Not seizing this chance to help them smacked of cowardice.

Pushing out of the stairwell a moment later, she glimpsed the back of Jake's head through the double glass doors as he left the building. A sigh of relief escaped her. She needed to pull herself together before running into him again.

Forcing a smile for the security guard, Maggie collected her Ruger. *What now?* She didn't need two hours to get ready for her dinner with Jake and Charles. She would find somewhere to sit by the East River and use the time to silence her uncertainties.

If she didn't want to be a liability in this rescue operation, she needed to get over her experience in Morocco and move on.

CHAPTER 3

Sitting across from Charles du Lac, the French Secret Service agent, Maggie struggled to retain the composure she'd summoned earlier by the river. The restaurant, located just off the hotel lobby, screamed art déco, with geometric patterns on the red carpet, chairs covered in gold and red upholstery, and crystal chandeliers cast a muted light onto every table, concealing—Maggie hoped—the tension creeping back into her.

Gripping her hands under the tablecloth, she kept up her end of a conversation with Charles while fighting her awareness of a silent Jake, to whom she hadn't spoken a word since their exchange by the elevator. Given the discerning glint in Charles's dark eyes as they swung from her to Jake, he could sense the undercurrent. But he didn't bring it up until their salads arrived.

"Forgive me, but I'm noticing a wall between the two of you." He drew an invisible line with his fork. "Perhaps you should get to know each other a bit better before passing yourselves off as man and wife."

Since Maggie had just taken a bite of her salad, it was up to Jake to respond to that. He turned his head, considering her profile. Her cheeks grew warm. "Actually, we already know each other. We both studied abroad during our junior year in college. Lena was my girlfriend."

Jake placed a hand on her back without warning, nearly causing Maggie to choke as she swallowed.

"Ah." Charles stabbed a fork into his salad while coming to private conclusions. "You call her Lena, that's good. You can keep doing that. And since we're all supposed to be French, let us assume that tongue from this moment, going forward. *Ça va?*" *Okay?*

Jake answered with a typical French shrug. *"Oui, ça va."*

Maggie glanced over, surprised that even that smidgen of French sounded native, not at all like the stilted way he used to speak. "What language will the peacekeeping team be using?" she asked Charles.

"Spanish exclusively. Although everyone is probably conversant in English, I've told them neither of you speaks English well. I don't want them hearing your American accents and wondering if you really are French—unless you can pull that off."

Maggie tipped her head at Jake. "He can." He'd made her laugh more than once, imitating a Frenchman speaking English. "But not me." Meeting Jake's eye, she added, "Did you go to language school for Spanish, too?"

He answered in French. *"Non.* I picked it up in the Peace Corps."

Oh yes. He'd been working in Guatemala that one time she'd looked him up. "How long was your French language course?"

"Only six months, and I don't have native proficiency yet, but—"

"You speak it well." She could give him that much. "With a perfect accent."

"Merci."

Across the table, Charles smiled as he stabbed at his salad again. "Well, this is more like it." He persisted in his native tongue. "May I recommend you two sit at the bar after dinner and catch up?" His tone grew subtly harder. "I cannot have you airing your differences in front of the UN team and jeopardizing our mission."

As Charles popped his fork into his mouth, Jake studied him with that same deceptively soft gaze Maggie remembered from Paris. Now that he was a SEAL, not just a twenty-year-old linguistics major, he didn't seem so harmless. Charles wiped his mouth with his napkin while regarding Jake warily.

"Sure," Jake finally responded. "We could have a drink at the bar after this." His gaze landed on her.

Maggie, who'd offered that very thing earlier, turned him down. "Actually, I don't drink." At least not while she was still taking antianxiety medication.

Charles frowned at her. "I'm sure they have nonalcoholic options."

Of course, they did, but sitting alone at the bar with Jake wasn't going to resolve the tension between them because he would use that time to try to talk her out of this assignment. She didn't need him undermining her wavering confidence.

Fearing the meal would last forever, she willed their waiter to bring their main course. But Charles proved adept at getting others to talk. Even before their entrées came, he had both Jake and Maggie offering up their opinions on current events. It came as no surprise that Jake's outlook was similar to Maggie's. They'd been equally like-minded in college—with one exception. Jake was a man after God's own heart, while Maggie simply had no use for religion.

Not hearing him mention God, not even once over dinner, she wondered if his faith had waned over the years. *Oh, I hope not.* She'd admired him for it.

When their entrées finally came, she ate most of her steak, which was more than she'd eaten since the fiasco in Morocco. Some of that had to do with Charles saying, "Eat up! You won't get food like this for two weeks."

That was the length of time they were expected to negotiate for Howitz and Barnes's release. As missions went, two weeks weren't long at all, which made this assignment perfect for getting her confidence back. Maggie could do anything for fourteen days.

Stuffed by dinner, they all declined any dessert. Charles paid for the meal with a company credit card.

After signing his name with a flourish, the Frenchman slid aside the booklet. "I'm sure you have much to do before flying out on Monday. Check your emails for plane tickets and itineraries. My apologies for flying you back to New York first, but according to your legends, you live here, so..."

Well, of course, she was traveling with Jake. The news shouldn't catch her off guard.

Charles produced his phone. "I'm texting you the address of the facility where you'll receive your microchips tomorrow morning. By Monday, the small incisions will be healed, and you'll be ready to travel. Speaking of which, you will each receive a box in the mail at your respective addresses. Each box contains a backpack, waterproof jacket, and quinine tablets to safeguard against malaria. Leave your phones at home. Bring a pair of sturdy boots. Pack only two changes of clothing, a toothbrush, and maybe a comb. Any questions?"

Maggie couldn't think of any. She turned to Jake, who shook his head.

Charles pushed to his feet. "*Bonne soirée*, madame, monsieur. Enjoy your time at the bar." With a wink that implied they should get *very* well reacquainted, he swiveled on his dress shoes and left them sitting in silence.

Jake drew a deep breath. "I can already tell you're not going to sit with me at the bar."

He'd reverted to English, so she did, too, sending him a tight smile. "Looks like you can still read my mind." Hearing sarcasm in her voice, Maggie winced and tried again. "Sorry, but you can't talk me out of this assignment, Jake, and I don't want you wasting your time." She pushed her chair back. "I'm going to hit the hay. I'll see you in the morning."

Not waiting for his response, she left him alone at the table and bolted toward the lobby, jumping into an elevator that had already started to close. She'd accomplished her objective for the evening—keeping Jake from taking sides with the worried voice in her head.

Truth be told, this new Jake was intimidating, and she was a teensy bit worried he might come after her. She would get to her room as fast as possible and just ignore him if he knocked at the door.

~

A thumping coming from the room next to his roused Jake from a light slumber. He glanced at the clock next to his hotel bed. It was two minutes to midnight, and by the sound of it, Lena was still awake—doing jumping jacks?

He already knew she had trouble sleeping. His source claimed she liked to run at night, up to ten miles at a time. Maybe she was warming up for a run.

At night in New York City?

He threw back the covers and rolled out of bed. She'd better be smarter than that.

In the dark, he fumbled for a pair of sweatpants and searched for his socks and sneakers just in case she left her room. He was jamming his head into a T-shirt when her door thudded shut.

Muttering Grandpa Carrigan's favorite invective, Jake crossed to his door and peeked into the hall just in time to see her step into the elevator. As she turned around, he ducked out of sight and went to grab his key card and his cell phone.

Not that he was going to try to stop her from running. He doubted he could do that, any more than he could stop her from taking this assignment. He would keep an eye on her, was all.

Approaching the closed elevator, he studied the display above the doors while pushing the button for the second elevator. She'd stopped at the mezzanine level—oh, yeah, where the indoor gym was located. Good. He knew she wasn't foolish enough to run outside.

By the time he spotted her through the long glass wall that looked out on the hallway, she was running on a treadmill, looking for all the world like a mouse flying on its wheel—and getting nowhere.

The look of dismay on her face when she spotted him was worth losing sleep for. At last, he had her to himself—though once inside the room, Jake glimpsed the earbuds in her ears, and a portion of his satisfaction waned.

Five other treadmills were available. Even so, he chose the one right next to hers. After powering up his machine, he began to walk, easing into a run because his knees protested, having run five miles just the day before. Maggie glanced over as he increased his speed incrementally.

Finally, he was running as fast as she was. Why would anyone punish themselves like this? Worried they were going to run for an hour and not even speak, he invoked divine aid. *Lord, please let me talk to Lena tonight.*

Not two seconds later, one of her earbuds tumbled onto her conveyor belt, which flung it under a stationary bike.

Jake hit the red button on his machine. "I'll get that."

"Thanks." She slowed her pace, craning her neck to look back at him as he teased the earbud out from under the base of the bike.

Ignoring her outheld hand, Jake dropped the earbud into the pocket of his sweatpants and remounted his machine, amused by the indignant flaring of her beautiful eyes. Then he spurred himself into an easy lope, timing his footfalls to coincide with hers. Now they could talk.

"Look, I'm sorry if I came across a little negative today." He tiptoed around his reason for it. Her appearance had thoroughly dismayed him. She didn't look like she was anywhere close to being ready for the rough assignment ahead.

She shot a glance in his direction. "How come you knew I'd be at the briefing? You show up in my life without any warning, and then you disappear on me."

Oh, so that bothered her, did it? Good. "My commander briefed me on this assignment two days ago. He mentioned you were the CIA's top pick." Jake had even agreed Lena was the perfect candidate until he'd seen her in person that afternoon and realized she wasn't ready yet.

She cut a frown at him while running with an effortlessness he envied.

"I can tell you have questions. Go ahead and ask them." This was exactly what Charles wanted them to do—to clear the air.

"Okay. How long have you been a SEAL?"

"Five years. I worked for the Peace Corps first."

She nodded as if knowing that much.

"When I saw innocent people tormented by narcotraffickers, I decided I could help more if I was a special operator." His decision had as much to do with wanting to be part of Lena's world, but he wouldn't tell her that—not yet, anyway.

Her gaze slid over him. "How'd you do at BUD/S training? You weren't very athletic when I knew you."

He could always count on Lena to be truthful. "Well, I got myself in shape first, but it still took me two attempts."

"Two is still impressive. And when did you request to be a SOG?"

"A year before I recovered you from Venezuela."

Another nod. She kept her gaze averted. "You disappeared on me pretty fast after that… and after Morocco, too."

Her disgruntled observation made him smile on the inside. "Not my call." Walking away from her, not once but twice, had gutted him. He'd worked so hard to put himself into the same theater as her, only to be ordered elsewhere the instant he got her to safety.

"And Paris?" Finally, she looked at him, allowing him to glimpse the pain in her expression. "Why'd you leave without saying goodbye?"

He blinked, confused by the question. "What do you mean? My parents came and took me away before I could catch you. I explained all that in my texts after I got a new phone." His old one had been useless after the blast; hers, too, probably.

Maggie was frowning at him. "You never sent me any texts."

He jabbed the down arrow to slow his pace. Was she lying? What would be the point? "I texted you for months afterward, wanting to stay connected. I knew I had the right number because I called your house to check with your mother. After that, I figured you must have blocked me."

Her puzzled expression appeared genuine. "I had no idea you had texted me." She sounded dazed.

Chewing on Lena's assertion, Jake decided she was telling the truth. He thought immediately of someone who had both a means and a motive for blocking his number. "Could your father have blocked me?" A section chief for the FBI, Drake Ellis had had big dreams for his daughter, none of which included marriage to her college sweetheart.

"I don't know." Her edgy tone told him she didn't want to live in the past. "It's water under the bridge now, isn't it?"

Given her reply, Jake doubted his texts would have changed the course of her future anyway. Rather than dwell on his hurt, he changed the topic. "So, you're running a lot these days."

That earned him a defensive glance. "So?"

"Like fifty miles a week or more."

"How would you know that?"

He knew way more than she realized, having befriended her half-brother while swearing Miles to secrecy. "Been keeping tabs on you."

"Why?"

Why? She was the love of his life, his muse, the woman he was going to grow old with, provided he kept her alive long enough. "Just curious." World's biggest understatement. "Sorry I offended you after the briefing today. I'm just…I'm worried this assignment isn't right for you."

It was Maggie's turn to slap the emergency STOP button. As her treadmill ground to a halt, she whirled to face him, her body rigid, her beautiful eyes burning with emotion he could only wonder at. Her bosom, supported by a black jogging bra, rose and fell above her flat abdomen. He could see her hip bones through the Spandex of her running shorts.

"Please, don't say another word to me about walking away from this assignment. Mike Howitz and Jay Barnes were my friends, my colleagues. Would you leave your teammates to die in captivity?"

Jake firmed his lips. Of course not.

"So, I'm going, *Jacques*. Have I been diagnosed with Post-Traumatic Stress? Yes, but it's *not* a disorder. I've got it under control."

That she confessed as much took guts; he had to admire her honesty.

"I *have* to do this," she continued. "For them. All I can do is promise you that I won't let you down. So please stop undermining my self-confidence and be supportive, okay? That's how spouses are supposed to act."

Spouses. He hid a bitter smile. She didn't want to be his spouse—except in pretend. Then again, pretending might be all he ever got of her, so, okay. He couldn't lie. He was thrilled to be able to work with her, at last. "You're right, Lena."

While she silently processed his agreement, he powered down his machine, then stepped off it, putting himself within inches of her. Her eyes widened, and her body stilled like that of a wary doe.

Well, this is new. She saw him as a real man now, someone to be reckoned with. It was a heady thing to realize he could grab her and kiss her, and she would probably soften and kiss him back. But that wasn't how Jake rolled. He took her earbud from his pocket and held it out.

She snatched it from his hand, as if afraid to touch him.

"I'm going back to bed," he told her. "Don't run too long, and remember to hydrate. We have that procedure in the morning." He patted the railing of her treadmill. "Good night." He headed for the door.

As he strode past the glass wall seconds later, he could see that she'd yet to resume her run. She was staring at the treadmill display, clearly muddled by their encounter.

Jake tamped down a smile and counted her confusion as a win.

Maggie regarded the two Advil in her palm, lit up by the sunlight beaming through the airplane window next to her. The 747 jumbo jet she had boarded three hours earlier sliced serenely through the atmosphere at an altitude of thirty thousand feet. She and Jake were on their way to Bogotá four days after their briefing in New York. Soon, something as simple as pain medicine might be unattainable, especially if the FARC seized all their possessions. Advil she could do without, but what about her antianxiety pills?

She'd joined up with Jake at New York's JFK Airport, in the international terminal. Wearing a white rain jacket identical to hers, he'd been easy to spot. The last time she'd seen him was when they'd gotten their microchips implanted three days before. Strangely, one look at Jake's broad shoulders and grounding stare, and a large portion of her nervousness subsided. She was alive today because of him. In his presence, nothing bad would happen to her, with or without her pills. Unless the FARC shot him dead.

Stop that.

Squelching her PTS, she asked a passing flight attendant for more Sprite so she could swallow the tablets. As she waited, her thoughts went back to the phone call she'd shared with her father at the crack of dawn that morning. He'd called to wish her well, to caution her not to rub any of the FARC leaders the wrong way with her feminist remarks.

"I want you coming home in one piece, Mags."

His reference to the beating she'd suffered at the hands of Farid hadn't helped her confidence. "Hey, Dad, I've got a question for you, and I want an honest response." Jake's insistence that he'd texted her after Paris had been eating away at her. "After the bombing in Paris, when I got a new cell phone, did you block Jake Carrigan's number without my permission?"

"Whose number?"

"You know who I'm talking about—my boyfriend in Paris. You should know he's the SOG who pulled me out of Venezuela and Morocco and got me to safety."

Her father's startled silence had said it all. "So, you did," she concluded.

He'd heaved an audible sigh. "You had to finish college strong, Mags, not be distracted by a love interest."

"Yeah, well, I had no idea he texted me after Paris. You had no right to do that." She'd hung up on him, inexplicably furious. It wasn't until she'd calmed down that she acknowledged her father had saved her from years of suffering as she tried and failed to strike a balance between growing her career and growing a relationship.

Jake cut into her thoughts as he dropped into the seat beside her, startling her with his swift return from the lavatory. His gaze went straight to the tablets in her palm.

"Qu'est ce qui te fait mal?" What hurts?

Since joining him for this flight to Bogotá, they'd spoken nothing but French.

She answered in the same tongue, "I have a headache. *Merci*—ah, thank you," she said to the flight attendant handing her a Sprite." The truth was the spot on her right hip, where her microchip had been implanted, was still irritated.

Behind prescription-free lenses similar to the glasses he'd worn back in college, Jake's blue eyes narrowed. She'd learned the Navy had paid for him to have laser surgery. The glasses he wore now were part of his cover, meant to downplay his over-the-top physical fitness and to make him look more harmless. Thanks to his intelligent demeanor, he almost pulled off the illusion.

"Are you sure it's not your hip hurting?"

His acuity brought her startled gaze back to his. "Why? Does yours hurt?"

"No."

Oh. She swallowed down the tablets to hide her concern.

"Are you taking the antibiotics?"

"Yes." And the malaria tablets. And her antianxiety pills. "How do we know the rebels won't take our meds from us?"

"We don't."

Terrific. She could get stuck in the wilderness with a raging infection and a case of nerves, with malaria to top it off.

Jake brushed her shoulder while inclining his mouth to her ear. "It's not too late to turn back, Lena. When we get to Bogotá, we'll just say you're feeling sick, and we'll buy you a return ticket. *Pas de problème.*"

She whipped her face toward his so their noses were mere inches apart. "I am *not* backing—"

He cut off her furious retort—spoken in English—by covering her mouth with his.

In an instant, she was in Paris again, being swept away by the kisses of the young man she adored. The taste and texture of his kiss was exactly the same, but his technique was layered with a confidence that sent her pulse skipping.

Maggie drew away with her heart trotting. *Oh, dear.*

"Fais attention."

Jake's cautionary word rankled. She didn't need to be reminded not to speak English. She'd slipped, was all. Steeped in chagrin, she turned her attention out the window and peered down.

Far below them, the coast of Venezuela resembled a flouncy green skirt with a hem of sand and a ribbon of peach against the blue-green waters of the Western Caribbean. Picking out landmarks, she pinpointed the area called Maiquetía, just outside of Caracas, where she'd worked for fifteen months inside a government-owned weapons depot. Her objective then was to discover which countries were supplying President Maduro with what weapons. If not for Jake's timely rescue, she might have gone up in a ball of fire as a rebel army, intent on a coup that had ultimately failed, was about to fire a missile at the warehouse.

Jake, with a direct line to the rebels, had gotten them to divert their missile, which ultimately struck a retreating convoy filled with the dictator's arsenal. Jake had then whisked Maggie to safety aboard the USS *Theodore Roosevelt* before vanishing on her.

How bizarre that she was now with him again, miles in the air, headed for another tenuous assignment.

Would she rather be alone—or worse—paired with some stranger while pretending to be that man's wife? No way. Jake would keep her safe while she got her gumption back. When all of this was over, she would be stronger and more self-reliant than ever.

CHAPTER 4

An hour and a half later, their plane began its descent toward Bogotá. Nine thousand feet above sea level, Bogotá filled a basin in the Eastern Cordillera Mountain range. Among the largest cities in the world, it covered the plateau like a patchwork quilt, home to nearly eight million people who clustered into neighborhoods of differing wealth and ethnicity, with the slums pushed up against the hills. Regardless of wealth, every citizen was privy to a mountain view.

As their airplane floundered through the thin air, the pilot addressed the passengers, alerting them to the local time and the weather. Maggie watched Jake adjust his watch, turning it back an hour to 5:32 P.M.

"You brought your watch with you?" She'd left hers at home. "You know they'll probably take it from you."

"I'm counting on it."

She was still puzzling his reply when their plane bounced three times before landing at El Dorado International Airport. Maggie had to peel her fingers off the arms of her chair. At least it wasn't raining, this being August and one of the drier months of the year.

"We're good." Jake's soothing tone told her he was conscious of her fear.

As the plane continued leisurely toward the terminal, she peered outside at the familiar mountain range. When the doors opened, admitting the one-of-a-kind scent of South America, she relaxed further, having had positive experiences in this part of the world. And when Jake clasped her elbow as they strode up the jetway with their carry-ons, a portion of her old confidence welled inside her.

It wasn't long before their identical jackets, which, in hindsight, they should not have been told to wear, caught the attention of the Colombian customs agents inspecting their backpacks. All they'd brought with them were limited items Charles had instructed them to bring, along with the first-aid kits that had come inside of the backpack delivered to her door.

"You're both with the UN?"

"Yes." Jake's dampening tone suggested to the official that he had better not ask any more questions. The UN's agenda needed to be kept secret since Colombia's counter-narcotics company, the JUNGLA, would jump at the chance to find out where the FARC were hiding.

To Maggie's relief, the customs agent asked no more questions. After pawing through their packs, he returned them with a dismissive nod. Then, it was time to have their passports stamped and their tourist visas scrutinized.

A dour-faced customs official eyed both items, comparing the photos in their passports to their faces. "Which area of Colombia will you be visiting?" He spoke in English, the universal language of travel.

Maggie's heart thumped unnecessarily. Their passports would certainly hold up to inspection, and Colombia's visa policy was a lax one.

"*Juust* Bogotá."

Jake's reply, spoken with a heavy French accent, teased a giggle out of Maggie, which she squelched at the last instant. Back in Paris, his impersonations of the French had never failed to make her laugh.

"Which hotel?"

Jake looked at Maggie, then shrugged. "We don't know yet. We have no reservations."

"Hmph." His mouth pursed in disbelief, the official nonetheless stamped their passports and handed back their Type-V visas. His suspicious gaze traveled from Jake's face to Maggie's. "Enjoy your stay."

"*Merci.*" Jake snatched up both passports and slid them into a zippered pocket on his thigh before he ushered her swiftly toward the exit.

Pretending to adjust the strap on her pack, Maggie glanced back at the official as they walked away. Her heart skipped a beat. "He's making a phone call," she relayed in French.

"Walk faster." Jake gripped her elbow again and drew her into the crowd thronging toward the exit, eyes peeled for Charles, who'd said he would be picking them up.

Maggie spotted Charles first, lounging beside an advertisement for the *TransMilenio* Rapid-Transit System. At their approach, the Frenchman turned and marched ahead of them through the sliding glass doors, giving no sign that he'd actually seen them.

Humid air, choked with the smell of car exhaust, enveloped them as they hurried after their French counterpart. Charles was waving down a taxi. As they caught up to him, he opened the rear door for Jake and Maggie, his dark eyes snapping with urgency. *"Montez."* Get in.

Maggie ducked into the back seat with Jake right behind her. Charles slammed shut their door, then slipped into the front seat. "Hotel Hacienda Royal."

"*Sí,* señor." The driver pulled away from the curb, immediately switching lanes to overtake the taxi in front of them.

Maggie groped for a nonexistent seat belt while she shrugged off her backpack. She caught Charles's eye as he craned his neck to peer out the rear window. "Do we have company?"

As if comprehending her French, the driver veered into the oncoming lane, playing chicken with a bus loaded full of passengers, before lurching back onto the right side. Maggie seized Jake's arm without thinking. *Dear heaven!*

Charles smirked, clearly impressed. "I dare anyone to catch us." He stuck to speaking French. "Javier is the craziest driver in Bogotá, but he works for us, and his record is flawless. How was your flight?"

"Good." Jake had to pitch his voice louder as they'd just turned onto a boulevard laid with stone, causing the tires to rumble. "Nothing out of the ordinary, although these backpacks drew some attention."

Seeing Jake untie the laces of his right boot and haul it off, Maggie watched with increasing perplexity as he reached inside it, pried up the sole, and then shook out an oddly shaped device. When he pulled up a retractable antenna and held down a number on the keypad, she guessed the device was a satellite phone. So, this was how they would keep in contact with the outside world.

"Hey, Hulk, this is Iron Man. We're here. Do you see us?"

Jake had switched back to English and, given the names of superheroes he was spouting, he'd lapsed into code speak. Hulk had to be one of his teammates situated at the Joint Intelligence Center within the U.S. Embassy, and Jake was asking him if their microchips were showing up on the Joint Intelligence Center's geodesic map.

"Great. Let Wolverine know, and I'll see you all this evening."

This was the first Maggie had heard of any kind of meetup. She waited for Jake to end his call with the JIC before asking, "Iron Man?" Her lips twitched. It suited him perfectly. "Did you pick that name yourself, or was it given to you?"

Jake worked to put his phone back into his right boot. "One of our teammates is obsessed with superheroes. He gave me the name. Not sure if it's a compliment or what."

Fighting a smile, Maggie watched him pull his boot back on. A question occurred to her. "How's that thing charge?"

"It doesn't. The battery should last a week, and there's a spare one in my other heel."

"Huh." That didn't leave them any wiggle room should they have to stay longer than two weeks. "Those heels had better be waterproof."

"Yeah." His flat tone told her he shared the same concern, which was in no way reassuring.

Neither was her first look at their accommodations once they reached the hotel. The single queen-sized bed raised a red flag. Considering Jake's broad shoulders, sleeping together on that thing would resemble a contact sport, which—recalling the allure of that one kiss on the plane— made her pulse flutter with the hope that she might get another one.

"*C'est une belle chambre.*" *Nice room.* Unaware of her unprofessional thoughts, Jake placed his backpack on the luggage rack by hers while sending her a nonverbal cue to help him sweep the room for bugs.

The methodical procedure cleared errant thoughts from Maggie's mind. *"Il n'y a rien ici."* *There's nothing here.* Sinking into the upholstered chair by the window, she winced at the twinge in her hip.

Jake's gaze sharpened. "Your incision's bothering you." Alarm colored his voice.

"Non, c'est bon. I'm a little sore, that's all."

"It hasn't healed yet?"

"Of course, it's healed." The lie slipped out of her.

He clearly didn't buy it. "Stand up. Let me look at it."

"Non!" She wasn't giving him any excuse to force her off this assignment. Bolting off the chair, she dodged past him toward the marble-tiled bathroom, where she promptly closed the door in his face and then locked it.

With a calming breath, Maggie flicked on the light and turned down the waistband of her slacks while regarding the upper curve of her right hip, where the microchip had been implanted. She sucked in a breath at what she saw.

The Band-Aid she had stuck on that morning was blood soaked. Peeling it back, she was disturbed to see a small, gaping cut. What had happened to the single stitch that was keeping it closed? Had it dissolved? Rubbed off?

Sterilize. As her training kicked in, she washed her hands under scalding water, soaping them thoroughly. After drying them on a towel, she tugged fresh tissues from a tissue box, applied pressure to the wound, then rolled her pants back up to keep the tissue in place while she went to fetch her first-aid kit.

Exiting the bathroom, she ran smack-dab into Jake, who was standing just outside the door.

She reared back. "Don't *ever* stand outside the bathroom when I'm in it!" In her outrage, it was all she could do to speak French.

He sent her an easy shrug. *"Pas de problème.* There aren't any bathrooms where we're headed."

Annoyed that he was back to undermining her confidence, she shoved him out of her way—which was a lot harder than it used to be—and crossed the room to get to her pack.

"It's bleeding," he guessed as she unzipped the pouch on the side and pulled out the first-aid kit.

As she marched back toward the bathroom, Jake stepped into her path. His hand closed like a manacle around her wrist.

"*Écoute-moi.*" *Listen to me.* His gentle tone was oddly menacing when paired with his steely grip. "Even the smallest cut will fester in the wilderness. I can't let you proceed with this assignment."

Tempted to stamp as hard as she could onto his booted foot, Maggie drew a deep breath and summoned logic to argue her case. "What are you going to do? Call Gordon and tell him I've got a little cut? I've also got a hangnail." She held her right hand up in front of his face, tempted to hold up just her middle finger. "Does that disqualify me, too?"

"I have a new word for your vocabulary." He seemed to change the subject while tightening his grip as she tried unsuccessfully to twist her arm free. "*Travail d'équipe.*" *Teamwork.* He articulated the syllables clearly. "That's how Navy SEALs operate. That's why our casualty rate is as low as it is. We watch each other's backs. I know you're used to working alone, Lena. But how's that been working for you?"

She'd needed rescuing twice, and he knew it.

"*Nous sommes partenaires maintenant.*" *We're partners now.* "That means if you're going to wind up getting sick over an infection, then I have the right to know."

She'd always admired Jake for his unflappable logic. Where she tended to be hotheaded and impulsive, he was ever calm and reasonable.

"*Bien.* Whatever. I'll show you the cut, and you'll see that it's nothing."

"Good." With a nod and a grimace of apology, he released her wrist.

As Maggie marched back into the bathroom, he followed, making the spacious room feel half its actual size. Planting herself before the mirror, she was conscious of heat stealing into her face as she rolled down the waistline of her slacks and pulled back the tissue, which, to her relief, had only the smallest speck of blood on it. "See?" She switched to English, speaking quietly. "No big deal."

Jake bent over, putting himself at eye level with the incision. A furrow appeared on his forehead. "Looks like you rubbed the stitch off. Have you been running? You were told not to run."

"No." An outright lie. She'd run at least twenty-five miles since Saturday.

He straightened with a disappointed look. "I'll need to stitch it again."

"What!?"

"Relax. I've had plenty of practice. Let's see what's in your kit." He opened the box she'd placed by the sink and peered hard at the contents while proceeding to sterilize his hands. "Good. We have two needles and even a vial of lidocaine."

"You're not stitching my hip. It's just a little cut. It'll heal."

The implacable look he sent her was one she didn't recognize.

"You will let me close the incision, or you're not my partner anymore."

Ouch. Well, when he said it like that, it hurt her feelings a little. "Fine!" Gosh, he wasn't leaving her much of a choice.

A knock at the door startled them both, making Maggie regret her switch to English.

With a look of frustration, Jake dried his hands while Maggie went to answer the door.

"It's Charles," she announced after peeking through the peephole. *"Bonsoir, monsieur. Entrez."*

"Bonsoir, madame." The Frenchman's dark gaze took note of Maggie's flushed face before addressing Jake as he approached from the bathroom. "I've just come from speaking with the lead negotiator, Boris Mayer. He says the Italian, Leo Bellini, and the Turkish woman, Esme Simsek, will arrive late this evening, so he's postponing our briefing until eight in the morning, which leaves you plenty of time to sightsee tonight."

His emphasis on the word *sightsee* was clearly code for something. Maggie glanced at Jake and guessed they were meeting with the other SEALs.

Jake nodded. *"Ça a l'air bien."* *Sounds good.*

The Frenchman pitched his voice lower. "Your destination is ten miles from here. I scoped it out this morning. You can either take a taxi or the *TransMilenio*. Either way, be careful. The streets of the city aren't safe after dark. *A bientôt.*" He swiveled toward the door.

The words *aren't safe* echoed in Maggie's head. She and Jake were a heck of a lot safer in Bogotá than they would be in the wilderness where they were headed.

The instant Charles closed the door behind him, Jake swung toward her. "We're not going anywhere until your incision is closed."

Maggie found herself back in the bathroom with her slacks rolled down just far enough for Jake to sew the incision shut. She eyed their limited supplies while switching back to English and keeping her voice low. "You shouldn't use the lidocaine. We might need it."

Seated on the closed toilet seat with a syringe in one hand and the vial of lidocaine in the other, Jake looked up at her. "I'm using it."

"You don't think I can handle the pain?"

He met her defiance with a wry smile. "I'm sure you can, Lena, but I doubt I could handle hurting you."

Lines like that were the reason she'd fallen for him in the first place.

Swallowing hard, Maggie watched him drain the little vial and prayed they wouldn't need it later. As he commenced injecting lidocaine around the incision with infinite care, tenderness quilted her heart. As gentle and considerate as he apparently still was, it astonished her that he'd become one of the toughest operators on the planet.

Once the site was numb, he irrigated the tiny wound with the bulb-shaped squirter, using bottled water. Then he dabbed the area dry before sanitizing it with an alcohol square.

Maggie couldn't feel a thing. Watching him thread the curved needle, she admired his hands, which looked powerful, with long, dexterous fingers. He slipped the thread through the tiny eye on his first try, proving his eyesight to be perfect.

"Is that self-absorbing thread?" She snatched up the box and read it. "Yes."

For the next minute, he plied the needle, pulling the edges of her skin together. A memory floated up from the depths of her mind: Jake treating her skinned palms after she slid down the banister on the steep run of stairs in Montmartre and wound up doing a face-plant. She'd always been the reckless one, him the caretaker.

"All set." Having knotted the thread, Jake snipped it with the tiny scissors in her kit. "Keep a layer of this ointment on the cut until it heals and cover it with a Band-Aid." As he went to squeeze the tube, Maggie took it from him.

"I'll do that. Thank you." His ministrations were clouding her judgment. "What time is it?" She stepped away, putting some badly needed space between them.

Jake checked his watch. "Time to start heading for the safe house."

She'd figured that was where they were headed. "Well, let's go, then." She covered the incision with a Band-Aid and rolled her pants back up. *"Allons-y."*

A short time later, they slipped from the hotel's fire exit wearing their rain jackets in anticipation of cooler weather. The sun had set behind the rim of mountains to the west, leaving the sky a mellow hue that beckoned darkness and cool night air.

Maggie swept a practiced eye up and down the steep, stone-laid street. Their hotel, like the majority in Bogotá, was situated in La Candelaria district, close to the historic center of the city, where colonial charm and museums abounded. "I used to live near here." She turned toward Jake. "Have you been to Bogotá before?" she asked in French.

"Non."

"Do we have time to walk a little? I could show you around."

Jake pulled his sleeve back to check. *"Oui,* we could walk for maybe twenty minutes, but let's at least travel in the right direction." As he adjusted his stance, she guessed the watch had a compass on it.

"What's the district called where we're headed?" Not that she didn't trust his compass to get them there.

"Quinta Camacho."

She knew exactly where that was. *"Parfait.* It's this way. Come on. We might have time to see the best of Bogotá."

As she struck out down the narrow street, the fresh stitches on her hip rubbed a seam on her slacks. *Not again.* Maggie was about to shift the way her pants sat on her hips when Jake threw a companionable arm around her shoulders. *Oh...okay...*

Given their legend as a married couple, his familiar behavior made perfect sense, but this was how they used to walk together, back in Paris.

Memories assaulted her. They'd toured the entire city in lockstep like this, like nothing could ever come between them. She'd forgotten how good it felt to fit snugly under his armpit. Her left arm stole around his trim waist, and the discomfort of her stitches was forgotten.

Down the narrow, cobbled street, they ambled through a small colonial-era neighborhood with stucco buildings painted in vivid hues, either gold or pink or blue. The complex cultural history of the conquest was apparent everywhere she looked. Lights in a café window blinked on, illuminating a colorful mural of an indigenous woman adorning the opposite wall.

"That's one of Guache's murals," Maggie explained. "His paintings are the most vibrant. There's another one coming up."

Jake studied them both with grave interest.

Finally, the narrow street spilled them onto Calle 11, a wider thoroughfare surging with traffic. Here, historic buildings gave way to twentieth-century architecture, including the occasional high-rise. Streetlamps blinked on, lighting their way along the cement sidewalks. The warmth and scent radiating off Jake's body stole into Maggie's awareness. How, after all these years, did he still smell like a summer rain shower?

A famous landmark caught her eye, as its whitewashed walls and arched windows were lit up by floodlights. "That's the Botero Museum coming up."

"Botero?"

"You know. The sculptor and painter from Colombia who makes his subjects look, uh, how do you say, *rondelet*." *Rotund.*

"*Ah, oui.*" Jake cut a look at her slender body and grinned. "He should sculpt a fat Lena."

Maggie scoffed at the vision that came to mind.

"You'd still be beautiful."

She let the compliment pass, pretending it didn't warm her. The gold dome gleaming over the rooftops ahead gave her something to say. "And that's the Museo de Oro on the next block."

"The one with the gold, er…?" He gestured to indicate the dome, clearly not knowing the word.

"*Dôme. Oui*, there are more than fifty-five thousand pieces of gold in there, most of them artifacts from the Incan empire."

"I'd love to see that." Jake checked his watch. "*Hélas*, there's no time tonight. In fact, we'd better grab a taxi at the next street."

Probably a good thing since she realized her incision was stinging.

Jake cut her an astute glance. "You good?"

"*Oui, très bien.*" She sent him a carefree smile.

A minute later, they were crammed into the rear seat of a tiny yellow taxi zipping along back streets headed toward Quinta Camacho. In lieu of hotels and apartments, the neighborhood of Quinta Camacho was filled with private homes, many surrounded by walls topped with broken glass to discourage thieves. The taxi slowed alongside a curb, Jake paid the fee, and they both got out.

As the cab pulled away, he put his arm around her shoulders again. "We walk to the next street over."

The neighborhood was dark and quiet, suggesting it enjoyed less crime than much of the rest of the city. On the following block, Jake drew her to a pedestrian gate with wrought-iron bars and an intercom but no house number. He poked a long finger at the button.

A gruff voice came out of it. "*Sí?*"

In perfect Spanish, Jake announced them.

Once the lock clicked open, they pushed into a lush little garden where they were met by a silver-haired gentleman wearing a white Guayabera shirt. The stranger inspected Maggie, then thrust out a hand. "John Whiteside, station chief."

She recognized the name. "Oh yes, you replaced Norris. He was the station chief during my assignment here."

"Welcome back to Bogotá."

"Thanks. It's good to be back."

Jake got a handshake. "Lieutenant Carrigan. Come on in. Your men are waiting for you."

Following Whiteside into the safe house, they entered a tiled foyer that led them into the building's large living space. Whiteside hung back as they ventured in, and four fit men sprang to their feet, eyes locked on Maggie.

"Evening, sir. Ma'am."

Their civilian clothing in no way disguised that these were special operators—Navy SEALs, to be precise. Maggie was pleased to recognize two of them from when Jake had plucked her out of Venezuela.

He drew her closer. "Guys, a couple of you remember Magdalena. Lena, this is Harm, aka the Hulk." He gestured to the bald, blue-eyed SEAL who had manned a .50-caliber sniper rifle while covering their retreat from the warehouse. "You've met Bambino, our resident Spider Man." The mid-twenties SEAL of Italian descent was grinning like he had the scoop on an inside joke.

Jake nodded at the next SEAL. "And this is Zen Suzuki, our communications specialist. He's the one obsessed with superheroes. His call sign is Daken."

Zen sent her a bow, betraying his East Asian influence while sending Maggie a peaceful smile.

Lastly, Jake gestured to a SEAL standing with his tan arm folded across his chest, unsmiling. "And last but not least, Lieutenant Villalobos, officer in charge. We call him Lobo. So, naturally, he's Wolverine."

That made perfect sense to Maggie since *lobo* meant "wolf" in Spanish.

As tall as Jake and intense in contrast to Zen, Lobo scarcely acknowledged her. "We're all set up over here." He gestured toward a laptop perched on the coffee table, where yet another, more senior SEAL could be seen on the screen jotting himself a note.

"Great." Jake guided Maggie toward the couch that faced the laptop and pulled her down next to him, catching the eye of the man on the screen.

"Ah, Jake, good to see you there."

"Thank you, sir. This is my colleague, Magdalena. Lena, meet Lieutenant Commander Strong, our operations officer."

Maggie tapped her memory. Why did the mid-to-late-thirties SEAL look so familiar?

Keen gray eyes studied her. "Well, it's all clear to me now, Jake."

Lena shot a puzzled glance at Jake. But then the briefing got underway, and then the ops officer's visage was replaced by the photo of a dense green mountain chain buried in mist. "You two are headed northeast of Bogotá into La Cordillera de los Cobardes in the Santander region."

Mountain Range of the Cowards, Maggie translated. She'd heard of the area while working at the embassy. Due to its rugged landscape, the inhospitable region was home mainly to indigenous farmers but also offered refuge to drug cartels and antigovernment militias, like the ELN and the FARC.

"The Cordillera de los Cobardes is part of the highest coastal ranges in the Eastern Cordillera. The only groups who live there are rangers at the national park to the north, an indigenous tribe, and outlaws. To give you an idea, the *average* elevation is eleven thousand feet above sea level." Strong zoomed in on the image. "But the FARC are believed to live on this fourteen-thousand-foot monstrosity right here, called El Castillo, 'The Castle.' You can see by how green the area is that it rains a lot, even when it's not peak rainy season. There are no roads beyond La Esmerelda, where the FARC have arranged to meet the UN team and then escort you to one of their camps. Given the muddy terrain, transportation is done mostly on mules."

"You can't run in the mountains, Lena. They're too steep."

Maggie focused on El Castillo. The lower four-fifths of it was covered in foliage so thick she doubted there was a drone out there that could pick up thermal images of life forms under that canopy, let alone human beings. And the top was rocky and rugged and dusted with snow. If she were a rebel, she would hide there, too.

Strong continued, "We need to know where in this vast wilderness the hostages are being kept so we can get them out. We also need intel on possible infiltration and exfiltration sites. Right now, the only place we know we can land a helo is in this valley to the east."

Strong panned toward the valley, crossing a river to get there. "Jake, you've got your watch with you?" The commander's earnest face filled the screen again.

"Yes, sir." Jake showed it to him.

"Okay. Let's hope it ends up in the hands of the leader, General Salvador Rojas, though that's not his real name, which no one knows. He's called Rojas because of the red beret he wears."

A grainy photograph of a rebel wearing a red beret filled the screen.

Maggie stared at the resolute expression on the leader's haggard face. In his mid-fifties, he looked as though he'd spent his entire life battling the powers that be.

She wrested her gaze toward Jake's wrist. So that was why he wore the watch, even though they'd been told to leave anything of value behind. No doubt it was rigged with a GPS device like her watch back home. If Rojas ended up with it, he'd become a much easier target. Very clever.

Strong reappeared on the screen. "A word of caution. Colombia's Counternarcotics Jungle Company, or the JUNGLA as they're called, may try to follow you to the dissidents' camp. Any altercation between the FARC and the JUNGLA could endanger Barnes and Howitz's lives, so we don't want this happening."

Maggie pictured her former colleagues helpless to defend themselves in a shootout.

"If you find yourself being followed by the JUNGLA, try to let us know. We can call them off if we must, but we'd rather not reveal that we have people on the ground. Jake, you'll touch base with the JIC whenever possible. The phone in your boot seems to work."

"Yes, sir."

"Any questions?" The commander tipped his head and waited.

Maggie's curiosity got the better of her. "Have we met before?"

Several SEALs snickered, including Jake.

Strong sent her a humble smile. "I used to play quarterback for the Dallas Cowboys."

"Ooh." No wonder he looked familiar. Her father was a huge Cowboys fan. She'd probably grown up seeing his face on TV.

"One more question, sir." Jake leaned forward. "Is there an escape-and-evasion plan in case something unforeseen happens?"

Maggie stiffened. Like what? Did Jake think she was going to fall apart on him? *I can't afford to.*

The former quarterback thought a moment. "I think Lobo was working on that. Why don't you check with him?"

They both looked at Lobo, who nodded.

"Will do, sir. Thank you, sir."

"Good luck to both of you. Lena, it was nice to meet you."

"You, too, Commander."

Strong disappeared, replaced by a screen that read *Special Operations Web Connect* before Lobo scooped up the laptop and started clicking keys. Maggie hid her secret worries. She had used the E & E protocol back in Morocco. She wouldn't need it this time, not if Jake was with her.

When Lobo put the laptop in front of them again, Maggie guessed she was still looking at a satellite view of El Castillo.

Lobo leaned over with a finger on the keyboard. "Okay, if I zoom in on the top of El Castillo"—he spoke with softened consonants that betrayed Hispanic heritage—"you can see between the mountain's twin peaks what's left of a glacier. And right here"—he pointed out the blurred image—"are a couple of solar panels providing electricity to a radio station the FARC used to use to promote their Marxist views. These days, it's used by a missionary to transmit his Sunday podcasts."

"Missionary?" Jake sounded surprised.

Lobo kept talking. "If your comms go out, you could always use the radio station to broadcast an SOS. The FARC have a repeater up there for their handheld radios. Disabling the repeater would hamper their communication, since radio waves can't bend around the mountain. If you need a quick exfil, it looks like there's enough room on the shore of the lake on this side to land a rescue helicopter." Lobo's jungle-green eyes trekked toward the other three SEALs. "Should we firm this up as our E&E plan?"

One at a time, each man agreed, including Jake. Then they all looked at Maggie, who shrugged, surprised to be given a say in the matter. "Sure."

Jake sniffed the air. "Do I smell food?"

Harm grinned. "Yes, you do, sir. The station chief insisted on feeding us tonight. Let's eat!"

In the dining room, Whiteside was laying out paper plates and plastic utensils for the food he'd already set out. "Good. You're done already. Come and eat while it's hot. I've got four traditional dishes for you to sample."

The men insisted Maggie go first in heaping food onto her plate. There seemed to be plenty to go around. A lighthearted banter flowed between the SEALs, making it apparent they were accustomed to each other's company. With a twinge of envy, she imagined what it must be like having teammates to rely on.

As the meal wore on, Harm and Bambino helped themselves to seconds. But Maggie was stuffed, having eaten as much as she could. It might just be her last big meal for a while.

Whiteside brought in brownies from the kitchen. "Who wants dessert?"

As Maggie declined, Jake wiped his hands on a paper napkin. "We should probably head back to the hotel."

All four SEALs at the table rose when Maggie stood.

"Luck to both of you, sir." It was Harm who said this, his bright-blue eyes full of encouragement. "What's that Irish blessing you taught us again?"

A smile danced at the edges of Jake's lips. *"Go n-éirí an bóthar leat."*

May the road rise to meet you. Maggie knew that Gaelic phrase, as well. But there weren't any roads where they were headed, just an impenetrable mountain, drug lords, and rebel dissidents.

Maybe Jake was right. Maybe she wasn't ready for this.

CHAPTER 5

By the time Maggie and Jake left the safe house, night had smothered Bogotá in total darkness, no thanks to the clouds stalled on the high plateau. Not a single star or sliver of moonlight helped to illumine their way as they wended through the suburban neighborhood, headed toward a road busy enough for taxis to frequent. A distant bell tolled eight o'clock as they flagged one down and slipped into the back seat.

In Spanish, Jake told the driver where to go. Glancing at Maggie, he transitioned to French. "You're very quiet. Feeling intimidated?"

Even after all these years, he could read her like a book. "Why would I be intimidated when there are four operators waiting to pick us up if there's a problem?"

Headlights from the oncoming cars spotlighted his small smile. "That's a good point. Any one of those guys would give his life for me—and for you."

His words made her think of the SEAL in the news last year who'd dived into a rough Arabian Sea going after his teammate who'd slipped and fallen in. Neither man was ever recovered.

With her thoughts turning gloomy, Maggie peered out the window, hoping to recognize more landmarks. As the driver turned onto an unfamiliar road, she questioned his decision-making. Perhaps the man knew a shortcut because this was not the way she would have gone. Or maybe he was luring them into a remote spot, thinking he had two wealthy tourists in the back seat.

She called his bluff, challenging him in Spanish. "This isn't the way to Hacienda Royal, señor."

At her words, Jake jerked to attention, casting sharp looks around.

"Hacienda Royal? Ah, my mistake." The bulky driver immediately slowed down and swung his taxi nose-end into an alleyway between two shuttered buildings. As he twisted in his seat to peer out the back window, he brandished a pistol unexpectedly.

"Give me your wallets!" His eyes glittered with malice.

Adrenaline flooded Maggie's bloodstream. Kamal's bodyguard had that same look in his eyes before he punched her in the face. She was only vaguely aware of Jake's reassuring squeeze telling her he would handle this, which was well and good because she'd forgotten how to breathe.

"*Tranquilo*, señor." Jake slowly raised both hands. "I alone carry a wallet. There is not much cash in it, but you are welcome to all of it. I'm taking it out now, slowly." Keeping one hand in the air, he reached into the pocket on his thigh while Maggie swallowed hard, battling to bring her panic under control. "Here's my wallet."

Greedy for Jake's cash, the driver held out a hand to take it.

If Maggie had blinked, she would have missed the lightning-fast jab that broke the driver's nose. In the same instant, Jake wrested away the pistol. While the driver yelped and clapped a hand to his injury, Jake put away his wallet, then removed the magazine from the gun and dropped it at their feet. He reached across Maggie to open her door, but she was already halfway out of it, adrenaline spurring her with a cowardly urge to run.

Get a grip!

Jake caught up to her before she got five yards from the car. Together, they ran away from the alley and up the quiet street. With a glance over his shoulder, Jake flung the gun onto the roof of a building next to them, then tugged her toward a covered entryway. "Let's lie low until he leaves." Given no one was around, he spoke in English.

"No, let's run to the hotel from here." The urge to flee was so strong that Maggie couldn't hold still. Her heart hammered, and her thigh muscles flexed. It was all she could do to slow her breathing so Jake wouldn't notice.

"Running will tear your incision."

"Jake, I have to run." There. She'd exposed her vulnerability.

Even in the dark, she could see him assessing her mental state. "Only a mile or two."

"Okay." She bolted, counting on him to catch up to her.

Once she was flying up the side street toward the wider boulevard, her panic subsided. The predictable pumping of her legs and her deep breaths lulled her back to normalcy. They sprinted past storefronts whose doors and windows were shuttered by extendible steel gates. She recognized the name of a family-run bodega. This was familiar. This was safe. Plus, she could hear Jake right behind her.

"Lena, slow down. You're going to hurt yourself."

She ignored him, reveling in the freedom of flying like the wind along a broad sidewalk. The mist that cloaked the city kissed her cheeks before turning into a drizzle that made her thankful for her UN raincoat. Turning the corner at Carrera 6, the familiar dome of the Museo de Oro brought further reassurance. It was all uphill from here to La Candelería district twinkling dead ahead. Jake finally overtook her, catching her elbow.

"Enough running." He slowed her into a brisk walk.

Their heavy breathing filled the silence between them, broken by the sound of raindrops hitting their jackets and occasional cars rumbling past on the paving stones. Maggie waited for Jake to bring up her overreaction to a mere stickup by a single would-be robber.

"How's your incision?"

That wasn't the question she was expecting. "Um…It's been rubbing the seam in my slacks."

He muttered a phrase in Gaelic. "I'll have a look when we get back."

The hotel came closer, its windows bright with lights that promised warmth and safety. At last, the lecture she'd been expecting came from Jake's lips.

"So, I could point out that what we just faced was nothing compared to what's coming, only I imagine you're aware of that."

Oh, she was well aware.

"You know, you can always say you got food poisoning at the last minute."

She rounded on him, switching to French like the professional she was. "I'm going with you, Jacques. Howitz and Barnes were my colleagues. If this had happened five years ago, it could've been me who was kidnapped."

Jake caught her wrist, tightening his hold when she made to pull away. "*Je comprends.*" His gaze held hers. "I do. Look, if it makes things any easier, I'm here for you, okay? I'm not going to let anything bad happen to you. It's called teamwork, and I expect the same from you."

Well. That made her stand taller. Squelching the urge to salute him, Maggie let his words sink into her. His assurance did make things easier. At the same time, she cautioned herself, *Don't get used to the teamwork. It's only temporary.*

"*Ça a l'air bien.*" *Sounds good.* She sent him a tiny smile, which he returned.

"Finally. Let's get out of this rain."

Plagued by visions of the forbidding El Castillo, it took Maggie hours to fall asleep. Her incision throbbed, even though Jake's stitches had held, despite their run after the holdup in the taxi. On top of that, she was hyperconscious of Jake's presence in the bed. Following her insistence that he *not* sleep on the floor, he had finally acquiesced, lying upside down with his feet where his head should be. Eventually, his soft snores had lulled her into losing consciousness. She awoke to him jostling her shoulder.

"Up you get, sunshine. You've got twenty minutes before we meet the other members of the team."

"Twenty minutes!" Maggie threw back the covers and scooted out of bed. "Why didn't you wake me up?"

"Because you just fell asleep."

Mulling over his statement, she riffled through her pack, then marched into the bathroom with one of the two outfits she was bringing into the wilderness with her: water-resistant trousers, a lightweight T-shirt, and, of course, the boots she'd bought for her birthday in May, using the gift card her stepmom gave her.

Jake tapped on the door. *"Comment est l'incision?"*

Half dressed, Maggie turned toward the mirror and eyed the angry flesh around the stitches with a twinge of concern. *"C'est bien."* What a lie. She squeezed a thick line of ointment on it and applied a fresh Band-Aid. There were only five left in her kit, but Jake had a full stash in his.

"I hope you're telling the truth." He said this in English, quietly, through the crack in the door.

"I am."

"Uh-huh. Don't forget to take your pills."

She shook the bottle into which she'd dumped all of her pills—Advil, penicillin, quinine, and her anxiety prescription. "I'll be right out." *Go away!* Man, if she was craving privacy now, what would it feel like when there weren't any walls between them?

Nineteen minutes later, they were riding the elevator to the lobby to meet the others. Maggie stole a peek at Jake. In his white rain jacket, khaki-colored clothing, and boots, he looked like a model for *Outdoor Living* magazine.

As they stepped out of the elevator, the small group in the lobby dressed in jackets identical to theirs made it apparent they were the last to show up. Charles caught sight of them and waved them over.

"Here you are. I thought French people were always on time," he chided in Spanish, the team's common language.

Maggie assessed the unlikely bunch of UN peacekeepers. *If these people volunteered to trek into the wilderness, then I have nothing to worry about.*

Charles introduced them to the lead negotiator first. "Boris, this is the couple I work with at the Secretariat in New York, Madeleine and Jacques Cotillard, originally from Paris."

Tall and brawny, with a large head, the German's hand swallowed Maggie's as he greeted her with a polite nod and serious gray-blue eyes.

"Good to meet you. *Y usted también*, Jacques." He turned to shake Jake's hand.

"*Un placer*," Jake responded.

Boris took over with the introductions, turning to the petite, middle-aged woman with a thick black braid. "This is Esme Simsek from Izmir, Turkey. Her Spanish is excellent."

The woman beamed at Maggie, clearly pleased to have another woman present.

Gosh, I hope she's tougher than she looks.

"And this is our Italian volunteer, Leo Bellini."

Bellini boasted a five-o'clock shadow already—or perhaps he hadn't shaved that morning. In his early thirties like Maggie and Jake, he divided a puzzled gaze between them.

"I was just at the Secretariat last week. I thought I'd met everyone in the Department of Peace Operations."

Uh-oh. Caught in a lie already.

Charles intervened. "Nearly everyone. These two were on vacation—a wedding anniversary."

"Oh." Bellini lit up at the news, making him quite a handsome man. "Congratulations. How many years?"

Maggie waited for Jake to answer.

"Twelve." He said it with gentle affection while taking in Maggie's response. "More than a decade now."

Her heartbeat stammered. He'd given her the promise ring twelve years ago. Forcing a loving smile while tears pricked her eyes, she replied, "*¡Cómo pasa el tiempo!*" How time flies!

Would this day never end?

Maggie caught Jake sneaking a peek at his watch. "*Quelle heure est-il?*" What time is it?

"Almost three."

They'd been sitting in the back of this stuffy little van for over an hour, going nowhere. The journey to La Esmerelda was supposed to take only four hours in total, the first two of which took them northeast away from Bogotá and along the ridge of increasingly rugged mountains toward La Cordillera de los Cobardes. Maggie inwardly sneered. How apt that the FARC would hide themselves in a wilderness area called "The Cowards."

When their rented van slowed to a stop behind a line of cars, Boris Mayer muttered something in German, then got up to query the driver in Spanish. "What's happening?"

Maggie overheard the driver tell him there'd been a rockslide at the mouth of the tunnel.

Peering past the cars in front of them, she spotted Colombia's equivalent of the National Guard working to clear large chunks of granite that had tumbled onto the road from the promontory looming up ahead. The tunnel beyond the pile of granite was the only way to get to La Esmerelda.

Huffing out a frustrated breath, she sat back in her seat. *"Je dois aller aux toilettes."* *I have to use the bathroom.* They'd kept strictly to French between the two of them, a language none of the participants spoke fluently, though they doubtless understood quite a bit, especially Bellini.

"I told you not to drink that whole carton."

Jake was referring to the carton of coconut milk she'd bought at the hotel before their departure. Maggie had figured it was just a two-hour ride from Bogotá to Barbosa, the town on the other side of the tunnel, where Boris had said they would stop for lunch.

"Not to mention it's a *laxatif.*"

"Hush." He was teasing her now, reminding her of all the times he'd made her laugh back in Paris.

"I saw a paper cup rolling around up front. You could pee in that."

"Stop!" But she couldn't keep from giggling.

Jake produced a little notepad and a pen taken from their hotel room. "Let's play Kill the Man by His Neck."

It took her a second to realize he meant Hangman. Not even *she* knew that word in French. "Sure." She shrugged, eager for a distraction.

For the next twenty minutes, she tried to guess what the thirteen-letter word could be. All she had so far were vowels, and her man was about to hang. "I need a clue."

"It's a place we've been together."

She shot him a warning look. Did he have to bring up the past? But her mind was already sifting through the place names: Versailles, Montmartre, Chantilly…"It's Fontainebleau, where Charles is from." A loud blare cut into her momentary victory, causing her to jump like a startled deer.

Jake put a hand on her knee. Peering out the front of the van, Maggie spotted the cause of the noise. "The road's been cleared, *Dieu merci*." *Thank God.*

Jake put away his pen and paper. They started moving, only to stop after a short distance. Maggie whimpered.

Jake articulated what she was seeing. "Looks like they're checking IDs."

Maggie groaned. The cup Jake had mentioned earlier was becoming a viable option.

Boris stood with a tight-lipped expression. "Everyone, hand me your passports." The FARC had assured them they were safe to bring along and wouldn't be confiscated.

As Jake surrendered both their passports—he'd insisted on carrying hers—Maggie shared a grim look with Charles. A group of UN peacekeepers, regardless of how small, was going to be noticed. How long before word of their travels reached the JUNGLA, who chafed to discover where the FARC hid themselves?

Ten minutes later, a national guardsman stood at the van's door reviewing their passports. Maggie watched Boris gnaw the inside of his lip. She overheard the guardsman ask, "You're all with the UN?"

"Yes."

"Where are you headed?"

"To Puerto Limón," Boris lied. "We're a medical team. There's been an outbreak of diphtheria."

Nice one, Boris, but this isn't the way to Puerto Limón.

It wasn't until Boris returned their passports to them and the van started moving again that Maggie realized every muscle in her body had tensed up. She forced herself to relax as the van lurched forward, eager to make up for lost time.

But then they surged into a narrow, unlit tunnel, and she went rigid again. Deepening her discomfort, Jake pinned her against the seat with an arm across her shoulders, as there weren't any seat belts. Dying in a head-on collision inside a dark tunnel wasn't how Maggie saw her life ending.

But they didn't die. The tunnel spit them out on the north side of the mountain. Almost immediately, they turned off onto a tight ramp that swung them down into a valley. Gazing out the window, Maggie's eyes widened.

All there was to see in any direction was lush, lumpy greenery, no civilization in sight, except for a sign stating Barbosa was just two kilometers away. She heaved a sigh, relieved she'd soon get to use a bathroom. A short time later, the brakes on their van squealed, and they stopped for lunch.

Seated at an outdoor eatery under a thatched roof in the small roadside town, the team enjoyed a meal of chicken, rice, and fried plantains.

"Eat well," Boris urged. "We have no way of knowing whether the FARC can afford to feed us."

While Jake slipped into the small restroom to place a call to the JIC, Maggie caught sight of a military Jeep wending its way down the only main street. As the occupants of the vehicle stared at the group in white jackets, Maggie's antenna for trouble twitched. Was the National Guard checking out their story? They'd better not inform the JUNGLA.

Yet, by the time the team piled back into the van to continue their journey, the Jeep had vanished.

The van slogged on, taking them back to the highway at the top of the Eastern Cordillera and pressing north. An hour later, they took an exit that put them on a steep, winding road that narrowed every hundred meters until branches and fronds brushed the windows. The road's surface went from asphalt to gravel to a muddy trail riddled with potholes that filled with water as the leaden clouds overhead buckled suddenly.

Windshield wipers beat a frenzied tempo but never succeeded in clearing the fogged glass up front. The music on the radio crackled and faded into static before the driver turned it off.

A somber silence descended over the peacekeepers. Maggie dragged air into her tight lungs. Were the others thinking what she was thinking: They'd come this far; now there was no going back?

Staring out the fogged window next to her, all she could see were lush hills covered with coca fields and banana groves. A swollen brown river ran parallel to the road for a while, then veered away. With every hundred meters, their isolation deepened, and Maggie's anxiety rose.

Jake nudged her suddenly, then pointed out the opposite window. "Look."

Following his cue, she recognized the distinct shape of *El Castillo* from Commander Strong's briefing. Seeing it in person, she swallowed down a surge of fear. Lushly green at its lower elevations, it stood with its twin peaks buried in rain clouds.

Somewhere on its massive surface, Mike and Jay were chained up, miserable and despairing of rescue. If they were ever going to make it home to their families, Maggie and Jake needed to find out exactly where they were so the SEALs could rescue them.

It was dusk by the time they arrived at La Esmerelda, their four-hour drive having turned into eight. The little pueblo consisted of just three main buildings, one of which was a single-story, clapboard *ranchita* advertised as an inn. Isolation wrapped around Maggie as she watched their van drive away. But the indigenous hosts greeted the team warmly, fed them bread and goat cheese for supper, and then led them to private bedrooms that were little more than closets with straw mattresses on bed frames.

"Sleep well," Boris instructed the group. "We awaken at dawn tomorrow." The FARC were supposed to come fetch them.

Lying on the crackling double bed, Maggie found herself shivering in the oversized T-shirt she had brought to sleep in despite the warmth of the wool blanket covering her. No way was she letting Jake sleep upside down so they'd fit in the bed. She needed him to hold her—just to keep her warm, of course.

The door groaned inward, and Jake ducked under the lintel, his head still damp from rinsing in the communal shower. At the sight of her huddled in the bed with the blanket drawn to her chin, his mouth firmed. He whipped off his glasses, set them by the bed, and bent low, murmuring in French, "You can't fight fire with fire, Lena."

She raised an eyebrow. "What's that supposed to mean?"

"It means you're trying to scare off your fear. It doesn't work that way."

"I am *not* afraid." Yet she'd taken a whole antianxiety pill instead of a half to make sure she slept.

Jake muttered something in Gaelic as he reached for the string dangling from the naked lightbulb. "Make room."

Her senses clambered for his presence. Once he squeezed in next to her, she would be okay. His shoulders took up an inordinate amount of space, forcing her up against the wall. But then, wordlessly, he slipped an arm around her and pulled her against him. His chest became her pillow. Her stiff body seemed to melt with relief against his solid frame, causing a memory to float up of that warm spring day in Paris when they'd napped like this in the Tuileries Garden.

"Comfortable enough?"

"Mmm." She clung to the memory while absorbing his warmth the way she'd soaked up the sun that day. If only they were still in Paris, still young and in love. Instead, they were heading into the wilderness to deal with hardened guerrillas who justified kidnapping and murder to further their ideals. A fresh wave of fear made her stiffen.

"Relax, Lena. I'm right here. Nothing's going to happen to you."

She snorted at the macho assertion while, at the same time, hoping it was true.

Not twenty minutes later, he had lapsed into sleep, given his breathing. Eventually, the steady rise and fall of his chest lulled her into doing likewise.

CHAPTER 6

The FARC dissidents made them wait, choosing not to show up at La Esmerelda until ten the next morning. The UN team had been up since dawn, waiting tensely under the *ranchita*'s covered porch, listening to the rain drum the tin roof. For hours now, they had stared up at the muddy track that led into the dense vegetation of El Castillo.

The landmass rose straight up, a wild tangle of thick vegetation. Rain clouds had stalled over it despite the wet breeze.

Nothing happened quickly in Colombia, Maggie recollected. Being in the wilderness, smelling it, she could imagine how Barnes and Howitz had to feel, cut off from the world, chained like dogs, starved and humiliated. Four months had to seem like a lifetime. Thank God she was only here for two weeks!

Jake's last communication with the JIC that morning had taken place behind a family-run supply shop down the street. While keeping an eye out for observers, Maggie had overheard him tell his teammates, "Don't lose us out there, guys."

Whatever was said to him in return made him frown. "When was this?" He muttered one of his grandfather's Irish invectives. "Well, you'd better call them off."

"What'd they say?" she'd demanded as he put his phone away.

"The JUNGLA might be headed this way."

Her thoughts had flashed back to the Jeep that had driven past them at Barbosa. "What do we do?"

"Nothing. The admiral of Southern Command is reaching out to them personally."

Hours had passed since Jake's call. Maggie was considering the possibility that the FARC were standing them up when she spotted them. "Oh, here they come."

"Where?" Jake and the others strained to see.

Dressed from head to toe in jungle fatigues, the troop of rebels remained virtually invisible against the jungle-like backdrop until they were less than a football field feet away.

"Oh, hello." Jake finally spotted them. "I count six—no, eight."

Boris stood. "We should greet them. Come on, everyone out into the open. Hold your arms away from your bodies and show them your hands are empty."

Maggie was grateful for her rain jacket as she stepped into the drizzle to wait. Her heart thudded erratically as she inventoried the rebels' weapons. Two carried pistols on their hips, while the other six had AK-47s that looked decades old, probably supplied by the Russians to Cuba in the eighties. Those rifles probably jammed on a regular basis, if they worked at all. But all the banana-shaped clips bulging in the pockets of their artillery vests gave the impression they were armed to the teeth.

We come in peace. Maggie sought to relay that message in her deport-ment while battling the urge to assume a fighting stance. A cold sweat breached her pores. Her anxiety only worsened when she noticed the six with AK-47s all looked like teenagers.

The older two were clearly in charge, given the insignia on their camouflage jackets and floppy hats. They marched ahead of the group to greet Boris, who stepped forward, approaching with cautious courtesy and greeting them in excellent Spanish. The three exchanged words, and then Boris waved the team closer.

Maggie suffered the scrutiny of every rebel present but most espe-cially its two leaders, neither one of whom was Salvador Rojas. The elder had a gray handlebar mustache and a barrel chest. His face was like cracked, old leather. Boris introduced him as Comandante Marquez.

His deputy or *mondo* was called *Gallo*, meaning "rooster." Skinny with a face inherited from Incan ancestors, Gallo's dark, suspicious gaze reminded Maggie of Farid's. Here was the one to watch out for.

Jake put a reassuring arm around her, drawing *el comandante*'s attention to the watch he was wearing. Marquez nudged his deputy, who stepped up to Jake five seconds later and pointed to the watch.

"Quíteselo." *Take it off.* "If you want to come with us, you will give it to my leader."

Jake feigned dismay. "But this was my father's," he protested in hesitant Spanish.

Gallo went to pull the wicked-looking pistol from his side holster, and Jake threw his hands up. *"Vale, vale."* *Okay, okay.*

As he surrendered the watch, Maggie marveled at how quickly it had been appropriated. They could only hope it would end up in the hands of General Rojas. Even as Marquez strapped the watch to his own sturdy wrist, he continued to stare at Jake, whose stature clearly made him nervous. He said to his *mondo*, "Tell him to take off his glasses."

Gallo approached Jake a second time and made a grab for them.

Jake clapped the glasses to his face.

"Por favor." He appealed to Boris. "Please, I can't see without them."

Boris looked uncomfortable. "Best to do as they say, I think."

Compelled to defend Jake, Maggie spoke up—not in French-accented Spanish like Jake's, but as she'd grown up hearing it. "He can't see without them."

Mondo Gallo stared at her a moment, then snatched Jake's glasses off his face anyway. To Maggie's dismay, he tossed them down on the muddy ground and stomped on them.

An uncomfortable silence fell over the two sides.

Boris cut his team an anguished look, clearly loath to protest.

"Basta," Marquez said to his *mondo*. *Enough.* Circling the air with a raised finger, he bellowed, *"¡Regresemos!"* and the troop of armed teens swung around to retrace their footsteps.

Mondo Gallo gestured brusquely for the UN team to follow.

Here we go.

Jake gave Maggie's hand a reassuring squeeze as they began their march into the wilderness. Within just a few steps, it became apparent that they would struggle to keep up. The FARC might be diminutive, but they were used to marching in the mud.

Mondo Gallo railed at them to hurry up. *"Apúrense. ¡Rápido!"*

The mud sucked at Maggie's boots, and the drizzle dampened her ponytail, but she refused to pull her hood up as that would compromise her hearing. Cutting a sidelong glance at Jake, she found him staring intently at their environment, pretending it was all a blur. She marveled at his acting ability while thanking God that she wasn't doing this without him.

The vegetation thickened as the terrain rose, creating a tangled wall on either side of the footpath that became an erratic corridor, surrounded by hedges too lush to penetrate. Then, finally, it closed over their heads, swallowing them in a green gloom with no sign of the sky when Maggie glanced up.

The trail grew steeper and narrower the higher they climbed. Rainwater had carved out the middle of the trail, turning it into a V-shaped gulley, murder on Maggie's ankles, even in her new sturdy boots. She pushed herself, wondering how the others on the team, those who didn't exercise regularly like her and Jake, would fare.

On the heels of that thought, Bellini and Esme began to fall behind. Boris and then Jake went back for them, forcing Maggie to do likewise. She took the Turkish woman off Boris's hands while Jake took over Bellini.

Gripping Esme's elbow, Maggie hauled her to ever higher elevations, with Jake and Bellini struggling behind them. Boris made his way to the front of the pack to ask Marquez if they could slow down, but Maggie could see by the commander's frown they wouldn't be offered any preferential treatment.

At last, they burst onto a hacked-out clearing where Maggie breathed a sigh of relief to see six mules dozing in a circle around a mound of cloth sacks, hides quivering to keep the insects off. A ninth rebel stood waiting with them.

Gallo rounded on them. "Come. Stand in a circle and throw your backpacks into the center."

Oh no. Maggie's fears were manifesting. The last to toss her pack onto the pile, she lamented the likely loss of her anxiety meds, not to mention the first-aid kits. Jake didn't look any happier than she was. Without the antibiotic ointment, the incision he'd stitched less than forty-eight hours ago might get infected. Worse still, she might have a nervous breakdown.

Boris spoke up for them, his tone respectful. "*Comandante*, may we at least keep our antimalaria tablets and our bug spray?"

"No." With that single word, Marquez dashed Maggie's hopes. "*Los medicamentos* are for all people, not just *capitalistas* who can afford them."

"But you promised the UN we could each keep our passports. We can't continue if you take those."

The question appeared to offend Marquez. "Of course, you can keep your passports."

At least their intel that they got to keep their boots was right, probably since the FARC couldn't afford to shoe them all, especially not the men. Keeping their pants was a boon, since Maggie's were water-resistant and covered the Band-Aid on her hip. Jake carried their passports in his side pocket.

As Maggie shrugged off her rain jacket and then her T-shirt, tossing both atop her pack, eight sets of eyes fastened on her slim torso and white jogging bra. Her skin seemed to shrink. She hadn't felt this vulnerable since running into Farid in the narrow street near her apartment.

Don't think of that!

Jake's bare chest garnered Mondo Gallo's attention. Circling the taller man, he eyed the slabs of muscle that roped Jake's arms and padded his pectorals.

"You're strong, eh?"

"I go to the gym." Jake mimed a chest press, holding a weighted bar.

Gallo punched him lightly in the stomach, and Jake's tortoise-shell abs flexed. He'd grown chest hair that he hadn't had when they'd gone swimming at Paris University's indoor pool. The soft-looking russet-brown hair tapered nicely toward his naval. It was hard not to stare.

The *mondo* didn't look convinced. "You know how to shoot a *pistola?*"

"No, no." Jake pointed to his eyes. "I can't see."

Gallo stepped closer, staring at him hard. "I'll be watching you."

Terrific. They were suspected already.

But then Gallo swung around and shouted at the kids to pick up their stuff and distribute whatever was in the burlap sacks. As the rebels dispersed armloads of clothing, Maggie was startled to realize two of them were females, maybe eighteen years old. One of them communicated an apology in her big brown eyes as she handed Maggie a camouflage jacket and a pea-green T-shirt.

Tunneling into the shirt, Maggie wrinkled her nose at the soapy smell it exuded. At least its soft fabric would protect her from the chafing jacket, which she buttoned up next. They were dressed like the dissidents now, minus the hats, which meant the JUNGLA wouldn't be able to tell peacekeepers from guerillas. Worse and worse.

Once dressed, they were told to mount the mules, one for each team member. The small concession was heartening. As Jake helped her atop the burlap and leather saddle, Maggie wedged her boots into the stirrups, then turned to watch Jake vault awkwardly onto his mule. As he went to put his boots in the stirrups, he discovered them too short for his long legs and too small to wedge his boots into. He had yet to find a way around his predicament when Gallo swatted their mules into motion.

Whoa! The saddle swayed from side to side. Maggie quickly realized she had to cling to the pommel to keep from falling off. Glancing back at Jake, she found him doing the same thing while also squeezing the mule's round belly with his thighs. How long could he keep that up?

As they meandered into a patch of bamboo, her gaze fastened on the razor-sharp spears lining either side of the trail. The product of machetes cutting through the undergrowth, those spears would impale anyone who fell off. She gritted her teeth, every muscle in her body rigid. Death by bamboo spike wasn't any more appealing than a head-on collision in a tunnel.

Maybe Jake had been right about fighting fire with fire. It wasn't working. But once they left the bamboo behind, she found she could relax her grip and catch her breath. Jake was still in one piece right behind her. So far, so good. If they could ride these mules the rest of the way, they'd be just fine.

As they reached the crest of a hill, gunfire ripped through the fronds and vines, startling their entire entourage.

Maggie's mule reared. With a stifled scream, she slipped sideways from the saddle. Her foot caught in one stirrup, spilling her upside down. With her head just an inch from the ground, she heard Jake shout her name. A barrage of gunfire drowned it out.

Comandante Marquez roared an order, and his little army scattered.

Jerking her foot free, Maggie fell onto the trail, barely avoiding being trampled by the frightened mule.

Chaos had broken loose around them. Bullets peppered the trees and thumped into the humus-covered earth. The FARC dissidents had started firing back, putting the UN team members, who no longer wore their distinctive white jackets, squarely in the crossfire.

A frightened glance under her mule showed Jake herding the others—all except for Bellini, who'd slipped in the mud—toward a low-lying area on the far side of the path. Jake's bravery roused her own. Not to be outdone, Maggie darted down the trail to help Bellini get up.

"Come on!" As she hauled the Italian in Jake's direction, the whistle of a mortar shell had her shoving Bellini into the ditch where the team lay.

The next instant was a blur. She hit the ground, and the air knocked clean out of her as Jake landed on top of her. Fighting to inflate her lungs, she felt the earth tremble beneath her. Globs of mud and spongy lichen rained down on them.

"It's the JUNGLA, isn't it?"

Jake clapped a hand over her mouth, making her realize that in her stressed state, she'd spoken in English,

Clearly, the SOCOM admiral hadn't managed to call off the Counter-Narcotics Jungle Company in time. Another barrage of gunfire echoed through the undergrowth, continuing for what seemed an eternity. With Jake draped over her, he was the one who'd be killed or at least horribly maimed if a mortar landed on him.

Oh, no way. Maggie tried to roll over, to squirm out from under him, but he had her thoroughly pinned.

"Reste immobile!" he grated in her ear.

The gunfire intensified. Adolescent voices shouted back and forth.

No way could nine FARC rebels, six of whom were kids, hold off a special forces battalion. When their ammunition ran out, the JUNGLA would swoop in and arrest the survivors—including the peacekeepers, and the mission to locate Barnes and Howitz would be over before it had scarcely begun.

An eerie silence descended over the forest. Maggie and Jake made eye contact. As suddenly as the gunfire had erupted, it stopped.

The cautious twitter of birds and the screeching of howler monkeys seemed to indicate that the interlopers had departed. Either that or the FARC were all dead.

"Espere," Jake cautioned as she tried to move. *Wait.*

"I can't breathe!" she protested in French.

He eased himself off her slightly while waving at the other team members to stay down.

One by one, FARC rebels began to creep out of the forest. Ten minutes later, Marquez called an order for everyone to rally up so he could assess the damage.

Asserting his leadership role, Boris began ushering the peacekeepers out of the ditch and back onto the trail. Jake clambered to his feet and pulled Maggie up after him, his blue eyes inspecting her from head to toe. *"Tu vas bien?"* He brushed leaves off her dirt-stained jacket.

Just then, Mondo Gallo slithered into view from higher ground and rushed at them with his pistol raised. *"¡Traidores!* They led the JUNGLA straight to us!" He lunged for Boris, gripping the front of his jacket and pressing the muzzle of his pistol into the German's jaw.

While Boris blanched, both Jake and Charles widened their stances, preparing to keep Gallo from murdering their leader if they had to.

Marquez approached, scowling. "Is this the thanks we get for having you as our guests? The UN is in cahoots with the JUNGLA now?"

In his haste to reason with them, Boris stammered, *"Claro que no.*

Our agenda is to find a peaceful resolution, so…so the hostages might be freed. We are not at war with you."

Maggie took offense at Marquez's accusation. "Why would we jeopardize our own lives, *Comandante?* We were shot at, too, if you hadn't noticed."

Her perfect Spanish, not to mention her defiance, rendered the FARC dumb. They all regarded her in amazement, especially the two young women.

Me and my temper. As Jake's grip on her arm tightened, Maggie mentally kicked herself. Her pulse ticked upward as Gallo stepped closer to her while sparing Jake a wary glance. "Where are you from?" He had lost his hat in the firefight, making the reason for his name immediately evident. His black hair grew straight up at the top of his head like a rooster's comb.

She held his stare. "I am French. My mother was Venezuelan."

"Ah." His suspicion cleared, giving way to an ugly smile. "Well, any Venezuelan is a friend of ours. Right, *Comandante?*"

Marquez agreed, telling Gallo to put his gun away.

Dizzy with relief, Maggie released the breath she was holding as the officers turned away to check on their troops.

It took ages to get moving again. The rebel in charge of the mules was fussing over the one that had been nicked by a bullet. As he staunched the animal's torn flesh, the peacekeepers sat on the muddy trail and waited. Unaccustomed to such hostilities, Esme and Bellini remained dazed and silent while Boris consoled them with words of solidarity and encouragement.

"Things can only get easier from here out."

Maggie raised a cynical gaze to Jake and Charles's carefully blank expressions. They knew as well as she did, things would probably get much worse.

Once the mule was deemed well enough, the climb to the FARC's secret outpost resumed. Within an hour, the Turkish woman started vomiting—altitude sickness, Maggie determined, as they'd done nothing but plod into steadily higher elevations.

Too weak to stay in her saddle, Esme was foisted off on Maggie since the men's mules were already overburdened.

Peering straight up, Maggie marveled at the height of the spiraling wax palms, growing alongside trees she couldn't name, many with enormous roots keeping them rooted on the sloped terrain. It had to be midafternoon, she guessed, since her stomach rumbled with hunger. Her skin chafed wherever her stiff jacket rubbed it. When they crossed another trail, she asked herself if they were being led in circles to confuse the UN team as to their destination.

The higher they climbed, the more exotic the terrain became. Vines, heavy with fragrant and unfamiliar flowers, coiled up trunks and draped from branches. Dozens of monkeys observed them from on high while brilliantly feathered birds winged through the branches, calling songs she had never heard before. Added to the noise was the croaking of tree frogs and the constant drone of insects. It wasn't any wonder Maggie didn't hear the rushing water until they were told to dismount from their rides.

They had come to a muddy creek that had carved a gorge in the middle of the path, making it impossible for the mules to cross.

As she helped Esme to dismount, the animals' caretaker turned the beasts around and began leading them back downhill. Did that mean they were close to the FARC's outpost?

Her gaze landed on the contraption that would take them across the creek. Glancing at Jake's raised eyebrows, Maggie easily read his mind: *Nách mór an diabhal thú.*

It was a wooden box, large enough for three or four passengers, dangling from a cable and pulley system. Semi-hysterical laughter bubbled up her throat before she could stop it.

Marquez sent the *mondo* and two teens across to show the peacekeepers how the contraption worked. By the time it was Maggie and Jake's turn to squeeze into the hip-high box, Maggie was confident the apparatus would hold them. Esme was not. She clung to Maggie, hiding her face against her shoulder. With no choice but to be brave, Maggie caught Jake's eye. "Fire with fire, darling," she said in French.

Jake just shook his head.

Once safely on the opposite side, they waited for the others to join them before slogging on. Only now, the going was slower as they had no mules to ride and no more strength to call upon. To make matters worse, Esme was so weak that Maggie practically had to carry her.

It had to be nearing the dinnertime when the trail spilled the weary troop into a partial clearing of relatively level ground. *Oh, thank God!* They'd finally reached a rebel camp occupied by several more teens, who stood eyeing their gringo visitors.

Three mismatched buildings stood in a thin mist with a firepit in the center and a field behind. The chickens pecking in the mud suggested this had once been the farm of an indigenous *campesino*, appropriated by the FARC and turned into an outpost, the perimeter of which was guarded by a .50-caliber machine gun, presided over by a grubby teen.

Esme tugged on Maggie's sleeve. "Are the hostages kept here, do you think?"

"I doubt it." They wouldn't let the UN team see the hostages unless they had to.

Marquez waved them toward the tree stumps surrounding the firepit. As they collapsed atop them, the two girl rebels worked to start a fire. A generator began throttling behind the only brick-and-mortar building into which Marquez disappeared.

Maggie's eyes wandered. In the field at the back of the camp, four crude bull's-eyes had been mounted to tree trunks, suggesting this was probably a training camp. The brick building was probably for the officers, the stand-alone lean-to for the teenage rebels, so was the long, frond-topped bungalow for them?

An older, light-skinned man stepped out of it. Like them, he was dressed in camouflage with no floppy hat.

Charles gave voice to Maggie's question. "Who's that?"

The man's fair complexion set him apart. Nor was he armed with any weapons.

Commander Marquez, emerging from the brick building, waved the man over and introduced him to the group. "This is Señor Arias. He will represent the FARC's interests in the negotiation process."

Maggie frowned. Couldn't the FARC represent themselves?

Boris shook the slender man's hand. "I'm Boris Mayer, with the United Nations."

"*Mucho gusto.*" But the older man didn't sound enthusiastic.

Marquez gestured toward his dwelling. "You may begin the process now. Go inside."

Now? They were all exhausted, and they hadn't eaten since early morning.

Boris responded with confusion. "Just me and Arias, or all of us?"

"Do as you please." With a shrug, Marquez distanced himself, taking Gallo with him.

Charles stood. "I'd like to be included."

"Us, too," said Maggie.

Esme put a hand to her head. "I really don't feel well enough."

Boris made a quick decision, requesting Bellini to find somewhere for Esme to rest.

Arias pointed to the bungalow. "You'll be bunking there where I sleep. There are mats and nets at the door. Help yourself."

As Bellini led Esme away, the rest of them crowded into the officers' quarters. Once inside, Maggie searched the cozy interior for clues as to Howitz and Barnes's location. The bright lightbulb and small refrigerator explained the reason for the generator. Given the bunkbed, only Marquez and Gallo slept here, enjoying cold drinks and a tin roof while their minions had thatched roofs. Clearly even Marxists recognized rank.

As they squeezed into the small space, the Argentine offered the only chair to Boris, who refused it. Taking it for himself, Arias left the rest of them standing.

Speaking Spanish in a lilting Argentinian dialect, he acknowledged them politely as Boris introduced them, then explained that he was a businessman with pipelines in northern Colombia. "I was kidnapped from my office in Medellín to do a job for the FARC."

Maggie didn't understand. "Why kidnap a stranger to represent them? It makes no sense."

"It makes perfect sense," Boris countered. "Mr. Arias is used to working with money, wire transfers and all that. He knows how much the FARC can get away with asking, how to use technology, and he probably speaks English perfectly, yes?"

As Arias nodded, Maggie made a note never to speak English in his presence.

Boris heaved a sigh for the Argentine's plight. "Did they say they would release you if you got them rich?"

"Yes." Arias closed his prim mouth and swallowed hard. "And they promised to kill me if I do not."

A pained silence filled the small space until Boris broke it. "We will do everything in our power to keep that from happening."

"Thank you."

Maggie's gaze wandered a second time. Several books of Marxist leaning lay atop the crude desk. A pen lay next to a closed notebook, which she longed to crack open. Catching her eye, Jake drew her attention to the handheld radio lying atop an old boom box that occupied the windowsill. Thanks to the repeater on the top of the mountain, the FARC could communicate regardless of their position on the mountain.

"Have you seen the hostages?"

Boris's question drew Maggie's attention to the Argentine. "No, no." He shook his salt-and-pepper curls. "I arrived here only a week ago, and I've been at this camp since I was kidnapped."

"Have you met General Rojas, the rebel commander? Do you know where he stays?"

"No, I haven't met him yet. I probably know less than you."

Maggie could tell the man was speaking honestly.

"But you will take our requests to Rojas, right? You're the middleman."

Arias spread his hands in a shrug. "I suppose so."

Maggie shot a frustrated look at Jake. This business of negotiations could take weeks, even months, to accomplish. They had to find Howitz and Barnes before the captives succumbed to starvation or illness, and the batteries for Jake's phone ran out of power.

Looking depleted, Boris went to sit on one end of the lower bunk, propping his elbows on his knees to keep from bumping his head. "The first thing we will need from you is proof of life."

Arias nodded, looking overwhelmed. "What would that look like?"

Charles shifted toward the screen door to warn of impending visitors.

"Well, a written message with their signatures would suffice. When we have that much, we will make our offer to the FARC."

The Argentine thought for a moment. "Then there's nothing more to discuss right now?"

"No, but we'll just stay right here until they come for us." Boris glanced back at the bed, as though tempted to lay back on it and fall asleep. "I hope they're going to feed us soon."

Jake bent down to examine the boom box. "What do they listen to out here?"

Arias smiled cynically. "You'll see. There's reveille every morning and every afternoon anti-American hour. Commander Marquez opens the window, and the trainees are made to sit and listen to a Cuban Marxist rant about *las capitalistas*. They have no idea what they're listening to. Most are just simple *campesinos* forced to take up arms."

Maggie pictured the girl who'd given her the clothes and wondered at her circumstances. "Why are there only teenagers here? Where are the rest of the FARC?"

Arias thought for a moment. "I have no idea. But I'm sure there are more."

Maggie was also sure.

With nothing else to accomplish, they basked in the luxury of electricity until Charles straightened abruptly. "Time's up."

Marquez pushed open the screen door and poked his head inside. "All done?"

"*Sí.*"

As Arias came to his feet, Marquez said to him, "We will travel to my general in the morning."

"How long until you return?" Boris bravely asked.

Marquez ignored him, gesturing impatiently for everyone to vacate his headquarters. "Out, everyone. Time to eat and then sleep."

Finally, they would get some food! Maggie's head spun with hunger.

"*Comandante*"—Boris stuck his neck out again—"could we possibly get our packs back? We're not strong like you. Without our *medicamentos*, we could sicken and die."

Despite the German's tact, the commander scoffed at the request. "You think you deserve more than what we have because you're rich?"

Boris firmed his lips and cut the others an apologetic grimace.

Marquez pointed firmly at the tree stumps. "Sit. Eat."

The promise of food made Maggie eager to comply. *Please let there be a ton of it.*

Bellini came out of the bungalow without Esme. "She's too sick to join us. But you'll like our accommodations. There's room for all of us and relative privacy."

When they were finally served, Maggie eyed with disappointment the contents of the wooden bowl she was given, filled with nothing but rice and no silverware with which to eat it. Her drink was a sweet beverage she had tasted in her youth. "What's this called?" she asked the same girl who'd given her the clothes she wore.

"*Agua panela*, señora. Boiled sugar cane and water." With a shy smile, she darted away.

Forcing herself not to wolf down her dinner, Maggie savored each little bite of rice.

Boris, who finished first, said that he would check on Esme, and Bellini followed him, taking an extra cup of *agua panela* for her.

Marquez had retreated into his quarters, and Gallo had gone to rant at a young rebel for some unknown trespass. Left alone, Charles asked them in French, "So where do you think we are?"

Jake glanced up at the darkening sky. "Given where the sun went down, I'd say the west side of El Castillo, at an altitude of maybe ten or eleven thousand feet."

Charles nodded. "I agree."

Maggie noted while the female rebels were hard at work cleaning up after their meal, the boys were subjected to Gallo's long-winded lecture.

"Well"—Charles pushed to his feet, handing his cup and bowl to the elder girl—"let's get some sleep. *Gracias,* señoritas."

Following his lead, with Jake right behind her, Maggie crossed toward the bungalow, pleased they would be sleeping off the ground. Made of sturdy bamboo, all lashed together and topped by palm fronds, she prayed the bungalow was waterproof. Mats and blankets had been left out for them on the small veranda. Stepping into the cool interior, it took Maggie's eyes a moment to adjust to the dark. When they did, she could see a long, protected walkway leading to five or six cubicles, each divided from the other by the same bamboo blinds that served as exterior walls, keeping out the bugs.

Coursing the walkway on one side, they passed the cubicles occupied by Arias and the other team members. After peeking into the last two available spaces, Charles waved her and Jake toward the last one while he took the one beside them.

When Maggie peeked out the back flap, Charles's reason for placing them here became apparent. From this cubicle, she and Jake could slip out the rear of the building and into the wilderness without being observed by anyone.

As she tossed down the mat she'd picked up at the entrance, Jake joined her, laying his mat right alongside hers. Maggie eyed their sleeping arrangement with mixed anticipation and concern. Could she sleep next to Jake for two weeks and not make a fool of herself?

As she stood there brooding, he shook out a blanket, then fluffed out the mosquito netting hanging from a hook on the bamboo crossbeam until it surrounded their bed like a tent. How cozy.

As the others settled down with groans of relief, Jake gestured for Maggie to remove her boots and socks. "Take off anything that's wet." Thankfully, her water-resistant pants had dried by the fire, requiring her to strip only to her jog bra, as she had earlier that day.

Darting self-consciously under the mosquito net, she reclined on the far side of the mat, draping half of the blanket over her. On the other side of the diaphanous netting, Jake was checking his chest and armpits—looking for parasites, she realized. *Gross.* Surreptitiously, she did the same, searching by feel as she regarded his immensely broad back. The effort it must have taken him to pack on so much muscle impressed her.

When he dropped his trousers unexpectedly, she rolled away to keep from becoming mesmerized. Grown-up Jake looked nothing like he had when they'd gone swimming in the university pool back in Paris. If skinny Jake could light her fire, imagine what grown-up Jake could do.

Chill out, Maggie. Act professional.

As he lowered himself onto the mat and joined her under the blanket, she scooted way over, sending him nonverbal cues that she didn't need him to hold her as he had the previous night in La Esmeralda. She wasn't afraid anymore. But her arm would go numb in this position.

Maggie spared a thought for her pillow back home. Then, as her hip began to ache, she longed for her mattress. She'd be a lot more comfortable rolling to her other side and using Jake's chest for a pillow.

Don't do it. You'll only get used to it.

Squeezing her eyes shut, she heaved a long sigh. *Just go to sleep.* Between the endless climb and the deficit of calories, she felt like a wet towel, wrung out and left to dry. That was her last thought as she tumbled toward oblivion.

CHAPTER 7

When Maggie woke up at the crack of dawn, her head was on Jake's chest, her arm around his waist. Shocked by what she'd done in her sleep, she froze. Heat flooded her face. When had this happened? Surely he'd noticed, unless he slept very soundly.

She ordered herself to ease away from him, hoping he wouldn't waken and catch her in his arms. But she lacked the will to move just yet. Instead, she lay there, enjoying the dense but supple texture of his upper chest and shoulders. She could hear his heart beating, slow, steady strokes. His manly scent still reminded her of rain showers. The chest hair under her arm made her want to comb her fingers through it to find out if it was as soft as it looked.

Don't you dare, Maggie.

Her heart had begun to thud. Breaking out in a light sweat, she managed to peel herself off him. With great exertion, she squirmed out from under his heavy arm, moving it out of the way so she could lie back down.

Then she closed her eyes and willed herself to fall back to sleep. Instead, she listened to Jake breathe. He didn't snore. She turned her head to look at him. His profile in the muted light was so familiar that her heart clenched. In college, she'd thought him handsome in a nerdy way. But there was nothing nerdy about the profile of the warrior sleeping next to her.

With difficulty, she tore her gaze to the blinds by her feet. The sun was brightening by degrees behind the bamboo slats, slowly filling their cubicle with morning light. How surreal that she was lying on a mat near the top of a mountain with the only man she'd ever loved—and romance was out of the question, regardless of how attractive he'd become.

The blare of a recording shattered the camp's peaceful quiet. *"¡Despiértense todos. Arriba y Ándale!"* Maggie bolted upright, startled by the unexpected reveille, bellowing for the trainees to wake up, get up, and get going.

Jake's hand coming to rest on Maggie's bare lower back made her want to throw herself at him. Appalled by her response to him, she tossed back the blanket. "Time to get up." She jumped into her remaining clothes and her boots and left the bungalow before he did.

Minutes later, Jake joined her in watching the young rebels exercise under Mondo Gallo's eagle eye. In the middle of the camp, the *mondo* had them doing burpees, push-ups, and lunges. Maggie had to laugh at their form. Jake couldn't watch.

Shortly after drills, the FARC and the peacekeepers shared an uninspired breakfast of leftover rice and more *agua panela*. The sickly-sweet drink was getting old already. Desperate for carbs, Maggie forced herself to drink it.

Once breakfast was over, Comandante Marquez jerked his head at the Argentine and said, *"Vámonos."* Let's go. "Mondo Gallo is in charge. We will be back in three days."

Watching Marquez and Arias cross camp toward the .50-caliber machine gun, Maggie met Jake's speculative gaze. Rojas was smart to avoid using the handheld radio for his communication, preferring to do it in person. Spy drones couldn't pick up face-to-face communication. But was his camp so far away that it took *three full days* to get there and back?

The good news was Marquez was wearing the watch he'd stolen from Jake, which meant the JIC would soon have the coordinates for

Rojas, if only briefly, unless Marquez gave the watch to his leader as a gift—or had it taken from him, as Jake had.

A vision of Gallo swaggering toward them tempered Maggie's hopeful thoughts. Uneasiness swept over her as he hitched his trousers in a gesture of self-importance while running a hostile gaze over the peacekeepers.

"Oigan." Listen up. "I am the commander now. If any of you cause mischief, I will lock you in there." He pointed to a wooden shack standing at the far edge of the camp, nearly swallowed up by the forest. It appeared so rotten and dilapidated that it might collapse at any moment. "It is filled with hornets and bats. Don't cause me any trouble." With a dark look, he stalked toward the officers' quarters to enjoy being king of the castle.

The UN team all regarded one another. What were they supposed to do in the meantime?

Boris suggested some team-building exercises. Maggie, used to working alone, wanted no part of that. Seeing several of the teenage boys heading toward the bull's-eye field, kicking a soccer ball between them, she suggested, "Why don't we play soccer with the kids?" What she really wanted to do was find out whether any of them knew where the hostages were kept.

Esme, who'd come out of the bungalow looking better that morning, immediately declined, as Maggie knew she would. Boris shook his head. "I'm too old for that."

Bellini laughed. "And I'm too lazy."

But Charles jumped to his feet enthusiastically. "I'm game. How are your *fútbol* skills, Jacques?"

Jake shook his head. "No, no. I can't even see the ball. Lena's the soccer player."

The Frenchman tipped his head at Maggie. "Shall we suggest a game? Two against four. You think they'll go for those odds?"

She raised an eyebrow at him. "You'd better be good."

The Frenchman gave a modest shrug. "I'm not too bad."

～

Curious to see what happened, Jake followed Charles and Lena so he could see the game better, allegedly. Positioning himself by the sandbags that surrounded the machine gun, which was currently unmanned, he watched the boys receive Charles's offer with surprise. In unison, they glanced at Gallo's brick quarters, then shared a look and shrugged. Sure, why not?

For the first time, Jake noted nets already strung up on either side of the field. They'd played soccer here before. The terrain was almost flat but only a little larger than a tennis court. Lena took up a fullback position, and Charles played center forward, letting the ball slip right by him as the game began.

Sitting on the sandbags, Jake glanced casually back at the machine gun. It had only a short belt of bullets, suggesting the FARC were as low on ammo as they were on food. Returning his attention to the game, he watched Lena defend the goal against two fleet-footed youths. Admiration put a smile on his face as she put her long legs to work and stole the ball from under one boy's feet, then passed it up to Charles, who let it slide right by him again.

The look of pure annoyance on Lena's face made Jake chuckle. Her passionate nature, as evident as it had been twelve years ago, was a cultural trait she'd picked up growing up in Venezuela. Being hotheaded wasn't the best characteristic for a case officer, but she made up for it with her awareness of the environment, something Jake struggled to emulate.

Stealing the ball away a second time, Lena bellowed at Charles to hold on to it. At that moment, the door at the little quarters creaked open. Turning his head, Jake was dismayed to see the disagreeable *mondo* glaring at them from across the camp.

Shoot. Jake fully expected him to interfere.

The players didn't notice. Three of the four boys were swarming the Frenchman. All at once, Charles shifted into a whole new mode of playing, dribbling past all three astonished defenders as he worked his way up the field. Lena abandoned the goal and sprinted past him toward their own goal. Charles booted the ball directly at her, and Lena sent it straight between the defender's planted feet, right into the net.

From the corner of his eye, Jake watched Gallo drop his gun holster back inside his building, hang a key ring on a nail outside, and head toward the field.

The players finally caught sight of him and stilled, no doubt figuring their game would be over. Gallo jerked his thumb at one of the boys, indicating he would take the kid's place. Well, at least he wasn't adding to the grossly unfair odds. Even so, Jake suffered misgivings.

The rebels took possession of the ball, with Gallo himself dribbling up the field. Jake held his breath as Lena defended cautiously against the *mondo*'s encroachment.

Wedging a foot between his, she managed to steal the ball back and punted it to Charles, who once more weaved between three defenders. With Gallo covering Lena aggressively, the Frenchman kicked the ball toward the goal himself. It went right past their goalie, who dived the wrong way.

The score was France 2, Colombia 0.

Charles sent Lena a subtle gesture that meant, *Let the FARC score next.* Jake agreed. No need to make their hosts unhappy.

Once more, Gallo brought the ball up the field, circumventing Charles. Even with two forwards wide open, he kept the ball for himself, bearing down on Lena, who put up a half-hearted defense. Gallo stalled, showing off his dribbling skills. Just as he broke forward, pushing toward the goal, he slipped on mud and landed hard on his back.

His four subordinates hooted with laughter. Marshaling her own smile, Lena nudged Jake's respect to a whole new level by stepping forward and offering Gallo a hand.

Huh. Maybe you could fight fire with fire.

When Gallo slapped her hand away viciously, Jake saw red. While Lena bit her lips and squared her shoulders, Jake pushed off the sandbags and stalked toward the field.

The soldiers saw him and stopped snickering. Charles whirled and intercepted his path, laying a deterring hand on Jake's chest. "Easy, easy. It's just a game. Relax."

It took Gallo another minute to roll to his feet. He sent Lena a murderous look as if she was the reason he'd fallen.

Mallacht air. This was just what they *didn't* need—a rebel leader with a bone to pick.

Muttering threats to his soldiers, Gallo limped off the field toward his quarters to nurse his injured pride.

Once he was out of sight, the four original players approached the newcomers wearing hesitant smiles. It seemed, by humiliating Gallo, the peacekeepers had won over the rebels-in-training. One youth trotted off, then returned minutes later with two hard-boiled eggs for the victors.

Lena accepted her egg with relish, peeling off the shell with fingers that shook. As she took a bite out of it, her gaze landed on Jake, who hadn't been given an egg since he hadn't played. Her wide eyes conveyed guilt.

"Mange-le." Eat it, he assured her, ignoring the rumble in his stomach. She probably had less body fat on her than he did.

Utilizing his supposedly limited Spanish, Jake applied himself to learning the kids' names—Julian, Estéban, Chucho, and David. Each young man was eager to share his tale of woe. Julian and Estéban had been forced into service, their families threatened at gunpoint if they did not release their sons to the rebel's keeping. Chucho had been sold by his family for three bags of rice. Only fairer-skinned David, who wore the insignia of a squad leader on his jacket, admitted he had dropped out of college to join the dissident's cause. His father had been a white anthropologist, and his mother an Arhuaco Indian.

Holding David's intelligent brown eyes, Jake read both caution and youthful idealism in their depths. The product of disparate social classes, he had chosen to identify with his mother's people, the downtrodden indigenous, whom the FARC claimed to represent, insisting the Havana Accord of 2016 had done nothing to make their lives any easier.

Lena, having listened in silence while savoring her egg, startled Jake by throwing out the million-dollar question. "Do you know where the American hostages are kept?"

The younger boys shook their heads with credible ignorance. Chucho joked that he didn't even know where his own home was. But David looked away and shrugged. *"¿Quién sabe?"* Who knows.

David definitely knew. Lena had timed her question perfectly, ferreting out their best informant within a day of their arrival at the

FARC's camp. Jake's admiration for her made him want to pick her up and kiss her, but he managed to restrain himself.

The sound of Gallo's door creaking open let them know their party was over. Within seconds, he was bearing down on Chucho, who'd offered the eggs to the winners.

Grabbing him by the scruff, he shook the boy forcefully. "Why do you waste our food on these strangers? Our own people are starving. You think they're here to help us? They are friends of the American spies." He began pulling Chucho toward the dreaded shed he'd pointed out earlier, the key chain back on his belt loop.

Jake made a grab for Lena as she started after them, but she shook him off.

"Excuse me, Mondo Gallo."

Her firm but deferent tone made Gallo wheel around with a look of incredulity. Out of the corner of his eyes, Jake saw Boris coming their way with a worried expression.

"I'm the one who caused you to fall. Perhaps you should take your anger out on me."

Gallo released Chucho immediately and stepped toward Lena. "You wish to take his place?"

Knowing Lena, she would sacrifice herself without flinching. Jake cut in front of her, then tugged her away from the *mondo*. *"Cuidado."* *Careful.* He stared hard at the *mondo*.

Boris rushed up to disperse the tension. "Come now, everyone. It's starting to rain. Why don't we lie down until the rain is over?"

As a group, the peacekeepers turned away, leaving Gallo to rant at his underlings.

On their way to the bungalow, Jake grabbed a hold of Lena's hand and squeezed it. "Look, I admire you for doing that," he said in French, "but I'm going to try and save you every time. So if you don't want me butting heads with our hosts, please think before you act."

As she shot him a frown, Charles, who caught up to them, said in her ear, "Jacques is saying he would die for you, madam. Don't be a fool like I was and take such devotion for granted." With those admonishing words, he brushed past them and headed toward their shelter.

Lena turned her frown at Jake. "You would die for me?"

The blunt question was so typical of her that he could only smile. "I'd rather not, but if I have to, absolutely."

For some reason, his answer didn't please her. With a shake of her head, she stalked ahead of him, hurrying toward the building. "I need a nap."

Jake heaved an inward sigh. When would Lena realize her well-being was all that mattered to him?

An hour or so later, Jake awoke for a second time that day to a voice blaring over a radio. Given the dialect of the announcer, this had to be the Marxist from Cuba whom Arias had told them about. Jake turned his head only to find Lena missing.

"Lena?" He jerked his elbows. No answer. Through the veil of their mosquito netting, he could tell her boots were gone. The sun was back out. And given the bend in the blinds, she'd slipped out of the rear of the building.

Berating himself for not wakening at her exodus—how could he have missed it?—he crawled out from under the mosquito netting. Surely, she wasn't wandering around the FARC's camp alone? He hauled on his own socks and boots before exiting the same way.

"Lena!" Encountering her tracks, he followed them along the back of the building, pushing away the fronds that brushed against his shoulder. No reply. When would she learn that partners did everything together, and that included taking potty breaks? Not only were jaguars and poisonous snakes on this mountain, but he didn't trust the rebels— Gallo most especially—not to harm her. "Lena!"

"I'm here."

The surly sounding response seemed to come from the earth itself. Jake looked down, then ducked to peer beneath the raised bungalow. There she was, crouched just around the corner, trying to lure a brooding hen toward her.

"Here chicky, chicky." She made kissing sounds that caused the chicken to cock its head.

Jake gave a laugh that was part relief, part amusement. "Are you planning to wring its neck and eat it raw if it comes to you?"

"I want to know if it's sitting on eggs."

Clearly she was as ravenous as he was.

Giving up on the chicken, she backed out from under the bungalow and joined him behind the building, out of sight of any others. Speaking in hushed French so as not to disturb the occupants still napping nearby, she grabbed his arm. "There's got to be something in the woods that we can eat. *Please* find us some food while the rebels are busy. I know you know how."

He didn't have it in himself to deny her. "All right, but listen." He waited for her to meet his gaze. "You can't just leave my side and vanish anytime you want. Something could have happened to you, and I'd never know what. We're partners now, remember?"

She had the audacity to cast her gaze toward the sky.

The urge to shake some sense into her surprised him. Catching her chin between his thumb and forefinger, he growled, "Promise me."

Color bloomed in her cheeks, giving rise to a rush of desire that made him want to crush his lips to hers. *Easy, Jake.*

"Fine. I promise. Let's go." Tugging his hand away from her chin, she hauled him straight into the forest.

～

Jake's assertion that he would give up his life for her was messing with Maggie's head. She didn't deserve that level of commitment, not when they would go their separate ways when this was over.

"No, this way." He pulled her toward a slope that wasn't so steep. The vegetation had already swallowed them, blocking their view of the camp, even though they weren't that far away. The chittering monkeys, birds, and insects gave her a false sense of isolation.

Maggie cast a nervous glance uphill. "You sure you can find the way back?" Out here, she stuck persistently to French. A rebel could be lurking close by, and they'd never know it.

"Sure. We'll follow our tracks back." Jake pointed to their prints in the mud. "*Allons-y*. I need to make a phone call while we look for something to eat."

All Maggie could think about was food. But then raindrops pattered on the broad leaves overhead, and she fretted that their tracks would wash away. "This is far enough, I think."

Jake must have agreed as he put his back to a tree and started taking off his boot. Maggie tamped down a growl. Phone call first, then food. She could wait another minute, only the process took far longer than it ought to—imagine if this was an emergency.

"Keep an eye out," he requested as he pulled up the antenna and then powered it up.

The high beep it emitted made Maggie jump. "*Pleurage*, that thing is loud out here!" She had totally overlooked the sound it made when they were still in the civilized world. A droplet of cold water struck her cheek. Seeing Jake pull the phone from his ear and frown at it, she guessed, "No reception?"

"*Non.*" He glanced at the weeping canopy. "Let's try somewhere else. This is a dead zone." After jamming his foot back into the boot, Jake shoved the laces inside instead of tying them. He grabbed Maggie's hand and pulled her with him another hundred yards, where he tried calling again.

"Anything?" Her stomach was literally on fire.

"Nothing. The canopy's too dense for the electromagnetic waves to penetrate."

For a second, she forgot about her hunger. "Well, what about the trackers we're wearing? They'd better penetrate, or the JIC won't know where we are."

Given the firming of Jake's mouth, he wasn't sure their trackers worked any better than the sat phone.

Maggie's agitation rose as she watched him put away the phone and lace his boot back up. "You're saying the only place that phone might work is in the camp."

"We can't use it in the camp. Come on. Let's find some food."

They hadn't gone ten steps when Jake caught sight of something. "There."

With hope, Maggie eyed the distinctive orange balls dangling among its spade-shaped leaves. "Are they edible?"

"*Non.*" Jake snapped off a leaf and showed it to her. "This is *cordon-cillo*, also known as *matico*. I'm surprised it grows at this altitude. Every time you see this tree, I want you to tear a leaf in half and rub the juice onto your incision. It's an *analgesic* and *antiseptic*."

The English words, pronounced as if they were French, made Maggie snicker. But then she coughed at the peppery odor the leaf exuded.

"Here." He squeezed some of the juice onto her finger. "Do it now."

Maggie delved a hand under her jacket to rub it on her incision. The resulting burn had her sucking air through her teeth.

"Stings, huh? That's not a good sign."

"No, it's fine." She adjusted her clothing. "Jaques, I need food *now*."

"Sure. Sorry." Jake peered around, then drew her over to a shade-loving tree growing in the understory. Whitish globes that dangled among dark green leaves.

"Is that fruit?"

"Yes, garcinia. Look for fruit on the ground that's not rotten."

Rain pelted their backs as they bent over, picking through the fruit that had already fallen. Lena found one that still looked intact and started peeling off the spiky outer casing. Her hands were shaking. If only she'd started this assignment a little overweight instead of underweight.

"Looks like lychee." She popped the translucent globe into her mouth and brightened as she chewed. "Mm. Tastes like it, too."

He wrested his attention upward. "Same fruit family."

Following his gaze, Maggie saw dozens of more garcinia fruits hanging on a branch too high for them to reach. A howler monkey hung on it, looking down at them.

"Hey, *mon ami*," Jake called, "would you throw some fruit down here for us?"

The monkey grinned as if laughing at their predicament.

Jake grimaced. "I'm not going to be able to climb this."

Maggie wasn't giving up that easily. The one piece of fruit had only whetted her appetite. "I'll climb onto your shoulders like I did in Fontainebleau. Once I'm on the lower branch, I can shake the fruit loose."

"*C'est une mauvaise idée.* You could fall."

"So, if I fall, you'll catch me." She grabbed the sleeve of his jacket. "Please, Jacques, I'm starving, and I'm *grincheux*, and I'll be cranky all the time if I can't get some calories."

Looking unhappy with his decision, Jake crouched as he'd done at Fontainebleau when she'd wanted to stand on a high boulder.

Holding the hand he held out, Maggie stepped on his upper thigh, then his shoulder, while grabbing the lower branch. He slowly straightened and turned, making it possible for her to sit on the branch.

"Fais attention."

She had no choice but to pay attention because the branch was slick with moss. While clinging to the higher branch, Maggie scooted along the lower branch so she could shake the higher one more effectively. After several scoots, she gave the upper branch a good shake.

Thump, thump, thump.

Just as fruit hit the ground, Maggie slipped off her perilous seat. *"Merde!"* Hanging now on the higher branch, she watched it bow and then break. "Jacques!" All she could do was close her eyes and pray he caught her.

She crashed into him, and both of them hit the ground with a squishy thud, sliding immediately downhill. Gravity lassoed them, dragging them over slick layers of rotting vegetation.

"Hold on!" Jake's English words were entirely unnecessary, as Maggie had a death grip on him.

As a sapling came into sight, Jake flashed out a hand and grasped it, bringing them to a jarring halt.

Lena, who was hanging on to his jacket, dug her toes into the loam to keep them anchored. Jake briefly closed his eyes, steadying himself with a deep breath. They were fine. He opened his eyes to Lena's remorseful gaze.

"Je suis tres désolée." I'm so sorry.

Man, she was cute when humiliated. He pretended her apology was for everything—for choosing her career over a lifetime spent together. But, of course, she meant for falling out of the tree. "No big deal. Are you hurt?"

She rubbed her right kneecap. "I hit a root on the way down."

The one that had whacked the back of his head, probably.

She stared up at the mudslide they'd created. "How are we getting back up there?"

If he'd said it once, he'd said it a thousand times. "Teamwork."

His frustrated tone brought her wide eyes back to his. For once, she had no reply.

Jake offered up directions. "Look for something to hold on to about five feet above my head. See anything?"

"Um…Oh, there's a vine by the root of a tree."

"Good. Now climb up me, onto my shoulders and grab hold of it. Once you're good, then I'm going to do the same thing and climb up you."

Her gaze darted back to his. She swallowed. All this physical contact was clearly getting to her. Well, good. Maybe she'd realize what she was missing, not living her life as his other half.

By the time they arrived at the camp, covered in mud, the rain was falling in earnest and anti-American hour had given way to music—not the native *cumbia* or traditional *vallenato* music Jake expected to hear, but modern, lyrical songs in Spanish.

Rather than return to their cubicle muddy and soaking wet, they sat by the empty firepit to let the rain shower down on them. Ten young rebels, including the two girls and their four soccer buddies, sat in the downpour singing to the radio,

Jake tuned his ear to the words.

Father, You are holy. In You, I put my trust.

What? He cocked his head, listening more intently. These FARC were Christians?

Remembering the missionary Lobo had mentioned in passing, Jake turned to Lena, who was staring at the kids like they wore halos over their heads. The two girls sang out with confidence while glancing self-consciously in their direction. The song came to an end, the music faded, and a voice came over the radio that was utterly unlike that of the ranting Marxist.

"Good afternoon, my children." The speaker with the warm, soothing voice was obviously an American, given his accented Spanish. "Peace and love to you from Father Joshua. I hope you are feeling happy today, for, indeed, your Father in Heaven knows every hair on your head and is with you wherever you go."

Jake met Lena's wide eyes. He'd give just about anything to meet this missionary in person.

"Today's reading comes from the book of Matthew, Chapter 14. 'When Jesus heard what had happened, he withdrew by boat privately to a solitary place—'"

The radio cut off abruptly, causing all ten teens to exclaim their disappointment as they looked toward the boom box sitting on the windowsill of the officers' quarters. In the next instant, the screen door flew open, and Gallo came swaggering out, railing at them to put their lazy backsides to work.

As they scuttled up to do the *mondo*'s bidding, Jake felt sorry for them. These kids were no different from teens in North America, looking for meaning, trying to find hope where hope was scarce. Did Father Joshua know what effect his work was having? Imagine what would happen to the FARC movement if they all became Christians. It would fall apart.

CHAPTER 8

A rooster crowed, and Maggie's eyes sprang open. The ghostly shimmer of the mosquito netting reminded her that she was in a bungalow, way up on El Castillo, pretending to be a UN peacekeeper while snugged up against her college sweetheart, to whom she grew more attached by the day.

As with the previous night, she must have rolled toward him and moved closer until her head was on Jake's chest. They were tangled together now like they'd been married all this time. And, for the life of her, she couldn't bring herself to move away.

Sleeping by his side, pretending to be married to him—it was so much easier than she'd thought it would be. It also filled her with something she hadn't realized she was missing.

Imagine doing this assignment without Jake. She would have slid down the mountain yesterday and never made it back. But they *had* made it back, just in time to hear Maife and Ixtabel—Maggie'd learned their names at supper—sing as sweetly as angels. Those two had cooked another disappointing meal of rice for all the mouths in the camp. Jake had tried offering Maggie a portion of his bowl, which, of course, she'd refused.

He was willing to *die* for her, if he had to.

In that instant, a memory, long repressed, returned to her unbidden. Following her return from Paris, she had cried herself to sleep each night. Jake had been her closest friend. The void in her life had seemed too deep to cope with.

Imagine if she'd received the texts he'd sent. The entire course of her life would have changed as she attempted to keep their bond alive. Ironically, even after all this time, the bond was still there.

The familiar groan of Gallo's door brought Maggie's head up. Through the thin slats of the bamboo blinds at her feet, she could tell the *mondo* was carrying a lantern to the far side of camp where a young rebel manned the .50-caliber machine gun.

A minute later, Gallo snarled at the youth to wake up. Maggie waited for him to carry his lantern back to his quarters, but rather than grow brighter, the light of the lantern faded completely.

Had Gallo left the camp? He was probably just heeding the call of nature. She listened for his return, but after what had to be five minutes, the camp remained quiet. Gallo's screen door never opened again, which meant the officers' quarters stood empty, as Marquez was still away with Arias.

Now was the perfect opportunity to examine that notebook on the officers' desk.

Recalling Jake's lecture the previous day about being partners, she started to waken him, only to change her mind. The two of them moving around was bound to be overheard by the others, while she herself made scarcely a sound.

As she had the previous afternoon, she eased out from under the blanket, managing not to waken Jake with her movements. Stealthily, she eased into her jacket, tugged on her socks, then wriggled her feet into her loosely tied boots. Dread swirled in her like a cold tide, but she ignored it and slipped out of the bungalow the same way she'd left it yesterday, right out the back flap.

Hugging the rear of the building, she crept through the darkness toward the front, her footsteps silent on the damp earth. A peek at the quiet camp encouraged her to dart across the open space to Gallo's screen door. To her relief, it gave the barest squeak as she opened it just far enough to slip inside.

The generator had been turned off. In the dark space, Maggie paused to feed her pounding heart oxygen before starting her search.

Predawn light brightened the window, showing her immediately that Gallo had taken his handheld radio with him. The notebook, thankfully, still lay upon the desk. She crossed the room to pick it up, then stepped toward the window to better see its contents. It was obviously an officer's log. She skimmed the last entry written by Gallo about his playing *fútbol* with the UN guests and beating them soundly. *Hah.*

Flipping back in time, Maggie came to an entry about eight months old and encountered a drawing—no, it was a map! A map of El Castillo, complete with a compass indicating which way was east, west, north, and south, with three sites clearly marked with an *X*, two of them named.

Adrenaline flooded her arteries. With no way to take a photo, she could either try to memorize the map or tear it out to show it to Jake. This was just the kind of intel the SEALs at the JIC wanted from them.

Opting for the latter, Maggie stepped back to the desk, then parted the page from the binding as seamlessly as possible. It tore away fairly cleanly, leaving only stray bits of paper that she blew away before folding up the map and slipping it into her pocket.

Next, she peered under the bed, seeing nothing because of the dark. Feeling with a hand, she identified folded clothing and extra pairs of boots. Next, she ran a hand between the lower bunk and the wall. When her fingers closed around the haft of a little dagger, she pulled it out, reveling in the sense of security it gave her. She was stowing it in her left boot to lie along her ankle when the approach of footfalls jerked her upright.

Was Gallo back? With no time to dive beneath the bunk and hide, she flattened herself against the nearest wall. The screen door gave a squeak, and a dark figure stepped stealthily into the building. She was about to be caught red-handed!

"Lena?"

Her whispered name turned her weak with relief. At her exhalation, Jake whirled toward her. In the next instant, she was hauled nose to nose with him, his grip conveying frustration. "You did it again. When are you going to realize we're a team?"

"I found a map." It was the only way to check his anger. She'd be mad, too, if she woke up to find him gone.

"A map? Where is it?"

"In my pocket. We need to go."

He apparently agreed, tugging her toward the screen door. "I'll go first. Wait until you hear my whistle. That'll mean the coast is clear."

The same whistle he used to make in college, when she'd stolen out of her dorm without her roommate's knowledge to accompany Jake to a late-night café.

A quick, unexpected kiss on her lips brought her abruptly to the present. As Jake slipped outside, moving too quickly for the hinges to make a sound, she processed the kiss. Had he *meant* to kiss her? It had felt so unpremeditated...so *right*.

Peeking through the screen, she waited. The sky had brightened, and the forest had come alive with monkey chatter and birdsong.

A minute crept by, and then another. Was that Jake's whistle, or was that a bird? The sky was now a deep lavender hue. On the other side of the camp, the kid manning the machine gun left his sandbag bunker to relieve himself against a tree. His back was turned. The coast had to be clear.

Maggie eased the door open and stepped outside. In that same instant, a figure she hadn't seen standing by the firepit turned and caught sight of her—David. Maggie neither stiffened nor gasped. *"When caught red-handed,"* her father had taught her, *"go on the offensive."*

Squaring her shoulders, she marched straight toward him.

"Where is Mondo Gallo?" Both her tone and her body language suggested annoyance, though she was careful to keep her voice down. "Esme has a high fever, and I need the medicine that was in my backpack. Where is that now?" It was the first excuse she could think of.

The suspicion that had creased David's brow eased. "Your *medicamentos* belong to the people now. It was given to the mayor of the nearest village to be distributed equitably." He spoke in a gentle voice, clearly believing his own words.

"Equitably?" Maggie propped her hands on her hips and raised an eyebrow at him.

"Yes. We are all equals. No one person should have more than another."

"And yet, your guests are people, too. Shouldn't we have access to medicine?"

"I'm sorry. It was given to the poor."

To his credit, he did sound like he felt bad.

"And you don't think Gallo kept some for himself?" She gestured to the hut she'd been searching.

"I doubt it. I've never seen him get sick."

She heaved a sigh. "All right. Well, you'd better hope Esme doesn't die. That wouldn't exactly endear the FARC to the rest of the world. When Gallo comes back, I'll ask him directly."

Pivoting, she left David staring after her as she loped casually back to the bungalow, entering through the front flap. She ran straight into Jake, who pulled her into his embrace and held her there. Maggie felt his heart thumping through the material of their clothing. He'd truly been scared for her.

"I'm okay." If anything, the event should prove to Jake that she could handle herself in the slipperiest of situations. Sure, he'd had to rescue her twice in the past, but those were the exceptions, not the rule. She was getting her confidence back. And the time would soon come when she could go back into the field, operating solo, the way she had before.

Sorrow stitched through the fabric of her optimism. Darn it, she was getting used to having a partner.

"Plus lentement!" Slow down.

Jake chased Lena down the same path they'd taken yesterday to the garcinia tree. Thunder rumbled above the thick canopy, and it was raining again, turning the ground to muck beneath their boots. Following a long, boring morning in which Jake had taught the teens a version of Mancala using their own marbles, the clouds had buckled. Both the rebels and the guests fled the deluge by retreating to their shelters.

Lena had tried to show Jake the map, then, along with the dagger still stowed in her boot, but Charles had hushed them, conveying that their whispers might be viewed as suspicious. Jake, wanting to seize this chance to test the sat phone again, had gestured toward their secret exit and Lena had nodded.

The only drawback to seeking privacy was getting soaked. Cold rainwater dripped from the spiked ends of Jake's hair. The ground was like one of those Slip 'N Slide mats they'd set up as kids to play on. Lena, of course, didn't slow her pace one iota.

Frustrated, he checked the impulse to chide her in English because he didn't know the French words. He managed to put a precaution together, "I can't catch you from here if you slip, Lena."

In typical Lena fashion, she ignored him. "I'm not going to slip."

To make sure of that, she was grabbing hold of the vegetation as they charged downhill. He wanted to tell her that wasn't a good idea either, yet being as eager to see the map and get back to their cubicle, he didn't say anything.

In the next instant, Lena yelped as a species of tarantula scrabbled up her arm. Before Jake could brush it off, she shook herself violently and promptly slipped on the mud.

The indignant look she swiveled up at him made Jake's ribs tickle.

"Ne dis pas un mot," she warned on a humiliated note. *Don't say a word.*

To keep from laughing, Jake imagined what would have happened if the harmless tarantula was a fer-de-lance pit viper. As he helped her to her feet again, he swept the weeping forest. Who but fools and spies would venture out into a rainstorm? "I think this is far enough. Show me what you've got, but keep it dry."

Lena found the closest tree to shelter them and pulled the map from her pocket. Putting his cheek close to hers, Jake examined the crude drawing with interest.

She pointed at two of the three *X*s. "These are the names of camps, I think. Which one is ours, do you think?" She stuck faithfully to French, a true professional.

Jake pointed. "Probably this one. We're pretty high up the mountain."

"*Cecaot-Jicobo.*" She attempted to pronounce the name beneath it. The other was called *Ki-kirr-ziki*s. "Are these indigenous words?"

"*J'en doute.*" *I doubt it.* Jake lifted his right leg and went to work, taking off his boot. Once the phone was in his hand, he powered it up, glancing around vigilantly as it emitted the beep. At last, he pulled up the antenna and prayed for a connection.

Lena watched his every move. "Still nothing?" She sounded as concerned as he felt.

"Nope." As he lowered the antenna, disappointed, she looked back at the map.

"So, if these names aren't indigenous, what are they?"

"Encryptions." Another word he didn't know in French, so he faked it.

She looked irritated that she hadn't realized that before he did. "Can you break the code?"

Her expectant, upward glance warmed him. "Possibly, but it'll take me a while."

"Hmm." She looked back at the map, pointing to what was clearly a depiction of water. "I wonder if this is the creek we crossed. If so, there's a waterfall near the top."

Jake peeked at the crude drawing in her hands. "There's got to be more than one river on this mountain."

"Why isn't this camp named?"

He considered the X she was pointing to, situated near the mountain's peak. "Maybe that's the radio station." Giving up on a connection, he started to stow the phone back in his boot, then changed his mind. "Let me take a picture first. Hold it still for me."

She angled the map obligingly. "But you can't upload photos without a signal, can you?"

"No. The pictures aren't going anywhere until we get coverage." He snapped off a shot of the entire map, then zoomed in over each X.

"You think your team is worried that we haven't checked in?"

He replied with more assurance than he felt. "As long as our trackers are transmitting, they're not worried."

As he put the phone away, Lena folded the map. "Can we bury this now? I don't like carrying it around."

"You don't have to." He plucked it from her grasp and stuffed it inside his own pants pocket next to their passports, which he carried everywhere. "And we can't bury it until we're sure the JIC has the photos. In the meantime, I'll try to break the encryption."

"*Cryptage*," she corrected.

"Oui. It can't be that complex. It's not like they have a lot of technology out here."

Jake hauled on his boot and quickly tied the laces. He wasn't going to tell Lena this and compound her stress, but even if their phone was working, it was only a matter of time before the constant moisture here interfered with the electronics, rendering it even more useless than it was already.

When a shout came out of the forest early that evening, Maggie's first response was relief. She hadn't joined the CIA to sit on her hands all day waiting for others to make things happen.

While Jake sat around the smoldering firepit with Boris, Bellini, and Charles, Maggie sat with Esme on the bungalow's front platform, listening to the Turkish woman's life story. The shout coming from the woods was a godsend.

But in response to it, Chucho, who was manning the .50-caliber machine gun, let loose with a stream of bullets that tattered the foliage. Maggie hit the ground, her adrenaline spiking.

Rat-tat-tat-tat-tat. On the far side of the camp, bits of bark and leaves rained down like confetti. One minute, Jake was over at the firepit; the next, he was hauling Maggie off the mud and around the building, where he pinned her against the spindly post.

"What's happening?" She eyed the pulse in Jake's powerful neck, her heart beating fast.

"Don't know yet."

The familiar grating quality of Gallo's voice reached their ears as the deputy returned from his mysterious departure to rail at poor Chucho, accusing him of trying to kill his own leader.

"Guess who's back?" Jake sounded about as thrilled about the *mondo*'s return as Maggie was. But then Jake stiffened. "And he's brought company."

"Who?" Maggie stole a peek around the edge of the building. In the overcast afternoon light, she made out four more men standing in the mist beyond the machine gun. Their uniforms, solid pea-green, were different from Gallo's. They carried weapons over their shoulders that looked like brand-new AK-74s, not the antique 47s like the FARC had, and vests jam-packed with artillery.

A taut quiet fell over the camp as its inhabitants eyed the newcomers. Even the chickens seemed to stop and stare.

"They're not FARC dressed like that," Jake observed. "Maybe they're ELN?"

Maggie narrowed her eyes. The uniform struck her as familiar. Her gaze slid to the mules they were leading, each one laden with burlap sacks, and her stomach growled. "Please, say they've brought food for us."

"I wouldn't get your hopes up."

Rather than lead the strangers closer, Gallo summoned David's squad over to unload the heavy-looking sacks. Maggie and Jake watched as the four boys who'd played *fútbol* hastened toward the mules and took one bag apiece, toting them toward the little hutch that housed the cooking utensils.

"Why don't they just bring the mules into camp and save the kids some work?" Maggie wanted to know.

"Maybe Gallo doesn't want us rubbing elbows with these guys."

"Why not?" She tugged on Jake's sleeve. "Let's see what happens when we offer to help."

He frowned at her. "Are you trying to get into trouble?"

"How is that trouble? We're peacekeepers. Helping is what we do."

He cut a thoughtful look toward the newcomers, clearly as curious as she was. "*Bien.* But stay behind me and let me do the talking."

They left the corner of the bungalow together, walking casually toward Gallo and his buddies when David stepped into their path.

"Stay back." His light-brown eyes conveyed worry.

"But we can help." Jake sounded like an eager Boy Scout. "I can

111

carry two bags at once. Look at them." He gestured to the young FARC rebels huffing and puffing under just one bag.

"No." David's tone brooked no argument. "Gallo will blame me."

The words convinced Maggie to change her mind. At least she'd gotten close enough to read the lettering on the sides of the bags: **_Frijoles negros_**. Thank God! Maybe tomorrow, they would get some beans with their rice.

With the foodstuffs unpacked, Gallo waved off the newcomers who led their mules into the mist on the same path both Gallo and Marquez had taken earlier, leaving Maggie with more questions than answers, like where did that path lead, and what about the other one near the bull's-eyes? No one had headed off on that path yet.

"I'm not good at this."

Jake lifted a wry gaze to Lena's longsuffering expression. It wasn't common for her to admit a weakness, but it wasn't like Jake hadn't noticed her frustration. With a weak morning sun brightening the clouds parked over their camp, they sat together on the front ledge of the bungalow, playing a game of tic-tac-toe in the dirt at their feet. Since she'd beat him in the last four games, she wasn't referring to her strategy, obviously.

"What, waiting?" he guessed in French.

"Yes. How are you not wanting to tear your hair out?"

He tapped his temple. "I'm busy thinking."

"About?"

"You know."

It took her a second to guess. Ever since yesterday, he'd been working on breaking the encryption.

"All in your head?"

"Do you see a pen and paper lying around?"

"There's some in the officers' quarters."

No sooner did she mention that building than the screen door swung open and out stepped Gallo, clutching his handheld radio. He yelled at David, who was cleaning his weapon along with the rest of the kids, to clean up the camp. Marquez would be back in half an hour.

Finally! Lena cast Jake a look of relief. "Let's pray Arias has proof of life so we can get the ball rolling."

The commander and the Argentine had been gone for three days. Between their two batteries, they were down to nine days of power left on the sat phone that had yet to connect with the JIC. "Amen to that."

A beat of silence followed his reply. As Lena turned her head and met his gaze, he could tell she wanted to tell him something. "What?"

"I hope you still pray."

He blinked. "I do. But you used to tease me about it."

"Well...that was before."

"Before what?"

She looked away, apparently self-conscious. "You used to tell me one day I would need to ask for God's help."

"I remember."

"Well, that day came in Morocco," she admitted unexpectedly, "when I wasn't sure I would make it to the"—she glanced around, making sure no one was close enough to hear—"to the place where you picked me up."

Picturing the way she'd looked with her face bludgeoned, crippled by pain, he could imagine she'd been terrified. "Did praying help?"

She raised her eyebrows. "It did, actually. Unless it was just adrenaline."

For Jake, it made no difference. "Think of it this way. If God created us with all of our marvelous complexities, then who made the adrenaline? God did. So, it was Him either way."

She cast him a tolerant smile. "I could never win an argument with you."

"Is that why we don't argue? And here I thought it was because we got along so well."

"Don't flirt with me, Jacques." Her request held a hint of desperation.

He was about to ask, "What are you afraid of?" when she announced, "Oh, here come Marquez and Arias now." Pushing off the ledge, she put several yards between them, making it abundantly clear she was done with their deep conversation.

Jake grimaced. Not to worry. They still had days to spend together. And with God's help, he would win her over yet.

Joining Lena and the other peacekeepers in welcoming Arias back, Jake's gaze went straight to the commander's left wrist as he marched into camp with the Argentine. The watch was gone, which meant either Marquez had sold it or he'd gifted it to Rojas. The CIA might know that man's exact coordinates without him even realizing it.

Marquez ordered Arias and the peacekeepers to get straight to business. They squeezed into the officers' quarters a second time, an even tighter fit with everyone packed inside, eager to discover what progress had been made. They gave the desk chair to the Argentine, who seemed to have aged overnight. In the last three days, he'd grown a prickly-looking mustache but no beard. Beads of sweat glimmered on his brow.

Speaking in a low voice, he forced all of them to lean forward so they could hear his words over the drone of the generator out back. "It takes three hours to reach Rojas's camp." He wiped his brow with his stained sleeve.

Jake met Lena's sidelong glance. Would that be *Ki-kirr-zikis* or the unnamed site near the top of the mountain?

"Yet I have brought proof of life, as you requested." Arias withdrew two wrinkled letters from the front pocket of his jacket and surrendered them to Boris.

The German tugged on the switch of the dangling lightbulb, which substantially brightened the room, before perusing both letters in silence. "These appear to be authentic." He passed one letter to his left, the other to his right.

When the letter from Jay Barnes fell into Jake's hands, he overheard the breath hitch in Lena's throat as she leaned in to peruse it with him. Given the water splotches and the smeared ink, it appeared as if Jay had been weeping when he wrote it—or getting rained on. The letter was addressed to his bride, Amelia, to whom Jay poured out his distress at being kept away. He hoped to be released by Labor Day, which was the only reference to time, apart from the date the letter was written, July

28, just over a week ago. The FARC had anticipated the request for proof of life even before Boris suggested it.

Passing the letter off to Bellini, Jake watched Lena take the letter from Mike Howitz and skim it briefly. As it was written in English, a language she professed not to know, she handed it to Jake, who waded his way through the sloppy handwriting, just managing to glean its message. He looked up. "Señor Howitz mentions that he missed his son's birthday. Does anyone know when that was?"

Lena was the only one to answer. *"El once de mayo."* *May 11th*. When everyone regarded her in surprise, she added, "Did you all not read the report?"

Jake looked back at the letter. "This letter was written a week ago, July 31, so, yes, he would have missed it."

Lena leaned closer to the letter in his hand, then plucked it away from him. *"Espera."* *Wait.* She shifted so she was standing under the light, then shook her head. "No. Someone else wrote this date. It's not in his handwriting, and it isn't even written with the same pen."

Her awareness of details amazed Jake.

"Let me see?" Boris took the letter and examined it. "It looks the same to me." He passed it to Bellini.

The Italian shrugged. "I think so, too." He gave the letter to Esme.

She regarded the date for a moment. "I really can't tell."

Charles got the letter next. Angling it toward the screen door, he examined it. "I believe Madeleine is correct. The ink and the writing are different." He passed it back to Boris.

Firming his lips, Boris stared at the date, then heaved a sigh. "I think, if there is a question about who wrote the date, then this letter does not prove Mike Howitz is still alive." He returned the letter to the Argentine. "I'm sorry, but this doesn't qualify as proof of life for Mike Howitz. He could have written this letter back in May, which is how it reads."

The once dapper Argentine seemed to shrink in his chair. Pity for the man kept Jake quiet. He was as much a hostage as Mike and Jay despite the modest respect the rebels had shown him.

Charles gave a push toward Maggie and Jake's agenda. "If we could only see the captives for ourselves."

Boris shook his large head. "General Rojas would never allow that. Would he?" he asked Arias.

"No. Not even I am permitted to see them."

A beat of silence passed.

Jake broke it by inquiring, "What about their voices?" He mimed talking via a handheld radio.

Lena jumped on the idea, taking over for him since Jacques's Spanish wasn't adequate enough. "Yes, whoever is guarding the hostages probably has a radio, as well. And, no, we don't need to see the hostages to determine who they are. Their accents would identify them. Barnes is a Texan, and Howitz is from..." She pretended not to remember.

"*Carolina del sur,*" Charles supplied, scratching his chin. "You know, that's not a bad idea."

Boris turned eagerly toward Arias. "What do you think, señor?"

The middleman gave a weary shrug. "I can ask." He sat a moment, brow furrowed, blinking as if to remember something. "Ah, yes. Rojas wishes to make a change to the FARC's demands: In addition to the ransom of five-hundred-thousand dollars for each man, he wants you to pressure the Colombian Army into releasing five FARC soldiers captured in Calamar three years ago."

Folding his arms across his chest, Boris didn't seem at all dismayed or surprised by the FARC's changing ransom demands.

Bellini gave voice to Jake's question. "How could we possibly promise the return of captured rebels? We can't speak for the Colombian Army."

The German's shrug implied he might have consulted with the Colombian Army prior to this trip to determine what, if any, concessions might be made. "Perhaps a trade," he suggested. "As I understand it, the FARC have also captured some of the JUNGLA."

Jake met Lena's startled gaze. This was news to them.

"And yet"—Boris looked back at Arias—"no arrangements can be made until we are assured the hostages are alive."

"Yes, yes." Arias seemed half asleep.

Boris swept an apologetic look over the group. "Then we are done here." Helping the Argentine to his feet, he thanked Charles, who held open the door for them. With a heavy heart, they all filed out, condemned to the soul-numbing task of waiting for better proof of life.

As they stepped into the hazy sunshine, the scent of simmering beans made Jake's stomach rumble. Marquez waved them over, clearly inviting them to eat.

Jake had to smile at the look of anticipation on Lena's face. Thanks to the mysterious delivery the previous evening, they would get to eat a halfway decent meal today.

More than that, Boris Mayer had revealed an ace in his deck of cards, which he'd hitherto kept up his sleeve. Colombia's Army was willing to release five rebels in return for the release of three captured JUNGLA. The prospect of a trade seemed reasonable, but only if the FARC let Howitz and Barnes prove they were alive by talking to the UN team via a handheld radio.

Sitting around the firepit's embers on the tree stumps, the peace-keepers consumed their midday meal while listening to the Cuban propagandist rant against North American Imperialism. Jake had to remind himself he wasn't a *norteamericano*, but rather a French citizen. He forced himself to nod from time to time as if agreeing with the commentator, who even had the gall to blame the uptick in protests on the "capitalist aggressor." Lena, he could tell, was fighting not to roll her eyes.

Just as Jake was scraping the last bean from his bowl, Gallo barked an order that had him and the other UN team members gaping at the man, confused.

"Get up! You're leaving."

"Where are we going?" Boris asked him.

"No questions. Follow the squad commander." Gallo pointed to David and his three sidekicks, Estéban, Julian, and Chucho, all of whom clutched their semiautomatics, urging haste.

With his meal sitting heavily in his stomach, Jake glanced at Lena's taut expression as they both rose. The rebels were notorious for relo-cating their hostages, but the UN peacekeepers weren't hostages, were they? Were they about to be marched to a different camp? How arduous would the hike be?

"You." Gallo gestured imperiously to Bellini. "Carry the bucket."

Looking mystified, the Italian did as he was told. With a cautious peek into the pail of hammered tin, his worry vanished. He sent the others a grin of relief. "Soap and towels."

Jake shared a smile of relief with Lena. They were getting to bathe? Where?

As they followed David across the camp toward the football field, he reached for Lena's hand, pleased when she let him hold on to it. It appeared they would get to forge the path nobody had used until now, the one by the bull's-eyes.

Confidence welled in Jake. Apart from the sat phone fiasco, things were looking up. It wasn't even raining for a change. Spindles of sunlight pierced the mist here and there, brightening the pink and yellow orchids sprouting on the bark of trees, on anything organic, really. The name for such plants surfaced from a college biology class taken long ago: epiphytes.

With Lena's hand tucked in his, Jake felt himself smiling. He had to be crazy because he was happier now on this wet, muddy mountain in the middle of nowhere than he'd been in the last twelve years.

CHAPTER 9

Maggie cocked her ear toward a sound in the distance. She caught Jake's eye. *"Tu entends ça?"* Do you hear that?

His gaze lingered on her upturned face. *"Oui. Je suis impatient."*

The sound grew from a hiss in the distance to a gushing enticement to hurry.

Bursting onto a clearing, they all chorused their appreciation of the twenty-foot cataract spilling over the cliff in front of them and thundering into a basin the size of a backyard swimming pool before tumbling over a series of smaller rapids that disappeared downhill into the verdant wilderness.

Was this the waterfall drawn on the map?

Bellini dropped the bucket, racing with Boris to see who could undress the fastest.

Sitting on a boulder, Maggie untied her boots. With her eyes on the men, she pushed the dagger she still carried out of sight as she pulled her foot out. Realizing Jake had the map in his pants pocket, along with their passports, she glanced over to find him contemplating whether to strip his pants off.

"Just take them off," Maggie told him in French. If Esme took umbrage with him stripping, she could look away. As for herself, Maggie's clothing needed a bath as much as she did.

Leaving her boots beside the boulder, she waded into the shallows in her socks, fully dressed. Esme, led by her example, did likewise. They both gasped as bone-chilling water lapped at their feet.

"Are you going in all the way?" The Turkish woman didn't seem too interested.

"You bet I am. The secret is to jump in all at once."

Demonstrating, Maggie performed a shallow dive. The shock of the water startled her at first, but as it cooled the myriad bug bites on her body, she remained underwater, enjoying her solitude. The thunder of the falls muffled the exclamations of the others as they waded in. Hanging on to a root at the bottom, Maggie looked around. It was nice to be alone for a second.

A sudden disturbance had her looking up. A figure flashed toward her disturbing her peace, and a powerful forearm hooked around her waist before hauling her abruptly to the surface.

Jake's worried face was the first thing she saw as she sucked in a breath of air.

"You okay?" Water spiked his eyelashes.

"Um, *oui*." She glanced self-consciously toward the others. *"Désolé si je t'ai fait peur." Sorry if I scared you.*

"I thought you hit your head or something." His powerful kicks kept them both afloat and away from the current that had tried to carry her downstream. "You never came back up."

"No. I just…wanted some time to myself." Glancing self-consciously toward shore, she spotted Chucho picking up one of Jake's boots. At her soft gasp, Jake turned his head and stiffened.

"Mira, Estéban." Chucho held up the boot for his friend to see. "Look at the size of Jacques's feet." He lobbed the boot at Estéban, who held it up and hooted.

He was holding the right boot, too, the one with the sat phone in it.

"Déjalo." Leave it. Jake managed to keep his tone mild. Towing Maggie behind him, he headed toward the shallows to intervene.

Estéban ignored him for the time being, examining the boot in his hands and clearly marveling at the quality. "You must be rich, señor."

Seeing the frown on Jake's face, the young man panicked and tossed the boot at him awkwardly. Jake, staying true to his cover, went to catch it and missed.

With a splash, the boot landed in the shallows by Charles's feet. That man plucked it immediately out of the water, freeing Maggie to breathe again. Surely, the phone hadn't gotten wet with less than a second of immersion.

Charles frowned up at David as he returned Jake's boot to him. "Who is in charge here? Do you want your guests to get jungle rot?"

"No, señor." David cast an apologetic glance at Jake before stalking toward Chucho and Estéban to admonish them.

As Jake went to put the boot back with its mate, Maggie's gaze fell to his streaming wet pants. He hadn't taken them off before jumping in to save her. If the map and the passports were still in his pocket, as she suspected they were, they might be ruined now.

The flat look he sent her as he went to wring the water from his pantlegs said it all. He'd opted to save her when she hadn't needed saving, over keeping their IDs and the map dry.

At least they had pictures of the map on the sat phone. If they could just get the stupid phone to work, they could get the JIC's help in decrypting it.

But the passports? It could take weeks to get new ones made. She drew a tight breath. Anything could go wrong out here, and she'd never see it coming.

~

Maggie stood at the entrance to their cubicle watching with bated breath as Jake tried the sat phone again, this time in the middle of camp, just after supper.

Desperate times called for desperate measures. And here, in their cubicle, they enjoyed a modicum of privacy—not that it was private enough to hold a conversation. All Jake could do was upload the pictures of the map to the JIC, assuming it worked where the trees had been cleared. Apart from the beep the phone emitted when it powered up, what could possibly go wrong?

Even so, Maggie's heart raced as Jake nodded in her direction. *Wish me luck*, said his blue eyes before he burrowed under their blanket, using it to muffle both the beep and the phone's glow.

Maggie bit her lip while glancing down the hall toward the entryway. They had retired to the bungalow early, feigning weariness. Hopefully, nobody else got the same idea.

Looking back at Jake, she witnessed the simultaneous beep and glow and shifted to block the latter, though surely it wasn't dark enough for someone outside to notice a faint luminescence through the bamboo blinds. Someone *might* have been close enough to hear that weird beep, though.

Ten seconds elapsed. Maggie realized she was holding her breath and slowly let it out. No one had come running yet. Everything was fine. Was Jake getting through?

In the next instant, the glow disappeared, and Jake pulled the blanket off his head, leaving his hair ruffled. He sent her a small smile. Not only did he look adorable with his hair ruffled, but that sexy, confident smile rocked her back on her heels even as desire tugged at her. She had to restrain herself from tackling him onto the mat for a victory kiss.

Only things wouldn't end with a kiss if she had her way. Sending Jake a brisk nod and a thumbs-up, Maggie turned her back on him, hurrying back outside to join the others telling stories by the fire. It was either that or giving in to her feelings.

I'm still in love with him.

The acknowledgment came as no surprise. Honestly, had she ever stopped loving him? Probably not. But grown-up Jake was like young Jake to the tenth power squared—and so appealing to her that even her teeth ached. On top of that, he was thoughtful, concerned, easygoing, and protective. In his company, her PTS was slipping away. But the only reason was because of Jake. *He* was the antidote to her fears.

Doubts assailed Maggie as she seated herself among the group of peacekeepers while willing Jake to stay away and give her space to breathe.

She'd thought she was getting past her post-traumatic stress. Fighting fire with fire was working. The more she overcame various dangers, the more confident she grew. But her confidence, she realized now, was an illusion.

And that spelled ruin for her. For when this assignment was over and she went back to her life, with no Jake around to give her courage, she would fall apart all over again.

Oh, help. I'm toast.

~

Jake scrubbed a hand over his six-day beard and sighed. He'd broken the encryption—at least, he *believed* he'd broken it, thanks to a thought that had occurred to him the prior evening when he'd sent the JIC the photos of the map. The phone's coordinates had blinked on at the top of the display, giving him an idea. All he needed was the JIC to confirm his hypothesis.

But to do that, he needed to talk to them, not just text, and talking in the bungalow was out of the question. For one thing, anyone walking by the building might overhear him. For another, Ixtabel and Maife had raised all the interior and exterior blinds to sweep the building and beat the mats and blankets, getting rid of any vermin. Lena was pitching in, broom in hand. Hearing her encourage the girls to sing, Jake lost his train of thoughts as he eavesdropped.

Lena had a knack for developing assets. And even in the frumpy jacket she was forced to wear, with her long raven hair in a ponytail and not a speck of makeup on her face, he couldn't take his eyes off her as she plied her broom gracefully. When she bestowed one of her rare smiles on Maife, Jake's chest ached. He'd never loved and admired her more. Regardless of his initial reservations and the challenges of this setting, being with Lena was making this assignment one of his best and most rewarding, to date.

Catching himself off task, Jake continued his brainstorming. Where on this mountain could he find privacy and a cleared canopy at the same time?

The officers' quarters was way too risky, especially after Lena's close call the other morning. His gaze continued to roam. Too many kids cycled through the lean-to that housed them. That decrepit shed way on the other side of the camp had bats and hornets in it. He kept searching only to reconsider the shed a second later.

Well, why not? Because hornets in equatorial regions carried stingers with twice the venom as those in North America, that was why. And the bats were bound to be vampire bats whose spit contained an anticoagulant that kept blood from clotting. By day, though, they usually slept. And Jake could handle a hornet sting or two if it meant getting through to the JIC.

It couldn't be any worse than Hell Week at SEAL BUD/S training or the waterboarding training they'd put him through at The Farm. With a deep breath of resolve, Jake rose from the stump by the firepit, wondering the best way to get himself into trouble.

Guilt pricked him as he glanced back at Lena. How many times had he lectured her on the importance of keeping her partner in the loop? In this case, though, telling her would put her in harm's way, as she would insist on getting into trouble with him. Since his first job was to protect her, not let her risk her life along with his, he had to keep this plan to himself.

Sorry, Beautiful.

Crossing the camp slowly, he hunted for the best way to vex the *mondo* without going too far and being shot by the man. Gallo stood in the field by the bull's-eyes, surrounded by the eight young male rebels. As Jake drew close enough to see what they were doing, he realized Gallo was teaching the boys how to bury mines. Talk about a sorry education.

Feeling Lena's eyes track his progress, he cast her a reassuring smile and a wave. *Better come up with a plan quickly, Iron Man, because it won't take Lena long to put two and two together.*

A solution presented itself in the form of the antique AK-47 Chucho had left propped against the trunk of a tree, in lieu of carrying it on his shoulder. Meandering toward the tree, Jake watched Gallo, who was down on one knee, take a mine from a box—hopefully a dud. He handed it to a boy Jake didn't know yet, ordering him to put it in the ground and cover it up.

Where were the FARC getting these mines, anyway?

Arriving at the tree, Jake reached casually for the eighties-era rifle and then picked it up. As he turned it over with the air of a man who'd never held one before, he sensed Lena's riveted stare from clear across the camp. Better act fast.

Hearing a rustle overhead, Jake made eye contact with a long-haired spider monkey peeking down at him. He said in French, "I would move if I were you." With a final glance at Gallo, who'd caught sight of him, Jake surreptitiously thumbed off the safety before firing straight up into the tree and missing the monkey by a mile.

Crack-crack! Bullets strafed the branches, raining down leaves and splinters.

"*¡Estúpido!*" Gallo sprang to his feet and stormed Jake while whipping the pistol from his holster. "Drop the weapon!" He thrust his pistol into Jake's face while calling him a string of unflattering names.

Feigning chagrin, Jake placed the rifle carefully back against the tree, leaving its safety off and hoping Chucho promptly reset it.

Lena and Boris Mayer were racing toward him, but not before Gallo transferred his pistol into his left hand and pulled back his right fist. Jake could have sidestepped Mondo's wild swing, only he wasn't supposed to see it coming.

Ouch, that actually hurt. Putting on an expression of wounded innocence, Jake pressed the back of his hand to his swelling lip. But it wasn't over yet. Gallo swung him around, shoved him face-first against the rough tree trunk, and thrust the point of his gun between his ribs. "You idiot!" he raged in Spanish. "Were you trying to kill my soldiers?"

"No, no!" Jake fretted that he may have overshot his goal. In mangled Spanish, he explained his intent. "I-I-I pretended to shoot the monkey and the *arma* went off."

Lena's feisty tone cut into the conversation. "He wasn't even aiming at your soldiers, Mondo. It was an accident. Leave him alone." She tried pulling Jake away from Gallo, who rounded on her.

"*¿Accidente?* There is no room for *accidentes* in this camp. He could have killed someone. He must be punished!"

"*Comandante.*" Boris stepped between Lena and Gallo, addressing the *mondo* by a title calculated to flatter him. "Please excuse Jacques. He knows nothing of weapons, and his eyesight is poor. I'm sure he meant no harm."

"You are sure?" Gallo turned back to Lena and Jake. "Well, I am not. I have watched these two. They are not like the others."

His comment struck Boris dumb. He divided a troubled look between the French couple.

Lena propped her hands on her hips and scoffed. "Are you scared of peacekeepers, Mondo?"

She seemed determined to get into trouble with Jake.

"Let it go, Lena." Speaking in French, Jake tried to convey his intent with his eyes. "I made a mistake, and I'll accept the punishment. Just stay out of it."

"Stay out of it?" Her passionate nature got the better of her. "You're my husband, and you want me to stay out of it?"

Jake winced as her tone alone demanded, *Whatever happened to team-work, buddy?"*

Boris placed a large hand on Lena's shoulder. "I am sure when Commander Marquez arrives, he'll resolve the matter at once. He should be here today."

Gallo very deliberately released the safety on his pistol, causing all three of them to fall silent. Lena tried to step between him and Jake.

"Back up!" Gallo snarled, and Boris hauled her to safety.

Fisting the back of Jake's jacket, Gallo prodded him into a walk. "You will wait in the shed until *el comandante* returns."

Lena's expression didn't alter one iota, save for a faint thinning of her lips, but Jake knew by her sudden silence she realized what he was up to.

He was going to sacrifice himself to make a phone call.

The villainous hornets had stingers the size of hypodermic needles.

"Ouch!" Jake slapped the insect stabbing the back of his neck and focused his efforts on keeping the intermittent signal. So long as he stood below the hole in the tin roof, straddling a puddle of fetid water, the signal was strong enough.

Holding down number seven, he speed-dialed the JIC, while praying no one had overheard the beep and that the call went through.

Surely only Lena, who hovered nearby, was close enough to hear either.

Bambino's deep voice, laced with his Philadelphia accent, was a balm to Jake's ears. "This is Spiderman in the Hall of Justice, over."

"Iron Man here." Afraid the call might drop, Jake wasted no time getting straight to the point. "Did you get the images I uploaded last evening?"

"Roger that, Iron Man. We've been lookin' at 'em all day. What took you so long to check in?"

"Technical issues with the equipment. Listen, the place names are encrypted, and I think I know how."

"Just a minute. I'm gonna put you on speaker so the rest of us can hear."

The speaker gave a click and Lobo's deep voice asked, "What's your idea, Iron Man?"

Jake pricked his ears to any sounds outside the shed, heard nothing, and proceeded. "Look at my global positioning right now. Convert my latitude, longitude, minutes, and seconds to decimal form. You follow me so far?"

He waited for confirmation before proceeding. "Now, convert those numbers to letters and you get *C* for the first letter, *E* for the second. See a camp that starts with those letters? It's *Cecaot-Jicobo.*"

"Hooyah!" Harm cheered Jake's success.

Lobo's response was tamer. "Sounds promising."

"And the *O* in *Cecaot* is probably a decimal."

"Good work, Iron Man. We'll play around with this and let you know via a text if you're right. Still no name on the third camp?"

"That's correct. That may be where the hostages are kept, I don't know."

"How are negotiations going?"

"We're awaiting proof of life for one of two targets. Texas appears to be alive, but there's some doubt about South Carolina. The team lead requested radio communication with the two, which would tell us right away if they're both alive. I think we'll find out today if that request is accepted. Ow!"

With his grandpa's favorite Celtic swear, Jake squashed the wasp stinging his temple. After brushing it off him, he teased out the stinger still lodged in his scalp. "Hey, before I forget, I think the top brass here has my watch. If my theory on the encryption is right, the watch's coordinates should match one of the camp's names, the one starting with K, I think."

"We'll work on it and let you know via text," Lobo assured him.

Harm asked with a smile in his voice, "How's the missus doing?"

The reference to Lena eased the stinging in Jake's temple. If only she were his missus. "She's alive and kicking." Which was how he intended her to stay.

"We were starting to worry when we didn't hear from you," Harm added.

"Yeah, well, the comms don't work under the dense canopy. Can you see our trackers, at least?"

"Perfectly. We figured the phone had problems."

"Yeah, you may not hear from me for a while, but I'll look for your text and send one back if I can."

"Roger that," Lobo answered. "Take care out there."

"Over and out." Jake forced himself to hang up. He would've preferred to keep talking—anything to distract himself from the hellish pit he was in. But the longer he talked, the more likely he was to get caught.

With the call complete, he put his phone carefully back into his boot, balancing on one leg as there was nothing to hold on to. Once his boot was securely tied, he went to stand where he wouldn't draw so much ire from the hornets. A rat scuttled under his heel, emitting a squeak.

Jerking the collar of his jacket higher, Jake eyed the vampire bats dangling unperturbed under the eaves. He would pretend he was one of them, putting himself into a deep meditative state while praying for the stamina to endure this.

$\approx$

"Madeleine, wait." Boris grabbed the back of Lena's jacket as she made to push off the bungalow platform.

A shout had just come from the forest, preceding Marquez and the Argentine, who'd finally arrived, hours later than expected. Up to then, when she wasn't circling the shed, calling to Jake to check on him, she was seething on the narrow deck of the bungalow, sweating in the humid heat, tormented by a flesh-eating fly.

Determined to be the first person to talk to Marquez, Maggie ignored the German's advice. Jake was her partner. And even though Jake had assured her several times that he was fine, her imagination spawned visions of his demise in there. She'd realized *why* he'd gotten into trouble, but even if he'd succeeded in having a full-blown conversation with his teammates, she was going to deck him when he emerged. He should've cleared his move with her first! That's what partners did.

Without having to try hard, she behaved exactly as any distraught wife would in her situation, shedding tears of frustration that looked to others like tears of worry for her beloved Jacques.

Jake had gone too far this time. What if the hornets in the shed were deadly? What if a few too many stings led to toxicity? He could *die* in there trying to make a stupid phone call, and what would happen when the FARC leaders opened the shed and found a sat phone in his hand, huh? They would kill her next, that's what.

The post-traumatic stress she was just beginning to vanquish returned with a double dose. Battling a panic attack, she hurried toward Marquez, furious when Gallo ran right past her, getting to his commander first. Gesturing grandly, he relayed the story of Jacques nearly shooting the rebels with their own rifle. It was all Maggie could do not to call the *mondo* a liar. She dragged air into her tight lungs and ordered herself to wait her turn.

Marquez was shooting a thoughtful frown in her direction, causing Maggie's stomach to cramp. Surely, he didn't believe the mild-mannered Frenchman had intended any harm. He listened at length, then raised a hand to stem the rant still coming out of Gallo's mouth.

"Release the man."

Maggie had just opened her mouth to speak. It remained hanging open.

Boris, who'd caught up to her, cast her an encouraging smile. "I told you."

"But, *Comandante*—" Gallo protested.

"I said, release him." Lowering his voice, he added something else that put a cold, resigned look on Gallo's face.

As that man swiveled toward the shed with the key needed to unlock the shed, Maggie shook off Boris's restraining hand and raced after him, hoping to reach Jake first—just in case he'd passed out with the phone in his hand. But, with a murderous expression, Gallo waved her back and released the lock before he swung the crooked door open.

As Jake stumbled out, blinking against the hazy sunlight, the desire to deck him disintegrated. A lump on the side of his head disfigured the shape of his skull. Another puffed out just below one eye. His neck was swollen and red.

"Oh, Jacques!" Her dismay was utterly genuine. "Somebody, get me a wet cloth, please." She eyed the welt on his temple with concern. Could the venom get into his brain?

"Je vais bien." I'm okay. But he weaved on his feet, prompting her to throw her arms around his sturdy frame.

"Did you get through?" she asked beneath her breath.

His nod was so faint no one else would have noticed, but Lena did, marveling at his courage and wanting, illogically, to sock him again.

"Come sit down," she urged. With Esme off looking for a wet cloth and the other peacekeepers offering moral support, Maggie led Jake across the field to the tree stumps. "Right here. Sit."

Jake collapsed on a stump, alarming her when he swayed so far, he nearly fell off the other side. Maggie tackled the buttons of his jacket, parting them to search for more hornet stings but not finding any. At last, Esme ran up to her with her personal wooden bowl and rag. They each kept one in their cubicles to maintain a modicum of hygiene.

Lamenting the filthy rag, Maggie nonetheless dipped it in the cool water before applying it to the welt on Jake's cheek first, as that was the most obvious.

As she fussed over him, concerned by his silence, she was conscious of the Argentine seating himself wearily on the stump next to them. In her frazzled state, she hadn't even noticed the man until then.

Boris was the first to greet him. "Welcome back, señor. What news, my friend?"

Arias looked toward Marquez for permission to speak. At the commander's nod, he drew a deep breath. "Rojas has agreed to let you speak with the hostages via radio."

Jake's head came up, letting Lena know he wasn't so far gone he'd missed the significance of the Argentine's words.

"When?" Boris sounded as pleased and excited as Maggie was.

"*Ahora.*" *Now.* Marquez marched up to them while holding out his handheld radio. "Only, do it out here where there is better reception."

Boris gestured for the others to step close to him.

Glad not to have to move Jake, Maggie placed a hand on his shoulder while Marquez switched on his radio, held down the button on the side, and spoke into it. *"Habla."*

When a voice responded, the commander handed Arias the device and walked away.

Maggie's blood began to thrum at the prospect of hearing her former colleague's voices. She would need to keep quiet, on the off chance they recognized her voice and blew her cover.

"Hello?" Arias began the conversation tentatively, in English.

"Yes, hello!"

The familiar tenor of Jay Barnes's voice hit Maggie like a blow to the solar plexus. His normally robust voice sounded weak, but the prospect of getting to go home clearly excited him.

Boris, who sat next to Arias, leaned toward the radio, speaking in English with just the faintest German accent. "This is Boris Mayer from the United Nations Department of Peace Operations. We are currently situated on El Castillo negotiating for your release."

"Oh, thank God." Jay's voice cracked with emotion. "Please, I appreciate whatever you can do to help."

"I appreciate," he'd said, not *we.*

Jake lifted his head to catch Maggie's eye. He'd picked up on the telling pronoun, too.

"How is your health, Mr. Barnes?"

"Fine. I'm weak, but my health is…it's okay."

"You make no mention of your companion," Boris pointed out.

"Oh, he's…he's here. He's not doing so well, though."

"Is he ill, Mr. Barnes?"

131

"Yes, yes, he's terribly ill. Cranial malaria, I think."

Maggie fought to keep her dismay from showing. Cranial malaria was deadly. The thick emotion in Jay's voice made her own throat close. She fought to keep her expression neutral. As far as the present company was concerned, she didn't know much English, so why would she be moved to tears?

Boris asked Jay, "Can Mr. Howitz speak? We need to know he's alive."

"Uh, yeah. I'll hold the radio for him."

"Hello? Mr. Howitz?" Boris called.

An unintelligible grunt followed.

"Are you Mike Howitz?"

Every team member leaned in, hoping to hear Mike's reply.

"Yes," rasped a voice.

Maggie cocked her head and frowned down at Jake. It didn't sound like Mike.

"Mr. Howitz, my name is Boris Mayer, from the United Nations. Can you tell me where you're from?"

"Charleston, South Carolina."

Boris brightened. "Yes, can you tell me the date of your son's birthday?"

A muffled whisper followed the question.

"Mr. Howitz?"

"Mikey." The man on the other end struggled for breath.

"Yes, when is Mikey's birthday?"

A long pause ensued. Either the man was too ill to remember or—

"The last day of April."

Boris raised an eyebrow at Maggie for getting the date wrong. She stiffened, certain the boy's birthday was in May.

"Have any doctors tried to treat you, Mr. Howitz?" Boris sounded gravely concerned.

"They gave me pills."

Maggie snapped her eyes shut, hiding her sudden devastation. Whoever this was impersonating Howitz, he wasn't a native English speaker. He'd pronounced pills as *peels*, which meant Mike was either too sick to speak or he was already gone.

Charles stood suddenly, pointing at the radio. "That man is not American."

Boris nodded shortly, letting Maggie know he had heard. "Thank you, Mr. Howitz. May I speak again with Mr. Barnes?"

"*Basta,*" growled a voice presumably belonging to their jail keeper. "Your time is up."

As the radio in Arias's hand emitted a low hiss, the Argentine flipped off the power switch and raised a weary gaze at the team.

Boris hung his head and pondered a moment. "I'm afraid," he articulated slowly, "we may assume Michael Howitz is dead or too ill to speak."

Even though she'd come to the same conclusion, Maggie felt a cold wave of shock roll through her. When she'd worked with him, Mike had been the life of the office, always firing off jokes, the first to offer a helping hand. He hadn't deserved to die on a remote mountain, being held against his will.

She pictured his son, who'd only been eight when she'd met him, a younger version of his father, all freckles and blue eyes, and her throat constricted. She leveled a glare at Arias.

"Did you already know Mike was dead?"

Jake reached over and squeezed her thigh in warning.

Arias spread his hands. "How could I? They tell me nothing. I travel from here to a camp on the other side of the mountain bearing offers to Rojas and counteroffers to you, nothing more."

Charles asked the question that jumped into Maggie's head. "Have you seen Rojas's camp, then? Where is it?"

"No, no. We meet at a small brick dwelling, not at his camp. Like I said, I know nothing, only that I am tired."

Charles persisted. "But surely you have an idea by now where the hostages are being kept?"

Arias darted anxious glances about the camp. Marquez had moved too far away to hear them. There were no other rebels about. He pitched his voice lower, speaking only to those in the circle. "I've heard rebels whispering of a place called *Arriba,* up there."

The *X* on the map that had no name! It had to be. Meeting Jake's upward glance, she knew he thought the same thing.

Bellini scraped a hand over the black whiskers on his cheek. "How does the death of one of the hostages change our situation?"

"Well, it gives us the advantage, I believe." Boris turned a compassionate gaze on the Argentine. "I understand that you are weary, Señor Arias, and I'm sorry. But the only way to put an end to this process is to press on."

"I know." Arias nodded, fully resigned.

"Please get word to General Rojas that because we have no proof of life for Mr. Howitz, we will not secure the money for his ransom. Moreover, because Jay Barnes is ill, we can only give half the requested sum for his safe return, two hundred and fifty thousand dollars. We will, however, arrange for the release of the five rebels captured at Calamar, but only in exchange for the three JUNGLA held by the FARC here."

Maggie wanted to protest that Mike Howitz's family would want his body back, dead or alive. Leery of sticking her head out, she bit back the words, relieved when Esme chimed in.

"We cannot leave Mike Howitz's body here." Her dark eyes flashed with affront. "His family must have closure."

"That's true." Boris rubbed his palms together, thinking. He nodded at Arias. "We will offer ten thousand dollars more for the return of Howitz's body."

Arias rubbed his eyes, then repeated Boris's counteroffer to make sure he had it right. "Very well. I will convey this to Rojas at our next meeting."

Maggie blew out a grounding breath. At this slow pace, negotiations could take forever, and their phone's first battery was about to die. The UN team, according to the terms of their visit, was only here for another week. Jay needed medical attention and could die in the meantime, the way Mike had. Yet he was doomed, just as they were, to wait for Arias to make another long march to the other side of the mountain, only to return with Rojas's counteroffer to *their* counteroffer, which would then require them to make yet another offer. Maggie, in the meantime, was going to lose it. If only Rojas would use a radio like everyone else.

Dark clouds of emotion descended on Maggie so suddenly and ferociously that she needed to remove herself from the group before they witnessed a meltdown and wondered at the reason for it. Only, she couldn't leave Jake in the state he was in. Where could she take him?

A glance at the bungalow brought an immediate surge of protest. Not enough privacy. She had to get away from here. A glance at David reminded her of their visit to the falls—that was it! The falls! If she could dive into the cooling water, she would feel better. Jake could also benefit.

"*¿Comandante?*" She dared to address Marquez as he approached them to reclaim his radio.

His eyes, buried within the leathery folds of his skin, focused on her. "*¿Sí?*"

"My husband is suffering from the stings of many hornets. Please allow David to take us to the *cascada* for an hour. Jacques needs the cold water."

The eyes of the other peacekeepers had rounded at her temerity but then lowered to Jake, who swayed intentionally on his stump, looking worse off than he hopefully was.

Marquez grunted, looked around, and caught David's attention before waving him over. "Take the French couple to the waterfall, but keep an eye on them."

"*Sí, Comandante.*" With a respectful nod, David crossed toward Jake, his brow furrowing as he studied his welts. "Can you walk, señor?"

Maggie grabbed Jake's arm, eager to leave before the others requested to go with them. "You take one side, David, and I'll take the other."

Together, they hoisted Jake off his seat and started across the camp toward the path that would lead them to the waterfall.

CHAPTER 10

The weight on Maggie's chest diminished as the sounds of the camp faded behind them. Lucky for her, it wasn't raining. Yet the spindles of sunlight shooting through the canopy and fingering the ferns at her feet seemed to mock Mike Howitz's death. The sun had some gall shining in the aftermath of Mike's brutal and unjust demise. Maggie's heart broke anew. How many more times would terrorism and political ambition kill good men, women, and children? She'd given her all to stop the madness, but the atrocities kept happening. Did her efforts accomplish *anything*?

Struggling to hide her distress from David, she blinked back tears of helplessness.

It made matters worse that Jake, who was her rock out here, leaned heavily on the two of them, stumbling over roots and rocks like he didn't have the coordination to avoid them. What if he wasn't exaggerating? What if he died of the poisonous toxins delivered by those hellish hornets?

Without Jake, she would become the jumpy, sleep-deprived mess she was before they worked together.

"David." She peered across Jake's chest at the squad leader. "You said your mother was from the Arhuaco tribe?"

"*Sí*, señora."

"Did she teach you any remedies for a hornet's sting?"

David reflected while struggling to bear his half of Jake's weight along the irregular trail. "She did teach me something, señora." He scanned the forest earnestly. "I don't know if it grows this high on the mountain."

"Please try." *Because if Jake dies, I'm going to fall apart completely.* The words in her head brought tears to her eyes.

"He is strong, señora."

David assumed her tears were for Jake. With a pinch of guilt, Maggie acknowledged they were more for herself and the loss of something she used to have—a confidence that had proven ephemeral. She wasn't ever going to get it back, was she?

At last, they reached the cataract, even more stunning today with a patch of blue sky visible through the break in the trees. She and David lowered Jake onto a boulder near the water's edge. Maggie took out the rag she'd stuffed into her pocket and immediately wet it in the cold water before applying it to the lump at Jake's temple.

The urge to walk straight into the water and wash away the panic swirling inside made her eye the pool longingly.

David backed away. "I will walk a short distance and look for a certain tree. You'll be okay, señora?"

Did she look as overwrought as she was feeling? "Yes, of course. Please, find something. He can't even talk." Unless Jake was faking it.

With a nod, David turned away, then vanished soundlessly into the shrubbery.

Crouched beside Jake, Maggie caught his face in her hands and looked him in the eye. She took care to speak in French lest David was still close enough to hear. "Don't you dare die on me, Jake."

To her relief, a small smile hovered on his handsome lips. "You've said those words to me before."

The fact that he replied in French reassured her he was lucid enough to cling to his cover. His words summoned a crisp memory, causing her to drop her hands and straighten away from him. "I don't know what you're talking about."

Since Jake was better off than he looked, she would tend to herself first. "I'm going in." Dropping onto a big rock nearby, she plucked at the laces of her boots, unable to get them off fast enough.

"You said you would marry me."

"What?" She pretended not to remember, even as the memory of Jake lying in the rubble with ash in his hair filled her mind.

"It was right after the bomb went off in Paris. I couldn't keep my eyes open, but I heard you. You promised to marry me one day."

Jake's remark drew her astonished gaze to his. He had heard her say all that? She hauled off her boots and shot to her feet, struggling to speak French and not English. "We'd just survived a bombing, Jacques! You were cut and bleeding, with glass all over you. I thought you were going to die on me. What was I supposed to say?"

The hurt that darkened his eyes made her want to take back the words because, of course, her words had meant *something*. But marriage?

Whirling away, she marched stoically into the water in her socks, welcoming the frigid shock as it climbed up her thighs, permeating her clothing. Careful not to dive in headfirst, she waded in until the water reached her waistline, then submerged herself, letting out all the air in her lungs to sit on the rocky bottom.

Why would Jake even bring up marriage when their jobs made that impossible? After this assignment, they might never even see each other again, let alone work together.

But what if there was a way? For the briefest moment, she imagined a future in which they remained together, and hope clawed at her heart.

Stop. With a return to reality, she banished the vision. Most case officers never married until they were retired. Their assignments took them to places that weren't always safe. Only a few, like Mike Howitz, tried to bring their families with them, and look what had happened to him? It would have been better for everyone if he'd never married.

Oh, Mike. I'm so sorry you died so far from home. I'm sorry I couldn't get here sooner.

Maggie wept underwater. If only its chilly current would carry away the ball of pain that filled her chest. Her lungs burned with a need for air.

By the time she breached the surface, Jake was kneeling at the edge of a flat rock, bathing his neck while keeping a sharp eye out for her.

At the sound of a rock clattering near the waterfall, they both whirled, astonished to see a middle-aged Caucasian male edging out from under the cascade. He boasted a mane of light-brown hair and a beard and wore plastic-framed spectacles and a cleric's collar over his blue shirt. Given the only thing he carried was a satchel and a walking stick, Maggie remained calm. The man was clearly no threat.

Sending them a wave, he continued to pick his way along a granite shelf while Jake clambered to his feet. "Peace be with you both," he called, heading toward them with youthful energy and a friendly smile. "You must be with the United Nations group. I'm Father Joshua." He held out a hand to Jake as he marched toward them. "My goodness. What got to you?"

"Ah, beeg bugs." Jake spoke English with his heavy French accent. "But where did you come from? You were hiding behind ze falls?"

"No, no, from the other side. I waved at you, but you didn't see me."

"Other side?"

The cleric pointed. "Yes, look just beside the cliff face, there. Can you see the trail now? It's a little treacherous skirting the waterfall but refreshing when you stand behind it."

Maggie's pulse quickened as she spotted the indicated path. Perhaps it went to the unnamed camp at the top of the mountain!

"What are your names?" Father Joshua's eyes glinted with curiosity.

Jake helped Maggie out of the water before introducing them. "My name is Jacques. And this is my wife, Lena. I believe we heard you on the radio the other day."

The missionary beamed. "Oh, good! The FARC are listening to my broadcasts, then. There's a radio station at the top of this mountain. That's where I've just come from. A pleasure to meet you both."

With water streaming from her hair and clothing, Maggie withheld her ability to speak English while taking note of how to get to the radio station.

"Are you two out here alone?" Unlatching the canteen from his belt, Father Joshua knelt upon the same rock Jake had knelt on earlier to fill it.

"*Non.*" Jake gestured toward the trees. "A rebel named David is going to look for something for these, uh, how do you say?" He pointed to his swollen face.

"Welts." The priest filled his bottle and stood. He studied them while screwing the lid on his canteen. "How are negotiations going for the release of the hostages?"

So, he knew about that. This man could prove a valuable informant. The opportunity to question him quickened Maggie's pulse. Seeing no sign of David, she stepped closer, pitched her voice low, and answered in English, "Not so good. One of the hostages is dead."

The priest, at first startled by her use of English, expelled a breath, clearly dismayed to hear it. "Oh, that's devastating news. What about the other man?"

With a warning glance at her, Jake replied quickly, "He is alive, and we're negotiating with the FARC for his release." He stuck with his French accent.

"Well, that is something. And thank you for the work you're doing here. Blessed are the peacekeepers." The man smiled at them benignly.

Maggie had never felt more like a sham. Keeping an eye out for David, she pressed for more information. "Do you live on El Castillo?"

"Are you American?" he asked instead of answering.

"French. But I studied in the States, and now we live in New York."

"Ah." He pushed his glasses up his nose. "Well, to answer your question, I divide my time between a village at the base of the mountain and the radio station at the top, pausing occasionally to visit the rebels on my way up. It's quite a hike, so I only do it once a week."

"And the rebels tolerate you?" She marveled at his temerity.

"They do, which is astonishing. They've been sufficiently hospitable, and the younger rebels are open to my message."

"What message is that?"

"Why the Good News, of course." He looked back and forth between the two of them. Before she could ask him about the hostages, he added, "Are you Christians?"

Maggie tipped her head toward Jake. "He is." Maggie acknowledged God's existence, but she'd never needed Him—until Morocco.

Father Joshua blinked. "I see." Father Joshua leaned in and pitched his voice lower, even as his gray eyes twinkled. "Well, the goal is this: If I can persuade the younger rebels that they are children of God, beloved by Him and charged by Him to love *others*, then the rebel faction will disintegrate. No one can love his neighbor as himself and kill him in the next breath."

"I like it." Jake glanced at Maggie to gauge her reaction.

"Huh." The subversive nature of the priest's plan appealed to her. The only problem was the grassroots effort would take too long. By the time the younger rebels had a say in what was going on, Jay Barnes would be dead, as well as Mike.

"You're very brave." She flattered him before asking, "Do you know where the hostages are located? Is it the camp near the top of the mountain?"

"Oh no. I am a coward." The priest chuckled at himself. "Trust me, it is not my courage that brought me here. But with Christ before me, behind me, and beside me, what have I to fear?"

Still ignoring her question, he reconsidered Jake's swollen face. "Well, I hope David finds just the thing you need, Jacques. He's a smart boy, well educated."

The man was going to walk away without telling them what he knew.

"Will we see you at the rebel's camp?" Perhaps she'd get another chance to pick his brain.

"Not today, but possibly before you leave. How much longer are you here?"

Jake persisted with his French accent. "*Juust* one more week."

"Well, I hope that happens." The cleric swung a gaze between them. "It would be a privilege to pray for you. May I?"

Maggie frowned at him. *Why don't you just answer my question instead?*

"*D'accord,*" Jake answered. *Of course.*

Smiling with pleasure, the priest clipped his canteen back on his belt. "Would you hold hands, please?"

Not knowing what to expect, Maggie gave her hand to Jake. To her surprise, the confusion and grief still roiling in her took a back seat to the pleasure of his firm grasp. And when the priest laid his own hand over the two of theirs, an unexpected calm stole over her, replacing her earlier despair.

She pretended to close her eyes along with the men, only someone had to keep vigilant in this environment.

"Loving Father—" The priest's resonant voice played a melody over the rushing of the falls. "Gift your blessing upon this gracious couple as they do Your work in the world, seeking the release of captives…"

Maggie's awareness shrank as she pondered whether Jake's and her assignment could be categorized as doing God's work. Studying the priest's round face, she could tell he was immensely focused on what he would say next. "Jacques and Lena, if you know the 23rd Psalm in English, would you say it with me?"

Was he testing them?

"'The Lord is my Shepherd," he began while they both stayed quiet. "'I shall not want; He makes me lie down in green pastures; he leads me beside still waters…'"

A memory popped into Maggie's head of this very psalm being recited in Spanish while she stared in shock at her mother's coffin. Her mother's car accident had left Maggie, at just eight years old, utterly alone with only a spinster aunt to take her in. Yet weeks later, Maggie had flown to the United States, where she'd been met at Dulles Airport by the father she had never known and welcomed into a family she had only ever dreamed of having. With a falling sensation, she returned to the present.

"'He restores my soul; He leads me in the paths of righteousness for his name's sake.'"

Her childhood had been unexpectedly salvaged.

"'Even though I walk through the valley of the shadow of death, I will fear no evil.'"

El Castillo was no valley, but the shadow of death held this place in its thrall. It had killed Mike Howitz. It could still kill Jake and her.

"'For You are with me; Your rod and Your staff, they comfort me.'"

Please comfort me!

"'You prepare a table before me in the presence of my enemies…'"

As Gallo and Commander Marquez came to mind, the missionary's voice faded into the background, and the memory of the firefight with the JUNGLA flashed into the foreground.

"'…and I will dwell in the house of the Lord forever.' Amen." The priest ended his prayer, squeezed their hands, and stepped back.

Maggie stared at him, strangely stunned. His words had shaken and strangely buoyed her.

Jake inclined his head. "Thank you, *Père*."

"Yes, thank you," she repeated.

The pointed clearing of a throat had them all spinning toward the young man standing mere feet away. David was back, bearing a familiar-looking branch in one hand. With the stealth of his Arhuaco ancestors, he'd materialized as soundlessly as he'd vanished, catching them all speaking in English, which Maggie wasn't supposed to know.

Concern pricked her. Could this become a problem?

"David, perfect timing." Father Joshua switched seamlessly into Spanish while waving the youth closer. "What have you got there?"

David's gaze remained watchful, keeping Maggie from relaxing. "My mother's people call it *matico*. I will wet the leaves and lay them on Jacques's skin, and soon the welts will subside."

Matico was the other name for *cordoncillo*, as Jake had pointed out when first showing the miraculous plant to her. The juice of its leaf had kept her incision from getting infected.

"Brilliant." The missionary clasped the youth's shoulder while looking back at them. "I leave you in good hands, then. Jacques and Lena, I hope to see you both again."

"*Au revoir, Père.*" Calling her farewell in French, Maggie sought to mitigate her mistake. The words of the psalm, still lifting her spirits, kept her from feeling too alarmed.

The missionary's appearance struck her as divinely choreographed. Only why would God go out of His way to comfort Maggie, of all people?

She kept quiet as David went to work treating Jake's inflamed flesh. With competent movements, the young man crushed the peppery-smelling leaves between his palms, then laid them along Jake's head, face, and neck.

Jake thanked him in Spanish. "It feels better already."

Something just happened to me. Maggie wasn't about to admit it to anyone, not even to Jake. But Father Joshua's words had taken her from despairing and overwrought to feeling like everything would be okay. Like God always had and always would look out for her.

"I will fear no evil." She held the words close. Maybe she wouldn't fall apart without Jake holding her together.

At the sound of a young woman protesting something in Spanish, Jake's eyes snapped open. Turning his head, he saw by the whites of Lena's eyes shining in their cubicle that she was already awake. They both sat up at the same time, ears pricked to the heartrending pleas of one of the female rebels, begging to be released.

When the light of Gallo's lantern filtered through the bamboo blinds at their feet, Lena threw off their blanket to investigate. Jake followed suit, crawling out from under their mosquito netting to peer through the bendable blinds that faced the camp.

Over by the free-standing lean-to that housed the rebel youth, Gallo was escorting both Ixtabel and Maife from their shelter by a rope wound around their wrists. Only Maife protested while Ixtabel clung to her older friend, clearly too afraid to protest.

Oh, this wasn't good.

Next to him, Lena went stiff with outrage. "Where's he taking them?"

At least she remembered to speak in French. "I can guess." The girls were being led away from camp toward the same path taken by Marquez and Arias and the soldiers in the pea-green uniforms before that.

Lena faced him abruptly. "We have to stop him."

"Lena." He shook his head. *"Ce n'est pas possible."* She had to know they couldn't risk drawing attention to themselves. The fact that these girls were being forced against their will had nothing to do with their mission of locating the hostages.

Perceiving a glimmer of moisture in her eyes, Jake's resolution slipped a notch. "You know why we're here. We can't save everyone."

A hushing sound came from the cubicle next to theirs, letting them know that Charles was listening to their conversation. The blind between them twitched as the Frenchman poked his head into their space. *"Pardon."* He spoke in a near-silent whisper. "We could follow them, Jacques. There has to be a camp nearby, as only a fool would walk into the wilderness at night."

None of the *X*'s on the map were anywhere close to *Cecaot-Jicobo*, but the soldiers who'd brought beans to their camp could have hacked out a clearing close by and set up camp. Here was their chance to find out who those soldiers were while counting on the dark to conceal them.

Lena reached eagerly for her boots. "Let's go."

"No." Jake clasped her arm to stop her. "You're staying here." She'd risked enough the other morning sneaking into the officers' quarters.

As Lena sucked a breath, clearly preparing to argue with him, Jake did the only thing he could think of to silence her. He palmed the side of her head, tipped her face to his, and kissed her soundly. "It's my job to keep you safe," he said against her mouth, then kissed her a second time, more gently. "Please, stay."

She fell perfectly quiet after that, making him think she might cooperate. After rolling away, Jake jammed his feet into his boots, stood, and grabbed his jacket off the bamboo pole it hung on. He then welcomed Charles into their cubicle so they could leave the bungalow together via the rear flap.

"Be careful," Lena breathed behind them.

Keeping to the shadows, they skirted the edge of camp rather than dart across the open space. Somewhere above the treetops and the ever-present clouds, there had to be a full moon shining because the forest wasn't as inky black as usual.

By the time Jake and Charles arrived at the path Gallo had taken, his lantern was like a fairy wisp floating in and out of the trees downhill but not too far away to follow. Maife, still vocal in her resistance, was slowing her captor down.

Jake winced as a shout from Gallo preceded the unmistakable sound of a slap. Maife commenced sobbing, and Ixtabel joined in, masking Jake and Charles's furtive footsteps as they closed in steadily.

Charles clearly had training in reconnaissance equivalent to Jake's. The French Secret Service agent's movements were practically imperceptible. They approached within fifty yards of the trio, so near that the glow of Gallo's lantern made the trail beneath their feet discernable. It sloped continuously downhill, taking them toward the northeast side of the mountain, possibly toward the site on the map named *Ki-kirr-zikis*.

As much as Jake wanted to attack the *mondo* and set the girls free, the repercussions were simply too far-reaching.

At the sound of coarse laughter up ahead, Jake's pulse ticked upward. Charles flashed out a hand, stopping him in his tracks as Gallo's lantern broke right. Calls of welcome informed Jake that they'd arrived at the *mondo*'s destination, illumined by a second lantern but no fire.

Next to him, Charles ducked and picked up a glob of mud, indicating they should smear it on their faces. Following his colleague's cue, Jake smeared a cold, smelly glob on his exposed skin. The scent of decomposing vegetation filled his nostrils.

With their faces, necks, and hands camouflaged, they closed in on the camp, pushing stealthily through the foliage, keeping their eyes peeled for a soldier standing watch. The unknown soldiers had obviously been drinking. Their boisterous voices masked the crackling of leaves and twigs beneath Charles's and Jake's boots.

With two lanterns lighting up the clearing, Jake made out a single structure, an elevated lean-to, surrounded by hammocks slung between trees. A field desk and an empty firepit stood in the center while three dozing mules surrounded a pile of boxed goods. Using the mules to screen themselves, Jake and Charles edged closer. One of the mules startled at Jake's advance but immediately calmed when he stroked its bristly, wet nose.

Over the backs of the mules, Jake counted eight soldiers in the flickering light. Several lounged on their hammocks, two sat on the platform of the lean-to, while the rest were checking out the young women Gallo had brought to them. Maife and Ixtabel stood hugging each other, their faces averted. Jake noted the end of the rope trailed from their wrists onto the ground. They could try running, but their fear of the dark would likely keep them rooted.

Disgust brought his blood to a simmer. He turned his attention to the soldiers. Were they ELN? If not, then who?

As one of them hunkered near the lantern, its flame illumined the band on his left sleeve—gold, blue, and red, with white stars stitched into the blue stripe. Recognition yanked Jake's scalp tight. Holy smokes, these were soldiers from the Venezuelan National Army! He'd had to contend with them two years ago while snatching Lena out of the warehouse in Maiquetía!

Wow, so the FARC *did* have an ally in the form of Venezuela. It curdled Jake's blood to think what these soldiers could teach the untutored rebels—fighting tactics that could easily turn the FARC into the menace it had been a decade earlier.

He had to inform the JIC as soon as possible. Catching Charles's eye, he pointed out the patch to the Frenchman, receiving a nod in return. Charles had seen it too, and with a jerk of his head, he indicated that they should leave. Outnumbered and facing an armed squadron, the worst thing that could happen would be getting caught by these men.

It soured Jake's stomach to leave the girls with these villains. Already, they were taunting the young women, sniggering and muttering crude remarks.

With a prayer in his heart, he forced himself to turn away. *You see this, right, Father?* In that instant, his gaze fell upon the contents of a box sitting on the pile of goods surrounded by the mules. Those shiny, black lumps were hand grenades. He and Charles could easily wreak some havoc here if they had the nerve.

Catching Charles by the back of his jacket, Jake directed the Frenchman's inquiring gaze toward the box. Charles frowned and shook his head, but a whimper coming from one of the women made him firm his mouth and close his eyes. When he opened them, he gave a short nod.

Let's do this right.

With determined stealth, Jake hunkered lower, striving to remain unseen as he slipped around the mule he'd petted to get to the box. Five more feet. He crept closer, scarcely daring to breathe. Four. His sole scuffed a rock, causing him to freeze. No one seemed to hear. He crept closer. Three feet. As a bout of laughter seized the group in front of him, Jake used the distraction to snatch up two grenades and back away.

Returning to Charles without incident, he passed one off to the Frenchman. Assuming both grenades were operational, they would certainly serve as a powerful distraction, allowing the girls to flee, provided they could overcome their fear of the dark.

The best tactic was to detonate the grenades downhill so the girls could flee back uphill to their camp and away from the disturbance. After that, Jake and Charles would have to stay small while the Venezuelans swarmed the area, searching for those responsible. Their first guess would be the JUNGLA, of course, which might spook them into leaving El Castillo altogether. Jake could only hope for that outcome.

He and Charles scurried downhill, where the darkness swallowed them, slowing their descent. As they ran into a centuries-old Andean oak choked in vines, Jake pointed it out to Charles, who headed straight for it. A minute later, they sat on a branch that gave them a bird's-eye view of the twin lanterns twinkling uphill.

Securing his seat on a moss-covered limb, Jake nodded at Charles. They pulled the pins on their grenades simultaneously, then lobbed them into the foliage.

Thwack, thwack, thumpity, thump. The grenades tumbled through branches and leaves before falling to the ground. Jake braced himself.

KA-BANG! BOOM!

Bright flashes of light lit up the wilderness. The shrieking of startled monkeys accompanied shouts of alarm as the soldiers responded. Snatching up their weapons, they scattered from the camp, seeking cover and searching for their foe. From his safe perch up the giant oak, Jake kept an eye on the swiftly emptying camp.

Maife and Ixtabel remained paralyzed, clutching each other. Jake urged them on under his breath. "Come on, girls. Run!"

In the next instant, Maife snatched up the trailing rope and pulled her companion with her. As they scurried up the path toward *Cecaot-Jicobo*, Jake met Charles's glinting eyes and grinned.

But then his smile faded. The lumpy bark of the oak tree was gouging his backside, and until the soldiers moved some distance away, they would have to stay exactly where they were. By then, the two girls ought to be lying safely in their hammocks—at least for tonight.

~

Maggie's pulse jumped as the sound of explosives silenced the drone of insects. Her heart threw itself against her ribs. *Jake!*

She couldn't do this mission without him. Shrugging on her jacket, she left the bungalow the same way Charles and Jake had earlier. Rounding the building, she flattened herself against the blinds as David and the teen rebels stumbled out of their lean-to and stared toward the path, conjecturing amongst themselves.

In the building behind her, Maggie could hear Boris and the others talking amongst themselves. She prayed they wouldn't notice her, Jake, and Charles's silence and then find them gone.

Despite her elevated pulse, the calm that had pervaded her spirit at the waterfall remained, assuring her everything would work out. Jake was trained to handle himself in the dark. And, unlike her, he was versed in guerilla tactics. He'd be fine.

Making up her mind to go back into the bungalow, Maggie was just about to retreat when David looked her way and stared. "Señora?"

Shoot, he'd seen her. Gritting her teeth, she forced herself to walk in his direction while looking completely natural. In the shadowy camp, it was impossible to read his expression. *"¿Qué ocurre?"* She hoped she sounded merely curious.

"Don't worry yourself." His tone was subtly harder than usual. "Why are you out at night, all alone?"

"I'm not." She gestured back at the tree. "My husband is in the trees over there, doing his business."

David eyed the area she pointed out with nothing to say.

He knows I'm lying. She stuck stubbornly to her story. "Ah, I hear him calling me now. Good night, David. I hope the JUNGLA aren't attacking us again." Turning her back on the squad leader, she marched straight back to the tree line, pretending to call reassurances to Jacques—*"Oui, oui, j'arrive"*—as she darted behind the bungalow. Then she peeked around the corner to gauge David's response.

He had turned away to greet Maife and Ixtabel, who'd just come running from the path Gallo had towed them down earlier. A grim smile curled Maggie's lips as she watched David usher them back into the lean-to. Jake and Charles had found some way to free the girls—only where had they gotten their hands on explosives?

Assured by the girls' return, Maggie decided to return to Jake's and her cubicle. Boris and the others had fallen silent. She deliberated on leaving her muddy boots on, just in case Charles and Jake needed her, then decided to trust in their training and to slip back into bed. There would be no sleep for her until Jake joined her.

Thirty minutes later, the camp had fallen quiet, layered again by the hum of insects. Still no Jake.

Fighting the pressure on her chest, Maggie drew deep, calming breaths. A craving for the peace she'd experienced at the waterfall had her clasping her hands together and reciting the 23rd Psalm in her head, surprised to discover she knew most of it by heart. Her stepmom would be happy to know all those Sundays of being dragged to church as a teen had taught Maggie something, after all.

At some point, she must have fallen asleep, for when she snatched her eyes open, the barest hint of dawn brightened the blinds. A draft had awakened her. Two men were crawling into the cubicle. Recognizing Jake's broad shoulders, even though his face was smeared with mud, her heart cartwheeled with joy. She sat up, bursting with questions, but the answers could wait until morning.

As Charles passed through their cubicle into his own, Jake went to work scrubbing his face, using the bowl of water and washcloth they kept in the corner.

Minutes later, he was back under the mosquito netting, wearing his shirt and pants. She embraced him warmly, savoring the gift of his presence, and received a heartfelt embrace in return. The memory of his kiss earlier made her want to pick up where they'd left off, but she could tell by his averted face that his thoughts were elsewhere.

"*Quelque chose ne va pas?*" she whispered. *Is something wrong?*

He put his mouth to her ear, scarcely speaking loudly enough for her to hear. "The soldiers who brought the beans the other night. They're from the Venezuelan National Army."

The unpleasant news slid like a thorn beneath her skin. That wasn't unexpected, but neither was the news good.

"You worked at their weapons depot in Maiquetía, Lena. If one of them sees you, there's a chance you could be recognized."

It touched her that he fretted on her behalf. "Come on, what are the odds of that? I'm not worried. So tell me how you freed the girls?"

"The Nats have a cache of weapons. We detonated two of their grenades, and the girls ran during the aftermath."

"Thank you." She hugged him more tightly. Her hankering for another of his magical kisses would go unfulfilled as Charles hushed them from the next cubicle over.

Battling the yearning inside her, she rested her head on Jake's chest and willed herself to fall back asleep. *It's better this way*. Soon enough, she and Jake would return to their separate lives. It would be tough enough to let him go without adding a layer of intimacy to the many ways in which they were already united.

CHAPTER 11

A t the cry of a masked mountain tanager, David jerked awake. Lifting his head off the pile of sandbags, he watched the irides- cent blue bird sail across the open camp.

What a night! Since being roused first by Gallo's mischief, David had scarcely slept. He'd worried about the welfare of his friends. Later, he had panicked at the sound of explosions. His first guess was the JUNGLA were attacking, prompting him to relieve Chucho of the .50-caliber machine gun. After all, with Gallo away, David was the one in charge of the entire camp's defense.

When Ixta and Maife had come running out of the pitch-black forest, it had seemed like a miracle. They'd rushed up to him, complaining of Gallo's behavior and declaring their intent to vanish at first light. David couldn't blame them. The *mondo* had treated them like trafficked women, not the freedom fighters they were.

As they retired to their hammocks until dawn, David stayed awake, alarmed by the furtive sounds emerging from the forest. Was the JUNGLA surrounding the camp, preparing to attack? He had stared into the darkness until his eyeballs ached, clutching the machine gun and praying to God he wouldn't be forced to murder anyone.

But the sounds abated, and the JUNGLA never attacked.

The sky was the color of beaten tin when Ixta and Maife emerged from the lean-to carrying just their packs. They needed to flee before Gallo could stop them. They would go to Medellín, they told him, to look for work. Sorrow tugged at David as they crossed toward the trail that would convey them to La Esmerelda. He would miss their friendship and their angelic voices.

He dozed after that, exhausted by his vigilance. If not for the cry of the masked mountain tanager, he would still be sleeping, making him a target for Gallo, who just then, stalked into view. Perhaps it was his whistle and not the bird's call that had awakened David.

This morning, Gallo's hair resembled a rooster's comb more than ever. The taut look on his face warned David to tread with caution.

Gallo marched up to the sandbags to question him. "Did anyone leave this camp last night—anyone in your squad or even you, yourself?"

David kept his face impassive. "No, Mondo." *Only Ixtabel and Maife, whom you took against their will.*

Gallo's eyes narrowed as if sensing David's reproach. "What about our guests from the UN? Did you see any of them out of bed last night?"

David hesitated as the Frenchwoman, Madeleine, came to mind.

"You did. Who was it?" Suspicion thinned Gallo's lips.

"Well, the French couple got up to relieve themselves." David hadn't fully believed Madeleine's story. Perhaps that was why he mentioned it now—that and to keep Gallo from asking whether Maife and Ixtabel were here.

"Where did you see them?"

David pointed to the area beside the bungalow. "I only saw the woman. She was waiting for her husband there."

"You say you only saw the woman?"

"Yes." He had neither seen nor heard the man, even though Madeleine had answered his summons, as she walked away. Another thought occurred to him. "I saw her leave your quarters the other morning." The instant he said the words, he wished he hadn't.

"What?" Gallo's dark eyes flared with affront. "Why would she have been in my quarters in the first place?"

"She was looking for the *medicamentos* we took from them because the other woman had a fever. She said she would ask you for the medicine when you got back."

David never saw Gallo's hand coming until his fist cuffed the side of his face, leaving his ear ringing. "*¡Estúpido!* You didn't think to tell me this before? That woman and her husband could be spies. Someone set off two grenades last night near the Venezuelans' camp." Gallo thrust two fingers in front of his face. "Who do you think that might be?"

"The JUNGLA?"

"I thought you were *educado en la universidad.*" Gallo sneered at the answer. "But you're a fool if you think the JUNGLA would throw two grenades into the air and *leave*. Maybe it was you who followed me last night, trying to save your little girlfriends, eh?"

David stared unflinchingly into Gallo's suspicious glare. He would not rise to the man's taunts. Nor would he tell Gallo about Maife and Ixta's desertion. For all that man knew, they had disappeared from the Venezuelan's camp, which would make their disappearance Gallo's fault. "Perhaps some of our guests are more than peacekeepers," he heard himself suggest. "I overheard the French couple speaking English—*American* English, which I heard often at the university." He didn't mention they'd been speaking with Padre Josué for fear of ostracizing the missionary, whose visits and podcasts he cherished.

Gallo's eyes rounded. "Are you saying they're not French?"

"I don't know. I only know what I heard."

Gallo went perfectly still, clearly processing the ramifications of David's allegations. Then, without bringing up either of the girls' names, the *mondo* stalked toward the officers' quarters while throwing suspicious glances at the peacekeeper's bungalow.

Uncertainty pounced on David as he watched the *mondo* stalk across the camp. Perhaps he shouldn't have mentioned his suspicions of the French couple. What would Padre Josué think of him vilifying his new friends?

～

Gallo tugged the cord on his generator, shattering the camp's quiet as he started it up. Normally, he roused the troops at dawn with the blare of his radio calling, *"¡Despiértense todos. Arriba y Ándale!"* But David's news that the Frenchwoman had entered his sanctum without invitation had him shoving through the screen door and snapping on the light to search the space.

What could she have stolen or—worse yet—discovered about the FARC, assuming she was a spy?

His gaze fell immediately on the officer's log. He snatched it up and pawed through the pages. Nothing seemed to be missing, relieving him at first. He flipped through the entire notebook, hunting for the map that detailed the precise location, in code, of two of the three main camps.

His heart began to thud. He knew where the map ought to be— right here. Yet there was only the faintest ragged edge that made it horribly apparent the page had been torn from the binding.

¡Demonios!

Gallo clutched the book to his chest in horror. He could not tell Marquez about the missing map, since its disappearance could be blamed on *his* negligence. After all, the camp was his responsibility while the *comandante* escorted Arias back and forth.

Staggering backward, Gallo sank into the only chair, thinking.

Who would have guessed that members of the peacekeeping team might be spies? If Madeleine had stolen the map, then her husband, Jacques, was likely also a spy. Spying for whom? Did they work for the JUNGLA who had followed them out of La Esmerelda and then attacked them? That could be. If only the Venezuelans, with their rough-edged humor and military savvy, hadn't lured him away from camp.

What to do? He should at least tell Marquez of his suspicions.

His radio crackled, breaking into his thoughts. Gallo snatched it off his hip and answered the commander's greeting.

"The Argentine and I are on our way. You may expect us both by noon."

Gallo wasted no time mentioning his suspicions. "Sir, I believe the

French couple in the UN team are spies. The woman was caught searching our cabin."

He waited with a held breath for Marquez to reply.

"Did you hear me, *Comandante*? Last night, someone set off two explosions near the Venezuelan's camp, and the French couple was seen outside of their bungalow at the time. Do I have your permission to question them?"

"No."

Marquez's definitive answer brought a scowl to Gallo's face. "*Comandante*, please—" He remembered how Jacques had picked up Chucho's rifle the other day. He could have killed them all!

"*Silencio*. The UN team is our best hope for getting our demands met. You presume too much to know whether they are spies or not."

"Then let me question them."

"You will *not*." Marquez's words came out in a growl. "We are just steps away from coming to an agreement."

The words derailed Gallo's argument. "They've agreed to our terms? The release of our compadres captured at Calamar and five hundred thousand per hostage?"

"It is not for you to know. Rojas makes the final decision."

Gallo swallowed back a protest. Two of the five *compadres* eligible for release were superior in rank to him. He would *never* be promoted if they came back to the FARC. Too furious to speak, he smoldered.

"You will treat our guests with respect. The sooner they leave, the happier Rojas will be. He doesn't want them discovering who is backing our cause."

Gallo muttered something to the affirmative, toggled off the switch on his radio, then hurled it onto his bunk bed, where it bounced harmlessly against his pillow.

Weak! Comandante Marquez was too weak to be a good leader. Thank goodness for the Venezuelans who would make the FARC strong again. But ignoring the potential for spies in their midst was a big mistake. Rojas wouldn't be so cavalier about the possibility. Gallo needed only a minute of the general's time to put a bug in his ear.

～

Crammed once again into the officers' quarters with Arias and the other peacekeepers, Maggie digested the news he relayed to the team: The FARC had accepted Boris Mayer's counterproposal—two hundred and fifty thousand dollars for Jay Barnes, ten thousand dollars for the body of Mike Howitz, and the release of the three JUNGLA captives in exchange for the five FARC captured at Calamar. There was just one caveat: The money had to arrive in the form of cash, via a helicopter, to a field designated by the FARC near the base of the mountain on the northeast side.

Maggie shared a stunned look with Jake. His SEALs might not have to rescue the hostages after all.

Bellini broke the silence. "How do we come up with that sum?" A bead of sweat rolled from his dark hairline.

With the approach of heavy rain clouds, the officers' cramped quarters were as humid as a sauna. Each UN team member eyed Boris with varying degrees of hope and cynicism.

Boris scraped a large hand over his bristly jaw. "It is possible," he said, each word carefully measured. "A better question is whether it is ethical to agree to such extortion, as it only encourages the FARC to kidnap again."

Bellini and Esme's faces fell. Those two were clearly willing to accept the FARC's terms.

"Then again…" Boris seemed to be thinking out loud. He sent an enigmatic glance at the seated Argentine, who appeared to have shrunk in size yet again. "I started a fund years ago that can cover the sum for Mike Howitz's body. And Jay Barnes has an insurance policy that pays up to two hundred and fifty thousand dollars in the event of his kidnapping. All that is needed to secure that sum is for Mr. Barnes to write a letter in longhand, requesting the amount be paid to a designated carrier."

Maggie caught back a cynical snort. Insurance, my foot. More likely, the CIA had reached out to the UN lead before this mission, informing him of what they were willing to pay for Jay's release. Once again, Boris had kept a card up his sleeve, waiting for just the right moment to play it.

The team members held a collective breath.

"So…" Bellini broke the silence. "We are agreeing to the FARC's counteroffer?"

Arias held up a blue-veined hand. "Wait, there is one more thing. The exchange must take place within forty-eight hours."

Everyone's eyes rounded. They looked to Boris for his response.

The mention of a timeline seemed to add another crease on the German's large forehead. Raising a hand, he tried to rub it away.

Maggie addressed Arias directly. *"Por qué tanta prisa?"* *What's the hurry?* "They kidnapped Barnes and Howitz four months ago. Now, suddenly, there's a deadline on their ransom?"

Esme, who rarely spoke up, suggested, "Perhaps they're just desperate for men and money."

Bellini nodded fervently. "Well, we have seen firsthand how hungry they are."

Until recently. Maggie kept her thoughts to herself. The world would soon discover that the FARC now had the backing of the Venezuelans. Maybe that was why the rebels were so eager to make a deal—they wanted the peacekeepers to leave before they learned who was backing them.

"The time constraint is problematic." Boris was frowning, deep in thought. "I would need to communicate with the outside world immediately so I can contact the right people and make the account transfers. Freeing the five captives from prison, securing the funds—there is always red tape involved." He drew a tight breath before blowing it out.

Maggie eyed him with concern. *Don't stroke out on us, Boris.*

Both Esme and Bellini seemed to wilt in the face of Boris's pessimism. Jake's steady blue gaze suggested the exchange was still possible.

Charles threw his hands into the air. "When does this time constraint begin? And what happens if the money isn't here in two days, eh? Are the FARC going to kill the remaining hostage?"

Arias blanched at the mention of anyone being killed. No doubt, he worried that might be his own fate. "I will tell General Rojas you are willing to cooperate but that you require a satellite phone and more time."

Boris nodded repeatedly. "Yes, yes, except high-speed Internet access would be better than a satellite phone. We must have seventy-two hours to make this work and access to the Web. Please convey this counteroffer to Rojas."

"Very well." Arias's final words were scarcely audible. A second later, he pushed to his feet and tottered toward the door.

As he pushed it open, Maggie's gaze went past him to where Gallo was sitting on a stump, cleaning his pistol. His dark gaze, full of malice, met hers, causing her scalp to prickle. She knew that look. What had she done, exactly, to exacerbate the *mondo*'s dislike of her? God forbid David had said something to rouse his suspicions.

As they prepared to file out of the officers' quarters, Boris said to his team in a quiet voice, "If they give us more time, then this will work." His encouragement was meant to raise Bellini's and Esme's flagging spirits.

Glancing at Jake, Maggie wondered at her lack of excitement. It wasn't like she wanted to stay on El Castillo any longer than necessary. But leaving this muddy mountain meant leaving Jake, whose company she wasn't ready to relinquish just yet.

Don't be selfish. This mission was about freeing the captives, not about her. Apart from Howitz being dead, negotiations were exceeding everyone's expectations, and both the CIA and Southern Command knew way more than they had a week ago. The last time Jake had checked his phone, a thumbs-up from the JIC meant they now had the precise location of two rebel camps. Thanks to the watch, they likely knew exactly where to find General Rojas.

Even so, Gallo's dark expression suggested things weren't as groovy as they seemed.

Marquez, looking disgruntled over Ixtabel and Maife's mysterious absence—who would cook and clean?—had ordered David and his squad to stoke the fire and cook the midday meal. Seeing the peacekeepers emerge from his quarters, he waved them all toward the firepit to partake in the teens' preparations.

Julian filled a bowl of rice and beans for each one of them. Thanking Estéban who delivered it to her, Maggie sat on the other side of Jake, as far from Gallo as she could get. An uncomfortable silence fell over the camp as they ate, broken only by the popping of firewood and the occasional cluck of a chicken.

"Your drink, señora." Estéban was back with a cup of *agua panela* for her.

Maggie thanked him and took a sip. If she never drank reconstituted sugar cane again, that would be fine with her. This particular mix left a funny aftertaste on her tongue. Lowering the cup to the ground, she concentrated on finishing her food while the teens joined the other boys over at the field with the bull's-eyes.

A moment later, David came loping up to them. "Jacques, could you help us? A tree fell over onto our *fútbol* field, and we're not strong enough to move it out of the way."

Jake, who was finished with his meal, glanced at Maggie's half-empty bowl. "I'll be right back." *Stay here*, his eyes said.

She was all too aware of Gallo watching them. "I'd rather go with you."

But Jake strode purposefully away, calling over his shoulder, "Finish your food."

The message that she needed every calorie she could get wasn't lost on her. Maggie forced herself to keep eating. Keeping Gallo in her peripheral vision, she pondered his weird energy.

She was scraping the last grain of rice out of her bowl with her fingers when her stomach cramped. Lowering the bowl to her lap, she waited for the feeling to pass.

"*¿Estás bien, chama?*" *Are you well, friend?*

The question, uttered on a silky note by Gallo, made her blood run cold, even as another sharp pain gripped her intestines. She shot him a glare of disbelief. Had he poisoned her food? No, in her *drink*—which explained the bitter aftertaste!

The urge to accuse him in front of Marquez and the others rode Maggie hard, but then they'd want to know what Gallo had against her. And clearly he had his suspicions, no doubt sown by David, who had led Jake away so Gallo could target her alone!

Desperate to signal her distress to Jake, Maggie craned her neck, peering across the camp in hopes of catching his eye. But Jake's back was turned as he helped the teens heave-ho the fallen tree from the field into the forest. In the meantime, her stomach was starting to churn in a way that suggested what she'd eaten was about to make a violent return.

Unwilling to alarm the other UN team members, Maggie stood casually, left her bowl on the stump, and marched toward the bungalow, since Gallo couldn't follow her there—not without raising eyebrows.

Once inside, she fled straight down the narrow hallway to their cubicle at the rear and right out the back flap, holding the urge to vomit in check. She pushed straight into the forest toward the *cordoncillo* tree, the leaves of which had kept the infection on her hip at bay, though the site had yet to fully heal.

Another pang hit her as she slipped and slid downhill. She crashed into the tree she was looking for and promptly emptied the contents of her stomach behind it.

Following a violent bout of retching, she wiped her mouth on a leaf and straightened, hoping she'd imbibed so little of whatever Gallo had put into her drink that her poisoning was unsuccessful.

The significance of her circumstances made her reel.

Gallo was on to her.

The sound of someone heading toward her had her turning with relief. This had to be Jake, who'd seen her leave, after all, and was coming after her. But when she turned around, still deciding what to say to him, her relief turned to dread.

Gallo, with his eyes fastened on her, sauntered closer, pushing fronds out of his way to maintain eye contact.

Back in Morocco, Farid had walked up to her with the same confidence; his dark eyes had communicated the same intent to hurt her. The vivid memories flashing through Maggie's brain kept her muscles locked. Fear banded her rib cage. She'd hoped she'd gotten over these flashbacks—apparently not.

The closer Gallo came, the harder it was to breathe. Maggie's heart threatened to jump up her throat. If she shouted Jake's name right now, her voice would crack. Instead, she demanded, "What do you want?" To her amazement, she sounded both defiant and *unafraid*, a circumstance that boosted her confidence.

He stopped within a yard of her. *"¿Dónde está el mapa?"*

Sure enough, David had told him about the other morning. Gallo had obviously searched the officer's log and found the map missing. "What map?" She propped her hands on her hips, hoping to look less vulnerable, though the sloped earth gave Gallo a height advantage.

"The one you took from my notebook, *chama*. That map." He stepped closer, his eyes glittering with hatred. "I know you took it. David saw you leaving my quarters."

"I was looking for the medicine you took from us. Esme was running a fever."

"You lie. You had something to do with the explosions last night, also. I know you are a spy. Tell me who you work for, and I won't kill you."

She managed to laugh at the empty threat. "If you would kill a member of the United Nations Department of Peace, you're even stupider than you look."

He hit her so hard across the face that she staggered backward. *Yeah, I probably shouldn't have said that.* A vision of Farid's fist arcing toward her eye robbed her of her bravado.

"Lena!"

At Jake's shout, her confidence surged anew. When Gallo glanced back, assessing how much time he had, Maggie snapped off a round-house kick that hit his midsection with a satisfying thump and caused him to double over. "I'm here!"

Jake came flying toward them with the fury of a mother bear defending her cubs. Gallo didn't even have time to respond before Jake was grabbing him by the scruff while, at the same time, raking Maggie with a protective once-over. *"Tu vas bien?" Are you okay?*

No doubt he could see the imprint of Gallo's hand on her cheek. *"Oui,* I'm fine." As she switched to French, she deliberated how much to say. "He thinks I stole a map from the officers' quarters."

Jake turned his attention to the man he was gripping. Maggie could see him struggling between the urge to thrash the *mondo* to within an inch of his life and the wisdom of sticking to his cover as the mild-mannered, myopic peacekeeper. Logic won out as it always did with Jake.

"Leave my wife alone," he said in halting Spanish before giving the *mondo* a shove in the direction of the camp.

Gallo shoved him back. But when Jake didn't move, the *mondo's* confidence faltered. With a scornful sneer, he wheeled away and plodded back uphill, leaving them in solitude.

Jake didn't wait for Gallo to disappear before folding Maggie into his embrace. He had to feel her heart hammering in her chest. "You shouldn't have left the camp without me."

"He put something in my drink. I had to throw up."

"What?" Jake set her away from him to plumb her gaze. "Are you sure?"

"*Oui.* I could taste it in the drink. I only took a sip, thank God."

"How do you feel now?"

"Better after getting sick. But I'm going to be hungry in ten minutes."

His grip tightened, and he cast a backward glance just to make sure Gallo wasn't hanging around. "Lena, you know what this means. He suspects us."

She didn't want to alarm Jake by telling him Gallo had called her a spy. "Well, he doesn't have any proof, does he? Besides, the mission's almost over. Let's just see it through and get out of here."

By the look on his face, that course of action didn't please him. Or was it the prospect of parting ways that kept his expression so grim? Her heart fluttered at the thought.

"I don't like this situation." Jake's jaw muscles jumped as he scanned the lush foliage around them.

"Me neither."

"Please. From now on, stick close to me. I don't trust Gallo not to come for either of us again." Lifting a hand, he stroked his knuckles over the side of her face that was likely still red from Gallo's blow.

At his pleasurable touch, the stinging vanished. Maggie forced a smile. If Jake knew how little she looked forward to this mission ending, it would probably put ideas into his head. Of course, separation was inevitable. In the meantime, though, she would wring selfish pleasure from every second they still had together.

"And another thing. I don't want you getting anywhere close to the Venezuelans. How long did you work at that weapons depot?"

"Two years. But I only worked the night shift. I doubt any of them would have seen me there."

Jake's frown didn't disappear.

"No one's going to recognize me." She wet her dry lips. "So, what's next?"

Jake stared at her a moment, as if memorizing how she looked in that moment. "We wait for Rojas to counter our latest offer. If he takes it, my guess is we'll be out of here in seventy-two hours."

That prospect was supposed to encourage Maggie. Instead, it left her feeling cheated.

~

It took the longest time for Jake to fall asleep. While Lena didn't seem overly worried about Gallo's suspicions, they spawned scenarios in his imagination, none of them good.

It was his job to protect her. But, ultimately, it was God who protected them both. With Lena's head on his shoulder and with her slow, even breathing telling him she was finally sleeping, he prayed.

Heavenly Father, give me the wisdom to know if and when I need to get Lena to safety. When I think of what she suffered in Morocco, I would never forgive myself if something like that happened to her under my watch. Be with us and protect us. In Jesus' name, Amen.

With his concerns thus surrendered, Jake slipped into a sleep filled with dreams.

He awoke to an uproar outside their bungalow. Amidst the shouting came Gallo's grating voice. "Find the woman who took the map."

The rough-cut planks of the bungalow shuddered as rebels stormed it, searching the cubicles for Lena. With no time to don their boots, Jake grabbed Lena's arm and hauled her out from under their mosquito netting. They had just slipped through the flap and jumped from the bungalow barefooted when the rebels raised the alarm that the spies were gone.

Jake tugged Lena straight into the cover of the forest while praying he could find them a place to hide. They couldn't flee in the dark with no shoes on. What a nightmare, to be stuck in this hostile environment without a single weapon, no shoes, and responsible for the woman he loved.

Wait, could this be just a nightmare?

With a start, Jake woke up. His heart still pounded. His breath sawed in and out over the drone of insects on the other side of the blinds. Closing his eyes, he breathed a great sigh of relief to find him and Lena still safe and still together. But could the dream be a warning? Hadn't he just prayed for the wisdom to know if and when it was time to leave?

Did he believe some dreams were divinely inspired? Sure, in the Bible, God had spoken to Moses, Jacob, Solomon, and even Joseph in their dreams. But Jake was a modern man. He'd been taught that dreams were the brain's way of processing sensory information picked up that day.

Uncertain of what to think, Jake prayed again. *Father, if I need to get Lena off this mountain, please give me a clear sign, one that I won't question. Sorry. Amen.*

CHAPTER 12

"Wake up, sleepyheads. We're leaving camp in thirty minutes."

Jarred from a deep sleep, Maggie raised her cheek off Jake's chest to blink at the Frenchman poking his head into their cubicle at daybreak, disturbing their slumber.

"Going where?" Jake articulated her question in a raspy voice.

"To the place where Arias has been meeting with Rojas. Arias himself is ill. Boris will take his place and speak with Rojas in the Argentine's stead, I guess."

Maggie sat straight up. Were they about to meet Rojas in person? From an intelligence perspective, that would be an incredible opportunity. On the flip side, if Arias was too sick to continue negotiations, he might end up dying like Mike had.

Hearing a light rain pattering their frond ceiling, she groaned at the prospect of leaving their warm, dry cocoon just to dress in damp clothing, then hike for hours, which would exacerbate her nearly healed incision. But Jake tossed off the blanket that was covering them, leaving her no choice but to rise and shine.

Sentimentality washed through Maggie as she rose from their cozy nest. She wasn't ready for this assignment to end. Her heart felt heavy in her chest as she donned her socks first, then adjusted the dagger in her left boot so she could pull it on. It wasn't until she was tying off her laces that she noticed Jake's preoccupied silence.

She searched his face in the gloomy light. "What are you thinking about?"

He shrugged into his jacket, grimacing either at its dampness or its muskiness. *"Rien." Nothing.* "Just...stick close to me these last few days."

Nothing would please her more—a circumstance that was starting to scare her.

"And if anything happens to me," he tacked on, "just find water and follow it downstream. The guys at the JIC will eventually find you."

Talons of fear sank into her shoulders. It wasn't like Jake to bring up worst-case scenarios. "Why are you talking like that?"

"I don't know. I had a dream last night, and I'm hoping it wasn't a sign."

"Oh, come on." She pushed to her feet. "You're worrying yourself for nothing. Watch and see. In a few days, we'll be flying out of here with Jay Barnes and Mike's body, and this wet, muddy nightmare will be a memory." A memory she would cherish for years to come.

He turned to face her, his quick smile flashing in the shadows. "Yeah, you're probably right."

"I'm always right." Stepping toward him, she succumbed to the urge to slip her arms around his waist and lay her head on his shoulder. Premonition tolled like a bell in her brain. "Even so, be careful."

"If we stay together, we'll be okay."

His words brought her head up. At this rate, they wouldn't be together much longer. "Teamwork," she heard herself say.

"That's right." He pressed a sweet, memorable kiss on her forehead. "Finally she gets it."

~

"Sir, they're moving."

Chief Harmony's alert brought Lobo across the floor of the JIC to study the topographical map over Harm's shoulder. Sure enough, the two dots, red for Jake and blue for Magdalena, were creeping toward the north side of the mountain, making slow but steady progress.

Lobo watched for a while. "Interesting. I wonder if they're headed to one of the other camps."

"Probably not to *Arriba* since they're descending. But they might be going to *Ki-kirr-zikis*."

Their intel, added to the piecemeal shortwave communications, photos, and thermal images picked up by military drones, was growing by the hour. They'd seen images of cargo trucks creeping across the border from Venezuela, headed for the northeast side of El Castillo and listened to conversations involving drugs and weapons shipments, all of which suggested what Lieutenant Carrigan needed to confirm before they took any action: that Venezuela was backing the FARC.

The door swung inward, bringing Lobo's head around as Zen Suzuki, loaded down with coffee and donuts from the cafeteria, pushed his way inside. "What's happening?" He came to stand next to Lobo.

"They're moving," Harm relayed.

Zen's expression never changed. Lobo could never tell what the younger SEAL was thinking until he asked a question.

"Should we be worried, sir?"

And there it was. "Not yet."

As Harm popped up to pluck a coffee from Zen's tray, Lobo occupied his vacated seat.

He stared hard at the monitor. One hair's width at a time, the red and blue dots were advancing toward *Ki-kirr-zikis*. If Jake could put eyes on Rebel Central and confirm Venezuela's suspected involvement, then the CIA and SOCOM could warn their Colombian allies.

Forewarned was forearmed. The rebel movement was going to be short-lived once the Colombian government, led by the JUNGLA and backed by the U.S.A., took measures to prevent an uprising.

Rain gushed through the forest canopy, turning the trail under the boots of the UN peacekeepers into a slushy gulley. Sweeping an eye up and down the line of hikers, it occurred to Jake that the same rebels who had greeted them in La Esmerelda were accompanying them again, minus the two girls, which suggested the team's visit to *El Castillo* was coming to an end. The telltale sign was supposed to cheer him, only it didn't. The sooner this assignment ended, the sooner he would be pulled away from Lena.

Perhaps because they traveled downhill, the hike seemed easier than their grueling climb up the mountain just over a week ago. Maybe the leisurely pace they set was because Arias had to be carried on a makeshift stretcher, David holding the front of it and Julian holding the back.

As with their last hike, Lena shepherded Esme along the treacherous snaking path, the same one Jake and Charles had followed the night before. The fact that the path led them right past the Venezuelan's encampment kept Jake uneasy.

He sought to reassure himself. The FARC weren't going to flaunt Gallo's new friends in front of the UN peacekeepers. And *surely*, after the scare with the grenades, the Venezuelans had packed up and moved somewhere else. But until they passed the spot where the camp had been, Jake would not rest easy.

When his gaze fell upon three mules, still roped to the same area where they'd been the other night, his fears surged back. Incredulous, Jake spotted the soldiers next, keeping well away from the traveling party but still watching with somewhat gloating expressions as the UN team straggled by.

Jake willed Lena to avert her face. The odds that any of those soldiers had visited the weapons depot were minimal, but still, why take any chances?

"*¡Chamo!*" A voice coming from the Venezuelans hailed Gallo.

Startled by the voice coming out of nowhere, Lena looked toward the encampment before quickly averting her face.

Gallo said something to Marquez, then, ignoring that man's frown, stepped off the path to hobnob with his buddies. With a rolling of his eyes, Marquez stopped their forward progress to wait for him.

Jake's mouth turned dry. *Oh, come on. Just keep moving.*

~

If the Turkish woman hadn't needed so much help to stay on her feet, Maggie would have seen the soldiers before the greeting startled her. The word *chamo* identified the nearly invisible group at once, even though they'd stripped off all identifying patches and bands to keep the UN team from guessing who they were.

Turning her back on them, she affected concern for her companion, who was battling a stitch in her side. "Breathe through it," she advised as Esme pressed the heel of her palms against her abdomen.

Over the woman's gasping complaints, Maggie strained to hear what Gallo was telling the Venezuelans. He seemed to be offering them shelter up at the camp they'd just vacated. Maggie rebelled at the thought of them sleeping in Jake's and her cubicle.

Marquez barked for Gallo to rejoin them. As the *mondo* made his way back, one of the Venezuelans followed him, loath to end the conversation. Maggie averted her face as much as possible while urging Marquez under her breath to start marching again.

From the corner of her eye, she tried to gauge whether any of the Venezuelans looked familiar. Of course, they wouldn't. There were tens of thousands of soldiers in the Venezuelan National Army, and yet…the man coming closer…Her breath caught. Her heart began to pound. It couldn't be *El Capitán* who'd cleared out the warehouse before the revolutionaries blew it up. The odds were a thousand to one.

But she would recognize his brutish features anywhere. Having duct-taped her to a chair so she would perish when the revolutionaries bombed the warehouse, how could she forget him? He'd haunted her dreams—same broad cheekbones, same reddish-brown eyes. God help her, it *was* him.

Finally, Gallo rejoined them, and their troop began to move. Feeling eyes on her profile, Maggie willed herself to be invisible. She must have squeezed Esme's arm too hard.

"What's wrong?" the woman demanded sharply.

"Nothing."

"Who are they?" Esme craned her neck to look back.

Maggie didn't answer. She dared not articulate what her brain was telling her—that she'd just been recognized.

Her heart did not stop pounding until they'd floundered another mile or more without a hue and cry raised. In her soaked jacket and pants, she shivered with cautious relief. Her knees trembled to support Esme's weight. Maybe she hadn't been made. Maybe things would be different this time.

Once the path gave a sharp turn, she peered back at Jake, who was helping Bellini over an exposed root. Across the space between them, he caught her eye, sending her a faint, encouraging smile. *If we stay together, we'll be okay.*

Maggie inhaled sharply. Man, she would miss having Jake as her partner!

The brick *casita* where Arias had met with General Rojas stood at the edge of a clearing filled with overgrown coca plants. One look at the old pipes and barrels thrown outside the building, and Maggie guessed this place had been used by *narcos* to process cocaine.

But as they ducked into the watertight building, she was glad to see all the old equipment had been cleared out, replaced by seven hammocks strung from hooks on the center beam and inner walls, each with its own blanket. A hearth occupied the wall by the door, faced by a couple of chairs. The tin roof, cement floor, and bags of rice and beans made this place feel like a five-star hotel.

Huffing with exhaustion, David and Julian carried in the stretcher bearing Arias. As Esme went to help them transfer the patient to a hammock, Maggie lingered by the door where she could overhear Marquez leaving Boris with instructions.

"Your team will stay here with Gallo and his soldiers while I take your counteroffer to Rojas myself. You may strike a fire twice a day to cook your meals, but no fires at night. Tomorrow, I'll return with my leader's decision."

Boris stammered, "Oh, I thought—well, I thought I would be talking to Rojas in person."

"No need. Stay here with Gallo and your team."

"Comandante," Gallo protested, "I have a message for Rojas from our

friends that I *must* convey in person. David and his squad can watch the Europeans."

The fine hairs on the nape of Maggie's neck prickled. From her present vantage, she could only see the back of Gallo's head and Marquez's answering scowl. Jake, who stood not far from them, caught and held her wide-eyed stare. What message did Gallo have to relay to Rojas? Could it be about the map and his suspicion of the French couple?

No, Marquez, don't take him with you.

"*Vale.* David and his squad will watch over you," the commander amended.

Looking as soaked and weary as the rest of them, Boris nodded. "What time will you return tomorrow?"

"Early." With that terse reply, Marquez gestured for Gallo to flank him as they walked away, continuing their trek.

Maggie stepped aside, letting the rest of the team into the *casita*. As they exclaimed over their deluxe accommodations, she crossed to one of the four windows, each fitted with a screen, to see which way the two FARC leaders went. They departed in the same northeasterly direction, downhill to what had to be *Ki-kirr-zikis*. Given Marquez's promise of an early return tomorrow, it couldn't be that far away.

Bellini knelt at once at the hearth to make a fire. As Boris went to help him, Jake joined Maggie at the front window. The look in his eyes told her he was dying to see Rojas's camp in person. Only, how would they slip away from the rest of the group, let alone get permission from David to wander off?

Esme straightened from hovering over Arias. "He is feverish, Boris," she conveyed to their leader while wringing her hands. "I think he may have contracted malaria."

Maggie eyed the limp Argentine with a wave of helplessness. *What can I do?* Her thoughts went to David, whom she had avoided since his betrayal of her to Gallo. In retrospect, her behavior had likely only affirmed his suspicions. With a glance at Jake inviting him to join her, Maggie crossed to the door and stepped outside, leaving him to follow. She found David and his squad members struggling to shore up a decrepit lean-to that listed off the side of the *casita*. That was probably where they meant to sleep.

"Need help?" Without waiting for an answer, she added her strength to lift the sagging end of the tin roof while Jake helped Chucho and Estéban wedge the post under the roof so it stood vertically, holding the roof up as it should.

"Thank you." David met their gazes, then looked away, clearly uncomfortable.

Maggie smiled, keeping her voice warm. "Any time, David. Listen, I was thinking of how well you treated Jacques' hornet stings, and it occurred to me you might help Señor Arias as well. He has a fever, and he doesn't deserve to die out here, so far from his family. You're the only one who knows enough about herbs to help him." Tears sprang into Maggie's eyes, surprising her. She wasn't usually so sentimental. "Please, would you look for something to lower his fever?"

Thoughts shifted behind David's light-brown eyes. He finally nodded. "I will make a tea for him, though it won't cure him."

"But that would help. Thank you, David. You're a good person." *Even though you ratted me out to Gallo.*

Turning her back on him, Maggie noted Jake's small smile as she grabbed his hand and pulled him back into the *casita*, where they found a warm fire blazing in the hearth.

Esme and Bellini were planning a midday meal. They would use a measured amount of their rice and beans each day, getting water from a cistern out front that caught the rain. The bags of food would last them several days, just in case their negotiations went awry. In an iron *cacerola*, they would boil the water for the rice first, then cook the beans.

Less than an hour later, the team had consumed their modest meal, sharing the surplus with David and the teens. Accustomed to napping in the rainy afternoons, each team member selected one of the hanging hammocks. Constructed out of fibers from the *hamak* tree, South American hammocks folded around the sleeper like a taco shell, which made sharing a hammock impossible. With a stab of nostalgia, Maggie rolled into the hammock next to Jake's, just an arm's reach from him. Would she be able to sleep without feeling him next to her?

Bellini was quick to nod off, his snores filling the *casita*. Boris and

Esme followed suit. Lying with her feet toward the front window, Maggie spotted David wading alone across the field in search of a healing herb for Arias. Charles saw him, too, and gestured for Jake and her to take advantage of his absence. The JIC hadn't heard from Jake since he'd been locked up in the shed days ago.

Jake signed to her that he would go alone, while Maggie stayed here.

No. She vehemently shook her head, at which Jake made a face of resignation and rotated quietly out of his hammock. Maggie's pulse sped up as she did the same. She really ought to stay put. After all, what would they say if David caught them at any significant distance from the *casita*? But waiting for others to act had never been Maggie's strong suit.

Slipping outside, they found the three other teens taking refuge under the lean-to, all of them sound asleep.

With a shared look of amusement, Maggie and Jake hurried away from the *casita*, striking out in the same direction Marquez and Gallo had taken earlier. Once out of view of the building, Jake grabbed Maggie's arm and urged her into a run. Hampered by the pain in her hip—which she admitted to herself was getting worse, not better—Maggie hobbled alongside him.

But as Jake had pointed out at the outset of their assignment, running in the mountains wasn't feasible. When she slipped and nearly wound up on her back, he slowed to a brisk walk so she could keep up with him. In just minutes, they came to a bluff where a mudslide had sheared off the slope of the mountain, taking trees and rocks with it.

"Wow. Let's have a look," Jake suggested. Grabbing Maggie's hand, he guided her over the spongy ground toward the edge of sheared earth.

As they neared the drop-off, he went down on his hands and knees, and Maggie followed suit. Peering over a felled tree covered in lichen, they were treated to a breathtaking view of the canopy at lower elevations. One area had been thinned out, making it possible to see tin and thatched roofs peeking through the leaves below them.

"Voilà." Maggie breathed. It had to be Rojas's camp, *Ki-kirr-zikis,* the only X on the northeast side of the mountain. Sawing and buzzing noises reached their ears, but the drizzle and the trees kept them from identifying the source.

"Are we hearing chainsaws?" Jake put his back to the log and wrestled off his right boot. He'd asked the question in English since he probably didn't know the word in French.

Still peering at the camp, Maggie glimpsed a motorized vehicle cutting across a break in the trees. "No, they're ATVs. There must be at least a dozen of them." Higher up, a flash of burgundy caught her eye.

Was that a bird? She squinted, trying to decipher what she was looking at. "Oh, look. It's a watchtower."

"Where?" Jake pulled up the phone's antenna as he turned to see what she was looking at.

Maggie leaned close so he could follow her finger. A log-hewn tower, draped in green netting, cleared the top of the canopy. She never would have seen it if one of the three men standing at the top of the tower wasn't wearing a red beret.

"Is that Rojas?" Jake tore his gaze away to frown at the phone in his hand.

Maggie's thoughts flashed to the photo they'd seen of the FARC leader at the safe house. "Looks like it." The two men with him also looked familiar. "And I think he's talking to Marquez and Gallo right now." Her heart sank as she imagined what Gallo might be telling Rojas about her, Jake, too, for that matter.

"Don't sweat it. Things are going well. Just picture us flying out of here in a couple of days."

Imagining Jake and her in a helicopter soaring away from these forbidding mountains failed to lift her spirits. *I don't want to go back yet, to say goodbye to Jake.*

When he stayed quiet, she looked over and found him frowning. "What's wrong?"

He grimaced. "It's the new battery. It doesn't seem to have a charge."

Her heart skipped a beat. Now there was no way to contact the JIC. Would that matter? Uneasiness coiled in her intestines. She looked back at the tower while wondering again what Gallo was telling Rojas. Was it about her possibly being a spy?

"Well, it's not the battery," Jake said a minute later.

Maggie tore her gaze from the tower to find Jake peering inside the phone's casing. "It's the phone itself. There's too much humidity out here. I can see condensation inside."

"Can't we do something about that?" The rain had started to pick up, drawing a silvery curtain between them and *Ki-kirr-zikis*. She and Jake would be soaked through if they didn't head back soon.

"Maybe. Question is, how do we dry it out?"

Maggie already knew. "We put the phone in the rice sack by the hearth and let it dry out overnight."

Jake's gaze flew to hers. "That should work, but it's risky."

"Yeah, well, it's our only option."

He nodded slowly. "Okay, then. I'll slip it into the sack tonight and sleep with one eye open."

His optimistic tone was for her sake, she knew, to keep her anxiety from rising.

"We'd better get back," he added, "before David does."

Together, they clambered up to the trail, then half-jogged, half-speed-walked toward the *casita*. "How's the hip?" Jake transitioned back to French.

"Ça va." It's fine. She wasn't going to give Jake anything more than the phone to worry about.

They were nearly back at the *casita* when the path gave a turn and there, blocking their way, stood David holding a stick.

Maggie was the first to recover. "Ah, *bueno*. Looks like you found something for Arias?"

David ignored the question and frowned. "Why are you so far from the *casita*?"

As Maggie scrounged for an excuse, Jake threw an arm around her, pulling her body flush against his. "*En serio*, David? If you had a wife as beautiful as mine, you'd want time alone with her too." As he nuzzled Maggie's cheek, a furious blush heated her face.

Jake's superb acting had the desired effect, at least. David's expression went from suspicious to indulging. "Well, don't wander so far next time. Come."

As he turned and led the way, they obediently followed. Maggie was all too aware of the arm Jake kept around her. The sensory memory of her body pressed to his filled her with a longing, unfulfilled. She would never get to experience the passion Jake had hinted at to David—not unless she was Mrs. Jake Carrigan. Jake made that clear twelve years ago.

If only that were possible. This shared assignment was a one-off, not likely to happen again. Once Maggie proved to the company psychologist that she was ready, the CIA would assign her wherever she was needed—somewhere in Africa or Latin America, given her language skills. Sure, so long as Jake remained a SOG, there was a chance she might see him briefly, in passing somewhere, but she'd never get to spend time with him like this.

All they had left was the present. She would wring every drop of pleasure from it while she still could.

CHAPTER 13

When the first hint of dawn silvered the screens of the *casita*, Jake swung quietly from his hammock to retrieve the sat phone. No one else stirred. The little house was filled with the sound of sleeping people.

The night before, when the building's interior had been darker than pitch, he had pushed the defunct phone into the open bag of rice. All night long, he had surface-slept, ready to pluck it out again before anyone awoke to measure the rice in advance of the morning meal. If their plan succeeded, all the moisture in the phone's casing would be gone, and the new battery would turn it on.

Feeling around in the kernels, he retrieved the phone, then brushed off the grains of rice before stuffing it deep into his pocket as he stood. Glancing over at Lena, he was surprised to find her still asleep. Of the two of them, she was the lighter sleeper. Perhaps she'd been awake much of the night, the way she was at the outset of their assignment.

Leaving her to sleep, Jake slipped out of the *casita*, inadvertently rousing Chucho, who slept closest to the door. As Chucho lifted the flap of his tarp to blink up at him, Jake gestured that he was heading into the trees to relieve himself, and the youth disappeared under the flap again. David and the others never stirred.

Confident of getting reception down by the coca field, Jake followed a muddy furrow past the overgrown coca plants to the forest on the other side. Yesterday's rain showers had finally subsided, leaving the earth smelling wet and clean. Droplets of moisture winked like diamonds on the ends of every coca leaf.

Serenaded by birdsong and the chatter of monkeys, Jake acknowledged the savage beauty of La Cordillera de los Cobardes. What a shame man had tainted this untouched wilderness with his greed and his warring nature.

Coming to the edge of the field, he tucked behind a bush, put his back to a tree, keeping a sharp eye out, and retrieved the new battery from his left boot. After inserting it into the newly dried phone, he murmured a prayer and powered it on.

When the phone gave a beep, he closed his eyes briefly. *Thank You.* As long as he could reach the JIC, everything would be okay. Holding down the number seven, he waited for his call to go through.

"Justice League, Hulk speaking."

Harm's deep voice was a welcome sound. "Hey, it's Iron Man. I need to keep this short. I'm about five klicks away from Rebel Central, which means my coordinates should be close to one of those camps, probably *Ki-kirr-zikis.*"

"Roger that. You're about four kilometers away as the crow flies."

"Cool, so listen, the FARC have an ally in the form of the Venezuelan National Army. I would have told you that days ago if circumstances allowed. Also, we might not be on *El Castillo* much longer. We're close to an agreement with our hosts. I'll try to let you know if it pans out."

"Hooyah. Roger that, we knew about the Venezuelans; just needed you to confirm it. And that's great news about your progress. Saves us a lot of work if that pans out. Bet you'll be glad to get out of there, huh?"

Honestly, Jake wasn't looking forward to leaving. "Sure."

"Sounds like we won't need the coordinates of camp number three, either."

"Hopefully not." *Arriba,* perhaps on the trail beyond the waterfall, could remain in obscurity forever.

"We'll wait to hear from you, then. If you can't get through, no worries. We'll know what's happening by your trackers."

"Roger that. Talk later. Over and out." Jake powered down the phone and put it away, making certain as he did so that the hollow space inside his heel was dry. After lacing up his boot, he turned toward the bush to relieve his bladder.

He was watering the leaves at the bottom, peering up at the *casita* through the branches, when the soft pad of a footfall made him turn his head. His stare collided with a set of large green eyes staring out of a round, spotted head with pointy ears.

God have mercy, he was being stared at by a jaguar!

But, as suddenly as he'd seen it, the creature wheeled and fled, scarcely making a sound as it leaped away. Jake kept stock still, rocked by the beating of his heart. He took one cautious step backward, then another, while zipping up his pants.

Keeping his eyes peeled for the giant cat to flank him, Jake hurried out into the field and up the muddy furrow, casting wary glances behind him all the way to the *casita*. What a surreal experience, coming face-to-face with an endangered jaguar!

With his blood still flowing, he ran into David and his squad, who were all awake by then and carrying wood into the *casita* for a fire. Glancing his way, they stopped and stared.

He explained his evident pallor. *"¡Vi un jaguar!"*

Their faces lit up, and they broke into grins.

"That's good luck, señor," David assured him. *"No se asuste."* Don't be *afraid.* "The jaguar protects men from evil spirits."

Pretending not to understand the second part of David's message, Jake followed them only to step back as Boris and Bellini emerged to do their business. "Don't go that way." He pointed downhill. "I just saw a jaguar."

As the two men marched warily into the woods, avoiding the field, Jake wiped his boots on the mat and reentered the *casita*. His alarm spiked to find Lena and Arias, the only two people still sleeping. Hurrying to her side, he placed his palm on her forehead and found it warm to the touch.

She awoke with a gasp, recognized him, and went to wipe a grain of sleep from one eye. "Hi."

"*Comment vas tu?*" He searched her expression.

"*Bien, et toi?*" She glanced toward the rice bag, clearly asking if he'd retrieved the phone yet.

"*Parfait.*" At his optimistic tone, she gave a small smile of relief that the phone was working again.

Her attention went to Esme, who was standing over Arias. Switching to Spanish, Maggie asked her, "How's the patient this morning?"

From where Jake stood, the Argentine's coloring looked better already.

The Turkish woman nodded. "His fever is broken. That tea David made for him certainly helped. Perhaps he can make more. I'll go ask."

As Esme left the *casita*, Jake watched Lena swing her feet out of the hammock and sit up stiffly. She'd lied yesterday about her hip being fine. Remorse for not checking her incision daily needled him, but it had looked good back at *Cecaot-Jicobo*.

Lena waited for Esme to disappear before asking him in French, "Did you call yet?"

Charles and Arias were the only people present, making it safe for Jake to answer.

"*Oui.* I got through." A glance toward Arias showed the man still sleeping.

"*Bon.*" Looking relieved, Lena started toward the door. "I need to use the facilities."

Of course, there *were* no facilities. With a wry smile, Jake followed in order to protect her. He decided not to mention the jaguar. Lena didn't need yet another reason to be anxious. Pressing into the forest, they ran into Bellini and Boris on their way back. Once out of earshot, Jake inquired, "How long have you been keeping your secret?"

She didn't even glance in his direction. "*Quel secret?*"

"You know which one. Show me the incision."

With a firming of her lips and a quick look around, she lifted her jacket and showed him. Her slacks hung so low on her skinny hips that she didn't need to pull them down anymore. They'd both lost weight on this mission.

As Jake stared at the angry red infection, premonition pulled his scalp tight. "Do your business and walk straight back to the *casita*. I'm going to look for another *cordoncillo* tree." *And hopefully not run into the jaguar.*

"Jake, don't bother. We'll only be out here a couple of days. I'll be fine until then."

David's voice calling for them kept Jake from going anywhere. He waited for Lena to tend to mother nature before they retraced their footsteps together. Maybe David would help him locate what he had called *matico*. Then again, no. David would want to know why Jake needed the medicinal leaves, and they'd roused his suspicions enough as it was.

Discovering why David was calling them, Maggie braced herself. Marquez and Gallo were back from their visit with Rojas. Nor were they alone. A squad of eight guerillas accompanied them, all of them hardened soldiers armed with brand new AK-74s, no doubt provided to them by the Venezuelans.

Leaving his men outside, Commander Marquez wiped his boots and squeezed into the little *casita* to speak privately with the UN team. Maggie watched him fold his arms across his chest in a stance of resistance that didn't jibe with the words coming out of his mouth.

"General Rojas has agreed to your latest offer."

The team members gave a unified gasp and shared eye contact.

"My men and I will escort Señor Mayer and Señor Arias to a pueblo, just down the mountain. Arias may be seen by a doctor there, and Señor Mayer will have access to a computer, the Internet, and a phone to make his arrangements. The rest of you will remain here with David and his soldiers."

So Gallo was leaving, as well? Maggie shared a hopeful look with Jake. Then again, was that a good thing?

"Once the arrangements are finalized, we will return for you. I cannot vouch for your safety if you venture beyond this *casita*, so stay put. This should not take long—a day or two at most." He swept one more look at the lot of them while avoiding eye contact with Maggie.

Her instincts niggled. *Why won't Marquez look at me?*

When the commander took his leave, everyone shook Boris's hand, wishing him luck. A short while later, the same stretcher Arias had used the day before was brought into the *casita*. The Argentine's expression of hope sent an arrow through Maggie's heart. She hoped he would make it home to his family alive.

The team trailed the stretcher outside to bid farewell to those leaving.

"Godspeed, Boris!" Rushing up to the German, Esme embraced him.

Watching the couple, Maggie realized a romance had bloomed between them. How more likely were they than she and Jake to share a future together? The question depressed her.

"*¡Vamos!*" Marquez bellowed, and the group set off, headed in the direction of *Ki-Kirr-zikis*.

Watching Gallo go with them, Maggie waited for hope and relief to wash over her. Instead, she was all too conscious that her time with Jake was dwindling.

Following their midday meal, the remainder of the team lolled in their hammocks. What else was there to do? Going outside became impossible, as a swarm of blood-seeking mosquitos surrounded the *casita*, driving David's squad indoors with them while David alone suffered the mosquitos to keep watch. Julian, Chucho, and Estéban hovered by the cold hearth, talking quietly amongst themselves.

Jake, lying in the hammock next to Maggie's, had turned himself around so they faced each other. Over the woven *hamak* fibers, Maggie met his steady blue gaze. What was he thinking? Did he wonder, like she did, how he was going to feel when they went their separate ways? Did that put a weight on his chest, as it did hers?

In the strained, dull silence, Charles tossed out a general question. "What's the first thing you intend to do when you return to civilization?"

Maggie, whose hip was aching, had a ready answer. "Sit in a jacuzzi."

"Hah." Bellini, who owned a vineyard, offered, "Open my best bottle of pinot grigio."

183

Esme held up a stockinged foot. "Get a pedicure."

Jake finally chimed in, "Take my wife on a—how do you say?—a honeymoon."

The unexpected comment startled Maggie into staring at him. She received, in return, a loving smile, which flooded her with tingly feelings, until she remembered he was role-playing.

"You never had a honeymoon?" Bellini sounded confused. "But you were off celebrating your ninth anniversary when I visited the Secretariat just a few weeks ago. Why wouldn't you call that a honeymoon?"

Uh-oh. Maggie offered a quick excuse. "Jacques is being facetious. Every anniversary, he takes me on vacation and calls it a honeymoon. He wants another one, is all."

Charles backed her up. "Yes, every year, they take an elaborate vacation. Where will you take her next, Jacques?"

Jake looked back at Maggie. "Well, I was picturing something memorable with a white—er, a white, sandy beach—and clear water."

He was so good at pretending not to speak Spanish well.

"I know." Esme shot them a bright smile. "You could take her to Istanbul. We have some beautiful beaches in Turkey."

Too close to Morocco. Visions panned through Maggie's head, but they weren't as crisp and debilitating as they used to be.

"Mmm." Jake tipped his head. "I was thinking maybe Phuket, in Thailand." He raised his eyebrows, looking for her reaction.

Knowing it was expected of her to play the loving wife, Maggie raised the bar by rolling out of her hammock and bending over Jake to reward him with a kiss. Lingering purposefully, she hoped to rattle his cage. But when he slipped his fingers through her hair, keeping her mouth trapped against his and deepening the kiss, it was she whose head was spinning by the time he released her. A honeymoon in Phuket looked mighty appealing in that moment.

Fighting to keep a smile on her face, she eased back down in her own hammock before narrowing her eyes at Jake. That was a low blow—tempting her with visions of what could never be.

And yet, once envisioned, Maggie couldn't stop imagining Jake and her sprawled on lounge chairs, sipping mai tais, while staring out at the aqua-blue Indian Ocean.

Marquez had told them to stay near the *casita*, but once the swarm of mosquitos abated, Jake approached David for permission to take Lena for a little walk. His excuse to the squad leader was the need to exorcise their restlessness as they waited for Boris to get back. The truth was, he had something important to ask Lena before they went their separate ways.

David's frown betrayed less suspicion than before.

"Por favor." Jake used his most persuasive voice. "We will walk on the *sendero* for five minutes and come right back." Pitching his voice lower so Lena wouldn't overhear, he added, "You know, my wife is a little crazy. She needs to get away from people."

"Bueno." David finally relented, but his eyes were full of thoughts as he gestured toward the path. *"Pero cuidado por el jaguar."*

Jake didn't wait for him to change his mind. Grabbing Maggie's hand, he pulled her uphill in the direction of their old camp. It hadn't rained since their march down to the *casita*. The forest was cool and perfumed by the many-colored orchids growing in crevices and the forks of the trees—a virtual paradise.

"Quel jaguar?" Lena demanded once they were out of David's hearing.

Jake gave his classic French hug. "David heard some snarling last night. He thinks there's a jaguar around here somewhere."

A tiny vertical line appeared between Lena's eyebrows as she peered around them.

"But I've heard it's good luck to run into a jaguar. How's the hip?" She seemed to be limping a little.

"It's fine."

He put her answer to the test. "So, you want to run some uphill?" The mud on the trail had dried, making it feasible.

"No, that's okay."

"So, it's worse."

Her head swiveled in his direction. "Drop it. We'll be back in civilization soon. I'll get on some antibiotics, and I'll be fine."

Jake heaved a sigh and swallowed the obvious retort. What would happen if they couldn't leave this wilderness any time soon? Peering into the lush vegetation, he hoped to spot the golden-orange berries of a *cordoncillo* tree. As he searched, he scrounged up the courage to talk about the future—their future.

"Listen, Lena, I was thinking…" He wished he could ask her this in English, but David could be following for all he knew. "When all of this is behind us, maybe we could see each other from time to time."

Lena, clearly startled, stared hard at him. "What are you suggesting?"

"Just, you know, to see each other again."

When she looked away, falling silent, Jake's heart sank. Still, he persevered. "I'm up in Northern Virginia at least once a month. We could meet for dinner or something." The thought of not seeing her every day, holding hands like they were right then, eroded his happiness. Even so, certain she would balk at the idea of dating him, he painted a deliberately casual picture.

Her step slowed and she faced him, causing Jake to hold his breath. He was conscious of the greenery surrounding them, the birdsong, the rustling of leaves that he hoped wasn't a jaguar about to pounce.

"Jake," she whispered in English, "please, don't do this. People like us don't do relationships. We've been over this before."

Disappointment gutted him, and his thoughts flashed to *Café du Jour*, right before the bomb detonated. "Right." But her eyes hadn't been filled with tears of remorse like they were now, shimmering like the precious emeralds for which Colombia was famous. "But there's got to be a way, Lena. I like being with you." *Understatement of the year.*

She blinked furiously, clearly battling her emotions. "I like being with you, too." Her words sounded strangled. "But, Jake, we would never get to see each other."

He forced a smile. "Look, I'm not asking for anything permanent. I just want to see you again."

She dragged her lower lip between her teeth. "I'll think about it."

Relief buoyed his spirits. Not that she'd said "yes," but "I'll think about it" was a heck of a lot better than "no."

Lifting his hands to her face, he ducked his head and lowered his lips to hers. Kissing her with all the pent-up hunger swirling through his body, he showed her exactly what she'd be missing if she didn't at least try. He knew he was succeeding when she matched his kiss with equal ardor, fisting the material of his jacket and pressing the length of her body against him. Desire stormed his bloodstream, making his thoughts reckless.

Danger.

Jake tore himself away, breathing heavily as he surveyed their environment, half expecting to see the jaguar about to leap on them. Alarm shafted him as he spotted a man standing twenty feet away draped in shadows—but then he stepped forward with an awkward smile on his face.

"You must come back now," David urged. "Padre Josué is here. He wants to pray for your team."

~

David hovered outside the door of the *casita* in turmoil. On the one hand, he had just caught Madeleine and Jacques speaking in American English—*again*. On the other, they had then kissed so passionately that it was clear they loved each other. And now Padre Josué was praying for the team leader's success as he was away securing the ransom money and facilitating the release of their *compadres*. As the priest prayed, guilt consumed David.

Because of him, Gallo was set on tearing Jacques and Madeleine apart. He might even kill them, making David party to their murder!

Hearing the priest bestow a final blessing on the peacekeepers, David quickly distanced himself from the *casita* door. As the priest emerged, he caught David's anxious regard and paused.

"Will you walk a short distance with me, David?" He gestured toward the ascending path.

"Where are you headed?"

187

"All the way to the top of the mountain. Just walk with me for a while. I enjoy your company."

David nodded, sending word to his underlings to keep an eye on their guests.

As he fell into step beside the priest, David waited for the older man to say something, but the missionary kept quiet. Perhaps climbing uphill required all of his energy. His breath flowed in and out as he plodded one step at a time. His walking stick thumped on the damp earth.

Unable to stand the silence anymore, David blurted, "Father, I have made a terrible mistake."

"Oh?" Padre Josué halted and faced him. The humid heat had summoned droplets of sweat along his thick brown hairline. "What mistake was that?"

David glanced over his shoulder in the direction of the *casita*. "The French couple. I consider them my friends. But they are more than they seem."

The priest blinked but said nothing.

"I saw the woman, Madeleine, coming out of Mondo Gallo's quarters one morning when he wasn't there. I saw her out of her bungalow the other night when someone set off explosives in the forest." David scuffed the ground with his toe. "I...I mentioned my suspicions to Gallo, and now I wish I had not. Later, Gallo ordered me to put a toxin in Madeleine's drink so he could question her while I distracted her husband. I'm afraid he will tear them apart...or even kill them."

The priest's eyebrows, resembling long-legged caterpillars for how bushy they were, had lifted with alarm. "Son, you must listen to your conscience. I suggest you warn the couple while asking for their forgiveness. Once that is done, you are blameless, and it will be up to them to respond."

David nodded, but dismay dragged his gaze back to his boot. The couple, who had always treated him well, would think badly of him. He would have to swallow his pride first.

A heavy hand settled on his shoulder. "If you find yourself needing help, I will be up at the summit through Sunday, perhaps even Monday if the weather is bad. You can find me there."

"*Gracias, Padre.*"

"You're welcome, David. Now, you've escorted me far enough. Go back and do what your heart tells you to."

David nodded, tried to smile, and turned away. Rather than relieve him, the priest's advice filled him with more turmoil than ever. He didn't want Jacques and his wife to think badly of him. They would know at once that he had plotted with Gallo the other day to sicken Madeleine. It was lucky Jacques had rescued her from Gallo's clutches before anything nasty happened.

Perhaps David was overreacting. After all, Gallo hadn't shared any more plans to cause the couple physical harm. And Marquez would have to approve of Gallo's actions anyway, and Marquez held no animosity for any of the peacekeepers. David might be fretting over nothing.

"Todo estará bien," he murmured to himself as he hiked back to the *casita. Everything will be okay.*

Lying in her hammock in the pitch-black *casita,* with rain drumming the tin roof and a cool, wet breeze blowing through the screened windows, Maggie replayed Jake's words to her that afternoon. He'd asked to see her again—nothing serious. But his kiss belied his words, as it conveyed a desire for her that went way beyond a casual friendship. Would he have stopped if David hadn't walked up on them?

Had the squad leader heard them speaking English, or had he only seen them kissing? For the rest of the day, she'd sensed his brooding gaze resting on her. What did it mean for Jake and her?

Surely, if Boris succeeded in arranging the agreed-upon terms, it wouldn't matter what David thought. They might all be leaving *El Castillo* any day now, which meant this mission with Jake would end shortly thereafter.

Loss rent her heart at the thought. Must it be the end, though? She dared to imagine what it would be like to see Jake again, as he'd suggested. Their meetings would be sporadic, at best. And once she was assigned overseas, next to impossible. She was crazy to even consider it.

Yet snuffing out the promise of that kiss felt *wrong*. If she never saw him again, she would be cheating herself of something truly splendid.

Wriggling onto her side, Maggie sought Jake's silhouette in the hammock next to hers. She ached for him, sleeping this way, so close yet so far apart. How she missed the warmth of his body touching hers, the comforting feel of his chest beneath her cheek, the steady beat of his heart. Yearning filled her eyes with tears.

I love him. I'll miss him.

It had taken her years to even look at another man. Yet if she kept Jake in her life, no matter how intermittently, she would only be happy when they were together and starkly lonely when they were apart.

I don't know if I can live that way.

Just go to sleep, Maggie.

She squeezed her eyes shut, undecided. It didn't help to know that she would be slumbering peacefully at that moment if only Jake were holding her. Memories of all those sleepless nights back in Arlington, turning in her bed, filled her with dread. She would have to take those antianxiety meds all over again.

Oh, help. She would be a mess without Jake.

CHAPTER 14

Daylight was just beginning to wane on yet another impossibly long and uneventful day when the door of the *casita* flew open, admitting a large moth that fluttered in as David poked his head in. "Someone is coming!" he said with a smile.

Maggie watched Jake step out of his hammock so he could look out the nearest screen at the mellowing landscape. "It's Boris and a few of the FARC. He's back!"

Anticipation and dismay warred within Maggie. She forced herself to get up, ignoring the discomfort that pinched her hip every time she moved. The lead negotiator had been gone for thirty-six hours. She'd been thinking about Jake's suggestion of a date for the last twenty-four, and she was no closer to a decision.

By the time Boris appeared at the door, Esme had scraped together what was left of their last meal into a bowl for him. Noting the German's satisfied smile, Maggie's emotions wheeled. It was obvious he had met with success.

"I have much to tell you." Stamping the mud off his feet, he crossed the threshold, leaving the door open behind him as a gesture of politeness.

Peering past him, Maggie glimpsed only Gallo and two of the hardened rebels from *Ki-kirr-zikis*. Marquez must have gone elsewhere with the rest of the rebels. She was glad when they remained outside, giving the team a modicum of privacy.

"Is it done?" Bellini demanded as Boris unbuttoned his jacket.

Esme rounded on the Italian. "Give the man a chance to sit and eat, Leo. We saved you some food just in case you came back, Boris. Here, rest." She gestured to one of the two chairs.

With a weary sigh, Boris sank onto the chair closest to the hearth's embers, then dug into his dinner with gusto.

Maggie gnawed on the inside of her lip as she waited for Boris's news. Would she and Jake be parting ways in a matter of days? Hours?

When Gallo stepped up to the still-open door, Boris stopped chewing, cutting him an uncomfortable glance. The entire team regarded Gallo with mistrust as he lounged against the doorjamb, a ceramic jug in one hand.

Charles broke the awkward silence. "What's the news on Señor Arias?"

Boris pawed his bowl. "Last I saw him was in the little town we went to, El Olvido."

The Oblivion, Maggie translated with a shiver of premonition.

"He was left with the local healer there, who was given instructions to call his family. I imagine he is home by now. Thank you, Esme." Handing her the empty bowl, he took the cup of water she held out to him and drained it.

Esme's face shone with hope in the dimming light. "Does that mean we'll be heading home ourselves, soon?"

"Yes, yes." Boris cut another uncomfortable glance at the door. "The process is underway."

Maggie sought Jake's gaze, drawing his attention to the doorway. Why was Gallo just lounging there, holding that jug? And what did his peculiar smile signify?

Perhaps sensing her disquiet, Jake stepped closer, looped an arm around her waist, and pulled her against him in what was blatantly a primal claim—one that Maggie didn't mind at all in this instance...or perhaps, ever.

Boris, lowering his voice, described his activities in the last two days.

"We traveled by ATV down the mountain to the small town I mentioned, El Olvido. There, I met a woman who gave me her cell phone to use, as it had Wi-Fi access. She took me to see a lawyer who is sympathetic to the FARC. With the lawyer present, making everything legal, I took a picture of Jay Barnes's request for his ransom to be paid—someone must have asked him to write it—and I sent it via email to the insurance company. The lawyer followed up with an email of his own, giving the company a routing and account number I wasn't privy to."

The kiss Jake pressed to Maggie's temple distracted her briefly—another memory to be filed away for later.

"Next, I made calls to my contact in the Colombian Army and arranged for the five FARC prisoners to be released. Then, I contacted the Red Cross and begged them to deliver the prisoners to the location specified by Rojas. All I had were the longitude and latitude to give them, but I believe it's in a valley on the east side of El Castillo. With all of that done, Gallo brought me back here while Marquez went to collect Jay Barnes, the body of his colleague, and the three JUNGLA. If all goes as it should, the Red Cross will fly us out and back to Bogotá tomorrow."

Tomorrow. Dismay steamrolled Maggie. She couldn't wrap her head around it.

"Morning or afternoon?" Bellini asked.

"Oh, afternoon. We'll have to travel to the valley first."

Stunned silence followed Boris's announcement.

Esme broke it. "Oh, you have done well, Boris!"

Cynicism kept Maggie from offering her congratulations. What about the red tape Boris had mentioned earlier? A whole host of things could go wrong, causing the entire plan to unravel.

Boris shrugged off Esme's praise while looking pleased. "Not I. All of us have done well."

"Then, you must celebrate." Gallo's declaration shattered the bonding moment as he swaggered toward the group with his jug extended. He thrust it at the team lead. "A gift from General Rojas."

Maggie pictured Rojas, Gallo, and Marquez all chumming in the camouflaged tower—saying what, exactly?

"Thank you." Ever polite, the German came to his feet and took the jug, though his tone was far from enthusiastic. "What is this exactly?"

"*Chicha.*" Gallo's broad smile shimmered in the twilight gloom.

Maggie had heard of it, but only Charles knew what it was. "It's fermented cassava."

Gallo gestured for Boris to take a swig. "Try it. It's better than *agua panela.*"

Never one to offend a host and likely still thirsty from his travels, Boris removed the cork and took an obliging sip. He swallowed, wheezed, and cleared his throat. "Not bad. A little like English cider. Thank you, Mondo Gallo."

Gallo gestured for Boris to pass the jug around. "Everyone must try it."

Maggie considered the offer with suspicion. After being poisoned by Gallo the other day, she didn't trust him not to kill them all, especially if arrangements for payment and the release of the five FARC soldiers were a done deal.

To her astonishment, Jake accepted the jug from Boris and took a hearty swig. How could he be so certain it wasn't laced with something toxic? He wiped his mouth with alacrity before passing it to her.

With all eyes on her, Maggie took a wary sip. Liquor seared her throat and left a sour-sweet taste on her tongue. *Chicha* wasn't half bad, though. Maybe it would numb the constant ache in her hip?

The others followed her example, all but Esme who declined. "No, no, I don't touch liquor."

"Drink," the *mondo* insisted.

With a sniff of disapproval, Esme left the group and went to lie in her hammock.

Bellini took the jug from Charles and held it up. "A toast to Señor Arias." Tipping it back, he swallowed down enough for him and Esme both.

All at once, the room seemed to shift. Maggie swayed against Jake, who cut her a sharp glance. Wow, chicha had to be a hundred proof, at least.

Bellini passed the jug back to Boris, who repeated the toast. "To Señor Arias." His eyes reflected the embers in the fireplace.

Jake took the jug next, taking another long draught.

In the belief that her hip pain was subsiding, Maggie did the same. She passed it on to Charles, who returned it to Bellini. That man spilled some on his face and giggled.

Without warning, Jake staggered. His grip on Maggie tightened, and they both fell against the cinder-block column that helped support the roof.

Gallo roared with laughter. The room's shadows turned his face into a grotesque mask.

"Sorry." Jake's speech slurred as he apologized to her, but Maggie wasn't even remotely hurt, as he'd kept his weight from crushing her.

"Jacques has no tolerance," she explained. Yet not once had he behaved like this in France when they'd drunk their fair share of wine, which meant he was faking it. Escorting him to his hammock, she held it still for him to climb into it. Even so, he rolled off the other side, falling onto the floor.

Gallo roared with laughter. Setting her teeth, Maggie helped Jake up.

"We should all retire."

Bless Charles for drawing a line in the sand. "The sun is almost down." He crossed to the hearth to extinguish the embers.

As the team members withdrew from him, Gallo sent them one last smirk before turning and walking out the door, pulling it shut behind him. Darkness descended with startling speed.

The instant Gallo was gone, Jake rolled smoothly into his hammock, even as he held onto her hands.

Boris's voice floated toward them. "Gallo meant no harm, I'm sure."

Maggie laughed at the naïve comment. "Are you? I'm not."

Charles deflected everyone's attention to Jake. "Are you okay there, Jacques?"

Jake's reply was a soft snore.

Maggie answered for him. "He's asleep already." Yet, even as she spoke, her sleeping prince lifted her hand to his lips and pressed a sweet kiss in the center of her palm. Poignant emotion lanced Maggie's heart.

His soft whisper just reached her ears. "*Je'taime*, Lena." *I love you.*

The words stole her breath. He had said them often, twelve years ago, back in Paris, his blue eyes bright with emotion. She had never replied in kind, for fear of raising his hopes.

I love you, too, Jake.

She stood over him now, awash with tenderness and yearning, as well as anticipatory grief. As she'd done twelve years ago, she would soak her pillow with tears. Unable to sleep without him, she would prowl around her shared apartment, and when sleep still didn't come, she would run, and run, and run, but the ache would never go away.

Twelve years ago, the choice between Jake and her career had been black and white. Since her early teens, her father had put ideas into her head about the importance of protecting democracy and about the advantage she had being a native Spanish speaker, attractive, and smart. She could make the world a better place.

"Look what happened to Venezuela," he would say. *"That's what happens when democracy breaks down. Tyrants like Maduro seize the reins of power and refuse to relinquish it."*

She'd heeded her father's words until they formed the foundation of her own ideology: Maggie was here for the United States of America, not for herself, not for Jake. Yet, look where that had gotten her? She'd been so traumatized by her experience in Morocco that she wasn't the same woman. It was only with Jake that she could be herself. That she could sleep without nightmares. But given their careers, they could never be together. One or the other would be away on an assignment. It would never be as it was now.

Still holding his hand, she envisioned the next twenty-four hours. If the exchange went off without a hitch, then this might be her last night in Jake's company. Yet, she couldn't even lie next to him, not in a hammock.

She did the next best thing. Without releasing his hand, she sank into her hammock, wincing with pain as her hip rubbed against the stretchy fibers. She would hold on to his hand for as long as possible, keeping their fingers entwined. She missed him already.

Her father's advice on the day she'd graduated from CIA training echoed in her head. *"Anyone can fall in love, Maggie. But if love means surrendering all that you've worked for and even what you believe in, then who needs it? A strong woman doesn't need a man to feel whole."*

Wallowing in loss, Maggie blinked back tears. *Clearly, I'm not as strong as I used to be.*

The descent to the valley on the eastern edge of El Castillo took place on ATVs. Jake held fast to Lena as their ATV, driven by a rebel they'd just met, bumped and fishtailed down the winding, rutted track.

Fortunately, Lena's hold on the driver was as tenacious as she was, and they didn't fall off. When they zipped past a familiar rocky outcrop, she let go of the man long enough to point out the landmark to Jake. Yep, he'd seen it before, too, which meant the rebels were driving them in circles, trying to confuse them. No doubt, they feared the JUNGLA would seek to debrief the UN team once they returned to civilization.

At least, the peacekeepers couldn't have asked for better weather for traveling. Patches of blue sky flashed here and there where the canopy thinned. Birds with vivid green, red, and blue feathers startled away at the roar of their ATVs. The air streaming past them was crisp and cool, smelling of freshly washed leaves. But when Maggie pointed out a pile of crates hastily concealed by cut branches, it was a grim reminder that the only thing about to come of the FARC's rebellion was death and destruction. He hoped the teen rebels he'd befriended wouldn't be traumatized—or worse, be maimed or killed.

The path forked as it had before, and, this time, their driver broke left, following Gallo and two other rebel drivers, each of whom carried two peacekeepers apiece, while David and his squad all rode an ATV of their own. Several hundred meters later, their convoy slowed to a stop, right there on the trail.

Confused by the sudden stop in the middle of the wilderness, Jake didn't know the reason for it until the ATVs cut their engines. The sound of rushing water made it evident there would be a river crossing, one that Boris hadn't seen before, given his look of confusion. Clearly, this wasn't the way to El Olvido.

In a silent procession, they walked until the trees cleared, exposing the view.

Lena grabbed Jake's hand in what was probably a knee-jerk reaction. A gushing river, about fifty yards wide, had carved a deep divide into the side of the mountain. It swilled toward the valley, churning up mud and tearing away bushes and small trees, which rode away on its foaming surface.

At the sight of the rope bridge that would take them across the gorge, the team members groaned in unison as Jake squeezed Maggie's hand reassuringly. At least they wouldn't be crossing via a wooden box on cables. Yet the bridge itself was narrow, built with fraying rope and rickety planks, clearly designed to be crossed single file. A fine mist rising from the water dampened both the ropes and the boards, making them slippery and subject to decay.

No way had the crates they'd glimpsed earlier been carried across this bridge. So, why bring the team this way when a safer route obviously existed? Either Gallo got his jollies out of scaring his guests, or the FARC didn't want them running into the Venezuelans bringing weapons in. That had to be the reason.

"Not to worry." Boris kept a reassuring grasp on Esme's arm. "Just picture the helicopter waiting for us on the other side."

Esme, pale with fear, managed to nod.

"Only two people on the bridge at a time." Gallo turned at the head of the line to issue instructions. He pointed at Jake. "You go last."

Oh? Why was that?

Lena glanced at him sharply, her expression taut. He sent her a wink. *I got this.*

The worry that creased her forehead testified to her feelings for him, though she'd yet to accept his suggestion that they continue seeing each other when life went back to normal. She had to say, yes. Jake clung to his optimism. Despite her silence last night when he told her he loved her, he could tell she loved him back. The magic they'd discovered in each other as young adults was just as powerful, if not more so, as it had been twelve years ago.

Inclining his mouth to her ear, he offered her advice. "Hold the railings on both sides and walk across quickly. Try not to leave the bridge shaking." The oscillations would get worse with every person crossing. That had to be why Gallo wanted him to go last—he was obviously the strongest.

The *mondo* sent David and his three underlings across first. The squad made it look easy, striding casually across the flimsy bridge like they did it every day. Charles and Bellini were sent across next. Heavier set than Charles, Bellini caused the bridge to ripple under his weight, but the planks held, suggesting the rest of them would have no issues.

It was up to Boris to coax Esme across the rickety suspension. She went before him, wailing with every step and racing the last twenty yards to arrive on solid ground.

The two older rebels who'd come back from *Ki-kirr-zikis* with Gallo went next. Only Lena, Gallo, and Jake remained.

His intuition for trouble niggled. "Let Lena go before you," he demanded, watching the *mondo*'s reaction carefully.

That man gave a careless shrug. *"Siga, usted,"* he said to Lena, using the formal imperative to show respect. *Go ahead.*

To Jake's delight, she went on tiptoe first and pressed a fervent kiss against his lips. The worry in her emerald eyes was unmistakable.

"Hey." He gripped her arms firmly. "I'll be right behind you."

As Gallo urged her to hurry, she backed away from Jake, drew a deep breath, and stepped bravely onto the slightly undulating bridge. With his chest tight, Jake watched her power her way across. As a result of her caloric deprivation, she'd lost some of her athleticism—not to mention her infected incision left her with a slight limp. Would she even have the strength to get across? *God, please.* If anything happened, Jake would be hard-pressed to help.

When she was two-thirds of the way across, Gallo proceeded to go next. With suspicion tightening his forehead, Jake watched the *mondo*'s every move. But he followed Lena without incident, and soon, she stood on the opposite shore waving back at him.

What a relief! Now it was Jake's turn.

He stepped out cautiously, still wary of a trap. If Gallo thought he was going to shake Jake off this bridge, he had another thing coming. Jake had traversed obstacle courses far more challenging than this, without incident.

The bridge oscillated gently, a consequence of those who'd crossed before him. Jake sought to absorb the bridge's energy rather than fight it. Dividing his attention between his immediate environment and

Gallo, who approached the opposite shore, he saw the *mondo* pause and look back. The man rested both of his hands on a post as he did so. His fingers curled over the knob at the top, pulling a piece of rope over it before he proceeded forward and stepped ashore.

A shudder whipped along the length of the bridge, catching Jake off guard. The rope under his right hand went suddenly slack. He released it, groping for the left railing, while the slats beneath his feet began to tilt. The rubber of Jake's boots squealed as he slipped.

Mallacht air! Clinging to the left railing, he kept himself from plummeting into the boiling water. Anyone else would have dropped straight in.

Lena's bloodcurdling scream reached his ears. Over the rushing river below him, Jake could hear his teammates shouting in consternation. A glimpse in their direction showed Charles fighting with all his might to keep Lena from clawing her way onto the distressed bridge to help him. Only once before had Jake seen that look of pure terror on her face. *She does love me.*

Still in shock, he encountered Gallo's gloating stare and knew. The man was dumping him intentionally. He should have heeded his dream and taken Lena away from *El Castillo* while he'd had the chance.

Gathering his wits, Jake assessed his options. He would slide his hands along this one railing and make his way to shore. With his powerful grip, he stood a good chance of making it. Eyes focused on Lena, he relaxed his right hand just enough to slide it a foot in her direction, then repeated the movement with his left hand.

Seeing Gallo head back in his direction, presumably to rescue him, dismayed him. "Get back," he yelled in Spanish, but the determined glint in the *mondo*'s eyes made it evident he intended to finish Jake off.

And now that Jake was closer, he could see the apparatus like the one Gallo had already dismantled. The left post, just like the right, had a knob of wood at the top, with rope looped under it. If Gallo slipped the loop over the knot, the railing Jake still clung to would go slack, just as the other one had. In hindsight, this bridge was obviously designed to dump enemy forces, like the JUNGLA, into the river.

Gallo, extending one hand to Jake, made it look like he was helping, but, in fact, he was prying the loop over the knob with his other hand.

Jake made a quick decision. Before the railing could give way, he released it, dropping onto his stomach atop the wobbling planks while wrapping his arms and thighs around them. A wet mist coated him as the bridge swayed, like those trick ladders at amusement parks designed to challenge nimble children. He shifted his objective toward survival.

What were the odds he would live if he fell into the river?

Another glance toward shore showed the peacekeepers looking on in helpless horror. Lena squirmed and wriggled and shrieked in her determination to get to Jake, but Charles—bless the man—kept her from joining Jake in peril.

Mondo Gallo, on the other hand, grinned with malice, telling Jake that even if he could save himself, the *mondo* would probably shoot him out of sheer frustration. The man was convinced Jacques and Madeleine were a threat to the FARC, which meant Lena was his next target.

Not if I can help it.

At this moment, there were only two things Jake could do. One, he could make his way toward Gallo, pretend to seize his hand for help, then rip the *mondo* off the bridge and into the river—only his minions would probably kill Jake for doing that. But option two was even less appealing. He could let himself fall off this flimsy crossing into the raging river below him and hope that he survived.

With a loud squeak, the nail holding down the board under Jake's left arm tore from the track, making up his mind for him. He groped for a different board, but the movement jarred his tentative balance. Gravity jerked him loose off the bridge, and all he could do was align his body so he wouldn't snap his spine when he hit the water.

With Lena's heartrending scream in his ears, he plummeted toward the river, arms tight to his side, breaking the impact with his boots.

Water slammed up Jake's nostrils and closed over his head. With the force of a collision, the current engulfed him and dragged him downstream at a sobering clip.

To protect his limbs, he curled into a ball. He could see nothing underwater but shades of dark brown. A log clipped the side of his head, leaving his ears ringing. His shoulder slammed into a boulder before he glanced off it. The branches of a submerged tree raked over him.

Desperate for air, Jake clawed for the surface and discovered his boots were too heavy to swim in. As they were filling with water, the sat phone in his heel was doomed. He wouldn't be calling the JIC anytime soon.

But if he shucked the boots, he'd at least get to breathe. Breathing would be nice.

Sluicing along underwater, Jake struggled to untie the laces. By the time he tugged off one boot, then the other, his lungs and nasal passages were burning. He tore off his jacket next, using it like a parachute to slow him down. At last, he shook it off and strained for the surface.

When his head broke free, he gasped in the smallest bit of air before the current yanked him under again. But he'd glimpsed his surroundings long enough to determine where the shoreline was. He struck out in that direction while fighting to surface again and sucking in another breath of air. If he could just find something buoyant to hold on to. *God, please!*

A log floating on the surface caught his eye. He groped for it, threw an arm around it, and then held on while recovering from his oxygen deprivation. Once he found the strength to swim, he started kicking for the shore.

Zen Suzuki relaxed from a full-bodied stretch and looked back at the red and blue dots on the screen in front of him. They weren't together anymore. In fact, the red dot was moving away from the blue one at a puzzling clip. "What the heck? Sir, you need to see this!"

Leaving his computer, Lobo came to stand behind Zen's shoulder. "Is there a road there? What's the terrain look like?"

Zen tapped a key, superimposing a topographical map over the image supplied only by coordinates and altitude. He blinked at what he saw. "Oh, he's on a river. Did he get on a boat?"

"Not unless he's whitewater rafting. Look how fast he's moving."

Silence fell between them as they watched the red dot travel farther and farther from the blue dot. Moving through water that fast without a helmet or life vest was a death sentence.

Lobo crossed to the nearest landline phone. "I'm calling the station chief."

Zen inclined his face closer to the monitor. "Sir, he's slowing down."

Lobo retraced his steps. "Can you zoom in at all?"

"Maybe a little." Zen toggled the appropriate key and stared. "Looks like he's headed for the shore."

Sure enough. The red dot was approaching the east bank. He and Lobo held a collective breath, waiting for a sign of life. "Come on. Move for us, sir."

The red dot gave a jerk, moving less than a millimeter, but it definitely moved.

"He's alive." Lobo sounded certain as he headed for the phone to contact Whiteside.

Zen listened with half an ear, curious to know what the CIA station chief recommended. When Lobo hung up and turned around, he wore a scowl on his face.

Zen braced himself. The muscles in Lobo's jaw were jumping. "What'd he say?"

"He wants us to wait an hour for Jake to contact us."

"Uh…I hate to point out the obvious, sir, but if the sat phone went down the river with the lieutenant, he won't be calling anybody."

"I know." Lobo thought for a moment. "Call in Harmony and Bambino. We're going to move on this."

Zen blinked. "Against the station chief's wishes?"

Lobo turned toward the phone again, likely to set up transportation. "He'll thank me when it's over."

The scream that erupted from Maggie's throat had raised gooseflesh on her own body. Something had snapped inside her as she watched Jake plummet into the river. Gallo had knelt on the end of the bridge holding out his hand, but she remembered him telling Jake to cross the bridge last. Why? Because he'd planned to dismantle the bridge and dump Jake in it.

"You monster!" The instinct to draw a weapon had Maggie reaching in her boot for the dagger she'd been hiding. Working it free, she curled it into her palm and charged the *mondo* just as he was starting to rise. She would drive it between his ribs and fling him into the river to die with Jake.

But Charles, who kept his arms around her waist, held her fast. "No, Madeleine!"

"Let me go!" She fought him, calling on every ounce of her strength, completely overwrought. *Jake was gone!* The thought utterly wrecked her.

"Lena, calm yourself!" It was all Charles could do to contain her. Boris and Esme gaped at her, as did Gallo's soldiers, too stunned by Jake's horrifying end to react.

Bellini stepped in to help Charles, wrestling the blade from Maggie's grasp. "Where did you get this?"

Charles hushed him, "Hide it!"

Now Gallo was striding toward them. Bellini swiftly hid the knife behind his back, but the other rebels, including David's squad, had taken note.

Gallo approached Maggie just as she expended her last ounce of energy. Still caught in Charles's unbreakable hold, she returned Gallo's impassive stare.

"Lo mataste." *You killed him.* Her accusation emerged in a scratchy voice, scarcely audible above the rushing river.

"Did you not see?" He gestured to the broken bridge. "I tried to help him."

"Liar."

His lips twisted into a dark, brief smile. "You are the liar." With those ominous words, he raised his voice to address the other peace-keepers as well as his own soldiers. "This was an unfortunate accident. Most unfortunate. But we must march on, or we will be late to the landing field."

For a moment, no one moved. Through her shock and devastation,

Maggie heard David protesting, "But, *Mondo*, shouldn't we search for Jacques downstream, in case he survived?"

Glancing at the other's faces, Gallo shrugged. "Of course. Go search for him, David."

Hanging in Charles's grip, Maggie processed Gallo's words belatedly and jerked her head up. "I'm going, too."

"No, Madeleine." Boris frowned at her, whether with pity or suspicion, she couldn't tell. "I am responsible for the team, and I say we stay together."

David came toward her, his gaze sympathetic. "I will look for him, Señora. Pray he is well."

"Ruiz." Mondo jerked his chin at one of the hardened rebels. "Go with David. When you're done looking, join us at the red-roofed building." Putting his mouth close to Ruiz's ear, he murmured instructions no one else could hear.

Ruiz's curt nod left Maggie suspecting Gallo had just given him orders to shoot Jake if he wasn't dead already.

As Ruiz and David started downriver, Charles turned her gently around. "Let's go, Madeleine. Come with me." Keeping one arm firmly around her shoulders, he propelled her forward.

Their trek continued. Encased in shock, Maggie scarcely noticed her environment. All she could see was Jake slipping off the wooden slats and plummeting into the river.

Blindly, she followed Charles's lead down a trail that wound toward the base of *El Castillo*. The microchip, jarring her hip with every step, was a reminder that at least the JIC still had her on their radar—Jake, too, for that matter. They could see they were separated. They were bound to respond.

Please hurry!

CHAPTER 15

Having kicked his way toward the branches bowing over a muddy shore, Jake crawled onto land, gasping in exhaustion. He rested a moment, then sat up, brushed a beetle off his arm, and took in his surroundings. On the other side of the river, El Castillo rose skyward in a precipitous tangle of vegetation, but on this side, the land appeared flatter.

As he clambered to his feet intending to get his bearings, the feel of mud and sticks beneath his toes made him grimace. His left foot was bare; the right one was covered in a muddy sock—not unlike his dream the other night—oh, man. He should have heeded it.

Once standing, Jake turned full circle to get his bearings. The terrain on this side of the river wasn't as jungle-like as the other side. With no land mass rising up to impede his view, he imagined the land sloped downward to the valley Marquez had mentioned. But had he been swept so far downriver that it would take hours to backtrack?

While knocking water from his ears, he considered his predicament and gauged his next move. It was only a matter of time before Lena became Gallo's next target. He had to get to her before that happened. Yet, here he was, kilometers away from her, and shoeless.

Charles would defend her; Jake was sure of that. But Gallo had a pistol, and Charles did not. And all Lena had was the little dagger in her boot. He pictured the consequence of her using it, and nausea roiled up suddenly. Bending at the hips, Jake vomited a stomach full of river water.

Lena, my brave girl. Don't lose your life over me.

Eyes swimming with tears, Jake slowly stood upright. This was no time to grieve what might be happening to Lena. For now, he would cling to the certainty that his teammates at the JIC had noticed their operators' separation and would come for them. In the meantime, he would fashion something to wear on his feet and go looking for her.

Dead or alive, he would find her eventually.

Maggie lost all sense of time as she stumbled along at Charles's side. Had it been minutes since Jake fell into the river or hours? Either way, the trees had begun to thin, and the sunlight beamed onto the ground at her feet. With a start, Maggie digested that they'd reached a valley—possibly the same one mentioned by Commander Strong in his briefing, since they'd crossed a river to get there.

Before her stood a bowl of open space filled with thigh-high grass and ringed with spiraling wax palms. To her left stood a cinder-block structure topped with a red-tiled roof, sporting several windows and a metal door.

Boris grew animated. "This is the building Marquez described to me! This is where the exchange will take place. The helicopter will land in this field."

Shading her eyes, Esme peered up at the sky. "There's no helicopter yet."

"It will come," Boris assured her. He turned back to Gallo. "Now what?"

The *mondo* pointed at the shady area next to them, right at the forest's edge. "Until the helicopter comes, you will wait here."

Boris turned his head, reconsidering the humble building. "Where are the hostages?"

"In there." Gallo nodded at it.

"Well, perhaps you could show them to us, so we know they're there?"

"Hmph." Pivoting away from Boris, Gallo ordered his men to follow him as he abandoned the peacekeepers to their own devices.

Boris regarded the shady area Gallo had pointed out. "Let's get out of this sun."

Joining the others in sinking onto the ground under a tree's sheltering branches, Maggie bore her weight on her good hip while struggling to shake off the lethargy of shock so she could read the situation.

If Gallo considered her a threat, why hadn't he tried to kill her yet? He'd made Jake's demise look like a tragic accident. After all, he wouldn't want UN peacekeepers telling the world that the FARC were ruthless killers. Therefore, if he intended to kill her also, he would be sneaky about it. She couldn't afford to let her guard down.

Maybe she should leave the group now and return to the river to look for Jake—for Jake's body. Charles would probably let her slip away, as his own integrity was on the line, especially with Boris, who considered him a trusted friend. And Jake had instructed her, if something were to happen to him, to find water and follow it downstream—the same way his body had been swept.

On the other hand, she had a job to finish here. The Agency had sent her to Colombia to bring the hostages home—even though one was dead. She was obligated to see that through, wasn't she?

Well, then, there was the answer. She wasn't going anywhere until Jay Barnes was on his way home.

Jake was using a stick to retrieve his jacket when a voice, floating on the breeze, caused him to freeze. Someone was calling for Jacques. Lifting his jacket from the rock on which it had been caught, he hoisted it ashore. The cry came again. It sounded like David calling for him, echoed by a voice Jake didn't recognize.

Should he answer? After all, he'd forged a bond with David. But the other man was an unknown, and armed, to boot. Gallo could have given them orders to shoot Jake on sight.

That didn't mean Jake should let them slip away, though. Assuming they would join up with Gallo once they gave up looking for him, it would save him time locating the other peacekeepers if he followed them.

First, though, he needed to fashion some booties to protect his feet.

Tearing the jacket into bands proved easier than he'd thought it would be. The canvas wasn't the same high quality as those worn by U.S. special operators. As he wrapped strips around his feet, he monitored the two voices calling his name. Were they getting closer or moving farther away now?

By the time Jake draped the remaining canvas over his head to camouflage his face, the voices had fallen silent. He needed to hurry. Setting off after the scouting party, he moved as quickly as the thin padding under his feet allowed.

Boris would push on with their agenda, regardless of Jacques's fate. Jake didn't blame him for that. The UN's priority was to make certain the exchange took place the way it was supposed to. Come what may, they had to meet the helicopter. That was the agenda.

It was Gallo's agenda that worried Jake now. No doubt, the *mondo* hoped to prevent the map, or knowledge of the map, from escaping. Too bad the information had already been disseminated and decrypted. But that didn't increase Lena's odds of survival one iota.

Wishing he had a machete to hack his way toward David, Jake pushed through vines and branches, scratching himself on thorns and disturbing a host of insects that either scattered or sought revenge. Sweat trickled between his shoulder blades. Mosquitoes swarmed him.

When he stumbled across fresh tracks, he breathed a huge sigh of relief. Given the deep impressions, the search party, consisting of just two men, had lingered here a moment before giving up. Then they'd taken off due east, leaving a machete-cleared path for Jake to follow.

The booties lent him stealth but offered scant protection. Again and again, he stepped on a thorn or a pebble or a sharp branch and swallowed a cry of pain. He pushed himself through the discomfort, all too aware that shadows were beginning to creep up the trunks of the trees in front of him. It was getting later.

And then he heard it in the distance: the unmistakable *whop, whop,*

whop of an approaching helicopter. The exchange was about to go down not too far from here! He had to know whether Lena would get on board.

Run! With his feet on fire, Jake sprinted down the torturous trail toward the sound. Thank God for the helicopter that drowned out the sound of his movements, for he ran right up on the two men—David and a larger rebel.

After reining himself in, Jake counted to ten, then stalked the pair, keeping far enough back that the others never saw him.

"There!" Boris Mayer pointed as a Red Cross helicopter burst into view from behind the gauzy clouds. With a reverberating crescendo, it approached the valley. Members of the team, including Maggie, clambered to their feet and waved a frantic greeting.

Maggie's eyes stung at the heartening vision of a red cross emblazoned onto the sides of the reconditioned "Huey" UH-1 Iroquois. If Jake were safely by her side, she would have gotten satisfaction out of watching its tail flare, watching the tall grass ripple under its rotor wash like rings on the surface of a disturbed pond. Wind, smelling of fresh herbs, whipped her ponytail into her eyes.

In just thirteen days, they'd accomplished what they came here for. But Jake's tragic accident had turned victory into defeat. How was she supposed to leave without him?

As the giant metal bird nestled onto the field and the thunder of the rotors diminished, Boris held them back. "Wait. The FARC prisoners are to be released first."

With a clank and a rumble, the helicopter door slid open, revealing a man in a navy blue uniform. He leapt to the ground, cradling an assault rifle. Scoping the area uneasily, he waved Boris over.

"Stay here." Boris gestured for his team to stay in the trees' shade as he marched across the field alone to speak to the man.

"Who is he?" Esme wondered out loud.

Maggie hadn't taken her eyes off him. "Prison guard, probably."

They all watched Boris shake the man's hand, then point at the red-roofed building. Peering into the chopper's cabin, Maggie made out several men in orange coveralls, under the armed watch of a second guard.

One by one, their ankles and wrists were uncuffed, and they jumped down from the helicopter, trotting with gleeful expressions toward the cinder-block building to join their fellow FARC.

Maggie tried to see into the building as they filed through the door. Was Jay Barnes even in there? What about Mike's body and the JUNGLA hostages? Would an exchange really take place?

With her thoughts still congealed by shock, it was hard to read their situation. Apart from Jake's horrible accident, everything seemed to be happening as planned. Even so, the suspicion that they would be duped kept her wary.

Boris reached for a briefcase being handed down to him. That had to be Jay Barnes's "insurance" money. Hefting the briefcase in one hand, Boris faced the building and waited. Now that the FARC had their rebels back, this was when the JUNGLA captives ought to be exiting the building; only they weren't.

Boris put his free hand on his hip and frowned. When the door on the building remained shut, he started walking toward it, guessing, perhaps, that Marquez wished to count the money before he let the JUNGLA go.

Maggie's intuition for trouble niggled. "He shouldn't go alone." Clambering off the ground, she started across the field after him. Charles seemed to agree and followed suit. A glance back showed Esme and Bellini bringing up the rear.

Uneasiness slithered through Maggie's gut as they approached the shuttered building. In addition to outnumbering them, the FARC held a strongly defensive position, considering the Red Cross helicopter was stripped of all fighting capabilities. Why had they cloistered themselves inside, exactly? It had to be hot in there.

Boris glanced over as they joined him, a look of gratitude on his face. "I'm sure they want to count the money before releasing the hostages."

Maggie wasn't so optimistic. The door swung outward, releasing the odor of unwashed bodies as Mondo Gallo blocked their entrance.

Peering past his smirking visage, Maggie spotted Marquez seated at a table. With a jingling of chains, a man sprang into view behind the *comandante* and waved at them.

Jay Barnes! Maggie swallowed her gasp of recognition. Seeing recognition flare in his eyes, she quickly touched her ear in the standard signal for "You don't know me."

As he tore his attention to the others, Maggie wallowed in pity while noting his condition. Her once-robust colleague was bent and thin. Four months of captivity had nearly killed him.

Without warning, Gallo stepped forward and wrested the briefcase from Boris, who protested with a, "Hey!"

"Stay outside," the *mondo* ordered, marching inside with the money. At least he left the door open.

Left standing in the sun, the peacekeepers all glanced at each other and then searched the interior of the building. Maggie was the first to articulate what they all had to be thinking. "I don't see any JUNGLA." They would be easy to spot, if they were as thin and haggard as Jay was.

"I'm sure they're here," Boris insisted. But he didn't sound sure.

Maggie didn't see any coffin either. Where was Mike Howitz's body? The suspicion that the FARC were about to cheat them added a layer of despair over the shattered remnants of her heart. If only this day had never happened. Jake would still be with them, reassuring all of them with his laid-back, this-is-easy attitude. She weaved on her feet, over-come with defeat, and Charles grabbed her arm, keeping her upright.

Marquez, who'd opened the briefcase and riffled through the money, slammed it shut, rousing Maggie from her misery. "Let the captive go."

Captive in the singular?

At the order, Mondo Gallo stepped up to Jay and, using a key on his key ring, unlatched the padlock that kept the metal collar around Jay's neck closed. Jay pried it off himself, dropping his shackles and chain with a *clink*. His huge smile displayed yellowed teeth as he hobbled toward the door as fast as his skeletal body would carry him.

"Bless you! Bless you all." With his arms outstretched, he crossed the threshold to greet his saviors.

They welcomed him with one wary eye still on the FARC inside. Where were the rest of the captives?

Grabbing her hand, Jay squeezed it extra hard. Maggie avoided his tear-filled gaze and merely nodded.

"Excuse me, *Comandante*," Boris called to Marquez. "Where is the body of Mike Howitz? And where are the JUNGLA captives whom General Rojas agreed to release?"

Marquez said nothing, just gestured for Gallo to show them something. Returning to the door, Gallo pointed toward the corner of the exterior, where a pine crate like the kind used to house weapons stood by itself at the corner of the building. "The body is there. Don't open it unless you like the smell of death."

The team members all stared at the box in horror. Picturing Mike's corpse folded over on itself and crammed inside, Maggie's blood heated to a boil. These rebels, in their quest for human rights, had snuffed out the life of an exuberant and fun-loving man, and they were getting *paid* for it? She shook with the force of her revulsion. Rounding on the FARC inside, she prepared to call them every vile name under the sun.

"Easy." Charles gave a yank on her arm. "Let it go."

Gallo pointed firmly at the helicopter. *"Ya es hora de que se vayan."* It's time for you to leave.

"But..." Boris floundered for diplomacy in the face of duplicity. "Where are the JUNGLA you were going to release?"

Gallo gave a careless shrug. "Rojas sends his apologies, but the JUNGLA escaped their escorts on their way here, and they fled into the wilderness. They are better trained than our soldiers, you see. At least they are free." He shrugged again.

His story was so obviously a lie. Boris gaped at him, at a loss for words.

Behind them, the helicopter's rotors began to spool faster. What choice did Boris have but to head out? The rebels weren't about to hand the money back. At least, the UN team had some of what they'd come for.

Charles thought the same thing. "Let's go, Boris." He tugged their leader away from the door. "Help me with the box."

As Charles, Boris, and Bellini hefted the box—which clearly contained dirt as well as a body—Maggie grabbed Jay's filthy sleeve and waved Esme with her as she struck out toward the helicopter. Would

Gallo really let her get away? A glance back at his expression sent shards of suspicion sinking deep beneath her skin. This wasn't the end of the FARC's treachery, was it?

Glimpsing movement at the edge of the field, she caught sight of David and the unknown rebel emerging from the forest alone. They hadn't found Jake. She faltered to a halt at the forceful reminder of Jake's death. Her knees turned liquid. The world seemed to spin.

This wasn't supposed to happen. How was she supposed to leave without him?

~

Jake pressed himself against a *kapok* tree, his heart thudding as he assessed the situation taking place in front of him. Across a field of tall, rippling grass, acid green beneath the rays of the low-lying sun, David and the unknown rebel marched ahead of him toward a red-roofed building while the five remaining peacekeepers—and one hostage—headed into the gale-force wind of the Red Cross helicopter. Boris, Bellini, and Charles struggled to carry a crate—*A Dhia*—that had to contain Mike Howitz's body.

Remarkably, the exchange seemed to be going off without a hitch—except Jake didn't see any released JUNGLA hostages. Perhaps they were in the helo already. He focused back on Lena. Even from a distance of a football field, he could tell his apparent demise was taking its toll on her. She moved like an automaton, looking around with a dazed expression that let him know she was thinking of him.

I'm right behind you, Beautiful.

As the UN team moved in a slow parade toward their noisy transport, Jake waited with dread for something to go wrong. David and his companion had slipped into the building, the door closing behind them. Jake could see faces pressed to the filthy glass of the two front windows, watching the team depart. Why had they all shut themselves inside like that?

As Jake looked back at the team, now arriving at the Huey, the field beyond it caught and held his attention. Darker green shapes seemed to slither among the stalks of waving grass. Jake blinked, thinking his vision was playing tricks on him.

When the first head reared up, alarm drove a shaft through his heart. Then dozens of heads appeared, covered in camouflaged helmets. Rifles rose next, pointed at the building. In one accord, the hidden army fired on the cloistered FARC.

A barrage of semiautomatic gunfire played descant to the helicopter's thunder. Caught utterly off guard, the UN peacekeepers froze and stared.

Fear raked Jake's spine as the red-roofed building bore the assault. The glass in the two front windows shattered. It had to be the JUNGLA who were firing at the FARC.

"No!" His shout of protest was never heard through the noise. The JUNGLA, who had jeopardized the start of this mission, were now wreaking havoc on its successful resolution. Why?

Certain to be shot dead if he moved from his concealed location, Jake stared helplessly as the male peacekeepers and a man in uniform struggled to lift the heavy box into the helicopter. Eyes locked on Lena, Jake wasn't surprised to see her heaving Jay Barnes into the big bird before turning to help Esme.

Get in, Lena!

Soon, she was the only member of the team with two feet still on the ground. The rotors spooled faster as the helo readied for takeoff. Thank God the JUNGLA's ammunition was being aimed at the rebels and not at the bird. For the moment, the FARC were pinned down and not yet returning fire.

Charles, kneeling in the doorway, stretched out a hand to Lena to help her up. Throwing a look over her shoulder, she hesitated. The temptation to step into view and reassure her he was still alive rode Jake hard. But if others saw him, too, what then? He gripped the tree, staying hidden.

Just go, Lena!

Movement within the building caught his eye. A rifle muzzle was now poking through a shattered pane. Jake's blood turned to ice water. Even before the crack reached his ears, he sensed Lena was the target.

Tat-tat! She crumpled where she fell.

Jake gave a hoarse shout. With his heart in his throat, he watched Charles leap out of the helicopter to retrieve her.

Rat-tat-tat-tat! The weapon that had fired on Lena discharged again, spewing rounds that *thunked* into the side of the metal bird. Struck by a bullet, Charles reeled and dropped. The helo began to rise. Charles crawled toward a running board and latched onto it. He then reached back for Lena, but with the bird rising, his grip on her slack arm slipped. It was all Charles could do to cling to the helicopter as it made its ponderous ascent.

Jake kept his eyes on Lena. Was she dead? *God forbid.*

He stared, desperate for a sign of life from her as the Huey continued to rise. A glance upward showed Boris and the two guards hauling Charles off the running board into safety.

To keep from racing to Lena's aid, Jake gripped the tree trunk with all his might. He would certainly get shot. The only way to help her was to stay hidden—and to pray.

Please don't let her die, Father.

This wasn't supposed to happen. His job as a SOG was to keep Lena safe, but then Gallo had pulled a fast one. No doubt Gallo was the one who'd shot her, too.

Through eyes that swam with tears, Jake tore his gaze off her long enough to note that the Red Cross transport was beyond the range of fire now. Its shadow streaked across the bright-green valley before banking south to fly along the Eastern Cordillera, headed to Bogotá.

Within the Huey, Charles scooted to the middle of the grooved floor and gasped his thanks. He met Boris's somber gaze. "We have to go back for her!"

Hunkered next to him, the German's jaw hardened. He looked Charles over. "Where were you hit?"

Charles rubbed the spot still smarting on his thigh, but he wasn't bleeding. There was no sign that a bullet had penetrated his flesh. He ran a hand over his other leg but found himself unharmed. "Were those rubber bullets?"

They had to be, in which case, maybe Magdalena Ellis wasn't dead. "Boris, she might still be alive. We have to go back for her."

"No." Anger burned in Boris's gray-blue eyes. "You played me for a fool, Charles. Madeleine and Jacques were never one of us. But you already knew that."

Charles cast an uncomfortable glance at the others, relieved to find them too far away to hear Boris's quiet accusation.

"For your sake, I will say nothing," the German added, "for I have long considered you my friend. But I will not put my people in jeopardy to return for two imposters. They are CIA, are they not?"

Charles set his teeth, refusing to answer.

"Let the CIA get them out." With those words, Boris left Charles sitting on the floor and went to join the others on the Huey's bench.

Swallowing convulsively, Charles remained on the floor, too spent to help the guards slide shut the still-open door. Lit by the setting sun, *El Castillo* had never looked so immense and formidable with its upper half buried in clouds.

Abandoning a fellow operative to fend for herself turned Charles's stomach, making him want to retch. The FARC had singled out the French couple for a reason. He was lucky they hadn't targeted him, too. The SEAL lieutenant might be dead already. And Magdalena, even if she hadn't been shot by a real bullet, would wish she were dead soon enough.

～

The strange and sudden quiet that fell over the field penetrated Jake's disbelief. He'd been staring at Lena's still form, trying to process that she might be dead and fighting every instinct in his body telling him to run to her side.

Wait a minute. Why weren't the JUNGLA firing anymore?

Tearing his attention from Lena, he studied the soldiers in the field with puzzlement. They had lowered their weapons and were beginning to stand up. Why weren't the FARC in the building taking advantage and shooting them all? Why wasn't *anyone* shooting?

The door of the beleaguered building flew open, and under Jake's astonished stare, the FARC poured out of it, pumping their weapons and *cheering* in victory. Only David and his friends hung back, not participating in the revelry.

Jake's jaw dropped as the JUNGLA countered with a cheer of their own, firing their rifles into the sky. Unable to reconcile what he was seeing, Jake focused again on Lena, who remained sprawled between the two parties. Bile crept up his throat as she continued to be ignored. No one made any attempt to staunch the blood that had to be spilling from her.

When Gallo sauntered up to her, nudging her with a toe, Jake could read the sneer on his face across the distance between them. Fury exploded in Jake. If he were armed, he would have cheerfully killed the man.

But then Lena stirred. She stirred!

Swallowing his cry of wonder, Jake watched Gallo nudge her again, clearly commanding her to rise.

How could she? She'd taken a hit square to the chest.

But she complied. Somehow, miraculously, she did. As the JUNGLA and the rebels mingled, exchanging handshakes and slapping each other's backs, Lena rolled to her knees and took in her surroundings with a mystified expression.

I don't get it either, Beautiful.

But then he caught sight of some of the JUNGLA shaking off their jackets as if they were covered in ants. At the sight of the pea-green uniforms beneath the jungle-patterned jackets, Jake nearly choked on his astonishment. *Nách mór an diabhal thú!* These weren't the JUNGLA, after all! They were wolves in sheep's clothing—Venezuelans. And they'd been using rubber bullets.

The scene suddenly made perfect sense. In a sneaky guerilla tactic that involved dressing like the enemy, the Venezuelan allies had just convinced the fleeing UN team that Colombian soldiers had shot and killed one of their peacekeepers while attacking the FARC.

The fallout would be tremendous. Within hours, both the United Nations and the International Red Cross would condemn the Colombian government, who would fly into a frenzy trying to prove their innocence—something that could take months to do. Only by then, the damage would be done. No one would believe the JUNGLA's claim of innocence. Colombia would lose big points with its allies, right when it needed them most.

None of that mattered much to Jake. The tragedy here was that Lena was now a hostage of the FARC. Worse still, the Venezuelan marching up to her and Gallo resembled one of the men they'd filed past on their way down from *Cecaot-Jicobo*. As that man planted himself before Lena, Jake's mouth went dry with fear. Even from a hundred yards away, Jake read contempt on the Venezuelan's face as he caught Lena's chin in one hand, turned her head this way and that, then nodded at Gallo.

The gesture was clear. He recognized her.

Jake briefly closed his eyes. His nightmare was manifesting. When he opened his eyes again, Gallo was clapping a steel band around Lena's neck, with a length of chain hanging from it. Dread banded Jake's rib cage, making it hard to breathe.

Lena had been branded a spy.

To prove his power over her, Gallo gave the chain a jerk, then laughed coarsely as she spilled to her knees. Jake couldn't see the look on her face, but he didn't need to in order to sense her fury as she rose slowly to her feet.

Don't do it, Lena. But, of course, she did. She kicked Gallo where it hurt the most. The *mondo* crumpled with a shout of pain. The soldiers who were watching all hooted with laughter. But the Venezuelan who'd recognized her clocked her for her gall, and Lena crumpled a second time.

Jake couldn't watch. Pressing his forehead to the tree's rough bark, he begged, "Enough. No more, Father. Please!"

The whine of motors cut through his anguish, dragging his attention back to the field as two ATVs shot into view and headed straight toward the two parties. As Marquez, Gallo, and the Venezuelan broke away from the others, it became apparent the ATVs were for the leaders.

Tugging Lena along like a dog, Gallo hobbled toward the first ATV, then forced her to climb on in front of him before sandwiching her between himself and the driver. Marquez and the man who'd recognized Lena boarded the other ATV. Then those four shot away from the field, leaving the allied soldiers to walk back to El Castillo.

Through eyes that burned, Jake kept Lena in his sights until the ATVs zipped behind the red-roofed building and disappeared into the tree line. He had an inkling of where Lena would be taken—to Rebel Central, *Ki-kirr-zikis*, where General Rojas could interrogate her himself. The thought of Lena alone in that heart of darkness made Jake want to throw back his head and howl.

Why, oh why, hadn't I listened to my dream? Instead, he'd prayed for God to show him a clearer sign, one he wouldn't question. Well, here it was.

He couldn't even go after her yet—not alone with no shoes to protect his battered feet and no weapon either. He had to wait for his teammates to find him first.

CHAPTER 16

Pinned on an ATV between Gallo and the driver, Maggie digested her circumstances. How had this happened? She'd been about to clamber onto the Red Cross helicopter, her heart ripped in two by the necessity of leaving Jake behind. Next thing she knew, a burst of gunfire erupted. She'd been hit so hard she'd blacked out. She awoke to Gallo prodding her with the toe of his boot.

Then—horror of all horrors—the Venezuelan *capitán* who'd recognized her, after all, was gripping her face and scrutinizing her features with those reddish-brown eyes she'd never forgotten. He'd nodded, identifying her as the same spy who'd been caught and left to die in the weapons depot in Maiquetía, two years earlier.

This has to be a nightmare.

But it wasn't, not when she could feel and smell every detail of her environment. As they bumped across the bridge made of split logs, crossing the same river as before but farther downstream, she thought of Jake.

He won't be coming to my rescue this time.

Isolation wrapped icy fingers around Maggie's heart. A sob choked her. Jake was *gone*. She was being driven up the mountain she had hoped never to see again, being led to her death.

Higher and higher they fishtailed, pressing deeper into the vegetation, past the shipment of hidden weapons, past *Ki-kirr-zikis*, where Rojas's tower jutted up through the canopy, past the site of the mudslide where she and Jake had realized their sat phone needed drying out—coming, at last, to the brick *casita*, where she and Jake had spent their final days and nights together. It felt like he should be here, but he was gone.

As they rolled to a stop by the door and the motor cut out, the second ATV carrying the Venezuelan rolled up next to them. Capitán Vargas—his name floated up from buried memories. Only Marquez was no longer in the vehicle with him. The driver must have dropped him off at Rebel Central to apprise General Rojas of their accomplishment.

Gallo dismounted first before tugging on the chain, forcing Maggie to step off. All the strength had leeched out of her. One look at the Venezuelan's brutish expression and she knew: This was not going to end well. He was going to want to know who she really worked for. How did a payroll secretary working for the National Venezuelan Army suddenly become a peacekeeper working for the UN? All Maggie could do was deny they had ever met.

She'd endured mock torture during her training at The Farm. She'd been deprived of water, roughed up, screamed at, and even waterboarded. But the knowledge that her torture wasn't real had kept her calm and in control.

She wasn't remotely in control now, as Gallo shoved her into the dwelling. And with Jake gone, the only force left in the universe who could protect her now was God.

David's last words to her tolled in her head. *"Pray, señora, that he is well."* She would be praying for herself now.

Seated with his back to the same tree he'd hugged earlier, Jake remained motionless all through the rest of the afternoon until nightfall. As the sun sank in the western sky, El Castillo's shadow fell over him before moving inexorably eastward, devouring the cinder-block building, the field of grass where the Venezuelans had hidden, crawling all the way to the line of wax palm trees on the other side, and up the face of the mountain opposite, until darkness covered everything.

Lena.

Just imagining her torment in that moment, he rocked himself and groaned. He'd been afraid something awful like this might happen. His job was to protect her. Yet, here he was far away from her, barefooted and weaponless. Only God could protect her until his Team got here. Hands gripped together, Jake pressed his forehead to his knuckles and begged for God's mercy.

~

"I told you this already. My mother is Venezuelan. I've never lived there."

"Liar."

As Vargas expelled his foul breath across her cheek, Maggie turned her head as far as the metal collar around her neck permitted.

The fire Gallo had built when they first entered the *casita* had died to embers, their only source of illumination. In the dim light, Vargas's face resembled that of a gargoyle.

"You were there in the warehouse in Maiquetía, you and that other white woman with the boy. You think I would forget your face, your eyes? Hmm? Who do you work for?" He repeated the question he had asked a dozen times, tugging on her hair so hard that her ponytail came undone, and her raven hair spilled over her shoulders.

Maggie ignored him, sinking deeper into herself, falling back into memories of Jake and her running through the rain, kissing at the top of the Eiffel Tower.

Gallo muttered with annoyance at their lack of progress. "It's growing late. Let's just leave her tied up and go to sleep."

"No! I will get the truth out of her yet." Grabbing her wrists, bound with the fiber cut from one of the hammocks, he hauled her arms over her head and strung her up on an L-bracket, still screwed into the rafter, a remnant of the cocaine processing days.

Maggie found herself on her toes. The new position made it hard to get enough air in her lungs to feed her thundering heart. *Now what?* As her pants slipped low over her hips, she feared they would strip her naked, and worse.

"What's this?" Gallo lifted the hem of her T-shirt, causing her to realize with a stab of fear, that he'd discovered her festering incision.

"It's just a cut. It's infected."

Vargas edged Gallo aside and prodded the wound with his filthy finger. "Does this hurt, señora?"

Maggie hissed in a breath at the searing pain.

He laughed maliciously and poked her again. "Tell me who you really are, and I'll stop. Wait…" His fingers stilled over her angry flesh. "There's something in here, under her skin."

Gallo snickered. "It's probably bot fly larva. They lay their eggs in human flesh."

Even through her fear and pain, Maggie registered the seriousness of her situation. If Capitán Vargas found the tracking device…She might vanish into the vegetation never to be seen again.

"No, it's hard, like metal or plastic—oh, I know."

The change in his voice and the flash of certainty in his eyes raised the fine hairs on Maggie's forearms. *No, please. Not this.*

"It's a tracking device. Watch and see."

The tip of a blade sank into her skin. Spots swam before Maggie's eyes as she held her scream locked inside. She needed more air! He dug deeper and the dark patches in Maggie's vision spread until they ran together. Darkness claimed her, bringing sweet oblivion.

Standing on the doorstep, David listened to the two men inside chortling. The evil tenor of their voices struck fear into his heart. What-ever they were doing to Madeleine, it was his fault. He put a shaky hand to the latch and scrounged for the courage to interrupt.

David's regret over sharing his suspicions with Gallo had grown into self-loathing. Padre Josué had urged him to warn the French couple what he'd done, only David had been too cowardly. When Jacques had been dumped in the river and David witnessed the Frenchwoman's grief, he'd realized *he* was the one who had murdered Jacques. And now, because of David, Madeleine was being mistreated by the very leaders David had looked up to.

Give me courage, Señor.

With that prayer, he thrust his way into the *casita*, drawing up short as Gallo and the Venezuelan captain spun around in surprise. The blood on Vargas's hands sent David's horrified gaze to the limp woman hanging from a hook by her bound wrists.

Gallo stalked toward him. "What are you doing here?"

David blurted the lie he had practiced. "I was sent by General Rojas to ensure the captive doesn't sicken." Glancing back at Madeleine, he was shocked to see a gaping cut on her hip, blood streaming over her low-hanging pants. What had they done to her? "The general says she is valuable and must not die like the last hostage." He held his breath, awaiting Gallo's reaction.

"Hmph." Gallo sneered and looked back at his friend. "That's Rojas for you, always milking the *capitalistas* for money. I guess he wants to ransom this spy. Show David here what we found beneath her skin."

Holding up his bloody fingers, the Venezuelan approached close enough for David to see what looked like a pill doled out by modern doctors. "What is it?"

Vargas's yellow teeth appeared in an evil smile. "A tracking device. With this, we can trick whoever comes for her and kill them all."

The words flooded David with horror. *Worse and worse.*

Gallo clapped him on the back. "So, you were right, David. She is a spy."

Did that change anything? David had left his studies at La Universidad Nacional de Colombia to fight on behalf of the indigenous poor, believing the FARC represented his people. From what he'd seen so far, that wasn't always the case.

"If she is a spy," he reasoned carefully, "then she is even more valuable. She can't be left bleeding like this. Take her down, and I will tend her wounds—as Rojas commands," he added. How long before his lie was discovered, before he himself was punished for his deception?

Gallo scowled, muttering something David was happy not to hear. It was clear these men had planned to inflict more punishment on the woman.

The *mondo* thrust a knife at him. "Here. You cut her down. She's your problem now. Tomorrow, we take her to *Arriba* to join our other hostages."

Accepting the knife, David digested this dismaying news. He'd only been to *Arriba* and to the radio station once, prompted by curiosity to see how far Padre Josué had to walk beyond the waterfall to reach his destination. The Americans were gone from there, but the three JUNGLA hostages whom the UN leader had expected to be released, likely still remained there, starving and sickening. How would David keep Madeleine from being chained there alongside them? He didn't have that kind of influence.

One moment at a time said a voice in his head. For now, David's priority was to comfort the woman whose misery he had thoughtlessly instigated.

Shrouded in the dark of night, Jake sat with his back to the same tree, unable to close his eyes even for a second without being tormented by visions of what Lena had to be suffering.

He had prayed for her protection until his chest felt like it was turned inside out. Keeping his ears pricked, he listened for the distinctive flutter of the MH-6M Little Bird light assault helicopter likely coming to support him, but all he could hear was the sonata of nocturnal insects and, once, in the distance, the distinctive roar of a jaguar. Was it the same one who'd looked him in the eye?

With every beat of his heart, Jake willed his teammates' arrival. What was taking them so long?

Worry kept his muscles locked and aching. After staring so long into the night sky hunting for the Little Bird's shape against the charcoal clouds, his eyes ached. Just when despair was about to claim him, a flurry erupted overhead. Relief broke over him like a sunrise, and he jumped to his feet, only to stumble as his battered soles protested.

The silhouette of the blacked-out mini helicopter, with special operators perched on its running boards, descended from the sky and nestled almost silently onto the same field that had hidden the Venezuelan Army hours earlier.

With a fervent word of thanksgiving, Jake hobbled toward the helo as his teammates, wearing helmets with their night-vision goggles lowered to look for him, slipped off the running boards and started in his direction. Behind them, the helo lifted off again, leaving to await further orders.

As the first man approached him, he raised his NVGs, revealing bright-blue eyes and a face covered in black greasepaint. "Sir, you hurt?" Harm grabbed Jake's arm, looking him up and down.

"No, but I lost my boots."

"Can you walk?"

"Barely."

"This way." Harm forced him into a trot that sent shards of pain up his legs.

In the cover of the trees, well away from the cinder-block building, the SEALs all came together—Harm, Lobo, Bambino, and Zen.

As they crouched in a tight circle, Lobo took charge. "Fill us in, Jake."

"The FARC have Lena." Fear turned his voice to sandpaper. "One of the Venezuelans came across our path and recognized her from the warehouse in Maiquetía"—he nodded toward Bambino and Harm—"where we extracted her a couple of years back. But the FARC were already suspicious. They had us walk across a rope bridge that came apart while I was still crossing it. I lost my boots and the sat phone in the river, but at least they think I'm neutralized. We need to get to Lena before they kill her, too."

Lobo dropped his gaze to regard the tattered remnants of Jake's booties. "Bambino, take a look at his feet."

As the soft blue beam of the medic's penlight shone in the inky darkness, Jake sank onto the ground to show his soles to the medic. "I'm fine. All I need is boots."

Given the sudden silence, Lobo hadn't considered that possibility. Bambino snapped open the kit he carried, then set about cleansing Jake's lacerated soles. It was all Jake could do not to betray his discomfort as Bambino poured a burning liquid over his soles.

Lobo scowled at Jake's feet. "You need to be medevacked."

"No." Jake had known those words were coming. "I'm Lena's partner, and I'm not leaving her here. Just get me some new boots and gear, and I'll be good to go." Hearing desperation in his voice, he snapped his mouth shut.

"We heard she was shot at." Harm's deep voice could not have sounded more gently apologetic. "Maybe dead."

Jake turned his head to look at him. "You heard that already?"

"The UN team touched down in Bogotá just as we were leaving, delaying our departure. We heard all kinds of strange reports."

Jake shook his head. "Whatever you heard was wrong." He briefly summarized the FARC and Venezuelan's clever duplicity, how they'd dressed themselves like the JUNGLA in order to sway public opinion against the Jungle Company and garner sympathy for the FARC. "We need to set the record straight. But first we're going to rescue Lena."

Lobo heaved a thoughtful sigh. While his preference to evacuate Jake was obvious, he couldn't dismiss his peer's wishes out of hand. "Zen, get on the radio and have the Little Bird deliver boots and gear for Jake, ASAP."

"Size thirteen," Jake inserted.

"Yes, sir."

As Zen pulled the high-powered sat phone from his vest and raised the antenna, Lobo shrugged the pack off his back and produced a rugged laptop. While it booted up, Harm thrust an energy bar at Jake. "Here, have some caffeine, sir."

"Thanks." Keeping one eye on Lobo's laptop, Jake wolfed down the snack, marveling that anything could taste so good. With a few keystrokes, Lobo brought up a 3D topographical graph of El Castillo. Realizing the blue dot halfway up its east side showed Lena's location, Jake's stomach lurched. He swallowed his food through a constricting throat.

Lobo worked the screen, homing in on her location and reading the results. "According to GPS, she's approximately seven klicks from here, due northwest, at an altitude of four thousand feet—looks like the same location you were both at for days.

"The *casita*?" Picturing Lena there without him made his chest hurt.

"Yeah. As soon as your boots and gear get here, we'll go after her. Depending on the situation, maybe we can ambush her captors and extract her on a SPIE rig."

The Special Patrol Insertion/Extraction rig could be lowered by a larger helicopter than the Little Bird. The rig went straight through the forest canopy to lift people out as a group, each of them clipped to a sturdy D-shaped ring.

Lobo made rescuing Lena sound like a walk in the park, which it wouldn't be. Still, compared to what she had to be enduring, the SEALs had the easier job, no question.

Just keep her alive, Father. Please keep her alive.

~

Am I dead?

Roused by the closing of the door, Maggie willed away the sluggishness that weighed her down like a heavy blanket. Her eyes opened to a familiar ceiling, patinaed by the first suggestion of sunrise shining through the four screened windows. She was lying in her hammock in the *casita*. Dare she hope the awful memories spurring her heart into a gallop were all a dream?

As she pushed onto one elbow, hoping to see Jake's hammock next to hers, metal bit into her neck and pain lanced her hip. *So, not a dream.* Gallo had shackled her with Jay Barnes's chains, and Vargas had used his filthy knife to pry the microchip from her flesh.

Sinking back into her hammock, Maggie willed unconsciousness to claim her. But the silence in the *casita* suggested she'd been left alone. Would Gallo and Vargas really leave her here? Wait, someone *else* had joined them last night. Ah yes, her unlikely savior, David.

She remembered rising to consciousness as he sawed away at the *hamak* fibers keeping her strung up and helpless. He'd been standing on a chair, and when the bindings gave way, they'd both nearly hit the floor as he struggled to catch her.

After that, he'd helped her into a hammock where she'd floated in and out of consciousness, vaguely aware that he was tending the gaping wound left by Vargas. Behind him, she could hear the

Venezuelan and Gallo making plans as they boiled rice and beans for their supper.

When she'd roused to awareness later, David had vanished. Feigning sleep, she'd watched Gallo and Vargas eat, petrified that they would attack her without David there.

But then he'd returned, whispering, "*Tranquila*, señora." He'd laid cool, wet leaves on her hip, then brewed her a tea and urged her to drink it. The pain had lessened immediately, and she'd grown sleepy. All the while, David stood over her, speaking a mix of his mother's indigenous tongue and Spanish. It took her a while to recognize that he was praying.

"Thank you," she'd whispered. He'd quite literally saved her from degradation and more torture. But death was still coming. There was only so long the slightly built squad leader could defend her against his murderous superiors.

The light in the windows told Maggie it was morning. Gallo and Vargas had just left—that must have been what woke her. Where would they be going this early? To speak with Rojas?

No. A chill washed over her—oh, she knew where. Armed with her tracking device, they were going to lure her rescuers into a trap. Hadn't she heard them planning such a strategy the night before?

Alarm made Maggie's heart pound, which caused her wound to throb. Jake's SEALs, who were doubtless on their way, would track her down by her microchip and fall squarely into an ambush. In the meantime, she would have to save herself, to flee from this place before the villains returned.

Braced for pain, Maggie sat up cautiously. The chain attached to the collar that gouged her chin gave a musical jingle before pulling taut and halting her movements. The end of it was padlocked to the metal ring that held up the end of her hammock. She wasn't going anywhere.

A dark lump on the ground drew her attention as it unfurled. "Señora!" It was David, shaking off the blanket in which he was wrapped and clambering to his feet. "How…how do you feel?"

All she could do was stare at him. *How do I feel?* Jake was gone. And for the foreseeable future, she was now a captive of the FARC.

Her gaze slid to David's ancient AK-47, still lying on the floor at his feet. She licked her dry lips. "Do you have the key to unlock me?" Her voice was hoarse from screaming when Vargas took his knife to her hip.

David's rounded eyes communicated pity. "No, señora. I'm sorry. Gallo has the key."

Her gaze fell to the rifle lying at his feet. "You could shoot the padlock with your weapon."

He shook his head with lament. "My rifle doesn't fire, señora. It's only for show."

Maggie just blinked at the bitter irony of a rebel's weapon not firing.

"Do not be afraid. I will protect you." He ruined the assertion by swallowing hard.

Maggie squelched the unkind urge to laugh. How could this young man possibly protect her, apart from keeping her well? "Where did Gallo and Vargas go?"

David hesitated. "I really don't know, señora."

He was an awful liar. She could tell by his tone alone those two were out setting a trap for her rescue party. An overwhelming lethargy had her sinking back into her hammock.

With Gallo and Vargas in possession of her tracking device, Jake's teammates would never think to look for her here. The only thing they might recover was Jake's body, downriver somewhere. Loss sucked her into despair's muddy undertow.

Oh, Jake. I'd give anything to see you again.

By the time Jake's boots and gear arrived, the sun was beginning to rise, brightening the sky from black to pewter. They'd waited for three agonizing hours, toward the end of which Lena's tracker began to move, suggesting she was being relocated. As her altitude climbed, Lobo suggested what Jake didn't want to accept: the FARC's newest captive was being taken to *Arriba*.

Soon, the SEALs might know exactly where the third camp lay.

It was not the Little Bird helicopter that brought Jake's gear but a Sikorsky SH-60 Seahawk that thundered into the valley at dawn. Lobo had made a quick and smart decision. Instead of chasing Lena all the way up the mountain by foot, which would have taken the better part of a day and added the risk of running into more FARC, they would fly up the mountain to within five kilometers of her location and drop in via a SPIE rig.

That was how Jake found himself dangling in the air over the clouds that ringed the upper half of El Castillo. Hovering in the thick white veil, the Sikorsky lowered them through the clouds, through a canopy of evergreens, totally unlike the trees that grew at lower elevations. The chilly mist dampened Jake's camo-blackened face as he and his teammates brushed through fragrant boughs, then touched down, one by one, onto a carpet of pine needles, where they detached themselves from the rig. Branches stirred over their heads as the SPIE rig was raised, returning to the helo hovering high above them.

Jake looked around, disoriented. He'd never been this far up the mountain. Was this where *Arriba* lay? The stunted, moss-covered trees looked nothing like the El Castillo he was acquainted with. He felt like he'd dropped into a *Lord of the Rings* movie. Moss grew up the sides of the gnarled and twisted trees. The mist kept him from seeing more than fifty feet in any direction.

As he rallied up with his peers, Jake could tell the air was thin by how fast his heart was beating. They all crouched around Lobo, pausing to catch a collective breath while their OIC consulted his laptop.

"We're five klicks away, but she's not moving anymore."

Foreboding skittered over Jake's scalp. That didn't mean she was dead, he assured himself.

Lobo pointed out the direction they should take. "Let's go."

Half an hour later, they came across a trail with fresh tracks on it. Jake tried to tell if the imprints in the dirt looked like Lena's.

Harm held up two fingers. Lena and one captor, then. Or two captors carrying Lena between them.

Lobo checked his laptop a second time. With a start, Jake realized they were practically on top of her location. Raking the eerie, misty surroundings, he tried sensing her proximity. The hairs on his nape prickled.

Lobo shut his laptop and signaled for them to separate and surround their target. Each man set off on his own, just fifty yards or so from his teammates. Forming a loose net, they would close in from all sides.

Jake cradled his M4 assault rifle, ready to flick off the safety at a moment's notice as he waded stealthily uphill. His new boots weren't just blessedly padded, protecting his feet, but they were designed not to leave discernible tracks.

As he climbed the steep, spongy grade, he queried his uneasiness. This forest was too quiet. Surely, howler monkeys lived at this altitude, but if they were here, they were mute. Even the birds were silent. A rumble of thunder portended rain. Maybe it was the weather keeping the animals listless.

What did it mean that Lena wasn't moving anymore? Either she was dead, or she was chained up in a hovel nearby, unable to move. Another possibility popped into his head, causing him to halt abruptly. He depressed the button on his inter-team radio, then spoke into it quietly, with the sense that someone could hear him.

"Lobo. What if she's not here? What if we're just following her tracker?"

Given Lobo's silence, he didn't like that suggestion. Obviously, if they were following her tracker, then this was a trap.

Jake's scalp tightened. Movement in his peripheral vision had him jerking his rifle in that direction. Shadows shifted within the mist. The silhouette of a deer had him releasing his held breath. "There's a small herd of deer at my three o'clock."

Four does and a fawn picked their way through the forest right where Lena was supposed to be.

The explosion that shattered the quiet knocked Jake to his knees. Stunned, it took him a second to realize what had just happened.

One of the deer had stepped on a mine. The memory of Gallo training the younger rebels how to bury explosives flashed through his head. This whole area was probably riddled with mines. This *was* a trap!

Dirt and lichen were still raining down on Jake when Lobo issued the order to retreat. Pushing to his feet, Jake wasted a moment trying to find his tracks. His high-tech boots were suddenly a liability.

There. The impression of his boot on a carpet of moss sent him in the right direction. He wouldn't blow up if he followed his own tracks.

Gunfire rent the air without warning.

Jake spun behind the closest tree. Bark sprayed his helmet as a bullet came within inches of striking him. The shot had been fired from higher ground.

Chief Harmony was the first to respond, retaliating with his .50-caliber sniper rifle, laying down enough heat for Jake to push off the tree and race downhill.

"Fall back." Lobo's ultra-calm order was echoed by the *BOOM!* of a hand grenade detonating feet from where Jake had just stood. Its blast propelled him so swiftly downhill, he grabbed at branches to slow his descent. Half-leaping, half-sliding behind the next big tree, Jake returned fire at the muzzle flare brightening the mist uphill. Now it was Harm's turn to fall back.

Moving with surprising grace for a muscular man, the bald chief bounded past him. In that same instant, Jake's rifle jammed. *Not now!*

With Harm left vulnerable, Jake gritted his teeth, set the safety, and shoved the charging handle forward. Working a finger into the front edge of the bolt, he forced it rearward. As the problematic round fell free, he thumbed off the safety and proceeded to fire. But a bullet cracked through the air before he got a shot off, flinging Harm to the ground.

Mallacht air! Jake spewed rounds to make up for his lapse. A gargle of agony up on the ridge assured him he'd hit a target, but with Harm on the ground, dragging himself to safety, it hardly felt satisfying.

Jake toggled his mic. "One tango down. Harm's been hit. Bambino, get over here."

"On my way."

The gunfire from the ridge above abated. Keeping a sharp eye out, Jake prayed the firefight was over. Even so, he laid up a wall of fire to cover Bambino's approach. The young medic tucked in next to Harm to assess the chief's wound.

Distracted by Harm's injury, Jake kept his eyes peeled, but the ridge, still veiled in mist, remained quiet. He could hear Bambino tearing into his medic kit and overheard Harm's growl of frustration. The sound of someone moving up on the ridge marshaled all of Jake's attention. Through the veil of mist, he thought he saw a figure drift away.

In the next instant, Lobo slid in next to him, still breathing hard. "What happened?"

"My rifle jammed. Harm took a bullet."

"Where are the shooters?"

"Not sure. I think one is down and the other might be flanking us. I saw him head that way." Jake pointed.

Lobo patted his shoulder. "Keep watch." Tabbing his mic, Lobo ordered Zen to follow him as they went after the squirter.

Jake scanned the impenetrable mist, ready for an ambush. Would one shooter be dumb enough to take on a squad of special operators? Or would he just hurl a grenade at them and be done with it?

Overhearing Harm's groan of discomfort, guilt burrowed into Jake. The chief had married Emma not too long ago, adopting her three young sons. To think Harm could've been killed all because Jake's rifle had jammed. Stuff like that happened. It wasn't like Harm was going to blame him, but why now, when finding Lena was the top priority? They didn't need this!

Twenty minutes later, Lobo reappeared, as stealthy as the wolf he was named for. "There's a dead tango on the ridge, Venezuelan by the name of Vargas if he's wearing his own uniform."

Satisfaction took the edge off Jake's frustration. Now, there was one less threat to Lena. Lobo checked on Harm, then returned and crouched next to Jake. The apology in his jungle-green eyes made Jake fear the worst. "Harm's losing blood fast. I'm calling for hot extraction."

In other words, they were leaving ASAP.

The blood drained from Jake's head to his pounding heart. "*No.* I'm not leaving Lena alone out here. Go without me. I'll be fine. I'll be your eyes and ears on the ground."

Compassion softened Lobo's hard features. He pitched his voice lower. "Look, I get it. She's your partner, and your job is to protect her. But the FARC and the Venezuelans know we're here now, which puts us in a defensive posture. We're not going to find Lena that way, not without her tracking device."

Jake couldn't accept the words coming out of Lobo's mouth. "I'm not leaving her alone." He spoke through his closed jaw.

His peer regarded him with rising frustration. "We're a team, Jake. We don't operate this way."

Jake's eyes burned as he held Lobo's stare. "She's *my* partner. She and *I* are a team on this assignment. I'm. Not. Leaving. Her. Here."

Lobo's mouth firmed. "You know I'll take the blame for your decision."

"Then tell Commander Strong I went AWOL. I don't care." His future in the Teams wouldn't matter anyway, not if Lena vanished from his life. She was the reason he was a SEAL and a SOG in the first place.

With a shake of his head, Lobo seemed to accept Jake's decision. "Fine. But we're not leaving you without our SERE kits and whatever arms and food we can spare. You could be stuck here a long time." He pushed away from the tree, leaving Jake to his thoughts.

A sense of calm stole over him, even as he kept a sharp eye out for the remaining tango. He didn't have to leave El Castillo. With supplies and weapons, he'd be fine out here. Hadn't he emerged from survival training in the jungles of Panama with mere cuts and bruises? It wasn't himself he was worried about. Lena was the one truly in peril here. *God have mercy on her.*

CHAPTER 17

Gallo burst into the *casita*, startling David as he applied the sticky mixture of *ajo sacha* paste over the señora's festering wound. His patient, lethargic with fever, nonetheless lurched up in the hammock, ready to protect herself. But it was David who needed protecting as Gallo bore down on him wild-eyed.

"What are you doing?" He hauled his pistol from the holster on his belt and pointed it at David's head, causing him to drop the wooden bowl with its potent-smelling poultice and back away from Gallo, his hands raised.

"I…I'm sealing her wound. She is feverish and could die."

Gallo raised his voice and waved his pistol in Madeleine's direction. "She is not your concern! She is a spy!" He had lost his hat. The hair on his head stuck straight up, and his eyes bulged. "Some soldiers came for her—" He cut himself off abruptly and spun away, dragging fingers through his hair as he commenced pacing the *casita*.

David divided his attention between the señora's glazed expression and the crazed *mondo*, whose energy was even more unpredictable than ever. Where was Gallo's partner in crime? He scrounged up the courage to ask. "Where is the Venezuelan captain?"

Gallo wheeled around, pointing a finger this time, even as he jammed his pistol back into its holster. "We don't know." His breath came in hard and fast.

We?

Gallo waved a hand at the door. "He went out last night to relieve himself, and he never came back. Perhaps a jaguar ate him. This is the story you will tell."

"But—" Gallo's wild look kept David from protesting, *"But you left with him this morning."*

Clearly, something had happened to Vargas that Gallo didn't want his superiors to know. Did that mean the Venezuelan was dead? Who had killed him—possibly the soldiers Gallo had just mentioned? Had they been looking for Madeleine?

Glancing back at his patient, David caught a glimmer of tears in her eyes before she turned her face away. She had obviously heard Gallo's words, gleaning that whoever had come for her was gone now—gone as in dead. But they'd managed to kill Vargas, at least, leaving one less devil to contend with.

Poor señora. Nobody would rescue her now. David gulped. It was up to him to look after her. Seeing Gallo head back outside, David snatched up the fallen bowl and continued to tend his patient's wound.

He was scrubbing the bowl in the bucket of water when Gallo returned. David watched warily as the *mondo* marched straight for Madeleine. Using a key on his key chain, he unlocked the padlock that had kept her chained to the wall. As Gallo freed the length of chain, the woman sat up slowly. She was right to be wary of the *mondo*, who then hauled her out of the hammock with a yank.

David abandoned the bowl, hurrying to catch his patient as she stumbled.

Gallo glared at him. "Tie her wrists behind her back. We're leaving."

David glanced at Madeleine's pale face. "But, Mondo, she's too sick to go anywhere."

Gallo flashed out a hand and cuffed the side of David's head, leaving his ear ringing. "I said, *tie* her wrists."

David stared at him a moment. For the first time in his rebel career, he wished his weapon weren't useless. "Yes, sir."

Turning away, he hunted down the length of *hamak* fiber that strung her up the night before. While securing the woman's wrists behind her back, as Gallo instructed, David asked himself when and how he would free her—how he would free them *both*.

Her health was not going to improve. Certainly, the *ajo sacha* would help to stave off infection, but stress and starvation would sicken her. "Are we taking her to *Arriba* now?" He was afraid to ask.

"We?" Gallo's dark glance should have incinerated him on the spot, it was so filled with loathing.

David wet his dry lips. "Rojas ordered me to keep her alive." It was only a matter of time before Gallo learned he was lying.

As the *mondo* huffed out a breath of annoyance, David's heart fluttered like a bird's.

"Then you must come along, I guess."

David nodded, though his victory was short-lived. Once at *Arriba*, it would be next to impossible to free Madeleine. The most he could do was to keep her alive longer. Perhaps Padre Josué was still at the old radio station, not far from *Arriba*, and could help David.

He dared ask one more question. "What if she can't make the climb, *Mondo*?"

Gallo sneered. "If she can't make it, you will carry her."

Rain drummed the broad leaves that sheltered Jake as he stood within the tree line, studying the *casita* where the UN team had spent their last few nights together. No smoke curled out of the crude chimney. No smell of food hung in the wet air. From his current vantage, he couldn't see through any of the screened-in windows, but he sensed the *casita* was deserted.

"Home sweet home." The memory of Lena bending down to kiss him while he lay in his hammock wafted through him, wrenching his heart.

It was almost evening. It had rained relentlessly since his teammates' departure, drenching the jungle fatigues Jake wore beneath his tactical vest and heavy pack. While carrying enough supplies to ensure his survival for days, his feet throbbed as he hiked downhill, finding his way using the GPS device Lobo left with him to Lena's last known location. In the dismal rain, the brick *casita* looked downright cozy, and Jake hadn't slept for more than thirty-six hours.

On the off chance someone *was* inside, he double-checked his weapons. Thanks to his teammates' generosity, he now carried an M4, Harm's KA-BAR knife, strapped to his right thigh, and Bambino's pistol in his belt holster. The mosquitos swarming his head couldn't get to his flesh through the grease paint covering his exposed skin.

Go. Jake darted across the open space, put his back to the wall, then reached out and pulled the door open. It swung outward with a groan, emitting a stillness that encouraged Jake to pivot around the wall and clear the building.

With mixed feelings, he discovered it empty. His gaze fell on the single hammock suspended right where Lena's had hung before their departure. Curiosity drew him toward it, and a stain resembling blood had him bending down for a closer look. He touched the damp stain, then smelled his fingers. The iron scent of blood, left right where Lena's hip might have come into contact with the woven fibers, made him fear the worst.

Not only had she been here, but she was injured. Her captors must have cut the tracking device from her hip.

His heart pounding and his stomach queasy, Jake searched the unlit space for more clues. Encountering a wooden bowl left in the soapy dishwater, he pulled it out and gave it a whiff. The faint smell of something herbal—garlic?—mystified him since the rebels never seasoned their food.

He dropped the bowl back in the bucket, then crossed to the screen that offered a view of the rain-soaked coca field. Disappointment cleaved his chest. Resting his forehead against the wall, he stared outside, drawing deep breaths until his unwieldy emotions subsided.

Had she been taken to *Arriba* from here or to one of the other camps? Rebel Central was the closest, located just four kilometers from the *casita*, where he would spend the night. Maybe Rojas wanted to question her in person. Jake could pop over there in the morning and hunt for any sign of her. If it didn't look like she was there, he would head next to *Cecaot-Jicobo.*

If she wasn't there either, he would capture the first rebel to cross his tracks and question that man until he learned of Lena's whereabouts. Regardless of how long it took, he would find her and free her.

I'm still here, Beautiful. I'm coming for you. I won't let you die alone on this godforsaken mountain.

Arriba. What an awful place to die. It did, in fact, lie beyond the waterfall, another mile or two of hiking that had nearly killed her. The place was unworthy of a grander name, as just two stone hovels and a couple of outhouses were all that was here, all built from the rocks that comprised the landscape at this ridiculous altitude. The lower hovel stood at the upper edge of the forest, while the second had been erected on the bare rock currently quilted in snow.

A chain-link fence topped by barbed wire hemmed in the second building and an outhouse. Nothing but wild grasses and stunted shrubs poked through the snow. A steady wind stripped all the warmth from Maggie's body. And even though the mountain's twin peaks loomed nearby, she couldn't see them for the clouds that capped the mountain, limiting visibility to maybe fifty yards.

Upon their arrival, Gallo had passed her chain off to a stoop-backed jailer, and for a brief moment, Maggie's optimism had risen, especially when Gallo sliced off the bindings at her wrists, freeing her to use her hands. The jailer looked like someone she could overcome with a well-placed kick.

But then a hulking, scar-faced brute stepped out of the jailer's hovel, and all hope of escaping withered. As the second jailer's soulless eyes slid over her, Maggie wondered if he was even human. One of Jake's favorite classic movies came to mind, causing her lips to twitch as she dubbed the pair Igor and Frankenstein.

Gallo had given the jailers specific directions. "Rojas wants her to remain in good health, so chain her well away from the others."

Her ears had pricked at the word. *The others? Were the JUNGLA still here?*

"As she is wounded, this soldier named David may check on her from time to time and bring her herbs for her recovery."

Meeting David's apologetic gaze, Maggie could see he regretted not being able to shoot the padlock back at the *casita* and escape while they'd had the chance.

Igor had tugged Lena into the stark enclosure, followed by Frankenstein, who locked the gate behind them. When Lena glanced back at David, the horrified look on his face confirmed what Maggie was thinking:

I really might die here.

Shoved into the hovel from behind, she could see nothing at first, for the dwelling had no windows. Chains rattled as the other prisoners took stock of her. The foul stench that made her hold her breath suggested they had been here for weeks, if not months. As her eyes adjusted to the dark, the familiar camouflage pattern of their uniforms informed her these were, indeed, the three JUNGLA who were supposed to be freed per the UN's agreement with Rojas.

Assessing their condition, Maggie was pleased to see the fire of resistance still smoldering in their eyes. Through some clever and cooperative effort, they stood a good chance of escaping, she assured herself. Enduring their fascinated stares for the moment, she waited for Frankenstein and Igor to withdraw before addressing them.

"My name is Madeleine Cotillard. I am a French citizen, born in Venezuela. I came here with the UN peacekeeping team to negotiate the release of Jay Barnes and Mike Howitz. You must have known Jay, at least, if not both men."

Her words were treated with skeptical silence. Perhaps she was too calm, behaving like the operator she was, not some traumatized UN representative. "Did you know we arranged for your release, but the FARC cheated us at the last minute, saying you had escaped from them?"

Her words got the response she was looking for. They spoke to her at last, introducing themselves, then peppering her with questions, which she answered as best a UN peacekeeper whose hip was throbbing and whose heart was shattered could.

When exhaustion claimed her, Maggie lapsed into silence, resting her head on the rock wall. Wrapped in a tattered and filthy woolen blanket, possibly used by her American predecessors, and seated on a cold dirt floor, Maggie shivered violently, unable to warm herself, even though her cheeks burned, suggesting her fever was climbing.

She must have fallen asleep, for she was kicked awake a while later by Igor—and subsequently every hour on the hour, even after nightfall, when he shone a flashlight into her eyes.

Recognizing the awakenings as psychological torture and dismissing them, Maggie fell right back to sleep with each stirring, embracing the vivid dreams that claimed her.

In one such dream, she was floating shoulder-deep in clear aqua-blue waters in Jake's embrace. The gentle rise and fall of the warm water cradled them. They were in Phuket on their honeymoon. White sand clung to Jake's dark hair. He smiled at her with so much love in his gentle blue eyes that contentment brimmed in her.

I've never been this happy. We should have married years ago. Laying a hand on his smooth shoulder, she put her nose to his neck, inhaling the scent of a spring rain shower. This had to be real.

But hadn't she seen him plummet to his death into the churning river, due to Gallo's treachery?

Querying the reality of her dream, Maggie roused to consciousness. Hunger and frigid cold hit her like the flat edge of a two-by-four, knocking the joy clean out of her.

In desperation, she grasped for the words that had comforted her before, surrendering herself to their promise because there was no other choice: "*I will fear no evil. For You are with me; Your rod and Your staff, they comfort me.*"

But the words rang hollow. Evil alone ruled this place. It was as if God had never even set foot here.

∿

The squeak of hinges roused Jake from a light slumber. He lay face down on damp soil. *Where am I?* The vision of a hen pecking his outflung arm brought it all back—how he'd spied on Rebel Central for hours the day before, even skulked around its perimeter and nearly grabbed a rebel to lead him to wherever Lena might have been taken. But the guards stood in pairs, and Jake only wanted one informant. And then he'd remembered: low-ranking rebels had no idea where captives were kept. He needed someone who knew something.

Giving up, he'd turned his back on *Ki-kirr-zikis* and hiked all the way up and around the mountain to *Cecaot-Jicobo*, that familiar camp where his joy at spending time with Lena had overridden all discomforts. As he'd hiked like an automaton, the rain had beaten down on him. It felt as if the entire world were weeping with him. Memories flowed through him of his and Lena's first hike up El Castillo, her defiance in the face of fear while crossing the river in a wooden box strung from cables. *Fire with fire.*

He loved her so much that his chest hurt. *Stay strong, Beautiful. Don't give up on me.*

Finally, just as darkness descended on his second day of searching, he arrived at the familiar camp. Exhausted, wet, and leery of sleeping with the creepy crawlies in the woods, he'd taken refuge under the bungalow, right beneath his and Lena's old cubicle. Memories of her sleeping with her head on his shoulder lulled him into a deep and restful sleep.

But now it was dawn, and Gallo had just stepped out of the officers' quarters, his door slamming shut behind him, which meant whoever was sleeping in the bungalow overhead—most likely Venezuelan soldiers—were bound to awaken soon with the blared recording of "*¡Despiértense todos. Arriba y Ándale!*"

As Jake pushed to his knees, the pack on his back—*THUMP*—struck the underside of the bungalow. A male voice mumbled in protest right above him, causing Jake to count the beats of his heart as he prayed for the man to fall back asleep. Finally, rewarded by the sound of a low snore, he scuttled backward, keeping low. Then he darted into the forest, just as he and Lena had done so many times before. Birdsong and monkey chatter muffled his footsteps as he charged downhill, retreating to a safe distance to strategize.

The best person to capture and question was Gallo, of course. Having whisked Lena away from the valley and back up the mountain, Gallo most definitely knew where she was taken. Jake just had to capture him, then make the *mondo* an offer he couldn't refuse: His life for Lena's safe return.

But the rest of the rebels and their Venezuelan counterparts would notice Gallo's absence and come looking for him. Some of them were bound to be good trackers. Jake's boots might not leave tread marks, but nothing could disguise the depressions his soles left in the soft earth.

Rethinking his strategy, he headed toward the garcinia tree and was pleased to find two of the prickly fruits intact and on the ground, as yet unnoticed by the active monkeys leaping in the branches overhead.

With his back to the tree, Jake tore off the protective outer layer and popped the first succulent ball into his mouth. He was just starting to peel the second ball when David walked soundlessly past the tree, his eyes fastened on the soil. Jake froze. With a furrowed brow, David turned, following Jake's barely discernable tracks. His head came up and his eyes flew wide. As he fumbled to aim the rifle that he carried everywhere, Jake threw his hands up.

"*Soy yo*, David! *Tranquilo, tranquilo. No me fusiles.*" Don't shoot me.

His jaw hanging open, the squad leader lowered his weapon. "Jacques, *estás vivo!*"

"*Sí*, I'm alive." Jake extended the second ball of fruit as a peace offering, but David waved it off. His light-brown gaze trekked over Jake's military attire and his many weapons.

"Are you JUNGLA?"

"No, no." Jake took a small step closer and pitched his voice lower. "I'm not here to cause trouble. I've come for my…my wife. Where is Lena, David? Do you know?"

The fear in David's expression gave way to cautious relief. He sent a worried glance toward camp, then gestured for Jake to follow him.

Led deeper into the forest, Jake was just beginning to question David's intentions when they came across a plant covered in dark purple berries. David began plucking berries and dropping them into a leather pouch tied to his vest. He flicked Jake a dry glance. "Your Spanish is much better."

Jake had to laugh at the remark. Dressed as an operator, he'd forgotten to speak painstakingly as Jacques would have done. Remembering his objective, he sobered. "Do you know where Lena is?"

The young man hesitated, plucking several more berries and feeding them into his pouch before pulling on the strings that closed it. *"Arriba."* He jerked his chin in the direction of the falls. "She is hurt, but I'm permitted to tend to her. I will visit her later today."

Hope surged into Jake's chest. "Will you take me to her? That's all I ask. Take me to her and tell no one. I'm not sure how to get there. Is it past the *cascadas*?"

Thoughts flickered in David's eyes, but he said not a word.

Desperation thrummed in Jake. "No one will ever know you helped me, David, I promise. I will take Lena from here and, God willing, you will never see me again."

David cocked his head. "Do you believe in God, Jacques?"

The question caught Jake off guard. He nodded earnestly. "Yes, very much."

"Yet, you will kill the guards to free your wife?"

David didn't want anyone dying, apparently.

"Well, not if I don't have to. There are other ways."

David glanced around before stepping closer. "I know another way, but I am afraid." He sucked in a breath and blew it out. "I am a coward."

"Be brave. Tell me what you're thinking."

Lifting a frightened look at him, David said quickly, "Gallo has a master key for all the padlocks used on El Castillo. I have heard him boast that he could free any hostage if he wished. He carries it on his key chain."

Intrigued, Jake considered the options opening up to him.

David patted the pouch he carried. "This afternoon, I will put these berries in Gallo's *agua panela* to make him sleepy. Once he's asleep, I will take his key ring and run for *Arriba* to tend your wife. I will unlock her chains, as well as those of the three JUNGLA captives. I thought if I freed them all at once, she could slip away while the others distract the guards. I planned to take her to the radio station. Padre Josué, if he is still there, will know how to help me."

David's clever plan, which closely resembled their escape-and-evasion plan, stunned Jake. "You're not a coward for wanting to avoid violence, David. You are the bravest man here, like young David in the Bible who slew Goliath with his slingshot."

"No, señor." The youth's brow furrowed. "I am the reason Gallo suspected you in the first place. All of this is my fault. I thought I got you killed!"

Jake squeezed David's bony shoulder. "None of that matters now. We can help each other. Make the *agua panela* for Gallo. When he falls asleep, take his key ring, and we'll go to *Arriba* together. We'll discuss our plan as we walk and finalize it once I see for myself what the area looks like. But tell me about Lena. How much did they hurt her?"

David grimaced, dropping his gaze. "She has a wound—here." He touched his right hip. "She needs a healer."

"Yes, I know. I'll get her the help she needs. Can she walk?"

David hesitated. "She could walk yesterday, but she was limping."

Jake would carry her to the top of the mountain if he had to. "Thank you for looking out for her, David. God will reward you for doing the right thing."

As the youth nodded, his gaze traveled over Jake's tactical vest to the M4 loosely held in the crook of his arm. "What are you? You don't look like a peacekeeper."

Jake sent him a small smile. "It's better for you not to know. I'm not a threat to you; I promise. When will you give him the *agua panela*?"

"Just before the evening meal. The sun will set soon after."

"How far is it to *Arriba*?"

"About an hour's walk, señor. Meet me at the *cascadas*. We will need to run to beat the dark."

Jake gave an inward groan as he spared a thought for his tender feet. But nothing would keep him from running his fastest.

Without medical help, she would grow septic and die.

Catching herself thinking gloomy thoughts—and it was only the second day!—Maggie applied herself to knowing the JUNGLA soldiers better. They were courteous and respectful to her, having speculated after discussing strategies for taking down Igor and wrestling the keys from him that Maggie must work for the CIA or MI6. But it was Frankenstein who checked on them in the morning, planting a heavy boot in Maggie's side to rouse her from feverish slumber.

Two hours later, as hunger gnawed at her like a tapeworm, Frankenstein brought them each a bowl of rice—and an extra bowl of roasted potatoes seasoned with wild herbs for Maggie. The guards had taken Rojas's supposed wishes to heart.

But Maggie, glimpsing the rabid hunger on the faces of the JUNGLA, who noted her preferential treatment with envy, weighed her health against the need to win them over and tossed each man a portion of her meal. Their attitude had shifted from speculative to accepting. She was one of them now.

Around midday, their chains were removed from the wall by Igor while Frankenstein stood watch, his AK-47 at the ready. *What's happening?* Following the lead of her fellow captives, she picked up the chain trailing from her collar and followed her companions out the door.

Sunlight bouncing off the snow blinded her as she limped into the frigid wind. As he shuffled along behind her, the JUNGLA named Diego inclined his mouth to her ear. "Once a day, they let us out to use the latrine and to take exercise."

Frankenstein prodded the man with his rifle. "No talking!"

Hugging herself against the cold wind, Maggie hunted for a means of escaping. The oldest JUNGLA, Fernando, carried his chain into the latrine and shut the door. The others walked around their shelter in a tight knot with Frankenstein stalking them, eagle-eyed. Igor, also armed with a rifle, manned the gate. Even so, Maggie recognized this was obviously the best time to effect an escape.

She considered the chain-link fence, ten feet tall and topped with barbed wire. Even in her injured state, she was certain she could climb it, but the barbed wire at the top presented a deterrent.

Diego spoke beneath his breath, his thoughts evidently on par with hers. "You could fit between the top of the fence and the barbed wire, señora. You're thin enough."

Maggie assessed the narrow space. Heavens, was she really that thin? She would have to count on the men to tackle Frankenstein and seize his gun before Igor reacted. It wasn't beyond the realm of possibility, but—"I'm not leaving unless we all leave."

Diego slanted her a grateful look. "Are you married, Madeleine?"

The pain that lanced Maggie's heart kept her from answering right away. Was she married? She ought to have married Jake years ago, but then she would never have become a case officer and never would have found that priceless information during her job in Venezuela.

"No." And now it was too late. Jake was dead. Picturing his plummet into the river, she reviewed it in slow motion, detaching herself from the denial and anguish that had seized her at the time. He had hit the water feet first.

Hope shot like a sunbeam through a crack into her desolate thoughts. Could Jake have survived that tremendous fall into roiling water without snapping his neck? Could he have weathered the rapids sweeping him down the mountain? Navy SEALs were practically drown-proof. What if he *wasn't* dead?

She had to be delirious to even consider the possibility. But if it turned out he was alive, and if he was well enough to get up and walk— well, then, he would come for her, no question.

Or was she just so gravely desperate that she would tell herself anything to stay alive?

CHAPTER 18

The sun was sinking behind the mountains to their west by the time Jake and David arrived at the illusive outpost called *Arriba*. Breathing harder than he ever had to extract the oxygen needed to feed his heart, Jake hid himself in the shadow of a stunted tree, while David identified himself to the guard in the first stone structure and was escorted to the gate of the enclosure, ostensibly to check in on the female captive, per General Rojas's supposed orders.

The sky was a pearly pink hue, suggesting sunset was on its way.

On their arduous hike, they had planned a strategy that hadn't changed once Jake glimpsed the layout. David would go in alone while Jake waited. His heart raced; his palms grew damp within the tactical gloves that kept his fingers warm. Jake's future with Lena depended on whatever happened in the next ten minutes.

David was going to slip Lena three things: Gallo's key ring, Jake's KA-BAR blade, and Jake's backup pistol. In English—which the guard hopefully didn't know—David was going to whisper that Jake was right outside the gate. David would apply the paste he'd brought with him to Lena's wound and leave. The rest was up to her.

Any number of things could go wrong. The hulking jailer who'd accompanied David into the second hovel might hear Gallo's key ring rattle or might glimpse the weapons as David passed them off. Even if the young man managed to make the transfer, the JUNGLA captives, rather than aid Lena, might subvert her efforts, though Jake couldn't imagine why they wouldn't take advantage of the dynamic situation and cooperate.

Oh, God. Jake sagged against the trunk of the tree he hid behind. Peering up at *Arriba* and the surreal color of the oyster-pink sky, he prayed, *Please let this work. Just get us safely off this mountain, and I'll take care of Lena from here on out, I promise.*

Maggie had decided David wasn't ever going to come back as he'd said he would. Feeling forgotten, growing more despondent by the hour, she had watched the feeble spindles of sunlight shooting through the cracks between the piled stone fade. Now, all she had left to anticipate were the vivid dreams brought on by her fever.

Just as she closed her eyes, surrendering to sleep, the grating of the gate outside the hovel caused her eyes to open. It was too soon for the hourly awakenings. Footsteps crunched across the ground outside, approaching the thick door. Both she and the JUNGLA captives braced themselves as Frankenstein pushed it open, admitting the glow of twilight and a slightly built figure.

"David!" Maggie dragged herself slightly more upright.

"Hola, señora." With his back mostly to Frankenstein, he dropped to his knees beside her. "How do you feel this evening?"

Noting his tense tone, Maggie glanced casually at Frankenstein, who shut the door behind him. For a moment all was dark before the guard snapped on his flashlight and shone it in their direction.

From under the woolen poncho he was wearing, David produced a small wooden bowl with a cork lid. "I've come to put more paste on your wound." With trembling hands, he pried the lid off, releasing the garlic-like aroma she had smelled before.

David's nervousness was obvious. His fingers shook as he dipped them into the paste. Was he simply afraid of Frankenstein? Keeping watchful, Maggie rolled onto her left hip, exposing the site of her injury now that her slacks were so low. David shifted so the guard's light upon her injury, a gash about an inch and a half in length, surrounded by angry red torn flesh in need of stitching. This was only her second time looking at it since Vargas had sliced her open.

With an anxious glance into her eyes, David began to dab a fresh layer of paste over the wound. Frankenstein watched his every movement, silently urging haste so he could go back to whatever he and Igor did on their own time.

When David's left hand lowered the small bowl to the ground, Maggie followed it. Easing aside the flap of his poncho, he showed her the vest he always wore. Maggie stifled a gasp, for in place of the banana-shaped ammo usually in his pockets, the haft of a blade and the butt of a pistol stuck out. Where had David managed to get such weapons?

The vision spurred her heart into a canter. And now David was slipping his fingers into his pants pocket, retrieving what looked like a set of keys—Gallo's key ring?! Before they could jingle, Maggie flashed out a hand under the guise of thanking him.

"*Gracias*, David." Curling her fingers firmly around the metal components, she took the key ring from his grasp and tucked it quickly out of sight behind her. Adrenaline coursed through her bloodstream, driving off her lethargy and sharpening her senses.

David wouldn't get away with passing off the weapons, though, not unless Maggie could distract Frankenstein from staring at them.

"Hey, Diego." She addressed her ally chained to the opposite wall while pushing the keys farther beneath her. "What do Colombians call men who are so hideous they look like monsters?"

As Diego chuckled, Frankenstein turned his glare on that man, giving Maggie the opportunity to snatch the pistol from David's vest and lay it by her leg out of the guard's view.

"Let's see. *Es un malparido*," Diego responded. *Badly born.*

Maggie's pounding heart rocked her where she sat. The pistol she'd just seized was heavy and modern; it had to have come from the Venezuelans. And the blade, from what she could see of it, looked like a straight U.S. military issue.

Diego must have sensed what she was up to, for he wasn't done insulting Frankenstein. *"Es una gonorrea de persona."*

The hulking guard whipped both his flashlight and his weapon at Diego. *"Oye. Cállate la boca!" Shut your mouth.*

By the time the guard swung his light back at David, Maggie had relieved him of the dagger and stowed it alongside the pistol. David, in turn, picked up the wooden bowl and recorked it while Maggie willed him to stay calm. A single line of softly spoken English emerged from his lips, the first she had ever heard him speak. "Jake is waiting outside the gate."

In the next instant, he was up on his feet and slipping out the door that Frankenstein held open for him.

Maggie's brain seemed to glitch as the door closed behind her visitors, sucking all light from the hovel. She sat in the darkness, stunned to the core. *"Jake is waiting outside the gate."* Had David just spoken those words, or had she hallucinated them? She had a raging fever, after all.

Whether real or imagined, she wasn't going to spend any more time in this cell than she had to.

Cotton-mouthed, with her extremities tingling, Maggie waited for the sound of footsteps to fade and for the hinges on the gate to groan. When the only sound to reach her ears was that of her own labored breathing, she shared her good news with the JUNGLA in a low-pitched voice. *"Muchachos*, how do you feel about getting out of here this evening?"

"What did he bring for you, señora?" It was Diego, who'd clearly seen her furtive actions.

"First, a key ring." She lifted it into view, letting the few keys on it jangle before grabbing one of them and trying to insert it into the padlock at her neck. When it didn't fit, she thumbed her way to the second key. "I think it belongs to Mondo Gallo, who chained me up. If I can get free myself, I will free you, as well. He brought us a pistol and a blade, too. Who's the best shot?"

"Jorge."

"Yes, I am." Eagerness strengthened that man's previously feeble voice.

The JUNGLA fell silent, no doubt listening intently as Maggie worked her way through the keys. The fourth one slipped neatly into her padlock, releasing it with a *click*. Prying the metal collar open and freeing herself was pure euphoria. Optimism soared like an eagle buoyed up by thermal updrafts.

"I'm free!" She rolled to her knees, grabbed up the pistol and the blade, and shuffled toward the men.

This was going to work. Already a plan was forming in her head. "Guide my hands to your locks." A pair of hands groped for her, caught her wrists, and drew her closer. For a split second, terror seized Maggie. What if this all went wrong, the way her plan in Morocco had veered off course?

No. This was a different place and time. And she wasn't alone, either. She had three seasoned soldiers to assist her. And—if she hadn't been hallucinating—the love of her life was just outside the gate waiting for her.

~

David rushed up to Jake, forcing him to raise his NVGs. The last ten minutes had been some of the most excruciating in his life as he relied on someone else to get the job done.

"It worked." David's quaking voice betrayed relief. The whites of his eyes shone brightly in the dusky light. "She took everything from me. I didn't have to do anything."

Admiration bloomed in Jake. *That's my girl.* "Then she still has her wits about her. That's good. Now we wait."

David looked like he could use a hug. But, with a grave nod, he moved away to crouch behind a nearby shrub. As they'd discussed on their way up from the waterfall, it would be rash for David to return to his duties as squad leader. Even if he managed to return the key ring to Gallo before that man woke up, David would be suspect number one when the captives turned up missing.

Without much persuasion, he had agreed to accompany Jake, Maggie, and possibly even the JUNGLA to the radio station. Earlier that afternoon, Jake had placed a call to the JIC using the heavy-duty sat phone Lobo had left him. After explaining his situation, he'd requested a possible extraction that night at the designated E & E site.

"This better work." Lobo's response echoed in Jake's head. *"I've taken a lot of heat for you, Jake."*

"I'm sorry. It's going to work, just as long as the Seahawk gets here when we need it, loaded with plenty of firepower, just in case."

As David quilted himself in his poncho and waited, Jake flipped down his goggles and looked back at the enclosure.

Viewed through his NVGs, the snow on the ground glowed a bright ghostly green. He studied the scene, seeking any hint of movement, whether in the guards' hovel or the prisoners'. Nothing moved except the smoke curling out of the guards' shelter and the stunted vegetation shuddering under a steady breeze. Apart from the wind whistling over the rocks, kicking up snowflakes, and rattling the barbed wire at the top of the fence, not a sound reached Jake's ears.

Time slowed to a crawl. What were the prisoners waiting for? Knowing Lena, they had a plan in place that would work—unless none of the keys on Gallo's key ring freed her lock. What if David had been mistaken about that?

Please, don't let him be mistaken.

It had to have been a full hour later when the door of the guards' shelter swung open and out stepped the larger of the two guards—Ugh. Why'd it have to be *him*? The corona of the man's flashlight bobbed as he crossed to the enclosure's gate. Using a key hanging from his belt, he unbolted it and left the lock hanging open as he stepped inside. This had to be a regular nightly inspection.

Jake's finger curled instinctively over the trigger of his M4. If only David didn't want him killing the guards. He could expedite Lena's escape with a double tap that would neutralize the large guard instantly, followed by his partner when that man emerged to investigate.

Still, Jake respected David's wishes and would do his best to abide by them. Killing was no small thing. Fortunately for Jake, the rules were different for special operators, who killed to save lives. Ben Harmony, the Teams' best sniper, had taught him that helpful truth.

Neither Lena nor the JUNGLA captives would suffer such qualms, thankfully. And surely this was when they would make their move.

The enormous guard was marching into the pen. He reached the rough-hewn door and stepped through it, taking the flashlight with him.

"David." At Jake's whisper, the drowsing youth jerked to attention, looked up at him, then craned his neck to see over the bush he hid behind. "It's about to happen."

Not five seconds later, a bloodcurdling scream issued from the hovel, raising Jake's hackles. The cry came again, only to curtail abruptly as the large guard met his untimely end.

Finally. Jake released the breath he was holding. Now the hostages could make their escape.

~

Frankenstein was hard to kill. It took Jorge, the JUNGLA who'd volunteered to slit the man's throat, two attempts before the beast finally crumpled. But not before his scream rent the quiet, alerting his colleagues to trouble. As Jake would say, *Mallacht air!*

Maggie's heart would not stop pounding. She rose on trembling knees, her thoughts fixed on one goal: to escape this awful place.

Fernando, their leader, waited for Jorge to wipe the blood off the KA-BAR onto his slacks before gesturing with the pistol. "*Vamos. Señora,* stay at the rear." He waved her to the back as they fell into a line and followed Fernando out the open door—Jorge first, then Diego, then her.

The cold air wafting over Maggie sharpened her fever-dulled senses. Even with adrenaline ricocheting through her bloodstream, her limbs felt weighted, her movements sluggish.

Scarcely aware of the pain in her hip, she slid along the hovel's outer wall behind the commandos as they headed single file toward the gate. Light jumped suddenly from the guards' hovel, and they shrank back as Igor came barreling out of it with his flashlight in one hand, his handheld radio in the other.

"Raúl!" The man's panicked cry echoed off the escarpment behind them. "*Raúl!*" He brought his radio to his mouth to alert the other FARC. "*Aviso! Aviso!*"

CRACK! Fernando felled him with a single bullet of the pistol. Was it Jake's? Both the flashlight and the radio fell into the snow.

Jake, are you here? Maggie squashed the hope that welled in her. She'd seen him disappear into the fast-flowing water. And, looking around, there was nothing but barren tundra, covered in snow and bone-chilling wind.

"Go!" Fernando powered forward, hustling them through the open gate.

The whistle that came floating out of the tree line made Maggie's heart cartwheel. She knew that sound! But what if it was just a product of delirium or the cry of an Andean Condor? "If you see a white man, please don't shoot him," she told Fernando, just in case. Her heart raced for a completely different reason. *Oh, Jake, please be here.*

If Jake was alive, she would do *everything* differently.

Their line fragmented as they dispersed, looking around, wondering, What now? There was nothing but snow and rocks, shrubs, naked branches, and clouds overhead with just a few stars peeking through. They might be free, but they were far from saved.

But then, a figure stepped out of the forest with his hands held high. The air backed up in Maggie's lungs. Her heart lodged itself in her throat. Behind him, with less confidence, emerged a smaller man in a poncho—David.

"Jake?" Maggie's strangled cry was scarcely audible. How could it be him? This man wore a helmet with night-vision gear mounted on it and a uniform. His face was blackened. Perhaps it was one of his teammates. "He's a friend. Don't shoot!"

As the soldier drew closer, she saw that he walked with a limp. But the breadth of his shoulders and the length of his legs were so like Jake's. Then his lips parted in a smile so familiar, so dear that Maggie's knees almost buckled. "Jake!"

She ran at him, heedless of the pain her sudden movement engendered. Joy like nothing she had ever experienced exploded inside her, seeming to lift her off her feet as she ran toward him, arms outstretched. He'd survived that fall into the river! Impossible! Yet here he was, rescuing her like he had done two times before.

Only this time, she was never letting go.

Lena crashed into him, her grip so tight Jake marveled that she still had such strength in her. She promptly burst into tears—the last thing she wanted to do, he knew, but she was overcome. Tears welled into his own eyes, and joy strangled his vocal cords—until he noticed the heat smoldering through the flimsy canvas at the back of her jacket. She was burning up with fever.

"You're all right now, Beautiful. We're going home."

Overcome by emotion, she nodded with her face hidden against his neck.

Looking past her, Jake met the wary expressions of the three JUNGLA commandos who should have been released days ago per the UN's agreement with the FARC. Reed-thin and grubby, they divided speculative looks between him and the boy in the poncho, whom they doubtless recognized.

Shifting Maggie to one side, Jake thrust a gloved hand toward the eldest of the bunch. "Lieutenant Jake Carrigan, SEAL Team Six."

The man's grip was surprisingly strong.

"Capitán Fernando Calderón. With me are Sargentos Diego Lopez and Jorge Peña. I imagine this is yours?" Fernando went to hand Jake's pistol back to him.

"Keep it. You may need it. Listen, our goal is to get to the summit as soon as possible." He jerked a chin toward the escarpment looming over them. "My Team is flying in on a *helicóptero* to get us out of here."

The men stood for a stunned moment, no doubt wondering if they were dreaming. Fernando was the first to recover, shooting a speculative glance at the steep climb ahead. "*Bueno.* Let's do this.*"

Cutting a look at the captives' feet, Jake was relieved to see they all still wore their boots. Their uniforms were made for this environment, helping them to survive as long as they had. They could make it just a few hours longer. "Is there anything you need before we start hiking? David knows the way."

"No, we're ready. *Vamos ahora.*"

Patting down his vest, Jake located his two penlights—one his own and the other left to him by Bambino. "Here, you take this. Let's grab the flashlight off the dead guy and his weapon, too."

Fernando went to relay the order, but his subordinates were already heading toward the dead guard. "Wait one second," Fernando called over his shoulder. Striding toward the guards' shelter, he gestured for his companion to follow him.

Jake focused back on Lena, who had lifted her head from his shoulder and stood wiping her face behind the fall of her long, tangled black hair.

Catching her lightly by the chin, Jake lifted her face so he could see her expression. "Can you walk, Beautiful?"

She sniffed. "Yes."

Her brave response made his heart swell with admiration.

"Hey, Jake?"

Even in the darkness, he could tell the words she was about to say were important. The hope that she'd realized they were meant for each other jacked up his heart rate. "Yes, Lena?"

A voice interrupted whatever she was going to tell him as it shouted from the guards' hovel. "We found a cache of weapons!" The commandos emerged with their arms full.

Jake looked back at Lena.

"I'll tell you later." Her teeth chattered. "We need to get moving. Igor warned the others. They'll be here soon enough."

Igor? The name briefly distracted him, calling to mind *Young Franken-stein*. But the sight of the commandos carrying two AK-47s apiece, extra clips, a couple of pistols, and a handheld radio caught his attention. They all froze as Gallo's voice came out of it, sounding gruff and disoriented.

"Repite, Oscar. *¿Qué pasa?"*

They all froze. Fernando reacted first, snatching the radio out of Jorge's hand and responding in what Jake hoped was a good impersonation of the guard. *"Falsa alarma. Todo bien aquí."*

Gallo's silence on the other end bespoke of his suspicion. "Tell me the passphrase, then."

Fernando looked to Jake for the answer. When Jake shrugged, Fernando answered belligerently, *"Tu madre."*

Oh, boy. The insult was sure to have consequences. Now Gallo knew the jig was up. At first light, he would head to *Arriba* to investigate, bringing a bunch of Venezuelans with him, just in case. Their tracks in the snow would make it apparent where the fugitives went. Even so, by the time Gallo got to the summit, Jake's party would be long gone, provided their escape-and-evasion plan worked.

"How far to the *cumbre*, David?"

"Er." David assessed the escarpment and scratched his chin. "As much as an hour."

Perfect, it would take Jake's teammates at least two hours to arrive by helicopter once Jake called for extraction. He would do that en route. "Okay, David. Lead the way."

Keeping Lena pinned against his side, Jake ushered her uphill, fighting to keep pace with David's nimble stride. As the commandos fell in behind them, the radio in Fernando's hand gave off a steady hiss of static, suggesting Gallo had wisely switched to another channel. Needing all his concentration to walk, the commando didn't bother searching for the new channel. The wind assaulted them, whipping snow into their eyes. Even so, the JUNGLA kept up without falling behind.

Jake had hoped to stop and place his call, but his hands weren't free. Adrenaline must have kept Lena upright earlier. Now she could scarcely walk, forcing Jake to put his arms around her and half-drag, half-carry her along with him. His own soles burned with the abuse he'd put them through these past few days.

Lena gasped for breath and shuddered with cold, but she never once complained. Casting worried glances at her, Jake was struck by her pallor. What had she been about to say before the JUNGLA cut her off? Might she finally be willing—after all they'd been through—to share a future with him? Or was Jake just setting himself up for disappointment?

First things first. They had to get off El Castillo. And then Lena had to heal, both physically and mentally, from what she'd been through. Guilt pricked him anew for not protecting her better. None of that was going to be easy. But surely, after everything they'd overcome, she could see they were meant to be together.

CHAPTER 19

S he never could have done this on her own. Even with Jake's arms around her, lifting her and guiding her up the steep grade of snow-slick gravel, climbing to the alpine crest was more than Maggie could do. She could tell by Jake's sidelong glances he was worried she wouldn't make it. She could also tell he was dying to know what she'd been about to tell him. But Jake, being Jake, didn't press her.

They came upon the summit so abruptly that her head spun—as much with vertigo as with relief to find herself standing on the pinnacle of the fourteen-thousand-foot mountain. It felt like they'd climbed up to heaven itself.

The night sky, adorned with patchy clouds and sequin-like stars, stretched as far as the eye could see in all directions, flaunting the vastness of space. However immense, she felt herself to be an integral part of God's great plan. There was a *reason* she was here, on Earth, alive.

Her gaze lowered to the mountain's twin peaks, then the saddle between them. Where there might have been nothing but ice a hundred years ago, a small lake glimmered in the darkness. Lobo's assessment had been correct. There appeared to be just enough room on one side of it for a helicopter to land, but the fit would be tight with water on one side and a granite sheer on the other. And then there was the wind to think of…

It buffeted them where they stood. If not for the warmth of Jake's body, Maggie would have turned into a human icicle, even with a fever burning her from the inside out.

The commandos, who came straggling up the rise behind them, panting in exhaustion, also stopped and stared. All three looked in danger of toppling over and never getting up again.

"There's the radio station." David pointed it out to everyone. "I've only seen it once before."

Maggie followed his pointing finger to the three solar panels Lobo had displayed on his laptop at the safe house. Hallelujah! They were a short walk away from shelter, not that Maggie could see one.

"Come!" Clutching his flapping poncho, David led the way down into the sheltered saddle. They passed the solar panels and a sturdy antenna, whistling in the wind, before coming upon a cinder-block wall and a sturdy wooden door. The building seemed to grow out of the granite itself.

The first to reach the door, David pounded on it to announce them. Maggie swayed against Jake. Just a few more minutes and she could pass out—providing somebody was here to let them in.

A light shone around the edges of the door. A bolt grated back, and the door swung outward, revealing the portly priest wearing a poncho like David's. As they flinched from the light shining over his head—an actual working lightbulb!—he greeted them with astonished silence, then exclaimed in Spanish, "David! You've brought me some companions. Come in, come in! Heavens, what a nice surprise."

They crowded into a blessedly warm but tiny dwelling. Maggie noted the radio equipment on one wall, a handcrafted cot, and even a rug beneath her feet. She was safe here. Jake would take care of her. She could let go.

"Where can I lay Lena down, Father? She's hurt."

"Oh, goodness. Right here." The priest stepped toward the cot, which was clearly where he'd just been lying. Whipping back the blanket, he held it up while Jake lowered her onto it. While little more than a stretcher, it felt as soft as down, compared to the rock she'd been sleeping on. There was even a pillow.

"There you go." The priest himself covered her with the blanket.

As Jake dropped to his knees next to her, she grabbed his sleeve. "Jake." Her eyes wouldn't open.

His gloved hand brushed the hair from her face. "Yes, Beautiful. Rest now. We'll be out of here soon."

"I want you in my life, always." There, she'd said it. She fought to lift her eyelids to gauge his response, but they were sealed shut.

His lips, still as cold as ice cubes from being outdoors, touched her burning forehead as he rasped in a voice thick with emotion, "I'm not going anywhere."

That was her last impression before she lost consciousness.

Jake straightened with his heart about to burst. *"I want you in my life always."* The assertion was way more than he'd let himself hope for.

One look at the expectant faces around him, and he filed away her words for later contemplation. Unless and until he got them all away from El Castillo, he and Lena wouldn't have an "always."

With the priest busy distributing juice packs to the JUNGLA, and with Fernando hunting for the new frequency on the radio, Jake raised the antenna on his heavy-duty sat phone, walked to the other side of the room, and made the call.

The phone rang three times before Lobo answered. "What's your status?"

"We're in position. You can head this way."

Lobo hesitated. "I'm afraid we've run into a glitch, an electrical problem on the Seahawk. We're scrambling for a replacement part."

No. There wasn't any allowance in this equation for a problem. "What about another helo? What are your options?"

"Only other option is the Little Bird."

That wouldn't work. The Little Bird required sitting outside of the cockpit on running boards. It was too cold and too windy for that, not to mention he had too many passengers for such a small helo. "How long to get the part?"

"Unknown. We're working every angle. I'll let you know."

"Out." Jake jabbed the call to a close.

In that same instant, a voice came out of Fernando's radio—Gallo's voice barking orders in what was clearly a mobilization effort. Surely, they would wait until first light to ascend to the mountain. Apart from desperate escapees, no one traveled on the mountain at night.

Something Lobo had said in their briefing returned to Jake. Pivoting toward the radio equipment, he hunted for the device that was re-transmitting the radio waves being picked by the huge antenna outside.

This was Zen's area of expertise, not Jake's, but the rectangular black box with lights jumping on the display had to be a transmitter.

He waved the priest over. "See this, Father? I think it's part of a repeater system for the FARC's handheld radios. If we pull the power, they won't be able to talk to each other unless they have a clear line of sight."

"Oh, I see. I didn't know that." If the priest wondered where Jake's French accent had gone, he didn't ask.

Fernando, who was listening intently to the radio, hushed them suddenly.

The cave fell silent as Jake strained to hear what was being said. The man speaking in a strong Venezuelan dialect was unintelligible to him, but the crease appearing on Fernando's grubby forehead spoke for itself. Jake braced himself. *"Qué dijo?"* *What did he say?*

"They're bringing mortars," the commando captain relayed.

"Right now?"

"No, no. At first light."

Mortars. Jake envisioned their Sikorsky SH-60 Seahawk helicopter blowing into a ball of fire.

Not on my watch. "I'm unplugging this transmitter. If they can't talk, they can't plan. *Vale?*"

Fernando nodded. *"Vale."*

As Jake unplugged the transmitter from its power source, the radio in the JUNGLA's hand gave a hiss of static. With a grim smile, Fernando turned it off and set it aside.

That ought to slow the rebels down a bit.

"Let's rest." Jake returned to Lena's side, passing Father Joshua on the way. "Sorry to kick you out of your bed, Father."

The priest waved off his apology with a worried look. "She needs her rest more than I do."

Back on his knees, Jake peeled off his glove to assess Lena's fever. He'd never felt a hotter forehead. What were the chances his team *wouldn't* get here before the FARC and the Venezuelans did?

Surely, God wouldn't have brought them this far only to deny them His protection at the last minute. Jake lifted a worried gaze to the priest hovering over him. "Father, please say a prayer for our safety."

The buzzing of his military sat phone roused Jake from a light sleep. Snatching it from his pocket, he checked the time as he answered, surprised to discover he had slept sitting on the floor with his head resting on the cot next to Lena's. It was zero-five-hundred hours, which meant the sun was starting to rise; impossible to tell in this windowless radio station, which was dark inside, save for the electronic equipment on the opposite wall.

"Go ahead."

"Status update." It was Lobo. "The electrical problem is resolved, and we're on our way—ETA, two hours."

Relief flooded Jake, followed by apprehension. "Copy." By the time the helo arrived, the sun would have been up for a while, giving the FARC and their allies plenty of time to hustle up the mountain to *Arriba* and then follow their quarry's tracks in the snow to the radio station. "We might have company by then, and they might be bringing mortars."

The beat of silence before Lobo signed off conveyed the same consternation Jake was feeling. Putting his phone away, he clicked on his penlight, shining it first at Lena, who flinched from the light but didn't waken. With a heavy heart, he palmed her forehead, then turned his penlight on the JUNGLA, finding all three of them sitting up and eyeing him expectantly.

"Let's move." As they came to their feet, David and the priest, who were also sprawled on the rug, stirred. The latter got up and switched on the light.

"I think I have some *salame de llama* here somewhere." Padre Josué went hunting in the cupboards for some sustenance.

A short time later, their stomachs sated with llama jerky, Jake stepped out of the radio station with the three JUNGLA and David and shut the door behind him. The sky was as gray as their granite surroundings, the air filled with flurries kicked up from the ground. Jake tugged his gloves back on while the JUNGLA secured the blankets Father Joshua had given them more securely around their frames. Poor David just had his poncho.

"We have firepower and the advantage of higher ground," Jake reassured them, getting earnest nods in return. "Let's spread out on the ridge overlooking *Arriba* and protect this summit from encroachment. David, we could use you to run messages between us."

"*Sí*, Jacques."

"*Bueno*. Let's have a look at our arsenal."

After assessing how much firepower they had, they dispersed. Jake climbed up the ridge closest to Lena, just above the radio station. As he settled behind a crag, using its breadth to block the wind, he checked on the JUNGLA, finding them nearly in position farther down the ridge. Seated, quite literally, on the top of the world, Jake absorbed the view.

The sky was the color of pewter and brightening by the minute. Eying the precipitous rocky slope down to Arriba, he realized that the clouds smothering El Castillo were actually *below* him.

Oh, that's not good.

They wouldn't see the enemy coming until they were close enough to shoot. Studying the impenetrable mist, Jake pricked his ears for any telltale signs of an approaching force. All he heard was wind rattling the tall antenna behind him.

The minutes crept by. Hugging himself to keep warm, he watched the sky brighten by degrees, turning from pewter to violet blue, reflected by the little lake in the saddle behind him. All at once, the sun burst over the eastern horizon, a golden orb that buttered the layer of clouds below him, spreading as far as the eye could see.

This must be what heaven looks like.

Under any other circumstances, Jake would have relished the splendor of this sunrise, seen from the top of the world. But not right now, not today, not with Lena's life hanging in the balance. *Come on, God. Lena needs a doctor.*

In the opaque veil below him, a shadow flickered. Jake tensed. Raising his M4, he focused on the spot where he'd seen something move, his gaze as sharp as a condor's.

CRACK!

One of the JUNGLA had fired his weapon, prompting Jake to sprawl on his belly and then squirm backward so only his head poked over the ridge. The enemy was here.

He heard them before he saw them. But as they emerged from the mist, his optimism floundered. At least thirty men, maybe more, were swarming up the east face of the snowline. Taking a bead on the nearest one, Jake fired, and the rebel dropped. *Please don't be one of the kids.* The remaining rebels scattered, taking cover behind stony outcrops.

Time slowed to a crawl. For the next hour, Jake and JUNGLA whittled away at the force below them. If the rebels had mortars, they didn't use them. Jake and company clearly had the edge, but their ammo couldn't last forever.

As if to manifest Jake's fears, David came running up to him. "Are there any more clips for the *pistola*? The captain has run out."

Jake patted down his vest, found a mag he had overlooked earlier, and passed it to David, who bounded away, taking it to Fernando.

Silence fell over the summit, broken only by gusts of wind that kicked up snow, concealing the movements of the FARC, who were probably discussing the strategy to flank them. Into the tense stalemate came the distinct throbbing of the Sikorsky Seahawk's twin turboshaft engine. Lifting his gaze from the snowline, Jake searched the brightening sky. *Come on. Hurry!* Lena needed antibiotics days ago.

There! He finally spotted her, a bird-sized speck growing larger by the second. Provided the FARC did *not* have mortars, their departure was imminent.

Jake started backing down the ridge. "David." Jake waved the young man up to him, even as he clambered down. "I'm going inside for Lena.

Get word to the JUNGLA to fall back toward the lake. We should be out of here in twenty minutes. It'll take the enemy longer than that to get up here, so we should be okay."

As David nodded, Jake put a hand on his shoulder, gave it a grateful squeeze, then continued down the ridge, headed for the radio station.

When he swept into the small room, his heart dropped to see the priest kneeling next to Lena, whose eyes were still closed. "Is she?"—he couldn't even say the word—"*dead?*"

"Not quite."

Not quite? That wasn't the reassurance Jake was looking for. His stomach pitched as he noted Lena's blue lips. She wasn't getting the oxygen she needed at this altitude. "Our transport's coming. I need to take her outside now." *Just focus on the next step.*

The priest got up wordlessly, backing away so Jake could scoop up Lena, blanket and all. As he reached the door, he glanced back at the priest. Sudden concern for that man's welfare prompted him to say, "You should probably come with us, Father."

"No, no." Father Joshua's determined smile conveyed confidence. "The Lord will protect me."

Jake stared at him, hoping with all his heart that was true. "Better plug the transmitter back in once we leave so they don't accuse you."

"Yes, I will. Here, let me get the door for you."

The Seahawk was close enough to make the stone walls hum. Jake held the missionary's eyes as that man pushed the door open. "Thank you, Father. I'm sorry for the violence."

A tight smile this time. "You didn't start it. I pray God watches over you and your wife, now and always."

The word *wife* stayed with Jake as he bore Lena toward the lakeshore. The wind was whipping now, made worse by the rotor wash as the Seahawk floated thunderously into view and then began its treacherous descent.

Given the *crack, crack, crack* in the distance, the enemy was firing at it. The helo's M30 chain gun retaliated with a *rat-tat-tat-tat-tat!* Jake watched with a held breath, not daring to look away, not even for a second, as the Sikorsky's substantive frame rocked in the wind.

All at once, Jake could see the shooter in the helo's open door. That looked like Harm! Recognition gave way to relief. He couldn't have been too badly injured if he was back in action already.

Centering itself over the lakeshore, the helo prepared to land.

Watch out for that sheer there.

Foot by foot, it dropped until, at last, it touched down onto the rocky surface at the lake's edge.

"We're going to make it, Beautiful." As Jake started for the bird, both Lobo and Zen jumped out, their M4s ready to defend their rescue targets. Jake saw Jorge trip and fall. David, with his poncho flapping in the wind, went to pick the man up, assisted by Zen who darted away to help.

Lobo came straight for Jake, grabbed the side of his vest, and drew him through the rotor wash to the door, where he gave him a heave-ho that made it possible to clamber inside without passing Lena off to Bambino, who grabbed for him and pulled them in.

"Over here," the medic shouted, drawing Jake toward a stationary gurney.

Lowering Lena across it, Jake relinquished her to Bambino's care, then turned his attention to the irregular terrain outside. Two of the three JUNGLAs clambered up into the cargo area and collapsed.

"Let's go!" Lobo shouted at Zen, who escorted David and a limping Jorge to the bird.

Beyond them, Jake caught sight of movement and fixed his stare on what could only be a human being, cast into silhouette by the sun shining on the eastern ridge. The acrid taste of fear filled his mouth as he spotted the unmistakable shape of a rocket launcher on the man's shoulder—a mortar mounted on a rocket. "Shooter!" Dropping to his knees, he pointed the man out to Harm.

"I see him." Harm swung his chain gun in the right direction.

Lobo all but tossed David into the cabin while Zen pulled up Jorge. "Go, go, go!" Lobo roared at the pilots.

The twin turboshaft engine whined as the pilots responded. "Hold on!"

Harm's M30 chain gun spewed empty shells onto the floor as he covered their liftoff. Jake, who hadn't taken his eye off the shooter, saw him duck behind a rock. Darned if the man didn't resemble Gallo.

The Seahawk rose, jerking in the wind like a malfunctioning thrill ride.

Watch that sheer! Jake threw himself across Lena's prone form to keep her from falling off the gurney as the helo tipped away from it.

David and the JUNGLA crawled toward the benches to grope for the straps on the wall. Harm, cool as a cucumber, slid on his gun rail, keeping their assailant in sight.

Rat-tat-tat-tat-tat! More shells rolled across the cabin floor.

But then the sound Jake dreaded to hear—the sizzling of an RPG ripping through the air—reached his ears. *This is it.* Holding on to Lena, he braced for impact. At least they would go to Heaven together.

The helicopter banked in the opposite direction, and the RPG sizzled past them, missing by mere feet. As Jake's adrenaline drained away, he opened his eyes to find them accelerating swiftly into the cerulean sky. They were too far from the mountain now to be targeted—not with the FARC's limited firepower.

With the danger over, Harm secured his chain gun to one side and rolled shut the large door, locking out the frigid blast.

In the quiet that followed, Jake met the eyes of his teammates, then David and the JUNGLA, who eased their white-knuckled grips on the wall straps and shared great smiles of relief.

Looking back at Lena, Jake's contentment fled. Bambino was slipping an oxygen mask over her face. She looked utterly lifeless. Nor did Bambino's grave expression offer hope as he proceeded to take her blood pressure. The worried tilt to the medic's dark eyebrows stripped the air from Jake's lungs.

He crouched beside the gurney and stroked Lena's dark hair. Tears of desperation stung his eyes as he bent over her, grating in her ear, "Don't you dare die on me, Lena."

She'd said those very words to him after the bombing. Never in a million years did he think *he* would be saying them to *her* just twelve years later.

CHAPTER 20

"Seriously?"

Maggie stared in disbelief at the empty armchair where she'd seen Jake sitting on the few occasions she'd managed to open her eyes. But this time, he was gone, and something told her he wouldn't be back. Uncle Sam must have crooked his finger, leaving Jake with no choice but to comply.

With a whimper of desolation, Maggie stared at the ceiling she had glimpsed now and then while floating in and out of consciousness. She'd wanted desperately to converse with Jake, who never left her side, only she'd been too sick to find the strength.

This time, her eyes stayed open. Even so, it took her a while to notice her warped, water-damaged passport lying atop the wheeled tray next to her. She extended a hand to pick it up and found a note tucked inside, written in Jake's vaguely familiar handwriting.

Welcome back, Beautiful. I wanted to be here when you felt good enough to talk, but I've been called back. Please remember what you said to me. We're going to make it work.
P.S. Your dad is on his way.
P.P.S. Here's my phone number. Call when you can.

Maggie memorized the number, then reread Jake's message before clutching the note to her chest and studying her surroundings. Where was she, exactly?

The sterile room was like any other hospital room, double occupancy with an empty bed next to hers. But the signs on the wall were all in Spanish. Peering through the wide window for clues, she caught sight of a distinctive, decorative panel mounted to the exterior of the building. The panel brought to mind El Hospital Universitario Nacional in Bogotá. Lifting the note again, she realized the letterhead said just that. She was back in the city where she'd done her first tour.

Maggie tucked the note back into her passport, laid that back on her wheeled table, and then took stock of herself. An intravenous tube snaked out of a vein on her right hand, while a PICC line disappeared into the underside of her left arm, delivering antibiotics straight to her heart. The infection must have been a bad one.

A peek under her hospital gown revealed monitors stuck to her bare chest, which explained the quiet beeping of a machine near her head. It also revealed how shockingly underweight she was. Gosh, she'd only been in the wilderness for what—two weeks and a day?

An abrupt knock at her door had her looking up. "Come in?"

The door cracked six inches, allowing her caller to peek at her before pushing his way inside. Recognition flooded her, along with relief and affection. Tall, dark, and distinguished, with silver hair at his temples and green eyes identical to hers, Drake Ellis commanded respect wherever he went. He crossed to her bed with a pained expression.

"Hey, Daddy."

He leaned over and hugged her fervently. "Oh, Mags."

"Gosh, do I look that bad?"

His chuckle sounded more like a sob, and his eyes were damp when he finally straightened. "You look wonderful. And you're alive, which is all that matters."

The words confirmed what Maggie had guessed: She'd come pretty close to dying. A memory niggled of Jake pleading with her while the helicopter swept them away from El Castillo's summit. *"Don't you dare die on me, Lena."* She'd had no intention of dying.

"I feel pretty weak," she admitted, if only to explain why she hadn't hopped out of bed to greet her father.

"The doctor said you had a serious infection. They've been pumping antibiotics into you for four days now."

"I've been here for *four days*?"

"Yes, and I would have been here sooner, but I was in the middle of a big case. Besides, your boss said you had someone staying with you?" He looked around pointedly.

Maggie glanced at the empty armchair. "He just left. Remember Jake Carrigan, Dad, my boyfriend in France whose number you blocked on my new phone?"

Her father's expression turned wary. "What about him?"

"He's a SEAL now. He saved my life in Venezuela and again in Morocco. We were partners on this latest assignment. And I'm in love with him." She astonished herself by blurting the last part on a defiant note.

"Well!" Her father looked stunned. "I'm delighted to hear that."

"You are? I mean, you're the reason we lost touch for twelve years. Aren't you worried that he's going to ruin my career?" Again, she sounded angry, blaming him for something that was ultimately her decision. "Sorry." She briefly closed her eyes. "I hate feeling helpless, and I'm taking it out on you."

"That's okay, Mags." He looked her over, then glanced around the room. "Is there anything I can get you?"

"Can you get me out of here?"

"Well, that's the plan, but you'll have to be cleared by your doctor first."

Maggie sighed. "How long will that take?"

"Not too long. We spoke over the phone. He said he'd release you in a couple of days."

"Days!" Maggie whimpered.

"Are you hungry? You look like you could do with a good meal. How about pizza? We could get it delivered."

Searching herself, she discovered she did have a bit of an appetite. She didn't want to be a stick the next time she saw Jake, so she'd better fatten up. "Sure, pizza sounds great."

"I'll order us some." But her father didn't move. He stood over her with a pensive expression. "So you really love him?"

The question brought a wistful smile to her lips. "Yes." She ached for Jake. "He's my best friend and *such* a decent person."

"Sounds like a great guy." Her father hesitated. "But you're not going to see him much if he's a SEAL."

"Right. I'm aware. Thanks."

Dad nodded several times, looked around, and slid his hands into his pockets. "Don't get me wrong. I'm not telling you to forget him. A good career is satisfying, Mags, but when there's nobody to share it with— well, it's a hollow reward."

Maggie raised her eyebrows. Miles, her half-brother, had tried telling her months ago that Dad was a different man now that he'd reconciled with Karen, her stepmom. He must have learned that lesson from their two-year separation.

"Nobody would blame you if you resigned. I mean, look what you've been through."

She didn't want to resign. But if the only way to have a future with Jake was to give her notice, then maybe she ought to. The realization sank into her consciousness like a rock falling to the bottom of a pool.

"On the other hand, your boss is thrilled with your accomplishments—not that he could tell me what they were."

With that, her father stepped toward the phone, switching seamlessly into Spanish after dialing the operator.

Accomplishments. The words stayed with Maggie. Her accomplishments were many. Jay Barnes was probably at home, deliriously happy to be reunited with his family. Mike Howitz's body was resting in peace on American soil by now. The U.S. Navy and the CIA had apprised the Colombian government of Venezuela's alliance with the FARC. Since they knew exactly where General Rojas was hiding, it wouldn't take long to topple that man's ambitions.

So, job well done. But her father was right. Her satisfaction felt hollow without Jake around to share it.

She would have to make a decision, obviously. She couldn't be in Jake's life always if he was a SEAL and she was in the CIA. One of them would have to give up their career. She gulped. Maybe she could try her hand at consulting or training, something that wouldn't take her overseas since Jake's tours would keep them apart enough as it was.

The math was pretty simple. *So I'll resign,* she decided, waiting for a flood of relief to hit her. All she got was a trickle.

～

"Good morning, Beautiful."

"Jake! I was hoping it was you. Good morning!"

Jake could hear the scratchiness in Lena's voice as she answered his 7:00 a.m. phone call, along with delight that they had finally connected after a week of playing phone tag. The initial message she had left on his cell phone this past Saturday told him she was back in Arlington, taking leave to recover her strength.

The desire to crawl into bed with her right then and hold her as he had on El Castillo made him ache with unfulfillment. But since he was sitting at his desk in the Team Building on Dam Neck Naval Annex in Virginia Beach, 210 miles away from her, his yearning was pointless. "I've missed you," he admitted, glancing through the crack in his door hoping none of the guys heard him.

"Oh, Jake."

She went silent, making his breath hitch with sudden consternation. Was she changing her mind already? Would she push him away as she had in Paris, even though she'd accepted his ring?

"I miss you, too. So much."

The breath came flowing out of him. *Thank God.* She still wanted to be part of his life. "Well, listen, I'm heading your way this weekend, and I thought we could meet up if you're free. I've got the whole weekend off, so maybe we could take the Metro to the National Mall, visit some museums, eat in China Town, whatever you want to do."

"Really, a whole weekend?"

"Yeah." He wasn't going to tell her what he'd be doing on Friday morning before they met.

"Okay. What day is today?"

He heard her sit up and pictured her rubbing her eyes while her silky black hair slid over her shoulders. Her room would be decorated with the mementos of her travels. He had a framed photo of her on a boulder in Fontainebleau for her to add to her décor. "It's Wednesday," he answered.

"Oh, wow, already."

There was something in her voice, something she was thinking about but not telling him. When she kept quiet, he added, "Seems like months since I saw you last." It had only been a week, not that she was conscious when he'd reluctantly left her side. "How are you feeling?"

"Good. I'm getting my strength back and putting on some weight. My sister-in-law's been cooking five-course dinners ever since I got home."

"Good thing, since you probably wouldn't cook for yourself."

She scoffed. "You don't know how I spend my free time."

He loved how easily he could provoke her. "Yeah, but I know you. Tell me I'm right. You never cook for yourself."

She tsked her tongue. "Fine, I never cook for myself, but I could still learn."

"Well, lucky for you, I can MacGyver any delicious meal with the barest of ingredients."

"Of course you can." The words were sarcastic, but her tone was admiring. "What else have you mastered as an adult?"

"Eh, besides French and Spanish, not much more than how to protect myself and kill bad guys."

"Well, you know, there's a need for people like you." The wistfulness in her tone suggested she was jealous of the Teams for having such a claim on him.

As if to prove that fact, a brisk knock sounded at his door. "Hold on a sec." Jake covered the mouthpiece on his desk phone as Senior Chief McLeod edged his door farther open. "Yes, Senior?"

Icy gray eyes conveyed McLeod's current displeasure with him. "The CO wants to see you in his office right away."

"Thank you. I'll be right there." Water off a duck's back. Jake didn't care how peeved his superiors were at him at the moment. Once Amos vanished, Jake growled his frustration. "I'm sorry, Beautiful, but I have to go." The time was soon coming when he wouldn't have to jump every time his commander summoned him. "I'll try calling you tonight. If you can't answer, look for my texts. Can't wait to see you."

"Can't wait to see you either."

There it was again, that peculiar thread running through her voice telling him something was up. Too bad he didn't have time to find out what. "I love you, Lena."

"I love you too, Jake."

He savored the words, aware that this was the first time—ever—that she'd admitted to her feelings. With a smile of true contentment, he added, "Bye, Beautiful" and ended the call.

In her bedroom on Friday morning, Maggie donned a different outfit than the one she'd worn to the clandestine CIA offices in New York City earlier that month. For one thing, that dress didn't fit her right as she was still twelve pounds underweight. For another, this bright-purple pantsuit with its lightweight, breathable fabric represented freedom and change. Wasn't purple the color of reincarnation? But some things never changed, like the emerald ring gracing Maggie's left hand, a reminder of why she was doing this.

It still felt unreal, being back in Arlington, and not slogging through mud on El Castillo. Despite how unpleasant so much of that assignment had been, it had felt so real that she still woke up in the middle of the night expecting to be there, sleeping with her head on Jake's chest.

Being apart from him now, even in this safe apartment, surrounded by artwork and artisanry that reminded her of her assignments to Colombia, Venezuela, and Morocco, she felt adrift, aimless, ungrounded. Her body was back in the States, but her thoughts were still with Jake on El Castillo.

If only she didn't have to give up her career to spend her future with him. But she did. Even then, his job as a SEAL and a SOG would pull him away, sending him into dangerous situations that would keep her on edge until his return. But at least they'd be together sometimes—versus *never*, if she stayed in the CIA.

Slipping amethyst earrings through the holes in her ears, Maggie contemplated her reflection. *I'll be fine. I'll find something else to do.* What she didn't want to do was spend more time apart from Jake. They'd lost twelve years as it was.

Plus, he was coming up to Northern Virginia tomorrow to see her. What better way to display her commitment to their future than by telling him she was all his? She would be Mrs. Jake Carrigan for the rest of their lives, if Jake still wanted that. She knew in her heart he did.

She had to admit, regarding her appearance in the full-length mirror, that despite being underweight, she looked better—less over-wrought. The taut expression that had been on her face since Morocco was gone, replaced by a little smile that came from having the hope of Jake in her life, not to mention a meaningful relationship with God, who had whispered to her spirit on El Castillo, who'd kept Jake from dying and brought her safely home. She had been a fool for thinking she could handle whatever life dished out to her.

Nodding at her reflection, Maggie turned from the mirror to slip into a pair of comfortable white sandals. No point in bringing her Ruger along, since she couldn't take it through the gate into Langley anyway. She left it in her bedside drawer without a second thought and strode out of her bedroom, through her well-appointed deluxe, high-rise apartment to the hall tree by the door. Miles and McKenzie were away at work—Miles at FBI headquarters, where he basically answered to their father. And McKenzie was painting another of her beautiful murals in someone's home today. Neither one of them—and especially not her father—knew what Maggie was up to today, aside from driving to CIA Headquarters to be debriefed on her last assignment.

After today, her world would never be the same.

Twelve minutes later, Maggie guided her blue Lexus SUV along the George Washington Memorial Parkway. In August, the forest was nearly as lushly green as El Castillo. Exiting into the CIA complex, she slowed at the gate to show her CAC card to be admitted.

What a relief not to be reporting to the office job she loathed! Even so, uncertainty knotted her stomach as she drove through the raised gate and over the directional spikes. Her palms felt damp. Gordon wouldn't like what she had to tell him after her debriefing. He might even try to talk her out of resigning, in which case, she would have to dig deep for the will to turn her back on everything she'd worked for, everything she'd ever known.

Shelving her doubts, she pictured Jake's face when she told him they didn't have to be apart anymore. He would be dumbfounded by her sacrifice, then grateful, maybe even humbled. She didn't want to dwell on how *she* would be feeling.

Finding a lucky spot in the shade in the front parking lot, Maggie made her way toward the original CIA building, where Gordon had his office. Most employees parked in the side parking lot, which gave access to the new building at the back of the complex. But Gordon, being a stickler for tradition, preferred to work in the original building.

The grand portico with its many columns never failed to stir Maggie's pride, followed by a sense of honor as she swiped her CAC card and stepped into the lobby, where her steps lagged.

The granite CIA seal, a mosaic on the lobby floor, measured sixteen feet across, catching Maggie's eye every time she went by it. How many times had she walked around it, finding it disrespectful somehow to walk right over it? As she followed its curved edge, her gaze alighted on the eagle's head, the shield, and the sixteen-point compass star.

Her steps slowed as her thoughts flashed to the moment she and Jake had stepped onto the ridge of El Castillo, giving her a sudden sense of vertigo followed by awe at the immensity of the heavens. The sequin-like stars pulsing in the sky were just like this one. They meant the same thing, though she wasn't sure what—something to do with honor, struggle, sacrifice.

Checking her watch, Maggie roused from her insight and started forward again. She only had a minute to get to Gordon's office on the third floor, and he was a stickler for punctuality.

The two analysts who shared her elevator wrangled over the viability of a new software. Their quarrel kept Maggie feeling unsettled. Was she really going to resign today? What if she was making a huge mistake?

Sooner than she wished, she was forcing a smile for Gordon's secretary. Gordon's door was shut. Maggie could hear him through the thick mahogany, his voice louder than usual, making an argument to which another male voice reacted in a steady and certain tone.

Wait. Maggie pricked her ears. No way was that Jake. She had to be projecting her thoughts onto someone else. Jake wasn't even in the area until later this afternoon. Well, no—he hadn't said that in so many words. He'd said they would *get together* this afternoon. And wouldn't Gordon want to debrief Jake as well as her?

A cataract of emotions rushed through Maggie. She wasn't ready to see Jake yet—not without accomplishing what she'd set out to do today. At the same time, every nerve in her body went taut in anticipation that he might step out of that door. It *did* feel like a month since she'd seen him last.

The door popped open, and there stood Gordon with a scowl of resignation on his face. He shook the hand of the man leaving. Jake's broad shoulders came into view. He wore the same heather-gray suit he'd worn to their briefing in New York City. As his head turned, their eyes met, and the same joy that had made her sob on the slope at *Arriba* winged in her again, reaffirming her intention.

"Take care, sir." Taking polite leave of Gordon, Jake crossed straight to her, folding her in a quick embrace. "Lena." As he straightened, his blue gaze raked over her, taking in every detail of her appearance. "You look great."

All the doubts that had been stacking up in her head blew away like dry leaves in an autumn breeze. "Thanks." Being with Jake meant more than protecting the country she loved.

"I guess you're next."

"Ahem." Gordon cleared his throat, not so patiently.

"Yeah." But doubts hovered on the periphery of her mind.

"Meet me in the courtyard after?" Jake suggested. "We'll catch up then."

"Sure."

With a glance at the ring she was wearing and a satisfied smile, he strode away, all confidence and contentment, leaving Maggie standing there, having no idea what she was going to say to Gordon.

When her boss raised an eyebrow, she marched dutifully into his office, aware of the pity that entered Gordon's dark eyes as he assessed her physique. She sank into the nearest seat, pleased to feel Jake's residual body heat on the cushions. She could do this for him.

"So." Gordon made his way behind his desk. "I've heard Lieutenant Carrigan's version. Now let me hear yours." Lowering himself into his large chair, he picked up a pen and held it over the notepad in front of him.

Gordon was surlier than usual. What had Jake said to upset him? Apart from Mike Howitz having succumbed to illness, their mission was a rousing success. She delivered her report without once having to consult the notes in her purse. Her memories were crisp and vivid, making them easy to recollect.

As she came to her conclusion, describing the conditions at *Arriba* and sharing the names of the three JUNGLA who deserved commendation for their assistance, she prepared herself to tack on her resignation. Gordon would assume, no doubt, that her imprisonment by the FARC had broken her.

To her dismay, she began to stammer as she described David and Jake's rescue. The moment was finally upon her. With a deep breath, she opened her purse, discovering a tremor in her fingers as she pulled out the envelope containing her official resignation letter.

"Gordon, I don't know how to tell you this, so I'll just give you—" She began to hand it across the space between them.

With an astonished expression, Gordon slammed his pen down onto his notepad. "He said you would do this!"

"What? Who said I would do what?"

Her boss gestured angrily at the door. "Lieutenant Carrigan. He said you would hand in your resignation letter unless he got to me first."

"What?" Maggie blinked her confusion.

"Didn't you hear me in here yelling at him? That man just handed in his notice. He's quitting the Teams and walking away from the Agency so he can follow *you* around the world." Gordon's eyes bulged. "Don't you dare hand me that envelope, Maggie. I know what's in it, and I'm not about to lose another field operative today."

Maggie remained speechless. Jake had tendered his resignation with the Agency? He was quitting the Teams so he could go wherever *she* was assigned? Astonishment kept her speechless. Second by second, relief eased the stricture in her chest. She didn't have to quit! Jake had beat her to it.

Very slowly, Maggie withdrew the envelope, slipping it back into her purse. It took a moment to find her voice. "Well, in that case, I'll just await my next assignment."

Gordon nodded several times, the whites of his eyes still visible. "You do that. And Maggie"—he stood, looking down at her from his impressive height—"don't you ever think about quitting again. You're one of the best case officers I've ever had. This country needs you."

Her heart swelled with gratification, pride, and contentment. She couldn't wait for her next assignment. She could still give her best in the struggle and the sacrifice—more so with Jake's support. Pushing to her feet, she stood tall. "Yes, sir. Can I go now, sir?" She and Jake were about to have an earnest conversation.

A reluctant smile crinkled the corners of Gordon's eyes. "Tell the lieutenant I said to take good care of you."

"Yes, sir." With those breathless words, Maggie let herself out of his office, tore past the secretary, and flew down the hall. She couldn't get to the courtyard fast enough. Jake had better be there like he said he would. Of course, he would be there. Jake's word was his bond.

To think he'd quit his career so they could be together! She had nearly done the same. My goodness, if Jake hadn't gotten to Gordon first, they would both be unemployed!

Maggie drummed her fingers as she rode the elevator to the ground floor. Leaping out, she headed straight for the courtyard between the old CIA building and the new one. She'd eaten many a meal alone in the covered picnic area off to her right. The rest of the courtyard was a large semi-circular lawn, comprising shade trees, picnic benches, landscaped gardens, and even a koi pond bookended by stone sculptures, ironically reminiscent of little mountains.

Spotting Jake admiring the crimson-colored fish in the pond, her heart gave a backflip. "Jake!"

Her tone had him whirling with a wary expression. Several people at the picnic tables watched her descend on him. Conflicting urges seized Maggie as she got closer. Falling back on her default mode of a tough girl, she punched him in the arm. "I can't believe you did that."

"Ow!" But he was trying not to smile as he rubbed his arm. "Which part?"

"You resigned from the Teams. You turned in your notice to the Agency. And you told Gordon not to let *me* quit!"

"So, all of it." Jake searched her face earnestly. "Did you quit?"

"No!"

"Phew. I'm glad I got to him first."

Maggie marveled at his selflessness. "Jake!"

He pretended to flinch. "Are you going to hit me again?"

"No." She softened abruptly, took a step closer, and wrapped her arms around his neck, her heart swelling with gratitude. "I don't deserve you."

"Yes, you do."

She blinked back sudden tears. "How'd you know I was going to resign?"

Glancing at their audience, Jake lifted a hand to stroke her cheek. "Because I know you, Lena. When you say you want something, you give it 110 percent. But I also know you were born to do your job. And I don't want you quitting it because of me."

She wrested his hand from her face but held on to it. "So you quit instead." She shook her head at the irony. "You gave up your career… for *me?*"

He cocked his head, his gaze watchful. "Can you still love me if I'm not a SEAL?"

She rolled her eyes. "Jake, I loved you when you were a scrawny linguistics major. But what are you going to do now?"

He smiled smugly. "Number one, protect you. Consider me your personal bodyguard."

PTS would never cripple her again.

"Number two, I'm starting up a nonprofit that brings food to those who don't have enough. Between the Peace Corps and the Teams, I've learned a lot about acquisition, distribution, and sustainability. I'll set up the infrastructure wherever you're assigned and hire locals to run it, so the company keeps working after we relocate."

Desire overwhelmed all decorum. Lifting a hand to the back of Jake's head, Maggie pulled it down so she could kiss him. He obliged with a smile on his lips, kissing with the same promise that she'd tasted under the trees on El Castillo.

The sound of clapping tore them apart. They both regarded the picnic tables where their all-male audience was just finishing up their coffee break. At Maggie's stern glower, they suspended their applause and got up hastily, taking their trash with them.

Her gaze fell on the briefcase one of them had left behind. Suddenly, she was back in Paris, staring at the Adidas backpack with dawning horror. *No way.* Her gaze flew to Jake's, who must have read her mind.

"It's okay." He raised his voice to address the departing employees. "Hey, one of you forgot your briefcase."

They all turned around. A chubby male threw his hands up, then hustled back to collect it.

As he toted it off, Jake pulled Maggie close again. "There, see. We're safe. We have our whole future together."

Her gaze locked on his lips. "Where were we?" She wanted that kiss to continue forever.

"You were about to propose to me," he stated with certainty.

That startled a laugh out of her. "Oh, I was?"

He sent her an injured look. "You weren't?"

"Well, I mean…" She blinked, wondering where he was going with this, but then narrowed her eyes at him. "You're teasing me."

He gave a little shrug. "Possibly. But I tried proposing to you before and that didn't work out so well."

Again, her thoughts flashed to the *Café du Jour*, but they weren't there anymore. She was older and wiser, and she wanted to spend her life with Jake. Tugging his ring off her finger, she thrust it at him. "Ask me again."

A flame ignited in his steady gaze as he took it. "Okay. I will."

Maggie glanced around. The courtyard stood empty. They had the place to themselves.

With a slow grin, he sank deliberately down on one knee.

"Oh, you don't have to get grass stains on your pants!"

But he ignored her, seizing her hand and gazing at her just as he had in Paris. "Lena, what we have doesn't come along every day."

He'd said those very words to her just seconds before the bomb in

Paris detonated. "I know." That had been her answer then, and it still held true today. It would always hold true.

"Would you marry me?" His voice thickened. "Not someday, but very, very soon?"

"Yes, Jake. I would be honored to marry you."

He briefly closed his eyes, kissed the knuckle of her left ring finger, and slid the ring back where it had been. Then, with a whoop, Jake surged to his feet, snatched her up in a bear hug, and spun her giddily around.

The green grass and the glistening pond called to mind the green pastures and still waters from Psalm 23. It really was true. *He restores my soul.*

EPILOGUE

PHUKET, THAILAND

There was only so much lounging by the pool, sipping mai tais, that Lena could tolerate. Jake watched with amusement as his bride glanced again toward the balcony on the fourth floor, the one immediately adjacent to their own room, using the brim of her straw hat to conceal her surveillance.

Phuket was everything he'd hoped it would be—white sand, blue sky, and a steady breeze wicking the sweat off his body. He would forever associate the scent of sunscreen with desire and bliss. To think he'd dreamed of this moment back on El Castillo, and now they were actually here on their honeymoon just one month after Jake's proposal in the CIA courtyard. He wouldn't have changed a thing about their intimate family wedding—his parents, her parents, their siblings, and a couple of cousins. It had been perfect.

"There he is on his balcony. Look, Jake. Just don't be obvious about it."

Indulging his wife, Jake peered casually up at their five-star hotel. The whitewashed balconies, all dripping with brilliant purple bougainvillea, were all empty, except for the one on the fourth floor, right next to theirs, where a man was pacing on his balcony, cell phone pressed to his ear.

They'd first seen him two days earlier, emerging from his hotel room, just when they were entering their own. Lena had remarked how much he looked like a Mexican fugitive named Lorenzo Nuñez-Aguiler. She'd seen a WANTED poster at the airport in Colombia while flying home with her father.

Jake had to admit, after looking up the man's name and finding him on the DEA's *MOST WANTED* page, their neighbor bore a striking resemblance to the renowned narco, sought after for multiple crimes in the U.S.A., including kidnapping and murder. Since he'd learned never to underestimate Lena's powers of observation, Jake had shot off an inquiry to the DEA using WhatsApp. To get his query noticed, he'd identified himself as a former SEAL affiliated with the CIA, and by morning, the DEA had sent him an old mug shot of the elusive criminal along with a message: *Does he look like this, only older?*

Jake plucked his phone from their pool bag, found the photo, and then held it up so he and Lena could compare a young Lorenzo with the man on the balcony. The man was holding still now, staring over their heads at the sea, while continuing his intense conversation.

There was definitely a resemblance, Jake had to admit, but what were the odds they'd be honeymooning right next door to a wanted fugitive?

Still hiding behind the brim of her hat, Lena divided a narrow-eyed gaze between the photo and the suspect. "Okay, so check out the way he holds his phone. See how the pinkie on his right hand sticks out?" She dropped her voice to a whisper as a server veered toward them to pick up their empty glasses.

"Would you like two more?" the pretty Thai girl asked.

"Two waters would be great."

"Yes, ma'am." With a bow, the server scurried off to fetch their drinks.

"What about the pinkie?" Jake had no idea where Lena was going with this.

"Look." She drew his attention to the mug shot and the letter board the young Lorenzo was holding. Jake blinked. The pinkie on the man's right hand stuck out the exact same way.

Whoa. Never in a million years would Jake have noticed that telling detail.

Jake reassessed his wife. He had underestimated her resilience and toughness at the outset of their assignment to Colombia. He wasn't dumb enough to do that twice. "You know, I think you're right, Beautiful."

She flicked him a disparaging glance. "Of course I'm right. Tell the DEA we'll keep him in our sights until they get a team out here to arrest him."

"Lena, we're on our honeymoon."

She arched an eyebrow at him, making it clear she wasn't going to let this go.

Jake dropped his head against the lounge chair and laughed to himself. He might not be a SEAL or a SOG anymore, but life with Lena was going to be every bit as adventurous and harrowing. Honestly, he wouldn't have it any other way.

SPEAK NO EVIL

THE LOST ARE FOUND, BOOK 2

Just you wait, Princess. Tonight's the night.

At oh-one-hundred hours, Gabe's squad packed up their possessions and slipped their packs on their backs. With their Sig Sauers cradled in the crooks of their arms, they left their hiding place for good. Cruz had parked his taxi on the street. They dropped their packs in his trunk on their way to the back of the school, and Cruz took off to await further instruction.

As they'd done the night before, they circled to the back of the school. Zen climbed onto Doc's shoulders and leaped over the wall so he could open the gate for them. The dog didn't bark tonight—a good omen.

While Zen and Doc guarded their perimeter, Gabe and Rodeo would fetch the princess, tranquilizing her if they had to, and carry her out of the Instituto and into Cruz's taxi.

Easy day, Gabe kept telling himself.

The climb was much as it had been the night before, only less frightening since he knew the balconies would hold. Reaching the second story, he secured a rope to the lower rung for Rodeo to ascend. Next, he clambered atop the flimsy upper railing and pulled himself onto the balcony jutting over him.

The feasibility of breaking in this way angered him. If *he* could climb up Rapunzel's tower, then so could any thug intent on harming her. Did Miss Clark not realize how quickly she could vanish—very much alive but dead to herself and dead to the world? The more he thought about the trouble and effort required to rescue her—not to mention the looter's pointless death—the angrier he got.

By the time he inserted the tip of his Gerber blade into the space between the two shutters, he didn't care if he was particularly loud.

Ping!

As the shutters drifted soundlessly outward, he sidestepped them before peering inside. In the darkness of the large, still chamber, a veil of mosquito netting shimmered around a small, four-poster bed. As its occupant rolled over, Gabe signaled over the railing for Rodeo to wait.

The SEALs didn't move again until Gabe was sure Miss Clark was sleeping. Waving Rodeo up, he stepped gingerly over the low windowsill, one foot at a time, until he was standing on the chamber's tiled floor. There, he drew his monocular from the cargo pocket on his thigh and IDed the woman in the bed. Yep, the mane of golden blonde hair, the piquant tilt of her nose—it was definitely Miss Clark, and she was just as pretty up close as far away.

As Rodeo joined him, ducking through the window with stealth that Gabe envied, he put his monocular away. As planned, they drifted apart, keeping to the shadows to approach her bed from opposite directions.

Once they boxed her in, Gabe would quietly announce them. Depending on her response, he would tranquilize her if he had to, using the loaded syringe in his other pocket. They couldn't make a furtive exit with a screaming woman.

But just then, someone outside the walls loosed a bloodcurdling scream, and the sleeping princess lurched straight up in bed, hair swirling around her shoulders, eyes wide and fearful. Gabe flattened himself against the armoire at his back. Rodeo, on the opposite wall, blended into a bookcase.

Well, this was awkward. How was he supposed to cue the woman to their presence without scaring her to death?

❦

Alarm crackled up Libby's spine as she eyed the open window. How had those shutters nearest to the corner of the room fallen open? She had taken great care, as always, to verify that each latch was fully engaged before retiring to bed.

Either the latch was faulty, and the shutters had swung open, or... someone had opened them.

Heart racing, Libby plumbed the shadows of the large bedroom, seeing nothing amiss. The croaking of tree frogs outside suggested all was well. Then again, only the scantest bit of light filtered the one open window, keeping her from seeing much.

Peeling back the sheet that stuck to her damp skin, Libby scooted toward the edge of the mattress, intent on crossing the room and closing the shutters—securely this time. As she went to duck under the protective mosquito netting, the sound of a man clearing his throat drove a blade of terror through her.

Shrieking, she scrambled back onto the bed. As she did so, a shadow detached itself from the armoire and headed toward her and murmured words she couldn't hear past the blood roaring in her ears. As he swiped aside the mosquito netting, she jackknifed off the far side of the bed, avoiding his outstretched hand and shaking off the mosquito netting.

With a squeal of fear, she bolted toward the door that faced the bed only to plow into a second man. A gloved hand clamped over her mouth from behind and pulled her backward, stifling the scream that erupted from her throat. Libby reacted instinctively, swinging an elbow up and back, right into her captor's nose.

Crunch. The man blurted a Spanish expletive, but his grip only tightened. Libby fought desperately to free herself.

"Now calm down, ma'am. We're not here to hurt you."

The words of the man in front of her, spoken with a Western drawl, were slow to penetrate.

"We're U.S. Navy SEALs, ma'am. We're on your side. I'm Rodeo, and that's Lobo." He nodded at the man subduing her. "We're here to take you home."

Relief liquefied Libby, turning her limp in her captor's clutches, though her heart kept trotting. So *that* was what they'd said earlier.

As the gloved hand came off her mouth, she sucked in a stabilizing breath, while staggering several steps away to reassess the pair.

Thank God, they weren't a threat, but—"You broke into my room to tell me this?" She gestured at the open window. "You snuck in through my *window*?"

Lobo, whose nose she'd broken, was gingerly clasping the wounded protuberance. "This is a clandestine operation." He spoke on a growl, clearly in pain and angry with her. "Did you want us to pull up in a Humvee and blow the horn?"

Libby narrowed her gaze at him. Given the swarthiness of her attacker, she could be excused for thinking him a local. His lighter complexioned partner, on the other hand, looked as *norteamericano* as apple pie.

"Wait." She was still processing. "So, you're here to take me home? As in, back to the States?"

"Do you have more than one *home*land?"

Granted, she'd probably broken his nose, but Lobo's surliness was bordering on rude. "Why would you come for *me*, though?" Surely, Navy SEALs had better things to do.

Lobo kept growling. "The State Department issued an evacuation *days* ago, Miss Clark. Your life is in danger, and your father wants you *home*."

Ah. And there it was. They even knew her name.

Libby smiled tightly. "My father. Of course." She should have guessed her silent refusal to leave wouldn't deter her overprotective Dad. "Well…as much as I appreciate your help, gentlemen, it's not that simple."

He cut her off. "We were told you wouldn't want to leave. Rodeo, hold her still."

"What?" As Rodeo started in her direction, Libby backed warily from the pair. He grabbed her before she could slip away, subduing her struggles with astonishing ease. Fright rose up as she watched the dark SEAL dig into the pocket on his pants. Something small and cylindrical shone in his hand. As he pulled off a cap, a needle glinted in the dark.

They were going to *drug* her? "Stop! I'll go with you. You don't need to do that."

Lobo drew up short, clearly weighing the truth of her statement. Whatever he might have said was interrupted by a knock.

Before Libby could blink, both SEALs were pointing pistols at the door.

"No, don't shoot!" she cried.

"*Profesora?*" A tentative female voice called through the thick wood.

"Who is that?" Lobo hissed.

"That—" Libby yanked her arm out of Rodeo's grasp—"Is a *student.* There are two young women still at this school with no one to protect them. Don't you think I would have left days ago unless there wasn't a reason why I couldn't?" Without waiting for permission, she marched imperiously toward the door.

◠

Available in Paperback and eBook from Your Favorite Bookstore or Online Retailer

ABOUT THE AUTHOR

Rebecca Hartt is the *nom de plume* for an award-winning, best-selling author who, in a different era of her life, wrote strictly romantic suspense. Now Rebecca chooses to showcase the role that faith plays in the lives of Navy SEALs, penning military romantic suspense that is both realistic and heartwarming.

As a child, Rebecca lived all over the world. She has been a military dependent for most of her life, first as a daughter, then as a wife, and knows first-hand the dedication and sacrifice required by those who serve. Living near the military community of Virginia Beach, Rebecca is constantly reminded of the peril and uncertainty faced by US Navy SEALs, many of whom testify to a personal and profound connection with their Creator. Their loved ones, too, rely on God for strength and comfort. These men of courage and women of faith are the subjects of Rebecca Hartt's enthusiastically received *Acts of Valor* series.

RebeccaHartt.com

Sign up for the Rebecca Hartt Newsletter Here

https://rebeccahartt.com/contact

www.ingramcontent.com/pod-product-compliance
Lightning Source LLC
Chambersburg PA
CBHW030648020726
47493CB00006B/1921